Conklin's

Corruption

The Third Book in
Conklin's Trilogy.

BROOKE PAGE

Conklin's Corruption

By
Brooke Page

Edited By: Samantha Hondorp
Proofed by: Emily Hamilton
Cover Design By: Perfect Pear Creative

Contact Brooke Page
www.facebook.com/authorbrookepage
www.twitter.com/brookepage05
www.goodreads.com/brookepage
Email: authorbrookepage@gmail.com

Table of Contents

Title Page...1
Copyright...3
Table of Contents...5
Prologue...9
Chapter 1...17
Chapter 2...29
Chapter 3...55
Chapter 4...63
Chapter 5...69
Chapter 6...77
Chapter 7...89
Chapter 8...99
Chapter 9...107
Chapter 10...117
Chapter 11...129
Chapter 12...149
Chapter 13...163
Chapter 14...181
Chapter 15...197
Chapter 16...207
Chapter 17...225
Chapter 18...231
Chapter 19...239
Chapter 20...245
Chapter 21...253
Chapter 22...267
Chapter 23...275
Chapter 24...283
Chapter 25...289
Chapter 26...297
Chapter 27...301
Chapter 28...309
Chapter 29...319
Chapter 30...329
Epilogue..335
Acknowledgements...341

If I were to die right now, in this very moment, I would know one thing: I experienced the most passionate love that could be found, and I was lucky enough to have gotten it for so long. The fantasy of our future would have to be enough to hold on to while in heaven where we'd meet again. I closed my eyes, preparing for the inevitable.

Only God can stop a moving bullet.

Prologue

I sat at my desk drumming my fingers anxiously against the mahogany. It was ten after eight in the morning, and Mitch was late for our meeting. Nathan sat across from me in one of the black leather chairs, his posture relaxed as he studied me.

"Where is he?" I grumbled, resituating in my chair. "I told him 8:00 a.m. at least three times. I texted, emailed, and called him for Christ's sake. He could have the decency to keep a schedule!"

I ran my hand through my hair trying to calm my nerves. But it was pointless. I was too furious with my younger brother.

He had some real nerve surrounding the house I built for Becca and myself with RJ bricks, and some huge balls to fill them with fucking cocaine. Feeling more agitated with every passing second he hadn't walked through the door, I stood and made my way to the photos of Wrigley Field being built that Becca gifted me last Christmas.

"You know he's never on time. Try to calm down, Tyler."

"I'm so fucking pissed off at him," I said through clenched teeth.

Nathan sighed and stood up, the leather squeaking as he did so. He made his way to the opposite side of my office, finding the tumblers of liquor.

I heard the ice from the bucket clank against the tumbler then liquid being poured.

Without taking my eyes from the photos I said, "You do know it's only a quarter after eight in the morning, right?"

Nathan walked over to my desk, leaning against it as he took a sip of the amber liquid. "Yes, Mother."

"As if our mother would care," I chided.

Nathan smirked into his glass. "That's correct. You know I can't operate without a little bit of the good stuff."

I smiled to myself. How do you call someone an alcoholic when they can function better with it in their system? I shook my head then checked my watch again. If Mitch didn't walk through that door in two minutes, I was going to call him and rip him a new one. I began to pace the room again.

"Tyler, try to relax. Mitch shouldn't have done that, and we'll make sure he doesn't do it again," Nathan said calmly, setting his drink down on my desk and crossing his arms. "How much overall was hidden?"

I let out a long breath of air. "Each brick I found had at least ten eight balls."

Nathan's eyes widened. "How many bricks?"

"Too fucking many." I ran my hand over my face and began pacing again, but this time behind my desk. I took off my jacket after the third pace and set it over my chair. Why was it so hot in this room?

"What did you do with it all?" Nathan asked.

I stopped dead in my tracks and stared at him. "I left it in the bricks."

"You left it there?" he asked, sounding puzzled.

I scowled at him. "How the fuck am I supposed to know what to do with that much cocaine?"

Nathan shrugged his shoulders. "Call Chino."

Anger fueled my body at his words. "We aren't getting involved with him and his drug scheme. Don't bring it up again," I growled.

Nathan rolled his eyes and stood tall from the desk to walk over by me. "Tyler, I hate to say it, but I think it might be his to begin with. You said yourself you didn't trust Mitch to be around Chino and not give in to his deals."

"I will break his hands so he can't smoke that shit ever again if he's dealing with Chino on our properties." My face must have been red and the veins in my forehead had to have been popping out because I was so livid with my younger brother.

Just as I was about to say something else, Mitch walked through my office door. He was wearing jeans and a hooded sweatshirt with his work boots, holding a cup of coffee. He had a lazy grin on his face, and I wanted to punch his teeth in when I saw him.

"Sorry I'm late. Ran into traffic problems," he said while yawning.

I glared at him as Nathan walked over to the side of my desk to grab his drink.

Mitch looked between the two of us, an unsure expression crossing over his face. "So, what's this meeting about anyway?" He didn't move to sit down but stood only a few feet in the doorway.

"Sit down," I said in a dangerously low tone. "We have an urgent matter to discuss."

Mitch raised his brows and walked further into the room to sit down on one of the black leather chairs. Coffee in one hand, he crossed his ankle so it was on his opposite knee as he relaxed into the chair. I just stared, feeling my heart race in my chest.

"Sit down Tyler," Nathan said sternly. I clenched my jaw and closed my eyes, attempting to calm down enough to hear Mitch's side of the story. But it was going to be almost an impossible task for me to handle.

"Tyler," Nathan said with more force. I rolled my eyes at him then plopped down in my chair, rolling it forward so I was leaning over my desk and facing Mitch. Mitch looked up at Nathan as he stood with his tumbler in hand.

"Are you drinking already?" Mitch asked.

"Yes. Now listen—"

"Tell me what you've been working on at my house," I said slowly, cutting off Nathan. My eyes were glued to Mitch.

He gave me a 'you must be crazy' look. "What do you mean what have I been working on? I've been busting my ass to get that shit done for you in a ridiculous amount of time. You weren't exactly willing to work within our normal time constraints," Mitch grumbled. "If something is wrong, I'll fix it."

"You're fucking right you'll fix it," I snapped, standing from my seat with my palms spread flat on my desk. "What about the fireplace? What exactly have you been working on with that? Huh?"

Mitch sat back, meeting my glare. "That fireplace is perfect. I laid it myself. Stop being such a prick."

I clenched my teeth together again, mentally doing all I could to keep my fist from going through his forehead.

"Mitch, stop being an idiot. I saw the RJ bricks," I growled.

A slow smile crept across his face. "Yeah, I thought they'd be a good touch."

I jumped from behind my desk so I was in front of Mitch. His eyes were stunned open by my deftness to tackle him. He was lucky Nathan was quick, rushing over to step in front of me.

"Did you really think I wasn't going to notice them?" I shouted. Nathan had a grasp on my arm.

Mitch stood up, meeting my glare. "Tyler, I don't know what you're talking about. I put in a safe box. I figured you'd be happy. Guess I was wrong. What the hell does Becca see in your moody ass anyway?"

The second her name crossed his lips I shoved Nathan to the side, causing him to bump into the wall, nearly knocking down the photos of Wrigley Field. I yanked Mitch across from me and pounded his head into my desk, palming his head with my hand and pinning him in place.

"Jesus, what the fuck, Tyler?!" he shouted as I used my elbow to hold him to my desk. A trickle of blood was spreading across some of my paperwork from Mitch's lip hitting the desk so forcefully. Even more reason for me to be pissed off at him.

"Don't ever fucking say her name again, you asshole. Why'd you hide cocaine all over our house?" I yelled in his ear. "Did Chino put you up to it?"

Mitch tried to flail from my grasp, but pure adrenaline was running through my veins. I hated to admit it, but Mitch could do a number on me if we were to get into a fight. He was broader and a touch taller, but with all the rage under my skin, I could hold my own.

"Cooper!" Nathan shouted as he stood tall from being rammed into the wall. Nathan cursed as he straightened his suit jacket. Cooper came through the door and had both hands on my biceps.

I tilted my head backwards, my murderous eyes meeting his. "Cooper, back off," I growled. "Answer me, Mitch."

Cooper glanced at Nathan then took a step back.

"It won't be there for long," Mitch muffled.

I practically roared as I pulled him back then slammed his head down again.

Cooper was back on me in a nanosecond, pulling me away from Mitch. I shrugged Cooper off and paced the office.

"Damn it, Mitch! I thought we agreed about Chino," Nathan scolded, adjusting his designer glasses.

"Who the hell said I was working with Chino, huh?" he mumbled through his hand then wiped the blood from his mouth on his sleeve. "You're a fucking psycho, Tyler!"

I saw red again, my moment of self-control vanishing again as I went to charge him. I grabbed his collar and pushed him against the wall.

"I'm a psycho? Who the hell hides over $100,000 of cocaine in his brother's house? Do you know what kind of danger you brought to MY house by doing that? Indirectly involving MY future wife with your fucking drug deals?"

I felt Cooper's hands back on me but more forcefully this time. I held my ground though, my forearm firmly placed on Mitch's neck. "I swear to God, if that shit isn't out of my house by tomorrow morning I will crush your face in with my fist so you won't ever be able to smoke or snort that shit again!"

"That's ENOUGH, Tyler," Nathan's said harshly. He nodded to Cooper, his signal to pull me off Mitch. Nathan took a step between Mitch and me. I was breathing heavy, my chest rising unevenly as Cooper still had a firm grasp on my biceps.

"Future wife? Can't believe she actually said yes," Mitch snorted, wiping more blood off his nose.

I tried to leap forward again, but Cooper kept a tight grip on me while Nathan raised his hand in front of me. Cooper had saved me from more than one fight back in college this way.

"I said ENOUGH! If we get any more blood on the carpet I'll have to have Sawla come and redecorate. I know how well that will go down," Nathan said with a threatening tone. I rolled my eyes. I couldn't stand Sawla, but I had my reasons why I stayed away from that crazy bitch.

Nathan turned his stern expression towards Mitch. "Where did you get the cocaine, Mitch?" He held up his finger and clenched his teeth. "And don't fucking lie to me."

Mitch took a few deep breaths, his eyes staring intently at Nathan. "It's a side job. It doesn't have anything to do with the company."

"Bullshit," I sneered, shrugging from Cooper's hold. Mitch's glare turned to me, eyes turning hard. I shook my head at him and wandered back behind my desk. "How many side jobs do you have with Chino, Mitch?"

"It's none of your business," he said arrogantly.

I turned and slammed my hands on my desk. "It is my business! It's all over my fucking house!"

Mitch winced and turned his head towards the floor.

Nathan flashed a look my way then looked back at Mitch, his demeanor calmer. "How many Mitch?"

"You don't need to worry about it," Mitch murmured.

Nathan and Mitch stared at each other for a moment before Nathan spoke. "Get it off Tyler's property. And if there's any hidden anywhere near a Conklin building, it better be gone by tomorrow."

Mitch scowled at Nathan with a clenched jaw then brought his eyes to me. My chest was still erratically rising up and down with anger. Mitch did a subtle nod then bumped Nathan's shoulder as he walked out the door. Cooper raised his brow as Mitch left then gave me a nod as he turned to follow Mitch out of my office, closing the door behind him.

"Way to stay calm," Nathan chastised. I clenched my jaw and plopped down in my chair, running my hands through my hair. Nathan let out a slight laugh as he went to find his tumbler of liquid.

"How much do you think he's helped Chino hide?" I asked Nathan.

"I'm not sure. But we're going to have to find out. I wonder if RJ knows."

"Of course RJ knows," I snorted. "He probably put Mitch up to it."

Nathan sighed. "You don't know that."

I leaned back in my chair, crossing my arms. "I know enough. RJ is the most money-hungry man on the planet. If

Mitch could easily hide $100,000 throughout my house, just think what damage he could do on a commercial site."

Nathan walked over to the window holding his nearly empty glass to his lips. "We're just going to have to believe he will get rid of it."

"Nathan, he isn't going to get rid of it," I practically shouted.

"Have a little faith. I told him to do it. Unlike you, he listens to me... most of the time."

I snorted and put my hands on my face. If Mitch were hiding drugs on Conklin properties, it would make our business complicated and far more corrupt than any other multi-million dollar company.

"So she said yes?" Nathan said calmly, trying to lighten the conversation.

I ran my hands along my face as I nodded my head. "Yes."

He turned and smiled at me. "Set a date?"

I blew out air, not really in the mood to discuss wedding plans. "Um... Becca was thinking October."

Nathan laughed. "How are you going to plan a wedding in six months?"

I furrowed my brows at him. "She wants a small wedding."

"You're not going to get away with that. Have you met Missy Stine? Have you met our mother?" He laughed.

"Mother will not have a say," I said through clenched teeth. I wasn't going to let her cause havoc on Becca; she was going to have to deal with enough from her own mother.

"Whatever you say. Becca will accept her help."

I rolled my eyes and ticked my jaw. Nathan was right. Becca actually liked my crazy, hair-brained mother. But Becca wanted a small wedding, and Mary Conklin didn't do small.

Nathan finished his drink and set it on the table next to the other tumblers. "Don't worry about this ordeal with Mitch. It'll get taken care of, okay?" I took a deep breath and stared at my screen saver of Becca and me kissing at Christmas. "I mean it Tyler. Don't dwell on this."

I know why Nathan wanted me to forget about it. The entire scheme was something he was still on the fence about.

Nathan had one too many of the same genes as RJ, and the money was way too tempting. *We could make this a billion dollar company* Chino said at our last meeting. I couldn't help but notice Nathan's and RJ's eyes widen for a slight second. I had to be the one to say the firm no first then Nathan and RJ reluctantly agreed.

"I'm finally happy Nathan. I don't want any more bombs to explode," I sighed.

He gave me a soft smile, his gentle blue eyes exuding happiness for me. "Nothing is going to explode, Tyler." I looked up from my desk, giving him a wry smile, worried gun powder was hiding everywhere in my life, just waiting for a match to fall.

Chapter One

Becca

I was livid. Absolutely furious.

I was sitting at my desk on the edge of my seat, staring down at the *Grand Rapids Press*, my eyes glued to the headline.

Maxwell Stine's eldest daughter to wed Conklin Architecture's CO-VP.

There I was, smack dab on the front page. A very intimate picture of Tyler and me on the Blue Bridge. He had his arms wrapped around me, practically nuzzling my neck, my eyes closed with a shy smile.

Why on earth would my mother do this?

I knew she sent the picture to the tabloid; she all but begged me to even get the stupid engagement photos. Tyler didn't help. After hearing my complaints about how I didn't want to get them taken at a family dinner, he made the brilliant choice to confess he wouldn't mind a few professional pictures of the two of us. It was all my mother needed to conveniently call the photographer and practically make the arrangements.

I even said, *these pictures are for family and no one else, but she did it anyway.* I didn't like the attention.

After Tyler's extremely romantic proposal in the dream house he built for me, for us, I couldn't wait to start making wedding preparations. Something small, personal, a day we wouldn't forget. We didn't need engagement photos. We planned to be married in October, only a six month engagement. We didn't need to send out save the dates.

The wedding list wasn't going to be that big. Boy, did I get an unpleasant earful at family dinner when I announced our plans.

"Becca, how could we possibly keep the invite list to only 100 people, including the wedding party? We have at least 300 people we must invite. I am sure Tyler's family has just as many!" my mother scolded, leaning forward in her chair. "Heather had a guest list of 750!"

I rolled my eyes. "Mom, I don't want a big wedding like Heather and Ray's. I just want something small and personal."

"Becca, it *will* be personal. It's your wedding day!" she tried to reason.

Missy Stine had that firm look on her face. She wasn't going to back down on this, and it irritated the hell out of me. "Besides, we have to include your father's business associates. It would be a poor decision business wise to not do so, same for Tyler's. I'm sure your parents have a large list of clients that attend functions," my mother said, turning to face Tyler. He gave her a tight smile and nodded. He chanced a glance at me, holding my gaze long enough to know I wasn't happy with his response to my mother. "See, Becca? You must have a bigger wedding," she said matter of factly.

I huffed and leaned back in my chair while crossing my arms.

"Sorry sweetie, but that's the way our world works," my father shrugged.

Needless to say, that day I knew I wouldn't be the one to plan my wedding. As my family said, that was the way our world worked. So I have been putting up with my mother's outlandish wedding plans. Even though my mother would try to influence my every decision, she wouldn't push my final choices. I was thankful and shocked. To be completely honest, I had no idea how to go about planning a wedding with the caliber that Tyler and I had to meet. But sending the engagement photos to the press was one step too far.

I picked up my phone, swiping Tyler's name on the screen.

"Hey," he answered on the second ring. "Are you having a good morn-"

"Have you looked at the newspaper? Or MLIVE?" I whispered harshly into the phone, cutting off Tyler's greeting.

"Um, no I haven't. I'm walking into the office now. Why?" he asked.

"She sent in our pictures. I told her not to! You heard me, I said I didn't want those pictures to be for anyone besides family!" I hastily whispered into the phone. My eyes left the newspaper on my desk to peek at my office door.

Yes, my office door. I no longer worked in a cubicle. I was now Will's assistant. Since Corey did such an awesome job with the prints for Edna Enterprise in Miami, he got offered a promotion. Nathan and Jamie marketed Conklin Architecture so well while in Miami that the company needed a permanent architect on staff. Corey was more than happy to take the job.

I knew I'd get offered the promotion to fill Corey's spot. I could practically feel the whispering behind my back about how I only got the job because of my relationship with Tyler. I'm sure once our engagement photo popped up on everyone's news site on their computer screens it would confirm their accusations. Becca Stine only got the promotion because she's screwing the boss.

Whatever, I'm over it. I busted my ass at this job. I didn't need to worry about what everyone else thought.

"Is it a good picture?"

"Tyler!" I scolded, stomping across my office to close the door. "It doesn't matter what pictures! Everyone in Grand Rapids is going to see them!"

I sank back into my chair and went to search MLIVE, the state's website, to see exactly how many pictures my mother had sent to the paper. Sure enough, there were six photos total on the website. Now everyone in Michigan was going to see.

"She sent in one of each outfit change, damn it!" I whined.

"I'm sure it's not that bad," Tyler said. I heard leather moving as though he were taking a seat at his desk. He was in Chicago and had been the past three days.

I heard clicking of his computer mouse.

"When is she going to learn? I'm going to say something to her tonight," I seethed. "We're going to meet with a florist."

"That will be fun," Tyler commented. Then I heard him suck in a breath. "Wow, you weren't kidding."

He must have seen the photos on the web page.

"At least she picked good ones."

"That's not the point! Oh my God, she gave them one where we are kissing!" I practically shouted. The last photo on the page was of the two of us sitting from behind on the pier in Grand Haven, our feet dangling off the edge and kissing. It was adorable. One of my favorites, and it was a picture I didn't want Grand Rapids, or all of Michigan, to see.

"They have that photo on MLIVE?" Tyler asked.

I rubbed my face with my free hand. "Yes, what site are you on?" I questioned. I had assumed he was looking on MLIVE just as I was.

He didn't say anything.

"Tyler... what website?" I asked, dragging out my words, terrified of what he might say.

I heard him take a deep breath and sigh. "I'm on the *Tribune's* website."

I audibly gasped. "No!"

Tyler still didn't say anything.

"So you're telling me our engagement photos are all over Chicago's newspaper, too?"

"Well, they are on the website. I haven't seen the printed newspaper yet today," he said quietly.

I threw my hands to my head and slumped at my desk. I didn't want this kind of attention. I know Tyler's name is big in Chicago, but why would my mother send the pictures there as well? My father periodically did work in Chicago but mainly stayed near Grand Rapids.

"Becs it's not that big of a deal. People will probably skip past the photos anyway."

I groaned into the phone. "I am so close to saying screw it and taking off to Vegas."

Tyler laughed. "I promise the wedding will be private; no photographers allowed besides who we hire. No photos will get out to the public, okay? I won't let them post or print any pictures of my beautiful bride. No one except for me is allowed to ogle you in your white wedding dress."

I leaned back in my chair and let out a slight smile, feeling a touch of relief from his possessive comment. "How do you know it'll be white?" I teased.

"I have an inkling," he flirted.

"You do?"

"Yes. Now get back to work and stop surfing the internet," he scolded, although amusement was laced in his words.

"Don't worry, I have back to back meetings all day since Will is off with his wife and new baby. No more staring at your handsome face," I laughed.

"I love you; enjoy your meetings. I can't wait to see you tonight," he said, his voice filled with so much promise. I couldn't help but feel my pulse increase.

Just as I hung up my cell, my work phone rang. My first meeting had arrived. I picked up my iPad and headed to meet with Lauren.

I graduated from high school with Lauren. We were always acquaintances and took similar classes. She was a curator for the art museum and happened to be very involved with ArtPrize. ArtPrize is one of the biggest festivities the city held each year. Artists and people from all over the world participate. They bring in their artwork and fill the city with any type of art ranging from huge sculptures that are placed outside on the streets to small paintings that are put on display inside various buildings. Art literally covers the city. My father is always a great contributor. He hosts many artists in his buildings and is a big benefactor to the winners. He loves seeing the city thriving with activity, and ArtPrize does exactly that.

Conklin Architecture, Construction, and Design sponsored an artist this year to participate in the city's festivities. Jamie had actually introduced the idea, encouraging Nathan to go along with the local support. She was meeting with Lauren and the artist. I was only attending because of my contact with Lauren.

I greeted Lauren with a hug then led her to the elevator. We were going to meet Jamie in the conference room on her floor.

"Becca you're going to love the artist. He's totally eccentric," Lauren said with excitement. I smiled warmly at her, enjoying her enthusiasm for the project. "Along with being eccentric, he's a touch scatter brained and thought the meeting was at 9:45am, not 9:30am. Sorry."

I shrugged my shoulders. Fifteen minutes could be made up easily throughout the day.

The elevator doors opened, and we made our way into the conference room.

"Hi Becca," Jamie said, standing from her seat at the conference table. "You must be Lauren. It's nice to meet you."

Lauren reached to take Jamie's hand.

"Thank you so much for participating in ArtPrize. We love when buildings hire local artists. I was just telling Becca you're going to love Louis Putters. He's an extraordinary man!"

"Great!" Jamie smiled then looked over our shoulders. "Where is he?" Lauren offered an apologetic smile as she told Jamie about his punctuality. We all sat down and started to discuss the location of the art. It was kind of hard to pinpoint anything without Louis being present.

Approximately 20 minutes later, Louis walked through the door with one of the receptionists. She looked uncomfortable, and I couldn't help but smirk at her uneasy look.

Louis was a medium size man in his 60s. His hair was long and unkempt, salt and peppery down to his shoulders. His skin was tanned but leathery. He was dressed in worn jeans that had holes and cement or paint with a basic white t-shirt. He gave a crooked smile as he walked through the door.

"Ms. Stine and Ms. Rae, Mr. Putters is here to see you," the receptionist said flustered.

I thanked her and stood to greet Louis. Lauren introduced us, and she was totally right. He was quirky and artsy.

"So Mr. Putters, we'd love to hear your ideas," Jamie said while taking a seat after shaking his hand.

"Please call me Louis or Lou. Whatever is easiest for you to remember," he said blandly. He set a stack of mismatched size papers on the table as he took a seat next to Lauren.

"Okay, Lou," Jamie said slowly, puzzled by his lack of organization. "What were you thinking?"

He raised a brow at Jamie then started to place his papers throughout the table in front of him. We all looked curiously at the intricate designs on the mismatched pieces of paper.

"I was figuring on making sculptures. Different miniature houses. I haven't decided what materials would work best. I typically work with metal, but as houses are different, I figure so should the pieces of art."

I reached for one of the pieces of paper, but Louis' hand flew out to stop me slapping his hand on the desk to keep the paper in place. "Don't move them. You must look from my angle to get the full spectrum of my plan."

I moved my eyes to meet Jamie's briefly, but she was too busy blinking at Louis. This guy was odd. Lauren was looking at him in awe. Jamie finally met my eyes then slowly stood so we could go stand behind Louis and see his "vision". When we finally made our way behind him, we both looked confused.

"Can't you see it?" he said in frustration. "It will be a masterpiece. I will need at least 18 spaces throughout the city."

Jamie looked at Lauren. "I thought we agreed on each corner of the building and the main lobby, five locations total."

Lauren shrugged her shoulders and looked pleading. Louis started to shake his head as he raised his hand in the air. "This is the vision. It must be completed. It will be a masterpiece. Top ten, no less," he said sternly. Jamie and I looked at each other then started to head back to our seats.

"Eighteen sculptures weren't in the budget, Louis. We'll have to renegotiate your wages, and Lauren might have a problem getting that many sites this late in the game."

Lauren bit her lip. "Actually, Louis told me it was going to be 18 sites. I have the spaces reserved."

Jamie narrowed her eyes at Louis. "Finance will have to approve this. Don't expect anything special," she snapped.

A crooked smile crossed Louis lips. "We'll see, Ms. Rae."

Jamie attempted to contain her huff as we continued on with the details. He really did have some brilliant ideas once he finally explained what he was thinking. I was leery if he could actually finish 18 art pieces in three months. It was towards the end of June, and ArtPrize would begin in September. My head started to spin. That meant I only had four months until the wedding. Thank God my mother was organized in her crazy ways. Maybe her helping was a good thing after all.

***

The last meeting of the day quickly approached. The client was interested in building warehouses. It was a first-time meeting, and I was a little flustered because Will didn't give me any information about the client. I didn't even know what his or her name was. I grabbed my drafting notebook and headed to the conference room where we normally met with our commercial clients.

I took a seat, spreading out sheets of information neatly on the conference table. I stood and stared down at my handy work and felt I would come across as professional. This was a very first meeting after all. I would be mainly gathering information and giving whomever it was company policies and procedures. Just as I was about to take my seat again, a figure caught my eye and my breath got caught in my throat.

"Becca, what a pleasant surprise. I had no idea RJ would give me the privilege to be working with his future daughter-in-law." Lee Chino smoothly walked through the door and entered my space. He was too close, and I took a small step back, attempting to put on a smile.

"Yes, what a lovely surprise," I said in the most convincing tone I could. His pearly white teeth flashed me a smile, and I held my composure as I shook his hand. I gestured for him to take a seat. I was not prepared to handle Chino's accounts. The last time I saw him was at Mary Conklin's Valentine's Day fundraiser for St. Jude Children's Hospital, the same day I got locked in the bathroom with Tyler's ex-pedo nanny and had tear gas infiltrate my system. A shudder went through my spine as I thought about the evening. Thank God my Ty was there to rescue me.

"I must admit, your father told me you worked in the commercial department, but I doubted I'd get the privilege to be working with you personally, Becca," he smiled.

"Will's out of the office; he'll be the one to normally handle your account. I'm just filling in for him." *Thank God,* I added in my head.

Lee Chino gave me the creeps. Even though he was shorter and had a pleasant smile, there was something else hidden behind it, something darker. Detective Anderson had been asking to see the mock up drafts for the warehouses he was developing, and I couldn't find them. I had assumed RJ was dealing with it, but apparently it hadn't been handled yet.

Relief washed over my body as Chino sat a chair away from me. I didn't like when he was close. According to Connor, Chino was heavily into the narcotics scene but had never had enough hard evidence to put him away. I needed to pull myself together and get through this meeting.

"So, Mr. Chino. I was told you were interested in building warehouses. What type of facility will they be utilized for? Storage? Manufacturing?"

"Furniture construction. I'd love to bring back that aspect of Grand Rapids. It used to be the largest furniture distributor. Have you been to the museum? They have an entire exhibit." Lee smiled, leaning closer to me.

I had seen enough of the museum for the rest of my life. It happened to be located next to the Native American exhibit. No need to rehash that night.

"That's a great idea. How many were you planning on building? Have you purchased the properties yet? We normally suggest a building inspector go on site to see what the land looks like."

Chino looked slightly puzzled. "We've purchased six old buildings and are remodeling them."

I flushed. This was the information I should have already known.

"Of course. I apologize for my lack of knowledge on the projects. Bear with me."

Chino gave me a smug smile. It made my skin crawl.

We discussed more of what his ideas were for the buildings. I was surprised with his visions; the man actually had a keen sense of structural design. Once we went over the original ideas and I had drawn up a few mock drawings, Lee felt satisfied with what we had accomplished. I even felt the meeting went smoother than I had expected it to when I first saw him walk through the door.

"Mr. Chino, the next step is for you to schedule a meeting with the finance department. I'll bring these drafts and ideas to them, and they'll be contacting you shortly with the next procedures."

Chino leaned back in his chair, putting his hands on his knees and cocking his head to the side while looking at me. I couldn't read his expression.

"So I'll be meeting with Tyler, I assume?"

"Honestly, I'm not sure. Usually Tyler isn't directly involved with these types of projects."

Lee's eyes hardened. "I would prefer to work with Tyler. I'm sure you can put the request in the next time you see him."

I took a long swallow, surprised there was any saliva for me to get down because of his unnerving stare.

"Of course. I'll tell him you'd prefer to meet with him directly," I said quietly. I didn't like Chino talking to Tyler. I always had the feeling something was going on between the two of them, and that something wasn't good. Breaking laws and criminal activity came to my mind when it came to Lee Chino, but his plans for these warehouses seemed to be legitimate. I didn't pick up any fishy vibe from his ideas.

Lee's demeanor relaxed as though a mission had been accomplished. "How is Tyler doing? I've only met with him once in the past few months. I assume his mother is doing well after the tear gas incident?"

I stiffened, remembering my own incident with the tear gas. "Mary had some permanent damage, but she can still see. She has to wear glasses now. I think she's embracing the new look."

"Wonderful. I was impressed Tyler didn't go searching for the culprit of the attack, with his personality and all...," Lee trailed, cocking his head to the side.

"What do you mean?" I asked slowly as I started to pile the papers together in the correct order.

"He has a past you know, a few assault charges against him. I think RJ and Robert did their best to cover them up though," he said nonchalantly, crossing his leg over his knee.

"Tyler got into a pretty ugly fight in college. Almost beat a kid to death."

I stopped rustling the papers and blinked. Tyler had a record? He got angry sometimes, but I never thought he was so angry that he would get physical with someone.

Lee leaned forward with all seriousness in his eyes. "Becca, if he ever hurts you, you can always come to me. I know it can be hard to tell those types of things to your family members, but I hope you feel safe around me. I've been very good friends with your father for a very long time, and I would hate if his little girl were being mistreated."

I took a long look at him. Was he being serious? Or manipulative? I couldn't tell. "Tyler would never hurt me."

Lee sighed. "Okay, but I just thought you should know, and watch for signs. He can be a very angry man sometimes," he said sincerely.

I just looked at him, trying to hold back my weariness from information he had provided.

"Well, are we done then? The sooner we can start remodeling, the sooner we can bring the furniture business back to life in Grand Rapids."

I gave him a wry smile and continued putting the papers in order. We walked out the door, and I was extremely uncomfortable when Lee put his hand on my lower back.

"It was great meeting with you Becca, a very pleasant surprise." He winked at me as he left for the elevator while I just stood dumbfounded as the doors closed

I couldn't wrap my head around the thought of Tyler having a record for assault. I was going to have to Google him. *Ask him. You are supposed to trust each other.* My subconscious scolded. I wasn't going to ask him. What had happened was in the past, and if he did have a background with assault charges, I probably wouldn't find them. One thing a rich family could do is buy off the police for those types of things to magically disappear.

Chapter Two

The past three days had been hell, and I couldn't wait to be home and spend the weekend with my Becs. Chicago had been crazy. I had a huge deadline for a new client, Cortez, who wanted to build multiple commercial buildings. Multiple buildings meant more money, but the finances were tricky. I finally felt confident and pitched the sale, happy that the client seemed impressed and eager to get started.

I was about to shut down my computer for the day when an unexpected knock came on my office door. Surprised the receptionist hadn't buzzed for me, I curiously looked over my computer screen as the door opened.

"Got a minute?" RJ, my less-than-perfect father, asked as he breezed into my office.

I cleared my throat, surprised he had come into my office. He never came to me. I was always summoned, in some way, to him. We typically didn't talk, mainly because we didn't get along. His persistence to piss me off and get under my skin was the number one reason we fought constantly.

"Yes, a minute. I have to catch a flight by 5:00pm."

RJ nodded and went to look at a framed photo of a half-built Sears Tower. "Did you get the finances for the Cortez account settled?"

Of course he wanted to know about that. I sighed. He never seemed to have faith in me to nail any accounts. "Yes. He just signed the paperwork this afternoon. I was about to send the copies to legal," I said flatly, sliding into my chair to the fax machine with the stack of papers.

RJ still stood in front of the picture with his hands in his pockets. "Good." Then he was silent for what felt like an hour. An uncomfortable thickness was in the air. RJ has always been right to the point, no nonsense. He didn't linger for small chit chat.

"Is... there anything else you need?" I slowly asked.

RJ turned his head towards me, a blank expression turning into a slight smile. "Yes, I wanted to talk about the wedding."

What? Since when was RJ Conklin interested in the personal life of anyone in his family? I stared at him blankly.

"Your mother and I wanted to know if we could throw a wedding shower. I thought we could have a guys' day. You, Nathan, Mitch, Becca's father, and brother if they could come. We could go golfing. Spend some time together."

I scowled in utter confusion, surprised my jaw hadn't hit the floor. RJ didn't spend quality time with his sons. He didn't give two shits about weddings and showers. Even if this was entirely my mother's idea, he wouldn't be pitching it to me.

He rustled his hands in his pockets and started to tap his toe on the floor, waiting for my shocked expression to subside.

"Um... yeah, I'll ask Becca what weekend would work for her," I said, attempting to not sound dumbfounded. RJ cocked his mouth to the side as though he were thinking about saying more. The ticking of the pendulum clock on my desk filled the room with awkward silence.

Finally, he spoke. "Good. It'll be good for us." It felt as though he was trying to convince himself. "This wedding is good. Becca is a good girl. You need to hold on to her. Cherish her."

I snorted at his words, anger filling my veins. Who was he to tell me I needed to cherish a woman? He had never been faithful to my mother or anyone. Not even business partners. Especially the really dangerous deal he had been tiptoeing around with Lee Chino.

"Are you kidding me?" I asked, baffled.

RJ blinked and shrugged his shoulders. "No. Why would I joke about that?"

"Because you've never had a functioning relationship in your life," I barked.

RJ narrowed his eyes. "Don't act like you know about my relationships."

"Exactly. I don't know you. I know nothing about my father," I said point blank.

His eyes softened a fraction, a hint of guilt passing through them, but quickly vanished into a smirk.

"Hence the golfing and the wedding shower."

Was he kidding? After 28 years, he finally wanted to start a relationship with me? I wasn't buying it. There had to be more, something in it for him that involved dollar signs and power. "This is about Chino, isn't it? You're trying to get me to say yes to his obscene business propositions," I said in a menacing low tone.

RJ groaned and rolled his head to the side. "I told you I would take care of that. Stop thinking I'm some money hungry business tycoon who only cares about my bank account."

I raised a brow at him. He just described himself to a T.

"Don't look at me like that," he scolded.

I shook my head and stood from my desk. "I'm going to be late. Are we done?" I asked grumpily, grabbing some paperwork to put in my briefcase.

RJ sighed and ran a hand through his hair. "Yes," he said softly. "Let me know about the party."

"Yeah, sure." I was distracted, blowing off his weird attempt at being a normal parent. It was all an act for something he wanted; it had to be. Once my things were gathered I started to walk to the door. He could stand in my office all he wanted, but I needed to get to the airport. Just as I was about to head through the doorway RJ's voice rang through the air.

"I'm proud of you son."

I stopped dead in my tracks, shock and confusion taking over my body. RJ had never given me a compliment. My heart tugged at my chest as unnerving emotion was trying to trickle out of my system. Every bone in my body wanted me to turn around and say *thank you, I've been waiting to hear that my entire life*, but I didn't. I merely continued through the door, mumbling, "I'll talk to you later."

***

My black Maserati smoothly pulled up at the Gerald R Ford International Airport. I tipped the valet and slid into the sleek leather seats. I sank into the seat with ease, rubbing my fingers along the steering wheel. This felt good; this felt like home. I loved my cars. They were a close second to Becca, and I was happy to make the 40 minute drive to our new home in Grand Haven. It would help me tuck RJ's weird conversation in the back of my mind as I tried not to look too much into his rare 'I want to be a better parent' moment.

All of the final furnishings for the house were delivered last week, and I had to admit it was quite cozy. Becca did a wonderful job filling the space to make it feel like ours. It was nautical and tasteful, a lot of creams and blues, very serene. She even found a few vintage batman posters for the theater room in the basement. I couldn't wait to "watch" our first movie in the room together this weekend. We had yet to make it through the entire most recent Batman movie. I wondered if I would ever be able to keep my hands to myself whenever she was near.

Nah.

The rest of the drive home I fantasized about how we could utilize the theater room.

It was nearing dusk as I pulled into the long driveway of our new home. The sunset was beyond beautiful to look at from the deck. We lived right on Lake Michigan, and I was surprised how much it felt like the ocean. I opened the garage and parked next to Becca's new car.

Her father had gifted her a white Lexus GS hybrid. I was a little disappointed. I wanted to purchase her a car, hide it in the garage, and surprise her. I guess I still could. She would need an SUV for the winter. I smirked to myself. It would make a wonderful wedding present.

I opened the door from the garage, dropping my briefcase next to our bedroom door then went in search for my Becs. A mischievous grin spread across my face as my eyes found her standing in the kitchen in her favorite yellow dress. It was strapless and flowed at the waist to just above her knees. She was barefoot at the stove, stirring something in a pan. I checked my watch. It was a little after 7:00 p.m. She moved swiftly to the fridge, pulling out a bottle of wine, not even realizing I was standing just outside the kitchen. She went back to the stove to find her glass and fill it to the top. If I had to guess, meeting with the florist with her mother didn't go well.

I crept up behind her, taking in her scent. I loved the smell of her citrus soap and shampoo. She slowly tilted her head to the side, her lip slightly quirking up into a small smile. She realized my proximity as my hands found their way around her waist, pulling her back into my front. I rubbed my nose along her shoulder, my lips grazing her skin softly. God, she intoxicated me. I was thankful for summer because she wore more strapless dresses.

"Hi," I said softly, finally kissing her shoulder. My dick twitched as I opened my mouth to taste her skin with my tongue. I was surprised he wasn't full blown ready to go with the thoughts I had on the drive home. A small giggle escaped her mouth as she put her hands over mine.

"Hi back, stranger." She spun around to face me, placing her arms around my neck, giving me a way too quick of a kiss, then spun back to tend to the stove.

I frowned. "That wasn't the welcome home kiss I was expecting." I grabbed her hips again, nestling myself behind her.

"I don't want your potatoes to overcook," she said, completely ignoring my wandering hands and mouth. I trailed kisses from her shoulder to the nape of her neck then started to pull the ponytail rubber band thingy from her hair.

"Ugh, Tyler, can you not? It's too hot by the stove," she said, pushing me away. She threw her hands to her head and fixed the ponytail as I put my hands on my own hips.

"Okay, what happened?" I asked, attempting to fix the uncomfortable bulge in my pants. She wasn't one to deny me, especially when I had been out of town for work.

"Nothing," she said in frustration. "I'm just tired and irritated with my mother."

Bingo. I must have been right about the meeting with the florist. My hands found her waist again as I patiently waited for her to continue. She always needed a moment before she started to slowly unravel. One thing I learned about my Becs in the last few months was 'nothing' really meant something, and she would eventually spit it out if I were patient enough to listen.

She spun back around to face me while rubbing her hands on her face. "Everything has to be extravagant with her. I don't need a bouquet that is a third of the size of me. I don't want $1200 arrangements at the end of each aisle." She pulled her hands from her face and looked up at me. I remained quiet, waiting for her to finish. "I'm sick of telling her over and over what colors I want. I know she doesn't like them, but that doesn't mean she needs to keep trying to get me to change my mind. I don't want to feel like I'm battling every decision I make. I mean I shouldn't have a reason for what I want besides liking something, right?" She sighed and rested her head on my chest, wrapping her hands around my neck.

I ran one hand up and down her spine while the other remained firmly around her waist holding her against me.

"It's your wedding, baby. You do what you want. You always have the final say," I said soothingly.

She sighed. "Yes, and she never says anything once I make my final decisions. It's the side comments skirting around why she doesn't like anything that drives me nuts."

I smirked down at her. I knew exactly what she was talking about. "Ignore it, hold your ground. I know you have it in you."

She looked up at me and smiled. "Yes. I'm just overwhelmed and probably overreacting. Dealing with the house, the wedding, and...," she trailed off, turning back to face the stove.

I frowned down at her. "And what?"

"Nothing, just stressed at work from Will being gone. I'll be fine."

"What's stressful at work? Is it the Arena remodel? Because you have been doing a wonderful job." She had been working on the plans for the past month, making sure they were absolutely perfect. She was terrified to disappoint her father. If anything, Max was going to be as proud as I was with her work.

Becca cleared her throat as she went to find a strainer for the potatoes. "Yes. The Arena has been stressful."

I watched her move, the tension in her body extremely noticeable. She shuffled to the sink then shut off the stove and drained the potatoes, her head tilting back to the side as she rinsed them.

I didn't like when my Becs was stressed, and I planned on pampering her tonight after dinner. Normally pampering would lead to other pampering. I walked back behind her, running a fingertip across her shoulders. "How about after dinner, you take a bath then I'll give you a nice long massage. I'll even clean up the dishes."

I could sense her grin as she shook the potatoes around in the strainer. "I could agree to that." I kissed her shoulder again then went to grab plates and silverware to set the kitchen island, our typical meal placement. Becca continued making me mashed potatoes and steamed vegetables. She had chicken roasting in the oven and the scent of the herbs was starting to waft through the air.

***

I placed the last dish in the dishwasher and headed towards our new bathroom. I think it was one of Becca's favorite parts of the house. We had a wonderful view of Lake Michigan. The moon lit the gentle waves of the water and the lightness of the sand. I walked through the master bedroom while taking off my tie. Typically the first thing I did was change my clothes. I hated wearing the fancy suits and shoes. If it were up to me, I would wear basketball shorts and t-shirts the rest of my life.

By the time I made it into the bathroom, my eye softened at the sight of Becca completely relaxed in the bathtub, located in the center of the circular room surrounded by floor to ceiling windows. Maybe it was odd to have that many windows in a bathroom, but we didn't have any neighbors.

Bubbles surrounded her body as candles were lit and placed on a rectangular sofa table. Her eyes were closed as she rested her head on the back of the tub, her hair piled high on top of her head, tendrils escaping down her cheeks. She looked calm and at ease. I almost didn't want to disturb her.

Almost.

I proceeded to silently unbutton my shirt, not wanting to infringe on her tranquility. Dropping my shirt to the floor, I knelt behind the white porcelain tub and my hands found her shoulders. She jumped at first but then relaxed again. I wasn't going to jump in with her, not unless she asked. I was craving a shower, personally, and I had other plans for our reunion.

"This is nice," she sighed, tilting her head to the side. I couldn't help but take her invitation, running my nose along her neck. "Are you going to join me?"

"I won't intrude on your quiet time. I just thought I'd rub your shoulders for a while then hop in the shower."

Her hands found mine, stopping their motion. She leaned her head to the side then moved one hand to my cheek, pulling my face to hers. Her kiss was soft and sensual, gently stroking our tongues in a slow rhythmic beat. It was sweet and loving and a constant reminder of why I fell in love with my Becs to begin with. She was attentive and caring, everything I craved my entire life but didn't realize it until I found her.

She pulled her head back to look into my eyes, still cradling my face with her hand. Her eyes formed big saucers as she stroked the stubble along my jaw. "Please," she whispered softly.

How could I say no? I stood and removed the rest of my clothing, not missing the look of satisfaction on her face.

Yeah, you own me, my love. She slid forward, exposing her beautiful back, silently asking me to sit behind her. I sunk into the nice warm water, my legs finding their place on the outside of hers, using my hands to pull her back to my front. She giggled when I did so.

"Do you enjoy having me wrapped around your pretty little finger?" I teased, kissing her neck.

She giggled again then held her left hand above the water, exposing her Cartier princess cut diamond engagement ring. "I enjoy having this wrapped around my finger."

I smirked into her neck and pulled her hand to my lips, kissing her fingers and the diamond that represented her agreement to be my wife. "I enjoy it too. Means you're going to be mine forever," I murmured, nipping her finger.

I heard her sharp intake of breath from my teeth gently wrapping around her finger. "I missed you, Ty," she said in a low and very enticing voice. My dick was responding faster than my words, meeting her backside.

I let go of her hands and palmed her chest. Fuck, they were so perfect. They molded into my hands, and I couldn't help but start massaging them.

"And now I can tell you missed me," she giggled, wiggling her body against mine.

"Yes. I believe certain parts of our bodies need to become reacquainted," I said, beginning to suck on her neck. She moaned with pleasure, arching her back and pushing her chest into my hands.

"What did you do at work today," I asked between kissing and sucking her perfect skin.

She let out a low groan. "Meetings."

I traced my tongue up her neck and to her ear, nipping her ear lobe. "Meetings with who?" Talking about our days while feeling each other up was such a turn on to me. Something about how her voice would get those little gasps whenever I would touch an extra sensitive nerve. But the second I asked with whom, her whole body stiffened and her back straightened. I reluctantly dropped my hands from her breasts and to her waist.

"I met with the artist for ArtPrize."

"Anyone else?" I slowly asked.

She cautiously turned and sat back on the opposite side of the tub, pulling her knees to her chest and biting her lip nervously.

"What?" I asked in confusion.

"I met with Lee Chino today."

It took all of me to not freak the fuck out when she said his name. Why was she meeting with him? Only RJ, Nathan, or I met with him. He wasn't a typical client, and I sure as hell wouldn't allow him to meet with Will, especially Becca. That man was dangerous. I couldn't pinpoint it, but RJ and I were pretty damn sure Chino was the one behind the tear gas incident at my mother's Valentine's Day fundraiser. RJ wouldn't give me any specifics on why he thought Chino was behind it, but I could read RJ. Any miniscule warm feelings about him and his piss poor attempt to be a father had melted into scorching lava. I was going to be a big molten wave of rage the second I saw him Monday morning. His ass better be ready for my wrath. I didn't want Lee Chino within a 500 mile radius of my Becs.

Keeping my face composed and unreadable, I went to respond to Becca. I didn't want her to think anything was up with Chino. She didn't need to feel scared around him, even though I was terrified for her to have any type of interaction with the biggest cocaine dealer in the Midwest.

"Something wrong with meeting with Lee Chino?" I asked quietly.

She fidgeted and stared down at the bubbles. "You tell me."

I had my mouth in a thin line. I needed to be careful how I reacted to her. She could read me like a book most days. "I understand why you'd be nervous. He's a very well known figure. I'm sure you handled it fine."

Good answer. Yeah, hopefully she fell for it.

Becca's eyes met mine. She was doing it. Trying to read into my expression. "I don't trust him. And I think you feel the same way."

I sighed and cocked my head. "Yeah, he does seem kind of sleazy, but most men of his stature are. It will be fine. I'm sure you had him eating out of the palm of your hand." I reached for her foot, gently tugging it so her knee would pull from her grasp. She reluctantly let go, allowing me to bring her foot into my hands so I could start massaging.

She relaxed. My lack of interest seemed to work.

"I wouldn't say that. He did seem to have good intentions with this project."

I cocked my head to the side. Good intentions? "What exactly would that be?"

She settled further into the tub, closing her eyes as I kneaded the arch of her foot. "He's building more furniture warehouses. He wants to bring that part of Grand Rapids back. It'd be good for the city."

Shit, he was actually going to build warehouses. Now I really needed to keep an eye on Mitch. "I see. So is this your account to handle from now on?"

She let out a pleasing groan as I brought my left hand up her calf, massaging further. "No, I was just filling in for Will. He's going to be in charge of the account."

"Good." Her eyes flew open. Maybe I said that too fast. "I mean, you have a lot on your plate. Chino's project sounds like a big account to add to your load."

Her leg tensed along with the rest of her body as she straightened her posture. "What does that mean? Are you saying I couldn't handle that big of an account?"

"Of course not."

"Then why can't I handle it? I don't have that much going on," she grumbled.

"Becs, you were just talking about how you were stressed about the wedding and the house," I said nervously.

"That has nothing to do with work."

Fuck. I was digging a hole. Blinking a few times, I went to my best way to distract her. I gripped her foot and pulled it to my mouth, gently kissing her toes and giving her big soft eyes.

She took a sharp breath as her mouth dropped open.

"You're right. You could handle it," I said as I nipped her big toe. "Forgive me?"

She closed her eyes briefly at the intimate contact. "I guess."

Hole averted.

"Shall we continue this in the shower?" I asked, picturing her delicious naked body beaded with water.

She smirked. "Mmm, I think I'll just get ready for bed."

I scowled. Was she toying with me?

She giggled and pulled her foot away to climb out of the tub. "Don't worry. I'll be waiting for you."

I gave her a lopsided smile, quickly turning to watch her throw her robe over her body. I couldn't wait to get out of the shower and show her how much I missed her.

***

I quickly washed my body and hair, trying to ignore the massive hard on Becs gave me just by flirting. I couldn't wait to get my hands on her. Shutting off the shower, I grabbed a towel and dried off. I pondered how I should play tonight. Should I tease her or not? She was in a playful mood, I could tell that much. I went into the closet and threw on a pair of blue boxers. If all went well, they would be off my body in no time but would be enough to help with the game I wanted to play with her.

I walked into our nautical themed bedroom to find Becca sprawled on her stomach on the fresh white sheets reading an architecture magazine. She was wearing one of my white shirts, and sweet Jesus, she had on a pair of white lacy boy short undies. My eyes were glued to the delectable curve of her ass cheeks. Teasing her might be harder than I thought. I got the urge to focus on my favorite part of my Becs as I crawled on the bed over top of her.

"That was a speedy shower," she flirted.

"It was. Take off your shirt. I want to continue your massage from the bath," I commanded, anxious to see her tanned skin. I sat back on the bed, patiently waiting for her to obey.

She sat up on her knees facing away from me as she slowly pulled the shirt over her head. My eyes greedily took in her bare skin and how her long, sun-kissed brown hair cascaded down her back. Fuck me, she was beautiful. She started to reach for her panties, but I grabbed her wrists from behind. "I want you to keep these on," I whispered in her ear. A shiver went down her spine from my voice. "Lay back on your stomach."

She relaxed into the bed, throwing the magazine to the side and resting her head on her arms. I straddled the back of her knees, my hands anxious to make patterns on her skin. My palms kneaded the backs of her thighs as my eyes were glued to her perfect ass. She had put back on some of the weight she had lost in December, and it all came back into her firm ass. It was mouthwateringly perfect.

She groaned as my hands came just below her behind, my thumbs grazing her sex. She arched her back slightly but quickly put her stomach back flat on the mattress. My palms pressed up her spine and to her neck, rubbing and kneading out any of the tension that remained from the day. I glided my hands back down but this time stopped on her beautiful ass. I grabbed each globe and firmly flexed my hands. Each cheek fit perfectly in my grasp, and the urge to nuzzle her skin was growing. I wanted to take her from behind, but all in due time. She needed to be primed and ready. I liked to wait until she begged for it. She pushed her behind back into my hands as my thumbs grazed her sex again then back down the inside of her thighs. She groaned with pleasure when I squeezed harder.

My nostrils flared as I stared down at my hands molding with her skin. My breathing was becoming deeper, and my dick was roaring and ready to go, pressing against her thigh.

Why did I put on my boxers again?

I shook my head; I needed to slow down and not get ahead of myself. Becs needed to be dripping for me before I greedily took her.

"That feels so good, Ty," she murmured.

I smirked to myself. She was getting there. I slid my hands back up her back then slowly traced my fingertips back down, hooking her lacy panties in my fingers and pulling them down her backside and thighs to her feet.

I was throbbing now, eager to move inside of her. The sight of her bare ass made me crazy with lust.

I yanked down my boxers and tossed them to the floor, straddling her thighs again. I felt her shiver as our bare skin touched. I firmly placed each palm on her butt again, kneading even harder than before. Becca moaned louder and attempted to spread her legs farther apart, but I had her thighs pinned down with my weight.

"Ty," she whimpered.

Oh yes Becs. Just wait a little longer. I shook my hands slightly, watching her skin move, making my mouth water with hunger. The carnal caveman in me was awakened, and the need to nip and kiss her overcame me. I brushed my thumbs along her sex again and felt her arousal. Then her scent hit my nose.

Oh fuck. I needed to taste her now. Her glistening skin and essence made me wild, and I had no idea if she would be game for what was going through my mind, but I was sure as hell going to try.

I took my weight off her thighs and pulled on her hips, wanting her on her knees. She took the hint and went on all fours.

"Oh Ty. I'm so ready," she groaned.

I gripped both of her hips as I brought my lips to the middle of her lower back, planting a big wet kiss on her spine. She moaned again and pressed her hips backward, looking for some type of friction. I moved one hand from her hip and spread her legs apart farther, watching her head tip backward as she arched her body into me. I moved my lips downward, gently nipping each cheek, my moistened lips making a trail closer and closer towards her sex.

Her legs were shaking with anticipation now, and I couldn't hold back any longer. I clutched her hips and ran my nose along her intimate lips. Her body stiffened.

"Whoa... Tyler what are you doing?" she asked with a shaky breath.

I ignored her question and gently ran my tongue up the outside of her folds.

She tried to pull forward. "You're very close to my, umm...," she said nervously.

She squirmed again as I squeezed her hips, digging my tongue deeper in between the lips of her sex.

"Oh! Tyler I don't know," she gasped.

I nuzzled her sex. "Oh, Becs. Please let me kiss you this way. Let me make you fall apart," I murmured into her skin.

Her breathing was heavy as her body stayed tense. If I could get a few more licks in she would relax some before that magic tightening happened throughout her body. It always took a moment for her to relax when I went down on her. Her dumbass ex-boyfriend wasn't into it. Fucking idiot. If I could make a flavored gum of Becca, I would.

I pulled my head back and gazed at her backside, the smell of her still fresh in my nostrils. "God this is so hot. I've wanted to kiss you from this position for so long baby doll," I rasped moving my mouth back on her, completely ignoring her insecurities.

She moaned louder and dropped her shoulders to the mattress, succumbing to my plea and opening herself up for a better angle. I groaned in pure pleasure as she pushed back into me, finally giving in to the sensation and forgetting about being apprehensive. My tongue darted out to enter her slickness, and I was in pure heaven. I loved to taste her. I loved how she quivered when I pulsed my tongue. I nuzzled her again, enjoying the feel of her glorious ass cheeks against my face. I withdrew my tongue from her entrance and found her pleasure spot, moving my tongue the way she needed to explode.

Her legs started to quiver, and her toes began to flex. Her movements into me were becoming more rigid and demanding the more I pushed my tongue into her. I squeezed my hands around her perfect globes and worked her over as she fell apart in my mouth, moaning and grasping the sheets while her body quaked. I lapped her arousal pleasingly, becoming more and more turned on knowing I caused her unraveling.

"Tyler please, I want you inside of me," she begged.

Usually, I liked to detonate her pleasure bomb twice before I gave in to my own desires, but I was so ready to feel her warmth tighten around me that I was willing to meet her demands.

I sat up, keeping my hands on her hips. I pushed her back down so she was flat on the bed, my eyes glued to her ass making those perfectly plump mounds. I was going to plow into her from behind so I could watch that beautiful butt move with each of my thrusts.

I straddled her again, guiding myself in between her legs and slowly filling her. She came up on her elbows, head bowing back as she sighed with relief. I pushed into her deep, holding still and relishing being completely surrounded by her. She tightened her walls, and I took a sharp intake of breath while rolling my eyes back. "Oh, baby, I love when you squeeze me like that."

She did it again but flexed her walls tighter. I growled then pulled out and pushed back in a fraction quicker than the first time. I opened my eyes and stared down at her backside, starting to move a touch faster. Her skin was doing just as I predicted, gently bouncing with each thrust. My hands found each cheek and squeezed again, causing her to moan.

I moved faster inside her, my eyes growing even hungrier as I watched her butt bounce back into me. I was doing all I could to not explode right then and there. I wanted her to come again; I wanted her to come with me. She needed more stimulation. I pulled out of her and yanked on her hips so she was back on her knees. She gasped as I pumped back inside of her with more force, then reached around her waist so I could rub her most sensitive spot.

She let out a garbled yes as I rubbed faster and thrust harder. I was losing myself inside of her, enjoying every small moan and cry that came from her luscious mouth.

Then she gave in, contracting around me, crying out and pushing her hips back so I was filling her completely. I pounded into her twice more, coming hard inside of her. I fell forward over top of her, gently biting down on her shoulder as I twitched with my release. Once the spasms subsided, I rolled with her to my side, spooning my Becs as we both caught our breath.

"God, I missed you," I sighed into her hair. My arms were firmly wrapped around her waist, our legs tangled.

"I missed you too," she said quietly.

Silence passed between us. I could have fallen asleep, but Becca seemed unsettled. She would normally roll over and snuggle into me, trace patterns on my chest and give me little kisses randomly. I liked that, even if it sealed the deal for my slumber. Yeah, I felt bad when I'd pass out after we had made love and she wanted to pillow talk, but most of the time I couldn't help it, and she rarely gave me grief.

"You're so quiet," I murmured, moving my hand up and down her arm.

"I'm just tired."

I sat up on my elbow and kissed her shoulder, hoping my movement would cause her to face me. She stayed put. "What else is bothering you, Becs?"

She finally rolled to her side and looked up at me through her lashes, apprehension on her face. I moved my hand from her arm to her cheek, urging her to open up to me.

"Talk to me, love," I said softly.

"Did you ever get into trouble in college?"

I scowled down at her. I played baseball in college. I couldn't get in trouble by mixing with the wrong crowd. I drank at parties but never got caught. That was the extent of my law breaking.

"I was an athlete. I couldn't afford to get into trouble."

She suddenly sat up, pulling a pillow to her chest, not looking at me. Confusion spread over me as I looked up at her.

"So you never fought?" Her tone was accusing.

Oh crap.

My silence caused her to turn and frown at me. I ground my teeth, not wanting to relive what she was talking about. "Who told you," I sighed, sitting completely up and leaning back on the white Beachwood headboard.

"I think you should be telling me what happened," she snapped. "Not asking how I found out."

I blew out air. There was no way around this. "It was complete bullshit is what it was."

Becca leaned back against the headboard and gave me her no nonsense look.

I sighed and reluctantly began to tell my story. "Sometimes when I would drink in college, I got a little hot headed. Cooper was normally with me and would calm me down if I started to feel threatened. But there was this one asshole..." I shook my head in disgust. "He never knew when to shut his mouth.

"Nathan and I were in the same fraternity in college. We would always go to parties together. Since he was older, I didn't have to do all the lame shit underclassmen had to do. My baseball team took advantage of this as well. Nathan wasn't your typical frat boy. He drank, you've obviously picked up on his habit."

She shrugged her shoulders. We all knew he was an alcoholic like my mother, but Nathan didn't recognize it as a problem.

"Anyway," I continued. "The only thing different about Nathan was his lack of attempt to hook up with women."

Becca's eyes softened. Maybe it was the change in my tone.

I turned so I was completely facing her on the bed, crossing my legs and meeting her eyes. "Nathan has never told me outright he's gay. I always just knew. But Nathan's tells weren't as obvious in college. There was this one asshole named Jonah. He was my age and was constantly on Nathan's ass about hooking up with the sorority chicks. I think I was the only one who could tell how uncomfortable Nathan was when Jonah would pester him to go after a girl or grind against one at a party. It seemed to happen more and more frequently. Every party, Jonah wouldn't let it go.

"Then he said something in front of everyone that made me lose all self control. I jumped him, literally beat the shit out of him. I remember blood running from his face. I couldn't tell you how many swings I took until Cooper could finally pull me off him."

I looked away from Becca, recalling the evening and how floored I was. Nathan meant everything to me. I wouldn't stand for someone bullying my brother for something he had no control over.

Becca put her hands on my thighs. "What did he say that set you off?"

"He shut off the music and called him a faggot. Everyone stopped talking and looked at Nathan. Then Jonah told everyone there was a queer in the house since he'd never go after a girl."

I chanced a glance at Becca, and her eyes were wet. I looked back down into my lap, not wanting to feel the emotion that was trying to show through.

"The look on Nathan's face was something I had never seen before. Nathan was always happy, always on a mission. He's always radiating success and compassion. I know he loves money and shares that same driven mind like RJ, but Nathan has a heart. To see him trying to hide hurt and inner turmoil because some inconsiderate prick called him out in the most obscene way was destroying. I went crazy and just... lost it."

I felt Becca's hands move from my thighs to my face as she straddled my lap. She forced me to look back at her. "Sounds to me like you were protecting your brother."

I gave her a slight smile. Only if the courts felt the same way. "I'm not proud that I put the kid in a hospital. That he had to eat out of a tube for a week because I fucked up his jaw so bad. Jonah's parents were going to press charges, but once they realized whose kid they were dealing with, they went for a settlement.

"RJ was furious, worried about how my actions would affect the company name. My grandfather was ashamed. I had never felt more awful then the day my grandfather wouldn't meet my eyes because he was so disappointed in me."

"But Tyler, you were standing up for Nathan. What he said was a hate crime. How could they not stand by you?"

I swallowed. "They didn't know why I attacked Jonah."

Her eyes went wide again. "What? Why?" she said in shock.

"I didn't want Nathan to be outed that way. Sure, kids gave statements from the party, but none of it would have been used in court because of the settlement. RJ saw the statements, and I think that just gave him more reason to give Jonah's family money to keep them quiet. As far as I know, all of it has been buried."

"So no one knows about Nathan? Surely Mary does. Would RJ really be that ashamed? I mean, would your grandfather? From how you spoke of him I would peg him to support Nathan 100% no matter what," she said in confusion.

I sighed. "I loved my grandfather dearly, but he was very conservative. I don't know how he would have responded. Nathan would never admit it, but he was as fond of my grandfather as I was. He couldn't face that kind of disappointment. I think that's why he keeps quiet."

Becca shook her head. "Nathan shouldn't be afraid to be who he really is."

I laughed. "Nathan is career driven. Yes, he's gay, but he isn't out to find the perfect partner. He cares more about his business life than love life. Trust me Becs, Nathan is and acts like himself. No hiding that. He just doesn't outright tell people his sexual orientation."

Becca looked down into my lap as she dropped her hands from my face.

"You said you got hot headed. Did you ever hurt anyone else like you did Jonah?"

I rapidly shook my head no. "The only other 'fights' I got into were petty ones, where we just pushed each other back and forth and got into each other's faces. I never threw a punch as hard as I did at Jonah."

She nodded her head, but still kept her eyes to her lap, hugging her pillow to her chest. She was thinking, and I had an idea of what might be going through her head.

I took her chin in my hand, forcing her to look at me. "Becs, I'd never hurt you. You know that right? No matter how mad I might get, I would never touch you that way."

She gave me a gentle smile. "I know," she murmured.

I leaned in to kiss her, softly sucking on her bottom lip. "I'll always throw a punch to protect you. I can promise that much. No one will ever hurt my Becs. I take care of the ones I love."

She kissed me back. "You love your family a lot more than you think," she whispered.

"You are my family."

"I mean your brothers, RJ, your mom. I know you love them, Tyler."

I rolled my eyes then pulled the pillow from between us, bringing her so we were skin on skin. "I love you. That's all that matters."

She frowned at me. "It's okay to love them too, Ty."

That similar uneasy feeling started to rise in my chest again. The same feeling that was attempting to poke through when RJ told me he was proud. I needed to do something to push that feeling away. It made me uncomfortable and exposed, and I didn't like how it tugged at my heart.

I brought my lips to Becca's and kissed her, squeezing her to my chest, my hands wrapped around her waist, holding onto her as though my life depended on it.

She gasped when I finally pulled away as I tackled her to the bed. I hovered over her, settling myself in between her legs and began kissing her again. She raked her nails down my back. I welcomed the delicious sting, helping to distract me from the unnerving feelings that awakened in my heart. Becca was all I needed, not the rest of my family.

***

I woke around 7:00 a.m. fidgety in bed. Becca was passed out, rightfully so. The second time we had made love was a bit rough and needy, and it lasted well into the evening. She literally passed out on top of me the second she got off for the fifth time that evening. The thought of making her come so many times stroked my ego.

I got out of bed cautiously so as not to wake her. It was Saturday, and she deserved to sleep in after I had kept her up late last night. I pulled on a pair of graphite boxers and a t-shirt then made my way into the library. I didn't want to take the chance of waking her by going into my office.

When I had originally made the plans for my office to be connected to our bedroom I thought it was a brilliant idea. I didn't think about how I might wake her when the spiral staircase creaked as I went up and down. And I didn't want her to hear any of my phone calls. At least not lately.

I grabbed my suitcase with my laptop and made myself cozy at the white desk. I logged into the Conklin server and went through my emails. Most of them were typical and mind numbing, until I ran across one from Chino.

Tyler,

    I met with Becca today about the warehouses. I wanted a plan and RJ has been side stepping my requests. My assistant called and set up the appointment with ease.

    Becca was very pleasant to work with. I will look forward to meeting with her in the near future. She assured me you would be handling the finances and getting back to me in a timely manner.

    I would like to meet with you and RJ Monday morning in Grand Rapids. We can discuss our other projects further as well.

    My assistant will be calling to confirm times.

-Lee Chino
Owner of Chino Corporations

I reread the email at least ten times. My blood was boiling with the fact that he went and scheduled the appointment without contacting RJ or myself. Who did he think he was? He has direct contact to RJ; why would he go to someone else in the company? He wasn't going to get what he wanted from the typical staff. Unless he was trying to do more than find places to hide his drugs. I was going to have to look at Chino's plans once Becca and Will were done with them.

What pissed me off the most was the fact that he said he was looking forward to meeting with Becca in the near future.

Not in this fucking lifetime.

I was going to have to make that perfectly clear Monday morning. Normally I would tell him we needed to change the time to Tuesday, but I was floored and wanted to set this asshole straight. He needed to know the Conklin men weren't going to put up with his outlandish demands. And we sure as hell weren't going to let him hide his drugs on our properties. I didn't care how many times he asked. I was fed up, and I was going to be an asshole.

Maybe I wouldn't even do his finances and tell him to fuck off and find some other architect and building company to try and push around. But Nathan and RJ would duct tape my mouth shut and backtrack my words before I knew what was happening.

The only reason they wanted to keep Chino on as a client was because of his residential properties. He had numerous subdivisions throughout Michigan and the suburbs of Chicago. Conklin built every single one of them. I would be lying if I said we wouldn't feel a financial blow if we lost his business.

Chino wanted to partner with Conklin on his subdivisions. He wanted our names to be on the signs as his co-owners and not just the builders. Great idea and profitable one might say, but no. The problem with Chino's subdivisions? He hides his drugs on the properties. It's one thing if our company is subcontracted to build the homes where drugs are found and completely something else if we are part owners. More questions would be asked and could turn in to a big sloppy multi-billion dollar drug bust that could be pinned on us.

Not cool. Not cool at all.

RJ and Nathan knew it was something we shouldn't get involved in, but Chino was persistent and constantly throwing dollar signs in their faces. RJ and Nathan loved money, and each day brought on new fear of them signing a contract without me being around to knock some sense into them.

My phone started to ring as I was going to respond to Chino.

"Hello, Nathan."

"You sound chipper this morning," he teased.

I rolled my eyes. I wasn't in the mood for his playfulness. "Maybe because that asshole Chino made an appointment to meet with Becca about building warehouses."

"Oh," he sounded surprised. "Guess he was sick of waiting on RJ."

I wanted to slam my fists down on the desk but restrained myself. "Why would he go through Becca?"

"Probably because Becca deals with our commercial plans," he said. "I'm surprised he didn't set up the appointment with Will though."

"Will is out for the week. His wife just had her baby. Becca is helping with his clients."

"I don't see what your problem is, Tyler."

I clenched my jaw. "I don't like Chino talking to Becca. She doesn't need to deal with him. And I want to be done with him. I think we need to completely cut our business from him. I'm talking to RJ about it first thing Monday morning."

I heard Nathan gasp. "We can't cut ties with Chino. You of all people know how much of our profit is from his subdivisions. He gives us what, 20% of our income?"

"27%," I sighed. "But we cannot get caught up in his scheme. Do you realize how screwed we'll be if his drugs show up on our building sites?"

"Tyler, we haven't agreed to that yet. Don't worry about him meeting with Becca. Is that really what this is about? Are you feeling threatened by him?"

"I know he was responsible for the tear gas, Nathan. Why would I want him anywhere near Becca?"

"Why would he let tear gas off in a room with his girlfriend inside?" Nathan asked smoothly. "He's been seeing Margo for awhile now to my knowledge."

"Margo sees everyone," I snorted. "I doubt they are serious."

"People change Tyler. We can't jump to conclusions, and we sure as hell can't lose a profit holder, especially a holder that makes up 27% of our assets!"

I put my hand on my head, frustrated that Nathan wasn't on my side. "Something bad is going to happen. I can feel it."

"God, would you stop worrying? Anderson hasn't been by the building in months."

Detective Anderson. How could I forget about him. For a while, he was constantly snooping around the building trying to find dirt on our company. We earned our way legally, at least as of now.

"I'm meeting with RJ about Chino Monday morning regardless. I don't want him going through Becca or Will when it comes to the plans for the warehouses. He has her fooled already. He told her it was for furniture building because he wanted to help Grand Rapids get back in the furniture industry. You and I both know those warehouses aren't for furniture."

"Maybe it is. Stop thinking the worst of him, Tyler."

"Nathan, this man wants us to co-own his subdivisions where he hides billions of dollars worth of drugs and drug money. Do you really think he's a good guy?" I was fuming. How could Nathan fall for Chino's charm?

"That's why we haven't said yes. RJ isn't being dumb about this. He won't jeopardize this company. I know you have no faith in him."

"You're right. He's a money-hungry asshole, and I know he will choose dollar signs over Papa's integrity. This company isn't just his. It was Papa's. He needs to remember that." I was floored now, standing on my feet and pacing the library.

I heard Nathan sigh in defeat over the phone. "Don't do anything stupid, okay. I am supposed to be in Cleveland on Monday, but it sounds like I need to be meeting with you and RJ in Grand Rapids instead."

"Do what you want. We're meeting with Chino after I meet with RJ. Chino was so nice as to email about the finances of his so-called furniture warehouses. He wants the numbers by Monday. Guess I will be busier than I planned this weekend." I was annoyed by that as well. Sometimes I wish I were better about setting my business to the side for the weekend, but it would consume my mind until the projects were finished. Becca was meticulous about her notes for projects. She would leave me a good report that would help with my research. She was so amazing at her job.

"I would offer to help, but we both know I'm worthless when it comes to working numbers."

I laughed. "I appreciate the thought."

"Now, I originally called about some weekend RJ wants to have?" Nathan began in confusion.

I groaned in annoyance. "Did he attempt to get all sappy with you, too?"

"Not really. He just said Mom was having a wedding shower, and we all were going to go golfing or something."

I frowned and a small part of me was disappointed. RJ really did just want something from me. If he didn't get sentimental with Nathan then it was surely a show for me. My heart made that weird tugging feeling again, and I shook my head to rid myself of the awkward feeling.

"I have to talk to Becca about a weekend still. I'm sure she will be all for it," I grumbled. The fact that Becs got along with my mother was irritating to me.

"Let me know. I'll be there. When are we going tux shopping? Has she picked out her colors yet? You are having the reception at Amway, right?"

God, he was just as bad as Missy Stine. "Jesus Nathan, I don't know about that shit. Becca and her mother are handling it."

"Well then I'll handle the tuxes. You clearly don't have a sense of style nor do you seem to care. I'll make the arrangements and call Becca. You can sit around and be your grumpy self," he said snarkily into the phone. "You really don't know what colors she's planning?"

I leaned back in my chair in frustration. I really didn't care about this as long as everything was what Becca wanted. Isn't that what little girls dream about anyway? Cakes, bridesmaids, the dress? All that shit? Just tell me what to wear and where to stand. I get the love of my life and amazing wedding-night sex. That's all I cared about. And seeing Becca in a white wedding dress. The thought made me shift in my seat. I might have to go wake her before breakfast.

"It's some type of purple," I mumbled.

"Pale purple? Dark purple? Plum?"

"I don't fucking know! Ask Becca!" I shouted.

"Well hand her the phone then!" he shouted back.

"She's sleeping. Look, I have to go. Maybe I will see you Monday," I said in a rush, opening a new worksheet on my laptop to try and work on Chino's finances.

"I'll be there. Relax a little, will you?" he pleaded.

"Yeah, yeah, goodbye, Nathan."

Chapter Three

Becca

"Want to hang out on the beach for a little while?" I asked Tyler as I towel dried my body from our very sensual shower.

His eyes lit up as he finished brushing his teeth. "Sure. Can I pick out your bathing suit?" I smacked his bicep with my hand as I went to get dressed. He smirked and followed me into our closet. Tyler came beside me and reached into the drawer I was skimming through. "Wear this one. It tends to ride up." He handed me navy blue Tommy Hilfiger bikini bottoms.

I shook my head at him.

"What? I enjoy the view when you lay on your stomach," he flirted, his hands finding their way underneath my towel. "Although, I doubt it will beat the view I had last night."

My face went scarlet. Last night was unpredictable and super hot, but that didn't mean I still wasn't embarrassed. That angle could not have been flattering, and he was just so close...

"What?" he asked, trying to hold in his amusement.

Not meeting his eyes, I murmured, "Nothing, it's just... your nose was right there."

Tyler looked at me questioningly, not following my drift.

I fidgeted and held my towel snugly around my body. "You know... and you almost licked it a few times."

Tyler thought for a moment then a wicked smile spread across his face. "Licked what?"

I smacked him again, and then proceeded to grab the matching top to the bikini he had picked out.

He laughed out loud at my uncomfortableness. "I guess I did lick a little high. I'll make sure to hit it next time," he teased.

Pulling up the bottoms and sliding on the top away from him, I snorted in disgust. "You are NOT licking my asshole. That's just crazy and awkward."

I felt his breath on my neck as his hands found my waist, traveling up my sides and to the string I was attempting to tie. He brushed away my hands and held the strings. "You moaned the loudest whenever I was close," he murmured seductively in my ear.

Was he nuts? I was probably moaning in discomfort!

He began to tie the string as he nibbled on my ear. "We are most definitely doing that again," he promised.

I bit my lip with unease. Tyler could sense my apprehension. Once he was done tying the knot of my swim suit, he turned me around so I was facing him. Taking my face in his hands, he said, "Last night fulfilled a fantasy. It was so hot, and you were so sexy. Please don't be embarrassed."

"Fantasy?"

"Yes. One of many, but we have a lifetime for that." His expression was mischievous.

I shyly smiled back at him, enjoying his playfulness. Tyler kissed my nose and held me tight. A profound amount of solace and security settled throughout my body. Knowing we would have each other for a lifetime made his arms that much more satisfying.

"You want to know another fantasy I have?" He grinned as he pulled back slightly to look down at me. "Sex on the beach."

I gave him a teasing grin back. "Good thing we have a private beach in our backyard."

Just as Tyler leaned in to press his lips to mine, the house phone rang. Tyler groaned. "Why is that so freaking loud?"

I laughed as I pulled away from his embrace. "You wanted top-of-the-line gadgets."

I ran to the bedroom and noticed the incoming call scrolling across the TV screen. It was Heather. I took the remote and put her on speaker phone through the television so I could finish getting ready.

"Hey Heather."

"Becca! I'm so glad you answered! I'm sorry to drop this on you, but I need you to watch Josie and Emmett tonight." She sounded flustered.

"Aren't you and Ray going to Tahiti tomorrow?" Heather had planned the trip to Tahiti with Ray a few months after Emmett was born. She said the second he turned six months they were reliving their honeymoon. I thought she was crazy.

"We are, but I guess Ray has something planned for me," she squealed with excitement. "It was a last minute surprise, and he didn't think to check if Mom was going to be around. I guess she has an all day function in Traverse City and can't watch them."

I bit my lip in contemplation. Normally I wouldn't mind, but I'd been looking forward to having Tyler all to myself this weekend. Plus, I had no idea if he would be up to being around the little ones for longer than a few hours. He told me he wanted to have babies, but he still seemed uncomfortable around Josie and Emmett.

"Heather, normally I would say yes, but—"

"Oh, Becca, please! Ray and I need this. The look on his face was devastating when he heard Mom say she couldn't watch them. Becca, he was heartbroken. Please!" she begged. I could picture her face, her big brown eyes pleading as though her life depended on it. She and Ray had been through a lot trying to juggle the new baby and Ray's workload.

Tyler emerged from the bathroom wearing a pair of black checkered Under Armour swim trunks. He glanced at the screen then over to me.

"Becca, Josie really wants to see you. Please!"

Tyler looked at me questioningly. I gave him an apologetic stare as I answered Heather. "Okay. What time can you bring them over?"

"Actually, we have to leave in an hour to make Ray's plans. Could you come here and get them?"

Tyler's eyes widened in horror.

"Yeah, I can try, but—"

"Thank you so much Becca! Josie can't wait to see you!" She cut me off and hung up the phone before I could respond.

I closed my eyes for a long second then looked towards Tyler.

"Becca, what did you just tell your sister we would do?" he asked, his voice low and unsure.

I gave him an unsettled smile. "We're watching Josie and Emmett tonight. I'm sorry. She sounded desperate. You can stay here if you want, and I'll go watch them by myself." I apologized.

He sighed and shook his head, walking back into our closet. "Of course I'll go with you."

I followed him in the closet, my eyes glued to his swim trunks falling to the floor and his boxers taking their place.

"Are you mad?" I asked quietly.

Tyler turned as he was pulling on a pair of khaki shorts. "No." He walked in front of me while fixing his button. "I was looking forward to spending time together just the two of us."

His eyes were like kitten's and his lip pouted. I leaned up to kiss him gently. "Thank you."

***

"We should've taken my car, Becs. Why haven't you gotten the sound system fixed yet?" Tyler scolded as we drove along I-90 to Heather and Ray's house.

"I haven't had time. I don't mind listening to the radio." You would think my father's extravagant present would have come with a sound system and radio that worked. I'm sure he paid top dollar for it, but I wasn't going to bug him about it. I had the money to fix it, and it might have been my fault anyway. I put a CD in, and let's just say it hasn't come back out yet. I haven't had the guts to tell anyone though.

"Bring it to the dealership. I bet they'll do it for free considering your father just purchased it," he mumbled. I could tell Tyler was a bit bitter. He wanted to buy me a car.

"I will. I just keep forgetting." The truth was, I had a mechanic I wanted to bring it to, but I wasn't so sure how well Tyler would react.

Tyler nodded. "So, what are we going to do with the little ones?"

"I was thinking maybe we should take them to the zoo? It's a beautiful day, and I know Josie will love it. Does that sound okay?"

"I haven't been to the zoo in almost 20 years," he murmured. "My gran would take us when we were young."

I reached for his hand and squeezed. I knew how much he missed and respected his grandparents. I couldn't help but feel a touch of his sadness laced with his words.

"I'm sorry you lost them, Ty."

He glanced at me then pulled his hand away, grasping the steering wheel with his jaw clenched. "Can we get lunch first?" Tyler asked while clearing his throat. "Our shower this morning made me work up an appetite."

He was changing the subject. Tyler rarely opened up to me about his past. I could count on one hand the few times he showed vulnerability when it came to his grandparents. For some reason, this time he seemed more affected by my mentioning them. I think it was best to change the subject along with him.

"Of course. I'm sure Josie and Emmett would like that."

***

"Uncle Tyler!" Josie shrieked, completely bypassing me to cling to Tyler's leg. Tyler flinched and put his hands up as though the police ordered him to the second she wrapped her tiny arms around his thigh.

"Hey, Josie," he greeted his soon-to-be niece. He slowly moved one hand down to pat her head.

Heather followed with Emmett on her hip. He gave me a huge smile when our eyes met. My heart melted as I reached for him.

"Hey little man!" I took him in my arms and snuggled him close, causing him to giggle. Josie's head whipped towards my affection for her little brother, and she detached from Tyler's leg and came to mine.

"Auntie B! Mommy said we get to have a sleepover!"

"A what?" Tyler asked in fear.

Ray walked behind Tyler and patted his shoulder, handing him a diaper bag. "Have fun, big guy," Ray smirked.

"Becca, you just said we were watching them tonight," Tyler said in a low tone.

"And tomorrow morning!" Josie cheered. She ran back over to Tyler and took his hand. "Uncle Tyler, can I stay up late tonight and go in the hot tub? Mommy said the city lights are really sparkly." She looked up at him with her big brown eyes and a small smile snuck across his lips.

"Not too late little miss. Come here and give me a kiss. Mommy and Daddy won't see you for a week." Josie ran to her mom and hugged her. I saw a tear fall from Heather's cheek. Leaving her kids was hard on her.

Ray scooped Emmett from my arms and blew a raspberry on his cheek then smothered him with kisses. They switched places and cuddled each of their children.

Heather rubbed under her eyes as she handed Emmett back to me. "There's breast milk in the cooler, and all of their things are over there."

Both Tyler and I looked to where she was pointing and nearly gasped when we saw the piles of luggage.

"Do they really need all of that?" Tyler asked in horror while looking at Ray.

Ray grinned in amusement at Tyler. "Yep. Every last bit. I'd say you two should stay here and watch them, but Josie really wanted to go to Auntie B's house. You know, since she's staying there still," Ray winked at both Tyler and me.

My mother and father told us it would be bad press if we were living together before the wedding. I countered with the fact that I was 25 and Tyler was 28 and people could get over it. We compromised on me keeping the condo with Jamie and remained "living" there. Jamie would find a roommate once we were married. Ray found the entire situation hilarious.

Tyler's shoulders slumped as he took in all of the luggage. He let out a huff and went to load the bags in the car.

I gave him an apologetic look as he walked past me, his expression uneasy.

"Heather, we have to get going," Ray urged his wife as he followed Tyler with their own luggage.

Heather took Emmett from me one last time, cradling him in her arms. "Mommy loves you. Auntie B and Uncle Tyler will take good care of you. So will Grandma and Grandpa."

She sniffled once more and handed Emmett back to me then picked up Josie to walk outside to our cars.

"Becs, this isn't going to fit in the car," Tyler grumbled attempting to cram the bags into the trunk.

"Oh! You have to take the Bentley! The car seats can't be moved!" Heather shrieked. "Ray we talked about this!"

Ray looked up from the trunk of the Bentley with wide eyes. "Baby, I can move the car seats."

Heather gave Ray a stern look. "No, they fit perfectly where they are. It will be easier for them to take the Bentley."

Ray glanced at Tyler then put his head down. "Of course sweetie. Here Tyler let me help you with those."

Heather turned and smiled at me. I returned her grin. Ray obviously didn't want to piss her off at all. He wanted this week away as much as Heather.

Tyler and Ray swapped luggage while Heather and I loaded the kids in their car seats. Of course Heather had to give me an in depth tutorial on the correct way to buckle each of them into their seat.

Both Heather and Ray gave their kids final goodbye kisses and headed to their car. I smiled when I saw Ray open her door. Heather had him wrapped around her finger since she was 16 years old.

Tyler hopped in the car and swore when his knees hit the steering wheel.

"OOOOO Uncle Tyler said a bad word!" Josie giggled.

Tyler rolled his eyes and crouched so he could move the seat back. I let out a giggle at his expression. This was going to be an interesting weekend.

Chapter Four

Kids made me nervous as hell. Yeah, they could be cute, say funny things, and speak their mind, but watching them over night was a brand new adventure I wasn't sure I was up for. Lunch was hard enough. Josie didn't stop talking. It was cute at first, but her words started to run together, and I got lost in what she was trying to tell me. Becca just smiled and nodded at her the entire time. Emmett was a pretty cool little guy. He just sat in his seat wiggling his toes. Every now and then he would spit the thing in his mouth out and fuss, but I would simply stick it back in and he'd be fine. Too bad there wasn't something like that for Josie.

"Do you want to get the kids out or the stroller and diaper bag?" Becca asked.

"Um, stroller?" I answered as I parked the car at John Ball Zoo.

"Okay, here we go!" Becca said enthusiastically to Josie as she unbuckled her seat belt. Josie threw her hands in the air and yelled in excitement.

The hatch popped, and I stood and stared at all the crap in the back of Heather's white Bentley. Of course, I didn't think to put the stroller in last and had to dig it out while nearly dropping three bags on the ground. Josie was on my side like lightning as I finally pulled out the stroller.

How the hell does this thing open?

"You have to turn that top part," Josie said in her tiny voice. I looked at her as though I was waiting for further explanation to come from the three year old. As Josie and I were having our stare down, Becca came over holding Emmett and reached for the stroller handle, quickly spinning it and popping it open, almost knocking me backward.

"Sorry, I should have told you how to work this thing," she apologized as she strapped Emmett in the front part of the stroller. Josie plopped herself in the back. Turns out she could either sit or stand. Good thing because I was predicting Josie wanting me to carry her the entire time.

Becca grabbed the diaper bag as I threw the luggage that fell out back into the Bentley.

"Ready?" she asked after handing both kids water bottles.

I nodded silently, straightening my Chicago Cubs hat.

"Uncle Tyler, will you push us?" Josie asked sweetly.

A small smile escaped my mouth at her innocent voice. She really was cute.

Becca looked at Josie adoringly as well and then moved her baby blues towards me. God, that look. She had the look of pure happiness and contentment on her face whenever those kids were around. Especially when she held Emmett.

I was in trouble.

We strolled through the little zoo at the pace of molasses. Josie had to get out at every exhibit and find each and every detail. Becca was right by her side, helping to point out where the animals were hidden. Every now and then Josie would tug on my hand, wanting me to look with her. I'd lift her so she could see better in some exhibits. I found myself mesmerized at how Josie saw her surroundings. She studied everything with wide eyes and a huge smile. The aquarium was her favorite, especially the penguins. I must have held her for 30 minutes straight.

"I'm going to change Emmett's diaper and get his bottle ready," Becca said as she started to unstrap Emmett. "Can you handle Josie?"

I nodded my head and took a seat on the bench. Josie was checking out a penguin statue. "Don't lose her. Heather will kill both of us."

"I won't lose her," I said, offended.

Becca gave me another sharp look as she took Emmett to the restroom.

"Uncle Tyler, can we get ice cream?" Josie asked as she spun around the statue.

"That is a wonderful idea Josie. Let's go." I stood from the bench as she skipped to me, reaching for my hand as we made our way to the concession.

Becca never ate sweets, even when that time of the month came around. I didn't bug her about it. It was one of those sore spots she had that I learned to leave be. She wasn't hurting herself by being picky about what she ate, and as long as she was eating, I wouldn't give her a hard time. I loved her for her. Her obsession with food was a shield to protect herself from her family's harsh comments about her appearance. I just hope one day Becs realizes she doesn't need to wear her armor around me. Her body was perfect in my eyes and always would be.

Just as Josie and I were sitting down with our ice cream cones, Becca came walking over with Emmett cradled in her arms drinking his bottle. She scooted next to me on the bench.

"Auntie B! Look what Uncle Tyler got me!" Josie jumped from the bench and squealed holding her ice cream for Becca to see.

Becca gave Josie a huge grin. "You're a lucky girl, Josie."

I slipped my arm around Becca's shoulders on the back of the bench. "We can share mine if you want," I flirted.

She shyly shook her head no.

"Auntie B, it's really good!" Josie garbled through a mouthful of ice cream. She was down to the cone. She had devoured it in the matter of minutes. You'd think we didn't feed the kid.

"Josie, slow down sweetie. You don't want to get a stomach ache," Becca said gently. Josie just giggled and started to spin around the penguin statue, ice cream cone in one hand while the other rubbed against the penguin.

"Yeah, come on Auntie B, have a little lick," I said seductively, leaning closer so I was a mere inch from her ear. "You know you want to," I whispered. Just as I was about to kiss her, I a warm liquid splattered all over the front of my shirt.

I jumped from the bench throwing my hands to the side, dropping the ice cream cone on the cement. Josie's big brown eyes found mine as her lip started to pout. She just threw up ice cream all over me.

Becca leapt to the side with Emmett then ushered a teary eyed Josie to take her place on the bench.

I leaned over, trying to get the fabric on my shirt to unstick from my stomach. Looking down was a mistake as the stench of regurgitated ice cream filled my nostrils. I gagged and almost lost my stomach as well.

"My tummy hurts!" Josie wailed, hugging her stomach. Before Becca or I could say anything, another burst of liquid shot out of her mouth. I dodged it before it made contact with my shoes. I gagged again, but this time I got a look from Becca.

"This is disgusting," I choked out, pulling my shirt from my skin.

"Would you go get some napkins!" Becca scolded.

Napkins for what? My drenched shirt? Josie didn't have a drop of puke on her. It all came projecting out of her tiny body onto me.

I gagged again as I looked down at my shirt when I leaned to get the diaper bag to hand to Becca. "I'm going to get a shirt from the gift shop."

Becca held Emmett with one hand and patted Josie's back with the other. She was crying inconsolably now.

"Hurry, please!" she said through clenched teeth. Emmett was starting to fuss from all the commotion.

I rolled my eyes as I made my way to the gift shop, the entire concession looking at me with scrunched faces as they tried to eat their food.

Yeah, ice cream was a dumb idea.

Holding my shirt from my skin with one hand, I browsed the gift shop t-shirts. I didn't care what was on it; I just needed one in my size. "Don't you have any in size large?" I grumbled.

The lonely worker in the tiny shop covered her mouth as she looked me over. "The only size large we have are in hot pink or lavender," she said through her covered mouth.

I stared at her. I knew this shop was tiny, but really? They didn't have any larges in other colors?

"What about extra larges?"

She shook her head no, avoiding looking at me. Only if we could switch places. It's a lot easier to look at puke than have it touching you.

I grumbled and grabbed the hot pink shirt and tossed it on the counter while pulling out my wallet. As she swiped my card, I pulled off the puke soaked shirt and tossed it in the garbage can, quickly pulling on the gaudy shirt. Thank God she didn't get any on my cargos.

The gift shop worker made a disgusted sound and looked in the trash can. What did she expect? I was going to take it home?

I left without my receipt and walked back outside to Becca. Now everyone was going to be blinded by my hot pink shirt instead of losing their stomachs because of the puke.

Thankfully, Becca and the kids had moved to a different location away from the splattered vomit on the ground. Emmett was fussing harder now, and Josie was still teary eyed. Becca stood the second I walked next to them, practically throwing Emmett at me.

I had never held a baby in my life. I didn't put my hands up to take him, but just looked at her with a blank stare. "Tyler! Hold him so I can take care of Josie!" Becca shouted. I winced and reluctantly put my hands out to take the crying baby. I held him at arm's length. He stopped crying as he took me in, studying who was holding him. I think he could tell the only thing I held with care that was around the same size as him was a baseball glove.

I raised my brows at his scrutinizing stare then his lip started to pout again. Emmett's little body squirmed as huge alligator tears fell down his face.

"Tyler! Hold him closer to you!"

I awkwardly tried to bring him to my chest, but he just squirmed more.

"Becca, he doesn't want me!" I said as I tried to comfort the little guy. He was flailing his arms and causing a scene.

"I can't hold him right now. Try bouncing him. I need to change Josie's shirt."

Change her shirt? "Did she even get any puke on it? I think she mainly got me!"

Becca groaned as she maneuvered a t-shirt from the diaper bag over Josie's pigtails. "Just try bouncing him!"

I pulled him as close to my chest as he would let me, awkwardly attempting to bounce up and down with him. We must have been fun to watch. A crying three-year-old stubbornly changing her shirt and a screaming baby thrashing its little arms and legs while Becca and I argued. I bet we looked like parents of the year. *Not.*

Just as I was getting into somewhat of a rhythm a rumble came from Emmett's stomach, followed by a squirting noise along with a warm, thick liquid covering my forearms. Emmett stopped squirming and his head drooped down on my shoulder. I attempted to maneuver him enough to see the explosion that went through his diaper and clothing all over my arms and hot pink shirt.

You have got to be fucking kidding.

Chapter Five

Becca

Tyler was quiet and stoned face as we left the zoo and got into the car. He was sporting a very feminine lavender t-shirt from the gift shop. I liked the hot pink one better, but after Emmett's blow out, he silently handed him to me and stalked back to the gift shop. Today went well until the end. An unsettled feeling took over as I feared Tyler would never want kids.

Emmett was in a great mood the ride home, jabbering away, while Josie sang quietly. It seemed her vomiting wasn't going to bring her down.

"So today wasn't too bad," I murmured.

Tyler kept his eyes on the road, his lip twitching in annoyance. He had his aviators on with his baseball cap.

"Okay... So it was a little rough towards the end."

"A little?" he huffed. I bit down on my tongue. "I think it's safe to say it was awful," he sneered.

I rolled my eyes. He was being a little too dramatic. How could we have kids if he couldn't deal with a little puke?

He shook his head in annoyance. "What time is your mom coming home?"

"Not until later."

"How late?"

"Tyler! I'm not making my mom move them from their beds while they're asleep! Look, if you don't want to stay with us, that's fine. Just drop us off at my place then you can stay at Union Square," I grumbled, irritated by his poor attitude.

He let out a loud groan. "I'm not going to stay at Union Square. We'll go to your old condo. Is Jamie there?"

"No, she's in Miami this weekend."

"Does she still have liquor stashed in the condo?"

"Glad little kids drive you to drink," I mumbled.

"Who said it was for me? How do you know I wasn't going to slip it in their drinks?" he muttered while pointing his thumb back at Emmett and Josie.

I noticed a small smile appear from the corner of his mouth. It was a poor attempt at changing the subject, but thank God his mood was shifting.

"By the way, I like your shirt," I snickered.

A full-blown smile crept across his face. "Remind me to donate to that little zoo. They need a bigger gift shop."

***

We ordered pizza from Vitale's for dinner. Tyler booked it to the shower the second we got home and was leery to stand anywhere near Josie after she ate. She changed into her jammies and fell asleep in the middle of the first Disney movie. It was just after 9:30 p.m. and Emmett was snuggled to my chest after his nightly bottle, warm in his baseball themed jammies with heavy eyes. Tyler was sitting on the couch with a passed out Josie on his lap.

"Want to bring her to bed?" I asked quietly as I rubbed Emmett's back.

Tyler cautiously lifted Josie from his lap and stood to take her to the office. Josie wrapped her arms around his neck, causing Tyler to let out a slight smile. Maybe he could get used to the idea of having kids. I followed carrying Emmett, laying him down in the pack-n-play next to Josie on the chaise lounge. Tyler surprisingly covered up Josie with a blanket and tucked her into bed. The gesture looked strangely paternal, and warmth spread throughout my body as I watched him move a loose strand of hair from Josie's face.

We both snuck out of the office and turned off the light, heading straight across the hall to my old bedroom.

"I'm exhausted," Tyler sighed as he started to undress.

Taking off my tank top, I nervously asked, "Was it really that bad today?"

He dropped his gym shorts to the floor and lay on the bed. "It was pretty terrible. I think you should make it up to me," he smirked.

I rolled my eyes and dropped my shorts then rummaged through the almost empty drawers for a t-shirt to sleep in for the night.

"I think the best part was looking at your butt in those cute little khaki shorts," he flirted, rolling so he was on his side to watch me finish dressing. "I especially liked when you bent over."

I smiled as I shimmied on a gray Tiger's t-shirt. "This shirt would have been better than those shorts."

"Take that shitty shirt off and come here," Tyler said playfully, holding his hands out to me. "We left that crappy shirt here for a reason."

I laughed and crawled into bed next to him. "Better than that Cubs tank top you got me."

Tyler let out a slight smirk and pulled me into his arms. Snuggling into his warm embrace was extremely relaxing after the event-filled day. Tyler was right; exhausting was the perfect adjective to describe our outing with Josie and Emmett.

Just as I was getting settled, Tyler rolled so he was on top of me, lacing his fingers with mine on the sides of my head. Running his nose along mine, he whispered, "It wasn't that bad."

I opened my eyes and gazed at him, a weight lifted off my shoulders knowing he could tolerate children, maybe even want them, and not just because I wanted them. I tilted my head to kiss him, meaning for it to be sweet and innocent, but Tyler had other intentions. His tongue parted my lips, coaxing for mine to come out and play. The grip of our hands tightened as Tyler's knees began to wedge their way in between my legs.

"Mmm... Ty we can't do this now."

Tyler kissed down my neck. "Yes we can."

Pulling my hands from his grasp, I yanked on his hair so he would look at me. "Josie and Emmett are in the room just down the hall."

Tyler gave me a puzzled look. "So? Are you telling me Ray and Heather never have sex?"

I raised a brow at him. "Why do you think they wanted to get away for the week?"

"If they don't have sex then I'm never having kids."

I giggled at the seriousness of his expression. "Maybe if we were at their house and they were cozy in their own beds. But whenever Josie stays the night with me, she normally curls up next to me in my bed."

Tyler slowly lowered his head so his lips were back on my neck. "Mmm, I don't feel like sharing you tonight, but just in case we have a visitor, I think we shouldn't waste any time." His hand slipped under my shirt, finding my breast. His hand and mouth felt too good, and a sudden urge to please him passed through my veins. Maybe we did have a little time on our hands.

I quickly rolled him to his back, straddling his hips, seductively looking down at him. "What would please my fiancé tonight?"

He slowly licked his lips while his eyes darkened. "You could honor my first request," he murmured, smoothly running his palms up my thighs and under my shirt to my waist. I bit my lip and took his hint, reaching for the hem of my shirt, pulling it slyly off my torso and over my head.

His eyes were on fire now. "Take your hair down," his voice was low and commanding and oh so sexy.

I obeyed, pulling the hair tie and shaking my head back and forth, running my hands through it to make it less flat. I smirked as I felt his excitement growing underneath me.

"God, you're beautiful." He traced circles on my thighs as he greedily looked over my body.

I used to be afraid of his stare. Now it turned me on more than anything, knowing he desired every single inch of my body. Every beauty mark and imperfection was all his.

"What's your favorite part?" I bravely asked.

Tyler raised a questioning brow. "Favorite body part? I'm not sure I can pick just one." His fingers ran past my thighs to my stomach. "I like this, a lot," he murmured, tracing his finger tip around my abdomen. I let out a small smile. I barely clenched my stomach when he touched it anymore. I wasn't ashamed of the faint stretch marks like I used to be.

He sat up with me still straddling him then bent down to kiss my tummy. "I really do, Becs. So sexy." He kissed it again then worked his way up in between my breasts. "These are pretty distracting too." His tongue darted out, circling and sucking, causing a moan to escape my mouth. My arms found his hair, guiding his head where I wanted it. His hands found my behind and squeezed. "I don't even know how to describe what this does to me," he mumbled in between my breasts as his grip on my ass tightened.

I giggled as he pulled me flush with his body.

"I love your beautiful eyes," he continued, bringing one hand to my face. "This cute button nose, and that mouth," he groaned, moving on to give me a kiss. I slightly pulled back, a flirtatious grin on my face.

"Mmm, let me kiss you," he begged, massaging my behind.

"Let me kiss you first," I whispered. "I want to show you just how much enjoyment my mouth can bring."

His jaw slowly slacked, and his eyelids became heavy. I guided him to sit back against the headboard.

As seductively as I could, I crawled backwards down his body, never letting my burning gaze leave him. I dropped my lips to his smooth and taut abs, tracing the pronounced curves with my tongue. His eyes were devouring every move I made. His hand found my hair, pulling it off my face so we could meet eye to eye as I slowly got closer and closer to working my magic.

Letting a devilish grin leave my lips, I kissed him overtop his black Under Armour boxer briefs. His chest rose, and his gaped mouth turned into a crooked smirk.

I met his smirk, rolling his boxers once then tracing kisses across his hip bone.

"You're going to draw this out, aren't you?" he rasped.

I nodded my head, my tongue darting out again as I rolled his waistband once more, continuing the same drawn out process. His hand was still in my hair, his grip getting tighter the closer and closer I got. His stare was so intense, goading me to get to the point. My mouth was watering now, my hands shaky as they finally rolled the fabric enough for him to spring free.

My eyes grew wide as I took him in, still amazed with his size. I glanced up at Tyler only to find his smug expression. He knew he was blessed, and I blushed at his presumptuous stare.

Gathering my thoughts again, I ran my tongue along his length, enjoying hearing his head thump against the headboard and watching his teeth graze his bottom lip.

"That's so fucking hot," he rasped.

Flicking the tip with my tongue, I scolded, "Don't curse."

Amusement spread across his face as I trailed kisses back down his length. "Those innocent baby blue eyes looking at me while your mouth does naughty things makes me curse."

I grinned at him, making my eyes wider as I finally took him completely in my mouth.

"Oh... Yes...," he groaned in satisfaction, his eyes rolling back.

I firmly wrapped one hand around him while I worked the tip with my mouth. Tyler gently cupped my cheek with one hand, his other pulling the hair from my face so our eyes could meet. His stare was carnal and filled with hunger and promise.

The slight inhales of breath that escaped Tyler's mouth made me feel powerful. I had him in the palm of my hand, taking him as high as I wanted. He was at my mercy now, his abdomen clenching as he touched the back of my throat.

"Oh, just like that Becs," his breath came out in a rush, his words raspy and filled with need. His hands dropped from my hair and face, squeezing the life out of the satin sheets. He was on the very edge but I wasn't ready for him to give in yet. Slowing down my movements, I glanced back into his eyes. They were scorching with passion as he cocked his head to the side, silently begging me to continue with the pace I had been using.

I teased and taunted with the tip of my tongue, making long strokes up and down, slow and steady. Tyler's jaw clenched as he let out a low rumble from his chest, now both his hands finding my hair as I continued my tantalizing pattern. His body was fidgety, his hips pushing upwards every time I'd reach the tip of his length, pleading for me to score the final point.

Tyler groaned in frustration after I wrapped my lips around him as though I were going to completely take him in my mouth, but I quickly pulled away, my tongue lazily wandering back downward.

Grabbing my head, he firmly forced my eyes to meet his. Tyler's hard, lustful eyes implored mine as he bit down on his lip then roughly released it as he lead my mouth back a mere centimeter from his length. My lip quirked up in a devious smile, and I had him. I could get whatever I wanted at this point, but I wanted to please him, wanted him to come undone. I ever so slowly opened my mouth then ravaged him so fast he moaned louder than I'd ever heard him while we were intimate.

"Mommy!" Josie shrieked, followed by little feet patting against the hardwood floors.

I jolted back, my mouth making a popping noise as I suddenly released him. Tyler flinched as he reached for the pillow, and I quickly grabbed the Tiger's t-shirt, yanking it over my head in the nick of time.

"Mommy, Mommy, Mommy! I want my Mommy!" Josie sobbed as she climbed into the bed. Tyler shifted uncomfortably as she crawled over his legs.

I held my hands out for her to climb in my lap, my heart still racing from my attack on Tyler. "Did you have a bad dream?" I gently asked, patting her back.

"I heard a noise," she sniffled, rubbing her eyes.

I shot Tyler a look as he shrugged his shoulders.

"Do you want me to come and lay with you?"

"Can I sleep with you?" her voice cracked.

Without thinking I said yes, tucking her under the covers.

"Becca?" Tyler said accusingly in a hush. "What about–"

"Shh! She's used to sleeping with me whenever she stays. I think you'll be fine for one night!"

Tyler rolled his eyes and stood from the bed, adjusting himself in his boxers as he awkwardly walked to my closet, probably to find a t-shirt and shorts to sleep in since we would be sharing the bed with a three year old. I shook my head in irritation as I snuggled next to Josie. *Men.*

Chapter Six

I opened one eye to the bright light beaming in from the window. I had an awful kink in my back caused by a tiny foot that kept finding its way into my ribs, side, and hip. I almost went to the couch, but Becca had already taken it, making herself comfortable with Emmett on her stomach. The little guy cried half the night. Between his screams and Josie's constant need to kick me, I hadn't slept more than a minute.

Babbles from Emmett rang through the hall, followed by a singing Josie.

Glad she slept well.

"Uncle Tyler! Auntie B says breakfast is ready! She made pancakes!" Josie sang as she came right up to my face. I looked at her with my one opened eye, the rest of my face still buried in the pillow.

Groaning, I sluggishly sat up, rubbing my face with my palms.

"Come on Uncle Tyler!" Josie badgered while pulling on my forearm. She dragged me through the hallway, continuing her song with a hop to her step, her pigtails bouncing from side to side.

Becca was standing at the stove with a spatula in hand, bouncing Emmett on her hip as he chewed on a different kitchen utensil.

"Morning," Becca greeted with tired eyes. She had a smile on her face, but no doubt she slept about as much as I did. "Hungry?"

Taking a seat at the island counter, I mumbled sure followed by a yawn.

Becca gave me an empathetic smile then went back to flipping pancakes.

"Uncle Tyler, can we go swimming after church?"

I rolled my eyes in her direction then back to Becca. She must have felt my glare burning a hole in the back of her head from how her body stiffened.

"We're going to have to stop by Union Square to get some dress clothes for you," Becca said quietly. She turned off the stove and dropped the rest of the pancakes on a plate then brought them over to the island.

"Exactly how long are we watching Thing One and Thing Two?"

Becca turned to grab some orange juice out of the fridge. "My parents will take them after church..." Her words faded. There was more that she didn't want to tell me.

"Becca....," I said sternly.

She impressively fixed Josie a plate with one hand then poured her a glass of orange juice. "We're having brunch with my parents after church."

I shrugged my shoulders. That wasn't that big of a deal. Some quick food and chit chat then off to Grand Haven to finish out our weekend, alone. I had a serious case of blue balls from last night and planned on taking care of the situation the second those tykes were out of our hair. Maybe I could get her to give me road head. As my mind drifted, I barely heard the next words out of Becca's mouth.

"Your parents are going to be there as well," she whispered, putting Emmett on a seat with a tray on the counter.

"My what?" I asked quickly.

Becca pulled out a blender from a cupboard and some fruit from the fridge. "My mom and your mom were talking earlier in the week and decided it would be good to get together to talk about the wedding. Do you want a protein shake with your pancakes?"

"Why are you just now telling me about this?" I scowled; irritated she was trying to deflect the subject.

She audibly sighed. "I found out this morning."

"Great," I grumbled while fixing myself a plate.

***

My grandparents took my brothers and me to mass every Sunday. Sometimes my mother would join us, but she'd normally be doing her own thing. RJ was never around, and my mother would drop us off Saturday night so she could hang out with the other trophy wives in the city.

Mother of the year.

Which was why I almost had a heart attack when I saw RJ walking down the aisle. How did he not start burning the second he stepped foot on holy ground?

"You didn't say RJ was coming?" I whispered to Becca.

She looked behind us to see him and my mother walking towards us. "I told you your parents were coming."

"Yeah, but I didn't think you meant RJ."

"Well, he's your dad. I didn't think I needed to specify. Normally parents mean mom and dad."

"Hi Tyler!" my mother squealed as she wrapped her arms around me. "I've been looking forward to this all week! Becca, it's so good to see you again!" she added, moving her grasp on me to Becca.

RJ gave my hand a firm shake. I was still pissed to hell at him for the entire Chino thing.

"When's the last time you set foot in a church?" I asked RJ.

He gave me his damn smirk. I hated that smirk. Becca was so kind to point out I share the same expression. I think she's crazy. RJ and I are nothing alike.

"I'd have to say... your grandfather's funeral."

He moved past me and reached for Becca to give her a hug. I hated him touching her, but seeing her attempt to hide her discomfort with his embrace made me feel better. I automatically reached for her hand when he let go then pulled her to the chair on my other side. She gave me a 'really?' look, but squeezed my hand with reassurance. She thought my jealousy with RJ was ridiculous but understood I needed her affirmation that she was mine. I pulled her hand to my lips, silently thanking her for not scolding me further.

"Mary, RJ, I'm so glad you both could join us for the service!" Missy said as she made her way back to her seat in front of us. She was busy mingling with others from the congregation. I suspected that was a traditional task for her; my grandmother used to do the same thing. Max followed behind her, holding his hand out for me to shake.

"I hope you're ready for the golf course after brunch," he said, giving my hand a firm squeeze. I nodded my head. I couldn't tell my father-in-law no, especially when he was Max Stine. So much for getting home early.

***

Brunch was... boring. All the women talked about were flowers, cakes, party favors, colors... blah, blah, blah. Poor Becs. I could tell she was uncomfortable for most of the conversation. Especially when she found out my mother was the one to send our engagement pictures to the *Chicago Tribune*. She smacked my thigh under the table when I began to scold my mother. I didn't understand; Becca was floored because of that. Why would she get embarrassed when I yelled at my mother for doing something that irritated the hell out of her? There are some things I won't ever understand about women.

I was thankful to be out on the golf course, even if I had to share a golf cart with RJ. I planned on giving him a piece of my mind about Chino talking to Becca and how he wanted her to make his plans. Once we were all set to go, Michael, Becca's brother, and Max lead the way in their cart to the first tee box. It was about a ten minute ride according to the golf course attendant.

"You did pretty good at brunch with all that wedding talk," RJ said.

I huffed under my breath. I mainly kept my mouth shut.

"You should try not to snap at your mother though. She gets really bothered when you don't treat her well."

"You're one to talk," I sneered.

He shrugged his shoulders. "I know. I'm working on it. She's in a much better mood when I'm nice, and she's very... giving," he smirked.

I rolled my eyes. "I don't want to hear about that."

"Just thought I'd let you in on the secret. Women put out a lot more if you're nice to them, act like you care."

"The difference between you and me is I actually care about my future wife," I snapped. "I don't pretend to care. She's the only thing that matters to me on this Godforsaken planet. I care so much that I'll kill you if Chino comes anywhere near her again."

RJ whipped his head in my direction, acting shocked by the change in conversation.

"Oh don't act like you didn't know. He met with her on Friday," I grumbled. "Since you delayed making his plans for him."

"I didn't know. I have the plans already drawn. He knows that." RJ said in confusion.

My jaw ticked. "Then why the hell was he meeting with Becca?"

RJ blinked then looked back in front of him. "I have no idea."

"RJ, we need to be done with him! He's trying to weasel his way into this company. I won't let Grandpa's name be ran through the mud because of him. We need to cut ties."

"Tyler, that's ludicrous. You of all people know how much we need his business," he scolded.

"Money isn't everything. I know that's a hard concept for you to understand."

"I know you don't believe me, but I do care about my father's name and this company. I care about leaving it to you and your brothers so you can leave it to your children someday. I'm not a money hungry monster," he said with all seriousness.

I let out a superficial laugh. He was really putting on a show now.

"I'm serious, Tyler." His tone was tempered with sincerity, and my chest tightened. I glanced at him, not sure what to say or how to deal with the uncomfortable feeling that was washing over me.

"I'll talk to him about meeting with Becca; let him know that we're the only ones he deals with in the company, no one else."

"And the subdivisions?" I murmured as though it was a dirty word.

"It's a lot of money to pass down." RJ stopped the cart and turned his full attention towards me. "But I suppose we're doing fine without that side of Chino's business."

I bit the inside of my cheek, waiting for the catch. When our eyes met, I was struck with an image I'd never seen before on RJ—honesty. I swallowed hard, unsure if I should believe the gut feeling that was running through my insides.

"Are you gentlemen ready?" Michael asked, coming up to my side of the golf cart.

The first nine holes were awful. Having to sit with RJ the entire time, constantly trying to deal with his act of being a normal father was making my skin crawl. What exactly was he getting at? That we were normal? Was he trying to convince Becca's family that we actually shared the same dynamics? Max Stine wasn't an idiot; he would be able to see right through RJ's attempts. And since when did RJ care? He didn't care if our business partners knew how he treated us. We were out to make money, not run some mom-and-pop company.

"Let's have a drink, shall we?" Max said, patting my back as I stood from the cart. I think he sensed I was tense and overly irritated with my father. A quick drink or two on the turn might help me relax a little.

"Yeah, sounds great."

We walked into the dimly lit bar that only had a few other golfers sharing a pitcher of beer. They must have been done with their game, and I was jealous. I had to endure nine more holes with dear old dad.

"Can I get a Rob Roy for both Michael and myself, and put these gentlemen's drinks on my tab," Max said, taking off his hat to sit down at the nearest table.

"Thanks, Stine. Next round's on me. I'll have a Whiskey Sour. Do you want the same, Tyler?"

I nodded my head and took a seat next to Max. Since when did RJ know what I liked to drink on the golf course?

"You did pretty good out there Tyler. I'd love to see you on the baseball field. Do you ever play recreationally?" Max asked.

"Thanks. I haven't played since college." Saying those words made me realize how much I missed playing. I loved baseball. While growing up, the game kept me calm. I have no idea where I would have been if I didn't have the solace of my leather glove and the sound of gravel under my cleats.

"Tyler had a pretty good swing," RJ intruded, bringing our drinks to the table. "He could have gotten into the Majors if we would've let him."

I resisted glaring at RJ, not wanting to cause a scene in front of my future father and brother-in-law.

"Why didn't you play?" Michael asked. "Being a professional athlete would be the coolest job ever."

"School is more important than jumping around the Minor Leagues hoping to get your call to the Majors. There would be no stability in that. And what if you got hurt? Then what would you have fallen back on?" RJ said as a matter of fact.

My teeth clenched as I burned a hole in the table with my eyes. I felt RJ put his hand on my shoulder, and it took all of me to not rip his fingers from the fabric. How dare he say that about my baseball career? Or I should say lack of a baseball career. Why wouldn't he tell the truth, that he wanted me to do the finances for his company instead of fulfilling my dreams?

"Wise decision, Tyler," Max said, lifting his glass. "Making the right choices for your future isn't easy when your heart is telling you otherwise."

RJ lifted his glass along with Max. "Tyler wasn't very happy with me for steering him in this direction, but I'm sure he's thankful now."

I snorted, raising my eyes from the table. RJ took a drink, his eyes never leaving mine. After he swallowed, he said, "You'd never have met Becca if you continued with your baseball fantasy."

I gulped, feeling like the wind had gotten knocked out of me. When he said that, for whatever reason it felt like a low blow. RJ's comment felt too personal, too involved in my life.

Using my relationship with Becca to make himself look like the good guy was outrageous.

"Becca is the only good thing I've gotten out of this company," I said in a low voice.

RJ smirked. "Keep telling yourself that, Tyler. You're pockets wouldn't be nearly as deep if you hadn't come to work for me."

That was a lie. The majority of my money came from reading the stocks. My start up money for my investments was from the Conklin firm, but nothing since that. Maybe if he knew my bank account was a lot fuller than his he wouldn't be so damn arrogant. There was only one reason why I didn't say screw you and leave my trust fund.

"I didn't come to work for you; I came to work for my grandfather."

RJ set his drink down, moving his eyes away from mine. For a split second he looked wounded. "God rest his soul," RJ said quietly. "Who knows where we would be now if he were still around."

I didn't like RJ's tone. He said it as though my grandfather did nothing for the company, as if RJ ran a more successful business than his father.

"Probably in more cities," I snapped.

Max cleared his throat while Michael kept his drink to his lips, awkwardly watching our tiff.

"Robert was a great guy. I'm sorry for both of your losses. I always enjoyed doing business with him, even if it was for a short amount of time. Shall we cheers to Robert Senior?" Max said, attempting to hold the peace.

You could tell Max was good at deflecting conflict. He always seemed to sit in the middle of situations. That's probably why he was on everyone's good side and well respected in this city.

RJ grabbed his drink and held it in the air. "Why not. *Papa* would be proud of his grandson. Helping run a successful, multi-location business, about to actually marry a beautiful and successful woman. Only if he could be here to share the moments with us, right Tyler?" RJ said. Even though his smirk was back on his face, anger shown through his eyes.

The dumbass was always jealous of his father. Why couldn't he just be grateful? From what I knew, RJ messed up numerous times and my grandfather always bailed him out. Robert Senior paved the way for RJ, and the fact that RJ was a huge asshole about all Papa did for him fueled my anger even more.

"Tyler, why don't you join me for a cigar outside?" Max asked while reaching in his pocket. "I know how much you love my Cubans." He stood from the table, silently ordering me to follow. "Please excuse us, gentlemen."

RJ tipped his drink in Max's direction and turned to talk to Michael.

Standing and grabbing my drink, I followed Max onto the deck. It was warmer than usual outside, and I was cursing the strict dress code of slacks instead of shorts. I set my drink on the ledge and leaned on my elbows over the railing, staring out at the greenery.

Max set an ashtray in between us on the ledge and pulled out the cigars. He took one in his hand and left the other next to the ashtray. "Looked like you could use a break," Max said as he attempted to light his cigar.

I tilted my head backwards and closed my eyes briefly then reached for the cigar. A good Cuban would help ease the tension from my asshat of a father.

Max handed me his lighter once he got his cigar going then proceeded to lean against one of the pillars. "RJ stresses you out, doesn't he?"

I puffed on the cigar until the tip was lit, inhaling the Cuban tobacco. This was the real deal, not blended with American tobacco, and I was already feeling more relaxed.

"Was it that obvious?"

Max smiled towards the ground with the cigar in his mouth. "You're not like him, are you?"

"I like to think I'm not. We hold very different views on life."

"That's good. He seems to care about you more than you think."

"Don't believe everything you hear," I mumbled, leaning back over the railing. "He knows how to put on a good show."

"Most successful businessmen do. I get it; he was gone a lot. I know his type. Late nights, long business trips, and unfortunately... infidelity. Those things, though, they don't always affect how a person cares for their child," Max said.

I let out a slight laugh. "RJ wasn't a parent. I don't understand his attempt to act like he cares about me lately, but he wasn't there for me or either of my brothers."

Max shrugged his shoulders. "Some could say the same about me and my kids."

My stomach dropped. Becca had mentioned how she didn't really know her father. How he was gone until late most nights. She basically only saw him on Sundays because her mother demanded it. Max tried to be there for his family emotionally and financially. He did a far better job than RJ. I felt bad for implying all good businessmen were the same.

"No, how Becca talks about you... You're nothing like RJ," I said sincerely.

Max let out a small laugh.

"You made time for your family. RJ made time for himself and other women," I said quietly.

We were silent for a few moments.

Max took a long puff of his cigar. "I think I can trust you to make better decisions than your father with my Becca, am I right?"

"Of course," I said without hesitation. A hint of jealousy spread through me when he said my Becca. "I would never treat her how RJ treats my mother. I love her more than anything." She was the reason for my every breath.

Max's white teeth shown through against his tanned skin. "Good. Otherwise, I'd have to shoot you in the foot," he said jokingly. I laughed at his expression. "Oh wait, knocking her up before marriage is a shot to the foot, cheating is in the arm." Max's smile faded into a slight grin, his eyes turning dark. The air and his demeanor changed, and his look sent a shiver of fear through my system, wondering if he was really joking.

His eyes flicked back to soft like a light switch. He leaned over the railing as I was, putting the cigar back in his mouth. "I've been meaning to ask you, what's your business with Chino?"

I blinked at him as the air caught in my chest. "He contracts our services," I said as calmly as I could. Stine didn't know about the possible subdivision deal. Even though RJ gave off the vibe that we would pass down partnering with him, I still didn't trust RJ to follow through with the decision.

"Anything else? Is he partnered with any of your projects?" he asked inquisitively as if he could read my mind.

"Mainly subdivisions. He's starting a new business with furniture. Just invested in six warehouses for remodeling. Other than that—"

"Nothing on the side?" he cut me off, acting nonchalant.

Max must have known Chino's game. I knew they were acquaintances from their younger years, but I had never heard of them doing business together.

I stood tall again, my business presence making an appearance. "No. I can assure you, we don't do those kinds of deals."

Max looked me from head to toe expressionless. I was glad for the warmth in the air, fear creeping up my spine that I might start sweating from something other than the heat. His probing stare turned into a smile as he stood tall from the railing in front of me. Patting my shoulder, he said, "You're a good man, Tyler."

Even though I only had a few inches on him, the chilling way his eyes turned from soft to hard so fast was damn near terrifying.

Chapter Seven

Becca

"Becca, are you sure you want to wait four weeks to go dress shopping when you come in for the wedding shower? We should really do it sooner," Mary asked as we sat outside on the deck.

Josie was playing on the play set while Emmett was napping.

"Mary has a good point. Can't you take a day off next week?"

I refrained from rolling my eyes. "I can't just take a day off of work, Mom. Tyler wants to take a long honeymoon, and I haven't been with the company long enough."

Both Mary and my mother laughed hysterically at my reason. "Becca, do you really think you need to worry about vacation days?"

"Neither Tyler nor RJ would care if you took a month off, sweetheart," Mary added while holding her hand to her chest.

"I care. My co-workers already look at me as though the only reason I even got the job is because of Tyler," I whispered.

"I hate to break it to you, but every person you meet from now on is going to think that," my mother said. "Come on, Becca! It'll be fun. We can have a girls' day. Just the three of us."

I didn't want it to be just the three of us. I was going to need Jamie and Heather to endure a day of dress shopping with my mother. They could provide a buffer when my ass wouldn't fit into the tiny designer dresses.

"I want Jamie and Heather to be there. If we wait four weeks, then they'll have enough time to schedule the trip."

My mother sighed and reluctantly agreed.

"Could you manage to take off Friday at least? We could spend the entire day shopping then only worry about the shower on Saturday," Mary pleaded.

"Let me check my schedule," I conceded. She did have a point. It would make the weekend not seem so full.

"Great!" Mary squealed. "I'll make the appointment at Bella Vie! I might even be able to get Acra to be there for the appointment!"

My mother gasped. "Acra? As in Reem Acra!? She designs outfits for celebrities!"

Great. The going size in Hollywood was a zero. She would be in for a rude awakening when my size six ass walked through the door.

Mary giggled and nodded her head. "Yes! We have lunch whenever she's in Chicago." My mother and Mary were having a ball together. I was thankful to hear Emmett cry over the baby monitor and save me from their trophy wife antics.

When I came back with Emmett, Josie was sitting on Mary's lap.

"It must be so amazing being a grandma," Mary said.

My mother nodded her head. "It's the best gift from God. I love my children, but there is something different about a grandbaby."

I sat down between my mother and Mary with Emmett. He was curled against my chest and fell back asleep as I swayed back and forth in my chair.

"I predict you will be a grandmother sooner than you think," my mother said, winking at Mary.

I let out a shy smile.

"I hope so! Tyler with a little baby would melt my heart. He softens so much for you Becca. I can only imagine what his own child would do to him," Mary choked. She ran her finger under her eyelid, worried a tear may escape and mess up her makeup.

"Hello ladies," RJ greeted, walking through the sliding door, my father and Tyler following closely behind him.

My dad took a seat next to my mother on the wide sofa lounger, putting his arm behind her and kissing her cheek. "Did you enjoy your afternoon?" my father asked.

"I think we got a lot of wedding plans sorted out. We even made a trip to the venue so Mary could see," my mom answered while leaning into my dad. I loved their affection towards each other.

Tyler came behind me and put his hands on my shoulders. "Everything good?" he murmured so only I could hear. Turning to look at him, I smiled and nodded my head. His lip quirked up then his eyes found Emmett resting on my chest.

"Tyler, we were just talking about grandbabies!" Mary teased as RJ sat down on the footstool where Mary's legs were propped. I tried to ignore his hand creeping up her leg to her thigh.

Tyler's jaw tensed at Mary's excitement. His traditional scowl formed on his forehead. My face fell. He really wasn't ready for kids.

"Being a grandma is going to be so much fun!" Mary snickered to Josie, who giggled at her expression. I felt Tyler's huff as his hands tightened on my shoulders. Josie jumped off of Mary's lap and ran towards Tyler, throwing her arms up for him to hold her. He ignored her at first but eventually gave in and picked her up in his arms.

"Uncle Tyler, can we *please* go swimming!" Josie begged.

"Josie, I don't know. Aunt Becca and I have to get home pretty soon," Tyler said.

She pouted her lip at him, her big brown eyes taking a hold over him. Everyone awed at Josie's attempt to get Tyler to do what she wanted.

"I'm sure you could use one of Michael's swim trunks," my mother said. "Becca, you have a suit here in your old bedroom I'm sure."

"Please Auntie B! I want to go swimming with you and Uncle Tyler!"

"Tyler, how can you say no to that little face!" Mary said.

Tyler sighed and agreed. Josie's little arms flew in the air with excitement. She squirmed her way out of Tyler's arms to go to my mother, dragging her inside so she could get ready to swim.

"I'll hold the little one so you can change, Becca," Mary offered with big pleading eyes. I smiled and handed over the still sleeping Emmett. Mary clapped her hands and snuggled him. She loved babies. I was surprised she didn't take to her sons when they were babies.

Tyler and I walked downstairs to find swimsuits.

"There are suits in the pool room," I said to Tyler as I walked towards my room in the opposite direction. I heard him grumble as he went to find a bathing suit.

I search through my drawers, trying to find something that wasn't outdated. While I rummaged, my cork board with pictures caught my eye. I saw the picture of Ashlynn and me and wrinkled my nose. I huffed and reached for it, taking it and crumbling it, throwing it in the garbage can next to the dresser.

Stupid bitch. I was so glad to be done with her.

Then I looked at a picture of Gage and me. My anger towards Ashlynn quickly vanished, and my heart fluttered for Gage. It wasn't a romantic flutter but a caring one. I loved Gage, but in a different way. I decided I was going to stop by his shop later in the week to get my CD player fixed. I wasn't sure if that was his specialty, but it would be a good excuse to see how he was doing. I wouldn't tell Tyler. What he didn't know wouldn't hurt him.

"I find it odd your brother only has a bright yellow bathing suit," Tyler said grouchily as he stepped in the room.

"I'm sure my mother picked it out." I shimmied out of the white summery strapless dress then reached for the top of my bathing suit.

Tyler was suddenly behind me, his breath hot on my shoulder. "Can we make this quick?" He grumbled, his lips grazing my skin. I felt his excitement growing against my lower back as his arms made their way around to my front. "This is going to be very uncomfortable," he groaned, his lips finding my neck. I giggled and reached for his probing hands.

"Uncomfortable how?"

"I have the worst case of blue balls from last night," he whined against my ear.

A smile escaped my mouth. "Sorry about that. I'll make it up to you tonight," I flirted.

"I was hoping you would make it up to me on the way home," he groaned, his excitement still digging into my lower back.

"Sounds dangerous."

"Oh, baby doll, you know I live for danger. Besides, I can multi-task."

"Multi-task?" I asked, putting on the top of my bikini.

His lips found my ear again. "Another fantasy. That dirty mouth working its magic while I'm driving."

I turned and playfully slapped his chest then started to tie the back of my top. I was relieved to see a full blown smile. I had no idea what kind of mood he would be in after golfing with RJ and future father and brother-in-law.

"We'll see if you behave while swimming," I said seductively, dropping my underwear and stepping closer to him. Now I could feel him on my stomach. He really was ready to go. "You are going to have to try and tame that big guy," I scolded, stepping back again to pull on my bottoms.

"I'm in need of a tamer."

I rolled my eyes and tugged on his arm to take Josie swimming.

Josie met us on the pool deck with her bright pink swimsuit and matching swimmies. It seems the older crowd had relocated to watch everyone swim. Josie ran to Tyler, throwing her arms to him like usual asking to be held. Tyler picked her up sooner this time.

"Throw me in, Uncle Tyler!" Josie begged.

Tyler looked to me for approval, and I nodded my head yes. Josie could swim, especially with her swimmies. "Just jump in with her right after."

Tyler smiled at Josie then counted to three, tossing her in and following with a cannonball.

I smiled and went to the table where both of our parents were lounging to set our towels down. Mary had passed Emmet over to RJ. There was a sight I never thought I'd see. RJ surprisingly held Emmett with ease, gently bouncing him on his knee while making goofy faces at him. I caught Tyler watching RJ, confusion written all over his face. Mary's eyes longingly watched as well, probably thinking this was how life was supposed to be.

"Becca sweetie, you look great! The gym has been on your side!" my mother complimented.

My hand was hovering over my stomach self-consciously. She wasn't one to make positive comments about my looks. Was she just saying it because she felt she had to after our run in at the Christmas party?

"Thanks," I mumbled while looking at the ground.

I felt a pair of wet hands on my hips. "She's always been beautiful." My face heated with embarrassment and gratitude as Tyler kissed my cheek from behind.

"Can't argue that," my father smiled. I looked at him to find his kind brown eyes. "Wait until you have a daughter, Tyler. The thought of shooting boys never sounded so easy."

Everyone laughed as Tyler dropped his hands from my waist and gave an uneasy laugh.

"That's why I'm glad I didn't have any girls," RJ said, tipping his glass towards my father.

Tyler huffed under his breath. I was sure I was the only one who heard him.

"A girl would've been wonderful to have. We'll just have to settle for a granddaughter," Mary said, reaching to take Emmett from RJ. RJ zoomed him back to Mary as though he were a rocket ship, making Emmett giggle.

RJ and Mary laughed, and the look on Tyler's face was one of disgust.

A wet Josie came out of the pool stairs and over to me, tugging on my hand to join her in the pool. "Come on Auntie B!"

"Okay, okay," I laughed as she pulled me to the edge of the stairs.

Once I was half way down the stairs, Josie scurried back over to our parents. "Why aren't you swimming?" she asked with her hands on her hips, her determined face meeting all of our parents.

RJ smiled and cocked his head at Josie. "You want us to swim?"

Josie moved over to him, her body still dripping with water. "Yes. You're Tyler's dad, right? So are you my Grandpa, too?"

RJ laughed. "Whatever you want to call me is fine. But I don't have my suit, sorry sweetie."

"I'm sure Max has a suit you can borrow. A swim with your granddaughter would be nice for you, too," my mother said, nudging my father's knee.

My father rolled his head and gave my mom a half grin then set his drink down. "I guess we could do that. RJ, I'm sure I can find you a suit if you're interested."

"Yeah! Please, please, please!" Josie begged.

RJ laughed again and stood to follow my father. "Only for you, Princess."

***

"Can you believe RJ?" Tyler roared as we pulled out of my parents' driveway. It was nearing 7:00 p.m., and we were at my parent's way longer than we had anticipated. "He must have thrown Josie around that pool at least 15 times and pushed her on the swing for a half hour. I mean, who is he trying to impress?"

Tyler was furious. I couldn't pinpoint why he was so mad. "And my mother! She wouldn't let that baby go. She has never held a baby that long in her life!" His knuckles were white from gripping the steering wheel so tightly. "The whole talk about how he was so proud his son is getting married and ready to really start living. He always made it sound like marriage was the biggest trap in the world!"

I sank into the seat next to him, unsure what to say. RJ acted completely different today around my family. He was still his mischievous self but actually acted like he cared. It felt normal, how a family should behave.

"Maybe he's trying, Tyler."

"Oh, now you're on his side, too? First my mother, then your father, now you? Why am I the only one who can see through his bullshit!" he shouted.

I crossed my arms and shut my mouth. If he were going to be an asshole every time I commented on the way home, then I wasn't going to participate in his rant.

"And RJ suggesting we all have dinner together? Offering to pray before we ate? What the fuck was that about? RJ has never said a prayer in his life!" Tyler continued to grumble the entire ride home while I stared out the window. Once we pulled into the driveway, he finally addressed me. "Are you going to say anything or just remain on their side?" he barked.

I whipped my head in his direction. "Who said I was on their side? And no, I'm not going to say anything when you just attack me for giving my honest opinion."

Tyler clenched his jaw and rolled his eyes.

"Don't roll your eyes at me. You know it's true. I'm not going to respond if you're looking for someone to argue with."

Tyler took a deep breath and turned off the car. He leaned back in his seat remaining quiet.

Breaking the silence I said, "If you want to talk about this afternoon, that's fine, but I won't be used as a punching bag."

He closed his eyes. "You're right, I'm sorry."

I nodded my head in acceptance. "Why does RJ acting that way make you so angry? Same with your mother?" I bravely asked.

He looked towards the roof of the Lexus. "I don't know. We've never spent time together like this. RJ has never made time for us. It's like he's doing this complete one eighty, and I can't figure out what his tactic is."

"Ty, maybe he truly wants to mend your relationship. He has been treating your mom better, hasn't he?"

"So she says," he sighed.

"Why not give him a chance?" I said sincerely.

He was silent for a long moment. "I don't trust him," he whispered.

I finally took off my seatbelt and started to crawl across the middle console and onto his lap. I was thankful for his long legs, causing the seat to be pushed back far enough for me to squeeze in between him and the steering wheel.

I took his face in my hands and said. "You have to trust people Ty. I know it's hard, but sometimes we all need to shift our faith into gear, even if the bridges we're driving over have been burned."

His eyes looked so pained, as though I were holding the face of a little boy who'd been crushed after his dad missed his baseball game for the umpteenth time.

"It's hard," he whispered.

I pressed our foreheads together and moved my hands to his chest. "Trust me, I know. But it's not worth being angry over things that happened in the past. All it will do is bring you down."

Tyler was very still for a long moment. Just as I was about to say more, his hands slowly slunk across my thighs and up my dress as his mouth found mine. This was how he coped with his emotions. Whenever we started to poke at the deep and damaged feelings he had for his family, Tyler became physical as though he was trying to block out his pain. One day I was going to have to resist him so we could tackle his feelings, but he felt so broken. His touch was so needy. He acted like our connection was the only thing that would save him from falling off the edge.

Chapter Eight

Tyler

The sun was setting by the time I was finished making love to Becca. I was exhausted, resting my head in the crook of her neck, my body snug to her side. I slowly rotated my thumb across her bicep. Her breathing was still heavy. I might have worked the aggression out of me a little too hard. I didn't understand the feelings that were rising inside of me. My heart told me to accept them, but my mind was telling me otherwise. How do you embrace a complete opposite perception of someone you've known your entire life?

Becca's hand found my hair, her fingers slowly making patterns along my scalp. I couldn't help but close my eyes, feeling her comfort. She didn't say anything, but her chest eventually began rising and falling into its normal calm pattern, helping to lull me to sleep.

Just as the sun completely left the sky, my office phone rang. No one ever called that number on a Sunday. I wanted to ignore it, but at the same time I didn't want Becca to wake. I cautiously rose from the bed, untangling our body parts as gently as I could. I was pleased when she rolled to her side without making a sound.

Pulling on a pair of shorts, I quietly made my way up the spiral staircase. The call went to voicemail before I could answer. My ears stung when RJ's voice came over on the message machine.

"Tyler, it's me. I just wanted to say I had a good time today. It was a good start at building our relationship. I really want our family to feel... normal, like an actual family. I know we have a lot of work to do, but I hope you're willing to keep trying. The way your mom glowed being around family, it's contagious. I'm with her totally now. I want what she wants, Tyler. I want my sons to play golf with me then go home and have a barbeque on Sunday evenings with my grandkids. I know I wasn't around when you were growing up, and I pawned you and your brothers off on your mother and grandparents, and I'm sorry. I want this to work. We should grab lunch tomorrow and talk more since we'll both be in Grand Rapids."

RJ paused, and I tentatively reached for the phone to answer his call, but he started to talk again. "I decided you were partially right about Chino. Tomorrow at the meeting, we'll discuss a better outcome for his projects. I'll tell him we won't, now or ever, be partnering on his subdivisions, and if he wants to badger us anymore, he can find himself a new architect."

I swallowed hard, fighting a lump in my throat.

"Anyway, that's all I needed to say. We can talk more tomorrow. I love you son."

My mind was screaming at me to pick up the phone, but my hand sat shaking next to the receiver. RJ paused for a moment before he hung up, as if he knew I was hanging by a thread intently listening.

I sat at my desk and put my head in my hands. Was he telling the truth? Can we really be normal after all we've been through? Could we possibly just start over?

I shook my head; he had hurt me so many times throughout life. Forgiving him felt damn near impossible.

***

My phone startled me awake. It was a little after 6:00a.m., and I hadn't slept a wink last night. I moved myself out to the deck, spending the night listening to the waves and staring out at the stars. My heart was heavy with indecision, wondering if I could ever truly trust RJ. My phone beeped again, and I reached to see what all of the messages were about. I had three text messages and one urgent email that kept beeping. I figured it couldn't be that urgent or else whoever it was from would have called me by now. I checked the texts. One was from Nathan while the other two were from RJ. The first was a simple, you around? Then the second was about lunch. I blew out air in contemplation as my thumbs hovered over the letters.

Sure -Tyler

Lunch couldn't hurt. If he wanted to be a part of mine and Becca's life, then he was going to have a lot of ass kissing to do for me to believe him.

I stood stiffly from the lounger and stretched. My back was going to hate me all day from attempting to sleep out here. I opened the slider as quietly as I could to find Becca still passed out from last night. A half smile crossed my lips as I watched her sleep. I was so lucky to at least have one constant in my life, and soon she would legally be mine forever.

Gently closing the slider, I tiptoed to the bathroom to get ready for meeting with RJ and Chino. Nathan's text was a confirmation that he was going to be at the meeting this morning as well.

I stepped into the warm water and thought about how today might play out. Nathan was going to be irritated as hell with RJ threatening Chino. Nathan was as money hungry as RJ and might not appreciate RJ's sudden change of heart.

I shook my head. I'd have to believe RJ's promises when he followed through. Getting out of the shower, I dressed for work, my heart not feeling as heavy as my mind began to accept the idea of RJ being a part of my life like a normal father. A glimpse of the possible future infiltrated my mind as I tied my tie. A little boy about Josie's age was sitting on my lap with a Cubs hat at a baseball game. RJ was sitting next to us, leaning down and pointing out the baseball players to the little boy. To my little boy.

My stomach fluttered. I had never really pictured myself with my own kid. Maybe an actual relationship with my father would be nice. I could start calling him Dad instead of RJ.

Becca was still sound asleep when I walked out of the closet. I sat down on the bed next to her, admiring her natural beauty. Her alarm would go off in a few minutes, so I didn't feel bad for running my hand along her back trying to coax her to open her eyes.

She slowly lifted her heavy lids, and a small smile crossed her lips before she buried her head into the pillow. I grinned at her shyness. Some things might never change.

"Good morning, baby doll," I greeted, leaning down to nuzzle the side of her neck.

She giggled and rolled to her back, stretching her arms above her head. "I don't think I moved an inch. I slept so soundly," she yawned.

Pride filled my lungs. What can I say, it was a pat to my ego fucking her so good she could barely move and automatically crashed for the entire night.

"Are you feeling better this morning?" she gently asked while rubbing my forearm.

I nodded my head slowly. She always knew when something was wrong, even if I wasn't exactly sure what my problems were.

"You're up early, do you have a meeting?" she asked, moving her hand to feel the fabric of my blue tie.

"Yeah, I'm meeting with RJ and Nathan at 8:00 a.m. Chino is going to be there as well to go over the finances for the warehouses."

"You finished them already?" she asked.

"Yes, I worked on them Saturday and some last night while you were asleep. Don't sound so surprised," I said, trying to sound wounded.

"You always surprise me," she said with awe.

I leaned down to kiss her, smiling at the quick peck verses a good lip lock. She always wanted her teeth brushed before she'd give in to my charm.

"Will you be around for lunch?" she asked sweetly.

I paused then looked out the window. "Actually, I'm going to meet RJ for lunch."

"Oh?" she said with hope.

I nodded my head, trying to look unaffected, still not meeting her eyes.

She reached for my face, forcing me to look at her. Her expression was soft and encouraging, just what I needed to see to feel sure about my decision to meet with RJ. "I love you, Ty."

I was about to reply back, but my phone cut me off. That damn 'urgent message' was still bugging me to read it.

"I guess it's time for work," I sighed.

I kissed her again and said I love you back. Grabbing my phone, I headed to the kitchen to make our protein drinks for the day. Becca was crazy and put a bunch of spinach in them normally. I enjoyed getting to the blender first so I could mix more fruit in with them.

I scrolled to the oh-so-urgent email and nearly dropped the almond milk as I read the contents.

Tyler-

RJ informed me the plans for the partnership are in full gear. I hope to discuss further finance and percentages later this morning. I know the numbers won't be set in stone, but RJ and I agreed on a legal contract last Friday to get things going and will sign this morning for preliminary action to move forward.

RJ and I also discussed Becca last night over the phone. I apologize for working with her over the two of you and wanted another perspective on the plans for the warehouses. Think of it as breaking her in with a larger client.

Looking forward to future business and seeing you later this morning.

-Lee Chino
Owner of Chino Corporations

I reread the email again and again. The time the email was sent was at 6:02am this morning. My teeth clenched as I almost crushed the carton in my hand. I can't believe I actually started to fall for RJ's game. The only reason he was buttering me up about this whole being closer was to get me to say yes to this dangerous contract. *Fuck him.*

Too pissed off to continue making our shakes, I marched directly to the garage and slammed my key into the ignition. I revved the engine a few times then peeled out of the driveway.

Just as I was about to get onto the highway, Nathan's name came across the screen of my console.

"I hope you're fucking happy," I shouted as I hit answer on my steering wheel.

"Whoa, good morning to you too," Nathan responded. "What am I supposed to be so happy about?"

"Like you don't know," I sneered. "RJ told Chino he was making the deal."

"Huh. That's not what he told me," Nathan said calmly.

"What?"

"RJ called me last night to tell me he wasn't going to partner. He said he was going to tell him to find a new architect if he made a fuss about it."

"Then why did I get an email from Chino about how he and RJ were going to sign the paperwork for the partnership on the subdivisions?"

"Interesting. Maybe after RJ slept on his decision he change his mind?" Nathan said.

I hit my steering wheel with my palm. "I'm going to flip the fuck out on him."

"You need to calm down. Where are you?"

"About 20 minutes from the office," I said, stepping harder on the gas pedal.

"All right, I'm about to leave my condo. Talk to me before you go ape shit on RJ."

I hung up without responding. I didn't want Nathan to calm me down. Everything was going to spill out. RJ needed to hear it, and he needed to hear how furious I was about him trying to use creating a relationship as a scheme to get me to agree with his ridiculous business proposal.

I made it to the Conklin building in record time. I slammed my door shut and power walked to the elevator, steam radiating from my ears. The elevator couldn't move fast enough to the top floor. I paced in the elevator as each floor passed, fidgeting and cursing under my breath. This company was about to be in huge trouble.

The doors slid open, and I slipped through the crack before it was completely open. I turned directly to the right towards RJ's office but was jerked backwards by my arm.

"I thought I told you we need to chat before you attacked RJ," Nathan said calmly, dragging me towards his office.

"The only person I need to talk to right now is our lousy, good-for-nothing father." My eyes burned with pure hatred as I said the words in Nathan's face.

He cocked his head to the side in frustration. "Is this really about Chino talking to Becca? It's not that big of a deal."

"It's not just Becca!"

"Then what is it?" he countered, his voice rising with mine.

My eyes went hard, but the tightening in my chest made the words even harder to speak. "He's used me one too many times. The tactic of trying to start a relationship with me so I'd say yes really pisses me right the fuck off."

"Tyler, he's trying," Nathan exasperated.

"No, he's not! I'm so sick of everyone saying that! He's not trying!" I shouted. "This bull shit business deal has gone far enough," I said through clenched teeth. I shoved past Nathan and stormed out of his office.

"Cooper!" I heard Nathan yell from behind me.

I pounded on RJ's office door.

"Tyler, you're being irrational right now. Calm down before you talk to him," Nathan tried to convince me.

I hit the door harder with both fists. "RJ, open the fucking door!" I yelled.

"Buddy, it's not worth it; don't lose your head," Cooper tried to reason.

"RJ!" I shouted again. I was going to break the fucking door down. I grabbed the door handles, figuring they would jiggle from being locked, but shockingly they clicked free.

"RJ I swear to God—" I lost my voice and my train of thought as the doors flew open.

The puddle of blood streaming out from under RJ's desk caused my breath to hitch, but the bullet in his forehead stole my breath completely.

Chapter Nine

Becca

The skyline was hazy as I drove to work in my Lexus. I took a drink from my protein shake, wondering why Tyler had left everything out on the counter instead of making the shake himself. I appreciated the gesture, but normally I'd find the shake mixed and in the fridge. Maybe his mind was focused on other things, like his father. He'd never admit it, but I could tell he had hopes of starting anew with RJ. Tyler needed to mend that part of his heart, and unfortunately, it wasn't something I could help with.

When I got a few blocks from the Conklin building, I saw flashing lights all down the street. Maybe there was an accident? Once I finally got to the basement parking ramp, I was greeted with yellow caution tape and a policeman guarding the entrance. Then I noticed the building was flooded with cops.

A shiver traveled up my spine as I drove past the entrance. What happened? What if Tyler was hurt? Picking up my phone as steadily as I could I went to call him, but he didn't answer.

I frantically searched the streets for a parking spot, desperate to make sure my Ty was okay. Finally finding a spot about four blocks down, I raced as fast as I could in my four-inch yellow heels.

Why did I choose to wear heels today?

It was overly warm, and I was cursing myself for straightening my hair instead of throwing it in a ponytail. I was sweating by the time I made it to the building entrance.

"I'm sorry ma'am, but no one is allowed in or out of the building," a police officer halted me as I tried to cross the yellow tape.

"I work in this building," I replied.

"Doesn't matter, no one can come in or out."

"What happened?" I asked, trying to stay calm.

"Murder scene. Like I said, no one can leave or come in," the officer said without blinking an eye.

My knees trembled as my breath hitched. "Please, my fiancé is in there, please let me through!" I begged, tears threatening my eyes. I started to walk towards the door. He firmly grasped my shoulders.

"Ma'am, you can not go in there. I have strict orders from the detective—"

"Detective? Detective Anderson? Radio him. Tell him Becca Stine needs to get into the building."

"Ma'am, I can't bother the detective, now please—"

"I'm begging you! I need to know if my fiancé is okay!" I pleaded, tears falling from my eyes.

He sighed then reached for his radio to call the detective.

Rolling his eyes after making contact, he moved out of the way. A gentleman stopped me as I got into the building, asking what I was doing.

"Can you tell me where Detective Anderson is? Or where Tyler Conklin or Nathan Conklin might be?" I said in a rush.

"Top floor," he said flatly.

I gasped then moved to find the elevator door, rapidly pressing the call button.

"Come on... Come on!" I said desperately. Finally the doors opened, and I paced the small space, anxiously waiting to arrive at the top floor.

When the doors finally opened, I was shocked with the chaos in front of me. Swat teams and medics, police officers in all types of uniforms. I stopped the nearest one.

"Have you seen Detective Anderson or Tyler Conklin?" I gulped.

"Becca." I heard Detective Anderson's voice.

I briskly walked over to him, trying to keep myself together. "What happened? Is Tyler—"

"He's in his office. You should go check on him," he answered, nodding his head in the correct direction.

I sighed in relief then moved as quickly as my heels would let me.

"Tyler," I choked as I crossed through the entry way. He was standing at the window, gazing outside. He didn't even turn when I said his name. Nathan was sitting in the leather chair, his forearms on his knees. I noticed blood on his shirt and pants.

"What happened?" I asked, slowly walking over to Tyler. He finally acknowledged my presence and put one arm out to me as I hugged his middle. I caught my breath as I felt him in my arms, relieved that he was all right.

"RJ," Nathan whispered. I looked up at Tyler, whose head was down, not meeting my eyes. Then I glanced at Nathan, waiting for further explanation.

Mitch came rushing into the room before he could finish. "What happened?" he asked with a heavy breath, nervousness on his brow.

"Your father's dead," Detective Anderson finally said.

Mitch took a sharp breath then found a seat next to Nathan.

"What?" I asked in confusion, my head bouncing from Tyler to the detective.

"He was shot," Nathan whispered again.

I inhaled another deep breath, my eyes beginning to finally shed tears. I looked up at Tyler, trying to see his face, but he was still looking down and away.

"Ty," I said quietly, reaching to touch his face. He gently swatted my hand away then let me go, heading over to his desk.

His hand burned my skin as it rejected my comfort. I stood dumbfounded, trying to grasp this awful situation.

"If the two of you think of anything else you need to tell me, please, call. I'm sorry for your loss. I'm afraid I can't hold back any more information from the news reporters once I leave the building. You have roughly an hour."

Nathan stood and shook Anderson's hand while giving him a nod. "Thank you."

Anderson returned the nod and walked out the door.

"I need to get to mom. Did she go back home to Chicago? Or did they stay at their condo here?" Nathan said, looking at Tyler.

"I'm not sure," Tyler murmured.

Nathan sighed. "I need to find her before she turns on the news."

"I doubt she'll turn on the news," Tyler said coldly. "I'd check their condo. They were in town last night."

Nathan nodded and turned to Mitch, who was staring blankly.

"Come on buddy," Nathan said, attempting to make his voice sound soothing, but hurt and pain was laced with his words. "Let's go find Mom." Once Mitch finally stood, he turned to Tyler. "Come on Tyler, she's going to want all of us to be there."

Tyler looked up from his computer, no expression on his face. "I have a meeting in Holland."

We all gaped at him.

"Tyler... I think they'll understand," I said cautiously.

He darted his eyes towards me. I took a step back, startled by the flame that was hidden behind them. "I'm not going to just cancel my meeting."

Nathan and I shared glances, unsure of what to say.

"Ty... go with your brothers. You have to tell your mom about RJ," I whispered.

His glare was almost deathly. "Becca, they can handle it." His eyes shifted to Nathan. "Don't you have to be in Cleveland this afternoon?"

Nathan took a step back, blinking. "Yeah, but..." He was stumbling over his words. I had never seen Nathan so disheveled before.

Tyler shrugged his shoulders, giving Nathan the 'so go to Cleveland' look.

I clenched my jaw. Tyler was putting up his guard, and this wasn't the time to shut us all out.

"If you're not going to go with your brothers, then come home with me," I said, making my way behind his desk.

He didn't turn his head to look at me, but I could tell annoyance was spread across his face. "No." Turning to face me, he continued, "Nathan and Mitch can handle it."

His look was way to calm and relaxed. I looked back to Nathan, whose expression was blank.

"Let's go Mitch," Nathan said softly, nudging Mitch along. He gently closed the door behind them.

Tyler began sorting through the papers on his desk as I stood there watching him. After what felt like hours, he finally looked in my direction. "Do you need something?"

I dropped my head to the side, my eyes pleading with him to open up to me. "Tyler, let's go home."

He rolled his eyes again then stood from his chair, reaching for his sport coat. "Becca, I told you I have a meeting that I can't miss. I'm sure you have a lot of work that needs to be completed with Will being gone."

I uncrossed my arms and walked over to where he was putting on his coat. "I'm sure the other junior architects can handle my share for the week. We don't have to go home, let's go somewhere... to talk."

Tyler focused intently on buttoning his jacket. "A week? A bit long for time off don't you think? Besides, there's nothing to talk about. RJ died; there isn't anything else to say."

He slid past me back to his desk to grab a few folders and put them in his travel bag.

"Okay," I said quietly. He needed time to process what had happened. Eventually he would open up to me. I needed to remember that Tyler didn't do well with real emotions, and when he was ready, I would be there to comfort him in a heartbeat.

When Tyler gathered his things to leave, he barely brushed my cheek with his lips. It was the most estranged kiss I had ever felt from him, and my chest tightened.

"Will you be home for dinner?" I squeaked.

"I was planning on staying at my condo tonight," he said tightly.

I gulped as a stared at his beautiful face, willing him to look me in the eye. I would have grabbed his face, but I was terrified he would swat my hand away again. "Am I invited?"

His eyes finally met mine, and a trace of sadness was in them. I was thankful. For a moment I thought he had turned to stone.

"Of course," he whispered. "I'll be late though. Don't wait up."

I nodded my head, wanting to wrap my arms around him, but he walked out of the office before I even got the chance.

***

No way was I going to be able to focus on work. I made my way down the stairs, not wanting the silence of the elevator. When I reached the 7th floor, I started to hear murmuring.

"It's okay, buddy," I heard Nathan's voice in a soft hush. "No one could have predicted this." I heard heavy, sporadic breathing then found Mitch sitting on the landing with Nathan kneeling down next to him.

My heels clicked as I continued down to where they were; both Mitch and Nathan shot a glance my way. Mitch wiped his eyes and started to stand, turning his head in the opposite direction of me.

My eyes began to water as well, not sure what to say. Mitch was closest to RJ, and I couldn't imagine what to say to console him.

"I'm sorry, I should have taken the elevator," I said quietly.

Nathan shook his head as he patted Mitch's shoulder. "It's fine. We didn't want to take the elevator either."

"I'm so sorry," I whispered.

Nathan gave me a sincere nod. Silence filled the space around us, making the air thick and uncomfortable. "Come with us, Becca," Nathan asked. "Maybe it'll soften the blow of Tyler not being there."

"She likes you better than Tyler anyway," Mitch sniffed, a small laugh escaping him. Nathan let out a soft chuckle as well, probably feeling a tad bit of enjoyment seeing his little brother gaining his composure.

Looking at both of them skeptically, I finally nodded my head, and we all descended down the stairs in silence.

The security guard shockingly let us out of the building without hesitation. He must have recognized Mitch's SUV. I was kind of surprised Mitch wanted to drive, but he gathered himself pretty quickly after I walked into his and Nathan's moment.

"I'm sorry Tyler isn't coming," I said, breaking the silence.

Nathan shrugged his shoulders. "I can't say I'm not surprised. But I really thought this would be one of those moments where he'd let his guard down. I'm sure he'll open up to you later tonight, Becca."

I swallowed hard, hoping Nathan was right.

***

The empty pit in my stomach wouldn't go away as I rinsed my body in the warm shower at Tyler's condo. Watching Mary earlier literally fall to her knees with her two boys comforting her was heartbreaking. She sobbed for over an hour before she could coherently speak. They didn't share any details, just that RJ had been shot. I still didn't exactly know what had happened.

Mary kept repeating herself once she could finally mangle a few words together.

We were finally connecting again.

Our relationship was stronger than ever.

He wanted us to be a family.

Why would God take him from me?

I began crying along with her, taking my turn trying to sooth her. I admired Nathan's strength. He never broke, but anyone could tell he was hurting. He was being strong for his family, like I assumed he always had to be with RJ being absent more than half their lives. Never once did he let go of Mary's hand.

Mary didn't ask where Tyler was, but thanked me over and over again for coming with Mitch and Nathan. "We're a family now. We all need to stick together when tragedies happen", she said, giving me one last squeeze before we left.

Shutting off the shower, I searched for one of Tyler's t-shirts and a clean pair of panties. Every light in the condo was on, and I planned on keeping it that way until Tyler was home. I didn't want to think about how RJ died, and the light was comforting to me as I blocked out my unsettled feeling.

I dove into Tyler's satin sheets and turned on the TV. I flipped through the channels, looking for something mind numbing to keep my mind from wandering to scarier thoughts. Grabbing Tyler's pillow, I inhaled his scent, causing me to ache even more for him to open up to me.

Finally, at 12:15 a.m. I heard the door to Tyler's condo open. I sighed in relief. My Ty was finally home, and for the first time, I hoped he'd greet me with sadness, wanting my arms wrapped around him. I waited to hear his footsteps come up the spiral stairs, but I only heard cupboards opening and the ice machine go off more than a few times. I frowned and squeezed his pillow tighter. Tyler was drowning himself in alcohol, and I wasn't sure if that was a good or bad thing. Maybe he would start talking once he had a few drinks in him.

Just as I was about to go down the stairs to check on him, the light from the kitchen shut off and I heard his footsteps slowly climbing the metal stairs. I shut the TV off as soon as he entered the room.

"Why are you still awake? I told you not to wait up for me," he said smoothly. His tie was undone and draped around his neck, the first few buttons of his white dress shirt opened, sleeves rolled to his elbows.

"I couldn't sleep," I said softly, sitting up on the bed. He nodded then headed to the bathroom, closing the door behind him. I laid back down on the goose feathered pillows. He wasn't ready to talk, and my gut was still twisted. How could I talk to him about the death of his father's effect on me if he wasn't ready to talk about it himself?

His shower was speedy, and I half expected him to maul me the second he got out. Sex always seemed to be his go to for problem solving. Really, it pushed his feelings deeper, giving him a distraction instead of a solution.

Unlike what I predicted, he casually slipped on his boxer briefs and shorts and walked to my side of the bed. "Can I turn off the lamp?" he asked.

"Yeah, that's fine," I answered. After switching the light off, he walked to his side and climbed under the covers. We lay silently next to each other for what felt like hours.

Why wasn't he touching me? He always touched me, even if we weren't going to make love.

Tentatively, I reached my hand to touch him, shocked by how he flinched. I quickly drew my arm back. "I'm sorry," I apologized.

I heard him let out a shaky breath then felt his hand grasp my arm, tugging me to him. I let out a soft sigh, grateful to be pulled into his arms. His touch felt different though. It wasn't warm but distant. He was distracted for good reason, and it hurt. I wrapped my arm around his chest while nuzzling his neck, wanting to bury myself in him.

His silence was torture, but the words he finally spilled gave me hope.

"Thank you for being here," he said in barely a whisper.

"I'm here for you, Ty. Always," I said with a crack in my voice.

His body shuddered as he rolled to his side towards me. He firmly wrapped his arms around me, nuzzling my hair and tangling our legs together.

I let out a breath of relief, rubbing my thumbs on his chest. His hold around me was so tight that I couldn't move my arms.

I waited for him to speak again, but only heard the sharpness of his breath turn steady along with the rise and fall of his chest on my hands and cheek.

An unspoken message passed through us with his tight embrace. His father's death affected him more then he put off, and I had a feeling it was going to be a very hard hurdle for him to jump.

Chapter Ten

Tyler

Black. That's what I was going to wear to my father's funeral. I was starting to feel like it matched my soul. What asshole still hates his father with a passion after he dies? Me. He had betrayed my brothers and me mere hours before his death.

My chest tightened, making it hard for me to concentrate on knotting my tie. My hand shook as I closed my eyes to focus on breathing.

A soft hand covered mine, and I bit my lip in frustration, turning my head away from Becca. She had been more than patient, not hounding me every five seconds like my brothers or mother. She never said a word to me, only spoke if I would speak to her. I couldn't look into her eyes; all they held were pity and sadness for me. If only she knew the feelings I had inside were of complete rage.

"Will you teach me?" she asked in her sweet voice.

I licked my lips, unsure what she wanted me to teach her.

I sensed her smile. "Teach me how to tie your tie. I've always wanted to learn." I chanced meeting her eyes, and my lip quirked.

"Why would you want to know how to tie a tie?" I asked, my eyes moving from her to the half-ass job I was doing in the mirror. Becca turned her head to look at me through the mirror as she started to unravel the mess I had made.

"Just another excuse to touch you." She grinned then brought her eyes back to my neck.

A moment of guilt passed through me. I wanted to touch her. I wanted to screw her nonstop just so I could have a calm nerve in my body for a small moment, but I didn't. I knew I wouldn't be gentle. I'd have nailed her so hard and forceful, and I couldn't do that to Becca. I wouldn't use her to relieve my stress when I didn't even know if it was what I really needed. I had been distant the past four days, afraid to let her see the confusion I had from the death of my father.

Her fingers paused for a moment then she began fumbling again. I took her hands and tried to explain what to do. Her first attempt was awful, but gradually she got the hang of it.

Her grin was wide as she looked up at me. "Hah! Third time's the charm," she said proudly while resting her hands on my chest.

I smiled down at her as silence passed between us. Her smile never faltered as she cautiously brought her hands to my face, running her fingers along the just more than scruff on my jaw. The moment was tender and well needed.

"Maybe I should shave," I contemplated.

"Nah, I think it's hot," she flirted, biting her bottom lip.

I took a deep breath, noticing the fire in her eyes. That look had an effect on me that she couldn't possibly understand. She desired me, but I wasn't ready. I still didn't trust myself.

"We should get going. Most likely we'll run into traffic once we hit Chicago," I said while clearing my throat, gently removing her wrists from my chest. She nodded, her smile fading as she walked past me to her side of the walk in closet.

I let out another deep breath, feeling like shit for denying her. It wasn't an easy task either, especially when I watched her bend down to put on those damn black heels. I didn't think she liked wearing them, but holy hell did they make her legs seem long. Her nose was to my chin when she wore those suckers. Confining the bulge in my pants from the effect those heels and her sleek, form fitted black dress was becoming very difficult.

"Do you want me to make you anything quick? Grab a power bar?" she asked kindly as she slid by me to the bedroom.

"No, I'm fine," I said following her, willing my eyes to not greedily travel down her body.

"I'll grab one just in case you change your mind then we can go, okay?"

I nodded my head as though she could see me while putting on my sport coat. I was going to be sweating bullets in this thing.

I was lost in my thoughts in the Maserati as we drove down the highway, wondering who would come and what each ass kisser would say. I didn't feel like dealing with business people today offering their bullshit condolences. Everyone who did business with RJ knew he was a slime ball and only gave a shit about money but would act differently.

"What time did you tell your mom we would pick her up?" Becca asked, interrupting my thoughts.

"Nathan's bringing her."

"Tyler," she scolded. "Your mom wanted us to bring her."

I rolled my eyes thinking back to the funeral home last night when we were making arrangements for RJ's casket to get to Chicago. My mother was all over me, hounding me about what to do and bugging me to talk to her. I was sick of her whining and crying. RJ was the biggest cheating prick to her. Why she was so upset was beyond me. I begged Nathan to take her the long three hour drive to the funeral home instead of Becca and me.

"Nathan handles her better," I said flatly.

"She just wants your comfort, and I think she wants to comfort you," Becca said quietly.

I snorted. "I don't need to be comforted." My chest tightened at the words. I was so messed up inside with all the anger and rage; I couldn't stand the thought of someone telling me everything was going to be okay.

Becca stayed silent, not commenting.

Just as I was getting lost in my thoughts again, her sweet voice rang through the car. "Can I hold your hand?" she asked while running her finger along the backside of my hand that was firmly holding the gear shifter.

"Yeah," I said, my mood becoming softer. She smiled and squeezed my hand, pulling it to her lap. She used her other hand to keep drawing circles along my knuckles and wrists.

Shockingly, my mind stopped spinning and, oddly enough, her gentle touch was comforting the entire ride to Chicago.

***

"I'm sorry for your loss, Mr. Conklin." I must have heard this over fifty times in the past hour and a half. I nodded my head to the gentleman making his way through the line, moving to Nathan next.

"I'm going to go get some air," I mumbled to Becca as I broke protocol and slid through the mass of people showing their respect to the owner of the Conklin empire. We had to do this for another two and a half hours, and I was feeling agitated.

She murmured something, but I didn't hear her. Being in this room, the smell of the flowers and the eerie feeling of death was overwhelming, and I couldn't help but think of my grandparents' funerals. Especially my grandfather's.

I stood in the hall, leaning against the wall covered in gaudy wallpaper. I closed my eyes and swallowed, fighting that awful feeling in my chest. Why was I feeling like I couldn't breathe?

"Tyler?" a sphinx-like voice whispered.

"What do you want?" I growled, opening my eyes and meeting the green-eyed monster.

Margo crossed her arms and leaned on her hip while looking off into the distance. "I would say I'm sorry, but I'm assuming this isn't having a huge effect on you."

I rolled my eyes and pushed off the wall, heading towards the porch. "Thanks for your concern."

She followed me, letting out a sigh. "You know, you really shouldn't hate him so much. That man may have been one of the biggest jerks in the world, but he did care about you. The least you could do is be there for your mother," she barked.

I stopped dead in my tracks, spinning around to meet her face to face. "Don't try to fucking rile me. That man cheated on her more times than any of us can remember. There's a line of them in there, maybe you should go join them and compare slutty stories. You weren't the only one he bent over his desk," I said in a harsh whisper.

For once her eyes didn't turn into slits, but grew big with pain, tears threatening.

I groaned and rolled my head back. "Don't act like I hurt your feelings. You knew you were just a piece of ass to him. Just like all the others."

"You know, I would have expected this from you a few months ago. Your mother said you and RJ started to hash things out, building your relationship again."

"Again? We never had a relationship. I don't know why she would tell you that because it's a load of shit. RJ wanted something, and thank God it fell through."

She shook her head, tears streaming down her cheeks. "I thought your heart unthawed with Becca. The poor girl doesn't know what she's in for— a selfish, heartless bastard who acts just like his father."

I stood tall, dumbfounded by her comment. How dare she compare me to that asshole. "Fuck you," I spat, nudging past her to the deck. I didn't need to hear this, not today.

I flung the slider open and headed towards the railing, my chest heaving with anger.

Then I felt lost. I looked to the sky, unable to control or understand why breathing was so hard. Why was the sky so blue on a day that was filled with sadness for many people?

"Need a breath of fresh air?" Detective Anderson's voice murmured through the thick humidity.

I was startled, and I didn't have time for his bullshit questions.

"It's crowded in there," I murmured.

"That it is. Want one?" he asked, taking a puff of a cigarette. "My ex-wife left me because of these, or so she said. She wouldn't admit it was because of another man."

I watched him as he pulled out the pack from his chest pocket then extended them to me.

I studied him for a moment, trying to figure out his game. The ex-wife comment felt personal, and I didn't need for anyone else to try and trick me again.

Giving in, I reached for the pack, took one, then swapped them for his lighter. The cigarette was strong, and it was a good distraction.

"You're holding up awfully well," he said, taking another puff. "All of you."

I leaned on the railing, looking out over the horizon. "We know how to handle stressful situations," I said calmly. "My mother on the other hand..."

His lip half quirked into a smile. "Women can be a little dramatic." I looked in his direction. "I guess when your husband dies there can be an exception, right? You've found love, I'm sure you can't imagine losing Becca."

My heart started to beat faster as I stared at him. Losing Becca would be miserable. I would have nothing to live for.

He gave me a smile. "You really do love her, don't you?"

"I wouldn't be marrying her if I didn't," I said defensively.

He nodded his head in agreement. "On a serious note. I'd like to talk about your father's death. See, homicide thinks it was a suicide."

I turned back to him. RJ killing himself had never crossed my mind. Even though I could picture what I saw in his office vividly, I still didn't put together him holding the gun.

"RJ wouldn't kill himself."

"See, most would say that about a strong businessman," he said as though he were weighing his options. Anderson took two steps towards me. "But suicide can be very normal if someone's in over their head."

My expression was blank. RJ wasn't in over his head. At least not yet. If he had lived to sign that deal with Chino, then he would have been. RJ had too much pride. He loved himself too much.

We stared each other down for a few long moments. He was so close I could see the wrinkles against his eyes. "Like I said, RJ wouldn't kill himself." I spoke the words slowly, letting the inner meaning sink into his thick skull. *Stop snooping, dick.*

He swallowed, studying my features, probably trying to read if I were telling him the truth.

Nodding his head once, he turned back to look out over the deck. "I'll try to have them look over it again, but unfortunately that's how his death is going to be declared. You seem to be the least affected by your father's death. I figured you'd take it the easiest."

I didn't say anything, taking a long hit off the cigarette. "You want me to tell my family. I get it."

The slider to the porch opened, and we both turned our heads in unison.

"Hey, I'm not interrupting, am I?" Becca asked, standing timidly in the door frame.

Anderson gave her a half smile then stubbed his cigarette on the railing, tossing it out. "Not at all. He's all yours." Anderson said calmly. He had the nerve to hug Becca in passing.

It was official. I hated him.

"I wondered where you went off to," she said, eyeing the cigarette in my hand. "I thought you only smoked cigars."

"I told you I needed some air," I answered then turned back to the railing. I felt her hand on my forearm then her head against my bicep.

She was quiet, and her presence was semi-soothing, especially when she traced circles on my forearm with her fingertips. My agitation was dulled from the detective. I felt like the air was finally returning to my lungs for the first time since she held my hand in the car.

"That feels nice," I whispered, risking looking vulnerable.

"Yeah?" she said softly, continuing her pattern.

I turned to nod my head, not expecting her nose to meet mine. "Thank you," I said so quietly I wasn't sure if she could hear me.

"You're welcome," she said in the same tone, rubbing her nose against mine.

This was true peace but soon brought on that uneasy feeling I had been fighting so hard to keep bottled up inside.

"Tyler, Mom's wondering where you are," Mitch said, interrupting our moment. He was dressed nicer than I had ever seen him and part of me was completely pissed off that he'd dazzle himself up for RJ's funeral and not our grandparents'.

I pulled away from Becca to dispose of the cigarette. "I'll be there in a second."

I felt both Mitch's and Becca's eyes on my back then heard his sigh followed by the sliding door.

"Only a few more hours then the service, reception, and gravesite" Becca said gently. I felt her hand on my back now, making the same patterns as she had been on my forearm.

I stood tall, shrugging her arm off my back. I didn't want to feel soft and tender today, not for RJ. For a moment it was comforting, but I needed to push any what ifs and guilt that I had hidden in my heart. Her delicate way of handling me was helping those feelings surface for all the wrong reasons.

I heard Becca's footsteps behind me as I finally went back into RJ's funeral hall. More people had arrived to show their condolences while I was hiding on the porch. My mother waved me over to come stand beside her and Nathan.

"Are you okay, sweetheart?" she asked with a scratchy voice and tear stained cheeks. She let go of Nathan's forearm to reach for mine.

"Yeah, I'm fine," I answered stiffly, moving my arm to straighten my tie so she had to move her hand.

"I'm so sorry for your loss," Lee Chino's voice rang through the crowd of murmurs. When I turned to look at him, Margo was on his arm, her head to the floor. I had never seen her so low and unconfident.

"Oh, thank you Lee," my mother sniffed. He leaned into her cheek and gave her a peck of condolence. "Thank you for coming Margo." Margo gave her a small smile and a hug. I ground my teeth, wondering how she had the nerve to show up to RJ's funeral and hug his wife when she had actively screwed her husband.

"Tyler, Nathan, Mitch, I'm sorry for your loss as well," Chino said, moving his greedy eyes towards Nathan and me. I felt Becca squeeze my hand. Did she realize how much this man got to me? I straightened, trying not to look affected.

"Thank you," I said stiffly, taking my hand from Becca's to shake Chino's.

"Thank you for coming," Nathan added.

Chino nodded and shook Nathan's hand. "My assistant will call your assistant Nathan to reschedule our previous meeting. When you're ready of course." He turned to look at me, his head cocked to the side. "Or do they call your assistant, Tyler? Did RJ leave you in charge?"

I didn't like the daring gleam that was in his eye, as though he were challenging me to go against RJ's wishes. My jaw was clenched, and it was difficult to keep my cool around the company I was with.

Nathan sensed my animosity. "Our assistants will contact you in due time," he said strongly. I glanced at Nathan, a bit of my tension released to see he was irritated with Lee's comment. Truth was, neither of us had looked at his will or knew who the company was left to.

All I knew was I would do everything in my power to keep that man out of the Conklin business.

"Lee, I think talking business is a little inappropriate at the moment," Margo piped in, her eyes glaring at Chino. My mother gave a slight smile in agreeance with Margo.

Lee's eyes grew narrow with annoyance when he turned to look at Margo. "Of course, I apologize, Mary. I truly am sorry."

My mother gave him a grateful nod then was approached by one of the funeral directors.

"Mrs. Conklin, the service will start in 30 minutes. I suggest you and your family meet the priest in the prayer room."

Mary nodded, cutting in front of Chino, reaching for both Nathan and my arms.

"We'll talk soon," Lee's voice trailed behind us, sounding more like a threat than a casual goodbye.

***

I hadn't looked at RJ yet. Somehow I had managed to avoid opening his casket. The psychologist on staff came to the funeral home for our first meeting. I guess Nathan thought we all needed to talk with him. He said seeing RJ in his final state of rest might erase the last image we had of him.

Nothing could erase that.

I felt a chill crawl up my spine, and I shook my head, standing from the table where my family sat in the reception. All eyes were on me.

"I need to use the restroom," I mumbled while pushing in my chair.

My mother's hushed whisper was impossible for me to miss. "I'm worried about him."

After vigorously rinsing my face with water and staring blankly at my pale reflection, I managed to head back out into the hallway. To my surprise, Becca was leaning on a pillar with her cell phone in hand.

"Hey. Jamie called. She wanted me to pass on her condolences and tell you she hooked a huge account in Miami." She ended with a smile, and I gulped trying to return the smile back.

Her smile faded as she reached to touch my face. I turned my head, afraid to meet her eyes.

What the hell was wrong with me? Get it together Conklin!

"Is it time to leave for the grave site yet?" I asked, staring off towards the reception room.

"About twenty minutes. Your mother wants us all to ride in the Bentley."

I rolled my eyes. "I'd rather we took the Maserati."

"I know, but it would make your mother feel better if you all arrived together," she said gently.

I closed my eyes for a long moment then nodded my head.

Silenced passed by us for a long moment. "Do you want to wait out here or—"

"Yeah, go ahead, I'll join you in a minute," I said, reading her mind. I sensed her big blue eyes looking at me, filled with concern, but I refused to look at her. Finally she strolled back to the reception hall as I sat down on a bench.

People began filing out of the reception hall as I blankly stared off into the distance, trying to contain whatever strange emotions were bottled up inside my chest.

Nathan quietly sat next to me on the small bench, leaning back into the wall with his hands on his knees. He didn't say anything.

"Mom wants us—"

"Becca already told me," I snapped, knowing what he was going say.

He sighed and ran a hand through his hair. "Don't shut her out, Tyler."

I rolled my eyes and stood from the bench, trying to get space from Nathan. "Mom will be fine."

"I'm not talking about Mom," Nathan said, standing, taking a step towards me. "Don't push Becca away."

My head shot up like whiplash. "I'm not," I said defensively.

"Well, you're sure acting like it. You need her," he said sternly. "Stop being such an introverted dick."

I glared at him. I wasn't being introverted, and I sure as hell wasn't pushing Becca away. God forbid I just wanted a little space to try and understand what the hell was going on in my brain. Becca understood too. She was handling me at an arm's length, which is exactly what I needed.

"Mom is waiting for us to escort her. Let's go," Nathan commanded in his older brother tone. I huffed under my breath and followed.

Chapter Eleven

Becca

Today was one of the most awful days I had experienced. I had never been in a room filled with such sorrow and hurt, but the only person's pain I had trouble feeling was Tyler's. He hid it too well, and the funny looks on people's faces after they shook his hand and offered their condolences was impossible to miss.

"*He doesn't look too effected.*" I heard an older gentleman say. "*Probably because he didn't get along with RJ. Everyone knows they butt heads more than Democrats and Republicans,*" another gentleman replied.

My poor Ty. If only he would let me into his head.

"Are you hungry?" I asked as we entered his lofty condo at Elysian. We had declined his mother's invitation to stay with her at their estate tonight. I wasn't surprised.

"No," he simply said, taking off his sport coat and walking towards his office.

Tyler hadn't eaten anything all day, and I was beginning to worry. His lack of appetite was his only tell that the day had affected him.

Watching him walk down the hall, I decided to give him more space. Tomorrow we would lay around, hopefully cuddle in bed, and he could finally mourn.

Wandering into the kitchen, I raided the cupboards, not surprised to find minimal food. The freezer had some frozen veggies, but they just didn't sound good. I grabbed my phone from my handbag and decided to call for a pizza. Yes, I hated eating pizza, especially when I had to go wedding dress shopping in a month, but Tyler loved watching me eat it and rarely turned it down.

After ordering the pizza, I stopped at Tyler's office to tell him I was going to hop in the shower, hoping maybe he would jump up and join me, but his eyes never left his computer screen.

The shower was lonely and big, and I never thought I would crave Tyler's touch more. Maybe I was being greedy, but today had been hard on me as well. I didn't know RJ that well, but death wasn't something I was familiar with. I didn't know how to respond to people when they asked me questions about our wedding. Was I supposed to be happy? Was it okay if I let a smile slip? Neither Tyler nor his family smiled.

Resisting the urge to throw on a t-shirt, I grabbed a silk nighty instead. I don't know why I wanted to be sexy for Tyler, but maybe I needed the intimate connection more than he did after this long and awful day. Hearing the buzzer, I threw on my silk thigh length robe to meet the pizza man at the door. Tyler beat me to it.

"I'm surprised you ordered pizza," he said stiffly, setting the box down on the kitchen island.

"I thought it might sound good," I answered, reaching into the cabinets for plates.

He wiggled his nose.

"Ty, you haven't eaten all day," I pleaded.

"Don't tell me I need to eat. You get pissed off at me whenever I say anything about food to you," he snapped.

I flinched at his comment.

He relaxed his shoulders and raised his eyes to meet mine. "I'm sorry. Some pizza does sound good."

I gave him a soft smile and pulled two pieces out of the box and put them on a plate. He took a seat at the bar, reaching for the plate.

"Want some wine? Water? I think I saw some Gatorade," I asked, turning to the fridge.

"Gatorade's fine," he said quietly while picking up his pizza.

I smiled and grabbed a Gatorade and a water for myself and sat next to Tyler to attempt to enjoy our Hawaiian pizza together.

***

"Do you like my new nighty?" I asked Tyler as I slipped off my robe to crawl into bed.

He turned his head to me as he undid his cuff links. "Yeah. You know I love that color on you," he said sweetly, except his voice didn't match his eyes. He barely looked at me.

My face fell as I pulled the covers to my waist.

Tugging his buttons free, Tyler tossed his shirt in the laundry basket, his pants quickly following.

"I thought maybe we could go to Millennium Park tomorrow," I started to say, trying not to feel rejected.

Tyler shook his head as he pulled his side of the bed covers back. "I have non-stop meetings tomorrow at the office."

I looked at him dumbfounded. Even Nathan was taking the day off tomorrow. "Why don't you take the day off. We can stay here through the weekend, just the two of us."

"Becca, I can't do that," he said, irritation laced with is words.

"Ty—"

"No. Don't 'Ty' me. The world has to keep spinning, Becca, including our business. With RJ gone, there is more work that needs to be done," he said flatly.

I sighed, starting to feel a small bit of defeat. "Do it for me?" I begged, pulling out my ultimate weapon. He turned to look at me, the same tiny hint of hurt filling his eyes. My heart broke for him with that one look. "Baby—" I started as I tilted my head in concern.

Tyler sat up in bed, holding his arm out as though to stop me from trying to comfort him. "Becca, I'm sorry, but I can't tomorrow or Saturday. Sunday we can do something together. Don't you need to work on the Arena project?" he asked skeptically.

I sat back, shocked he would bring up my own work. "I've got a handle on it," I said defensively.

His eyes met mine, hard and fast. I bit my lip, his look flipping a switch inside of me. If I could beg with one look, I was doing it. I needed him to touch me. It had been too intense of a day, and only his firm hands could make my unsettled feeling go away.

Tyler's eyes dilated then he closed them, lowering his body to the mattress. "We should sleep," he said quietly, reaching to turn off the bedside lamp.

I stayed sitting on the bed in the dark. I had just been denied. So, it was only a seductive look, but that was normally all it took. I shook my head. He was hurting, no matter how much he was going to deny it. I laid down in the silence, pushing away any doubts about his feelings for me. He loved me still, didn't he?

"I love you, Ty. Goodnight," I said quietly, terrified he might not respond.

I felt the bed move then his hands pulled me to his broad chest. "I love you too, Becs," he whispered in the darkness.

His breath was hot against my cheek while his chest rose quickly. Tilting my head to meet his, our lips were barely an inch apart. "Please kiss me," I said softly.

The yearning in my voice was undeniable. The need for him to hold me, to comfort the both of us, was empowering. His mouth slowly met mine, locking tenderly around my lower lip. He sucked gently, reassuring that this whole mess wouldn't come between us.

We kissed slowly for what felt like an hour, our hands never wandering, merely holding each other.

With a shaky breath I broke away from our kissing. "Sleep baby." It was my way of telling him I understood he was tired and had possibly one of the longest days of his life. I knew that he wasn't ready to talk about it, and I would be there for him when he was ready.

But, I didn't know how long *I* could keep him at an arm's length.

***

The weekend was horribly long and quiet. Tyler worked long days in Chicago both Friday and Saturday and was holed up in his office most of Sunday. Even the car ride back to Grand Rapids was long and silent. He was doing it, pushing me away.

His demeanor was his old self, quiet and focused, not flirty and loving like he normally was with me. I really thought he would break by now. I thought he would start mourning and need me to comfort him. Even our nights felt distant. The only way I would get attention was if I showed interest. Otherwise, he would roll over and go to sleep, or at least pretend to.

Last night I woke around 2:00 a.m., catching Tyler staring wide eyed at the ceiling. I was thankful he didn't flinch when I rested my hand on his chest. His eyes still remained open, but his hand covered mine. It was the closest thing to comfort I had gotten from him all weekend.

Tyler had already gone into work when I woke. How did he sneak out so fast?

I showered with a heavy heart. Dressing in Tyler's favorite yellow summer dress, I straightened my hair and slid on heels, heading out the door with my protein shake in hand.

The Conklin building felt normal again. People moving in and out. The security guard who used to give me the slightest glimpse when I walked through the building doors was shockingly friendlier. I guess that happens when you have a diamond on your finger from the company owner.

Or at least partial owner. Today, Tyler and his brothers were going to find out who RJ left the company to. Most people would assume the company would rightfully be passed down to all of his boys, but who knows with RJ's crazy mind.

Walking off the elevator, I found a sense of security. My life had been full of ups and downs, but the past six months I had found true peace in my work. It was constant, and I thrived to succeed.

"Becca, how are you doing? I'm so sorry to hear about RJ. I wish I could have made it to Chicago," Will greeted with open arms.

I gave him a friendly hug back. "Thank you, I'm all right. Chicago is a long trip to do with a newborn. Congratulations! How are things going for you and your wife?"

Will smiled and filled me in on the details of his new daughter and how happy his wife was now that she wasn't the only female in their family.

After Will and I caught up on our personal lives, we discussed our latest prints and project deadlines. Once we were back in order from both of us being out of the office, we hurried to work and back into our typical routines.

My mind was distant from my work though, worried about Tyler. I glanced at the clock noticing it was nearly lunch time. Maybe I could convince him to leave the office before his meeting with the lawyer to grab some food?

Finding a stopping point, I headed to the elevator. As soon as the doors opened to the top floor, an eerie feeling came across me as my feet hit the carpeting. RJ had died on this floor. Was shot and killed. I still didn't know the details, and I didn't think Tyler was ready for me to ask, even if he acted like he wasn't affected.

Shaking off the uneasy feeling, I headed to the other hallway to Tyler's office. His door was closed, and Cooper greeted me with a warm smile.

"Hey Becca. Tyler just got back. I'm sure he would love to see you," he said looking up from his screen.

I gave him a polite smile and opened the door. "Thanks Cooper," I said as I closed the door. When my eyes found Tyler, my heart dropped.

He was pacing the length of the windows, one hand in his hair with the other pulling on the collar of his shirt. Heavy breaths escaped him, and his chest was heaving.

Was he having a breakdown?

"Tyler?" I asked cautiously, taking a few steps towards him.

His head swung in my direction, startled by my presence. His eyes were wide and lost, his jaw slacked in confusion. By the way he was panting you would have thought the oxygen was evaporating in the room.

"Baby, what's wrong?" I asked with concern, taking a few more steps towards him.

He was searching the room, as though looking for an answer. "I just... I..."

Tyler was frazzled and stuttering, and my heart was breaking for him. His breath hitched and became quicker and shallower the closer I got to him. His eyes were on the ground now, still rapidly moving to find something to focus on.

One hand was on his chest now while the other still tugged at his collar.

"Tyler... just breathe," I said gently, finally filling the space between us. I bravely moved my hand to cradle his cheek.

His chest still heaved, and I could tell he was internally fighting whether or not he wanted me to see him in this state.

"I'm... I have to..." He was panicked, his jaw slacking then swallowing hard and long. The sweat on his brow was glistening in the sunlight from the windows.

This was it; he was broken. The time for him to let me in was now.

"It's okay. It's okay," I soothed, bringing my other hand to his face. I massaged his cheek bones with my thumbs, trying to coax him to look at me.

"I need to... I just..." He was lost, and I hated it. Tyler didn't know how to handle his feelings, and the only way to get him to calm down was lingering in my mind.

"Take me," I murmured.

His eyes darted to mine, confusion and then contemplation crossing his face.

"It's okay, take me... please," I said, my words barely a whisper.

Tyler's breathing slowly evened as he studied me but was still hot on my skin.

Taking one hand from his face, I curled his tie around my wrist then slowly pulled him until I was backed against the opposite wall. His nostrils flared as his hand found my thigh, slowly creeping under my skirt. His grasp was firm and strong, finding my hip.

His head was turned away from me now, his eyes slowly blinking closed. Tilting my head, I brushed the side of his mouth with my lips. "Take. Me." I said as a command.

Tyler's hips pinned me hard against the wall, his arm snaking around the curve of my waist, his other hand finding its way to grip my panties.

I met his move, slipping my hand to undo his belt. When I met skin, a low growl escaped Tyler's mouth, and the hand that had a hold of my panties tugged the lace, ripping it with ease.

Letting out a gasp of excitement, I pulled him from his suit pants, enjoying the increase of his breath on my neck as I squeezed his length.

Tyler moved one hand to my thigh, aggressively hitching it around his hip, causing our skin to finally meet. This time Tyler wasn't gently easing into me, he was going full speed, his hands firmly pulling me into him.

"I'm here... it's okay," I whispered through his harsh breaths.

Tyler groaned into my neck, his teeth grazing to my shoulder, biting my skin. The pain from the grasp his teeth held was erotic and welcomed.

This was his way of coping. His escape from whatever was haunting him in his head. If only I could escape with him, help him understand his feelings towards the death of his less than involved father.

My hands were gentle on his neck and shoulders, the complete opposite of his tight hold. His bite on my shoulder became hard as his thrust deeper and faster. He came with a muffled grunt, his teeth digging into my skin, causing me to whimper from his rushed and forceful finish.

Tyler's grip remained strong as his breath finally calmed. I continued my way of soothing him, my fingers delicately tracing circles on the nape of his neck.

Just as I was about to softly tell him I was here, his hands left my skin as he cleared his throat. Stepping back from me, he grabbed his tie again, fiddling trying to tighten it from his exertions.

"I have a meeting in ten minutes with the lawyers," he said, his voice deep and raspy. He leaned down to pick up my ripped underwear and threw them on his desk chair.

Smoothing my dress back down my hips, my face blushed slightly knowing I would be without panties the rest of the day. I waited for him to say more, to even look at me, but he didn't.

Was *that* his dismissal? I just let him pound his frustrations into me, the least I thought he would do was talk to me afterwards. Say something reassuring that would help me slightly understand.

"Okay. Can we meet for lunch after?" I asked, trying not to feel awkward from what had just happened.

"I'm not sure," he murmured, letting out a long deep breath.

"Why won't you look at me?" I said, my voice cracking.

His eyes slowly worked their way to mine, the sad greener-than-blue color being pulled from his brown dress shirt and olive tie.

"Because I hate doing that to you," he said softly.

"You needed it," I responded, stepping closer to him. His eyes left mine again, but sorrow filled his face. "Tyler, why won't you open up to me? I'm here for you, and I've been patiently waiting to help you deal with this. I know you're affected by RJ's death, and you should be. He was your father, absent most of the time or not."

"I'll be fine," he muttered.

I didn't believe him. "Didn't look like you were fine when I walked through that door."

He shook his head then walked to his office door. "I'm just stressed out. That was nothing. Forget it ever happened." He opened the door and ushered for me to leave.

"Tyler, I can't just forget that—"

"Well, it was extremely embarrassing," he snapped, cutting me off from finishing my sentence.

I marched towards him, grabbing his arms before he could walk out the door. "You never have to be embarrassed with me, Ty. That's what I'm here for, to love you unconditionally. Don't feel like less of a man because you need to be comforted."

He stared at me, that same lost boy look in his eyes. Before I could wrap my arms around him, he shook his head and his bleak expression was back as though no vulnerability took place in this room. "I have to go meet Nathan in the conference room on the sixth floor."

I studied him, trying to understand his point of view. Finally giving up, my shoulders slumped as I said, "Okay. I'll walk with you. I have my meeting with Jamie and the ArtPrize artist."

Tyler rolled his eyes. "That guy is a loon. He wants me to pay him double. His work better bring in some new clients," Tyler grumbled.

I let out a small giggle, agreeing with his loon statement. Tyler gave me a soft smile, the first one I had seen in awhile as he lead the way to the elevator.

Entering the elevator, my good feeling from Tyler's small moment of happiness was gone when he didn't touch me. Normally he always would put a hand on my lower back, around my waist or grab my hand as soon as the doors closed.

"Maybe we could get away this weekend," I said softly, trying not to be offended by his lack of physical touch.

"I have to be in Chicago this weekend," he said flatly.

Tears pricked my eyes. I didn't like this distance, and even though I knew he needed the sex in his office, I wasn't expecting his mood to be the same as before. I thought the sex would help open him up to me, not help him bury his feelings deeper.

"Hey," he said quietly, turning his head towards me. I couldn't bear to look at him, scared what his expression might be. "Give me a month, Becs. Then all of this will be sorted out."

I nodded my head, closing my eyes and forcing the huge lump down my throat.

I felt his proximity become closer as the elevator started to descend. His hands cautiously traced my forearms and biceps, causing goose bumps to form on my skin. Once his hands found my face I opened my eyes, feeling unbelievably exposed by his stare.

"I mean it, just give this time," he swallowed hard, looking away from me for a moment. "Give me time," he whispered.

His hands were still on my face when the elevator opened.

"Becca, there you are! I was worried you had forgotten!" Jamie said. She was a sight for my sore, tear-threatening eyes. Tyler dropped his hands from my face as I ran to give her a hug. I missed my best friend. We rarely got a chance to talk anymore, and I hated it. She was so busy in Miami, and I was busy here.

Once Jamie pulled away, she looked towards Tyler. "I'm sorry for your loss Tyler, and I apologize I couldn't make it to the funeral."

"Thank you. You were needed in Miami. Please don't apologize," Tyler said stiffly as he turned towards me. "I'll be late tonight. See you at home."

"Do you want to stay at the condo?" I asked quickly.

He shook his head no. "I need to pack for Chicago and Cleveland."

The elevator doors closed before I could say anything else.

"Well, he looks like he has been a real gem to be around," Jamie scoffed as we made our way to my office.

I let out a deep breath. "Yes, things have been a little tense. Honestly, you're the first one to notice him acting strangely."

"The death grip he had on your face was the first clue, along with the intense stare. RJ's death not settling well?"

"He needs more time to let everything marinate," I murmured.

"Good luck with that. Putters is going to be late. I swear, if he doesn't have a model of whatever the hell he is building for ArtPrize I'm going to flip shit on him," she grumbled.

I laughed as we entered my office, taking a seat at my conference table.

"I booked my flight to Chicago to go dress shopping," Jamie said, changing the subject. "I swear to God, if you make me wear yellow..."

"No, it's a deep purple. Plum I believe is the exact color title." I laughed.

"One good thing, there is no way your mother can say anything about your smokin' body. My God, Becca."

I shook my head in discomfort. "We will have to see."

Truth was, I was terrified of the weekend. The more I thought about it, the more it crossed my mind that this fancy wedding dress designer was used to tiny size zero models. How was she going to look at me coming in as a size six or eight? Especially when all of the women I would be arriving with are smaller than me.

We spent the next 15 minutes catching up, mainly about the wedding. Everything was touched from the cake to the DJ's playlist. Jamie was super thankful she would be walking down with Nathan and not Mitch.

"I'm surprised Mitch is standing up for Tyler," she commented with a wiggle of the nose. "If he hits on me one more time, I might smack him with one of those damn bricks he's constantly bragging about."

I cocked my head at her. "Bricks?"

"Yes, those RJ bricks. He was gloating to me the other day about how he had perfected them. So annoying. I hate that he has been in Miami. Why he constantly comes to our office is beyond me." She groaned.

I picked through my brain. I remembered RJ talking about one with pride the very first time I went into his office. What could you do with a brick that was so special anyway?

"Did he say what was so great about the bricks?"

Jamie shook her head. "Who gives a shit about those bricks? If that punk 'accidentally' brushes against my ass one more time..." She raised her fist in the air.

"He is a Conklin," I said, shrugging my shoulders.

"Ugh, Conklin men. Of course the only half-way normal one is gay."

We both laughed as the phone rang. "Becca Stine."

It was Putters. "Did you and Miss Rae forget about our meeting?"

I looked at Jamie dumbfounded. "No, of course not. We're on the commercial architectural floor where we discussed meeting."

There was a loud saw sounding noise in the background. "No, we're meeting at my studio. I'll be here the rest of the day."

"I'm sorry Mr. Putters but I was under the impression we were meeting at the office... Mr. Putters?" I heard dial tone next.

"He hung up on me!" I said, surprised.

"Did I hear that correctly? What a pain in the ass. We are NOT working with any more artists next year to this extent. I mean it Becca," Jamie said in a huff as she stood from the desk. "Let's go to his freaking studio."

I rolled my eyes and followed Jamie, grateful for the fresh air and the distraction from Tyler's odd mood.

***

I got caught in traffic on the way home. For the first time, I didn't have road rage. I knew Tyler wouldn't be there yet, and part of me wanted to stall until we could be home together at the same time. I still wasn't used to the big house all by itself in the woods. Even though Tyler had a state of the art security system installed, the darkness in the air at night was chilling, and lately I have been easy to jump at anything out of the ordinary. I needed to get better about turning the alarm on once I got home instead of leaving it off until it was time to go to bed.

I ran through the day in my head, everything from the craziness of Tyler's assault to the unexpected change of plans to visit Lou Putter's art studio. His studio was more like a giant warehouse, the ones I predicted to be a lot like Chino's fixer uppers. I couldn't help but examine the structure of the building while Putters took us through his work space.

He'd finished a few models, and Jamie and I were pleasantly surprised. They were well constructed, creative structures of the city. My father's building, Riverhouse, Union Square, the Cathedral of St. Andrew. They were stunning, and I couldn't help but think he might have a shot at winning something from ArtPrize.

As I suspected, Tyler wasn't home when I pulled into the wooded driveway. It was just after 7:00 p.m., and I needed to find something to do.

I found myself going through the Arena plans. They were turning out beautifully, and I was about ready to show them to my father. I couldn't wait to hear his opinion. I'd hoped to make him proud. His approval meant so much to me.

I finally gave in once the sun went down, lying in bed and watching T.V. waiting for Tyler to come home, curious what his mood would be like.

My eyes flew open with a loud crash. I bolted upright in bed, pulling the sheet to cover my chest. I was in a tank top and shorts but still felt bare. I swallowed hard, listening for other signs of commotion.

Did I turn the alarm on? Shit, I didn't!

My body started to shake as I reached for my phone to call Tyler.

I heard ringing from the other side of the house as I sighed with relief. It was Tyler making the noise. I jumped out of bed, my racing heart wanting a hug. Hopefully he would give me one that was warm instead of cold.

I traveled through the nautical themed house, my feet comforted by the plush carpeting once I found the living room. Another crash sounded through the hall, and I was startled when I found Tyler fumbling aimlessly with a set of shot glasses on the breakfast table.

"What are you doing?" I asked as I studied his slouched position. Another crash sounded as he slammed another shot glass on the table after pouring it down his throat.

"Hey...," he slurred.

Shit. He was drunk. Did he drive home drunk?

"Hi," I said cautiously as I approached him.

His tie was off and thrown on the kitchen island, his shirt unbuttoned at the top with his sleeves rolled up to his elbows. "Want a drink?" he asked with a hiccup, holding a bottle of Jack Daniels that had maybe two shots left.

I shook my head no. Tyler tilted his head then shrugged his shoulders, tipping the bottle to his lips. If I suspected, he killed it himself.

"Why don't you come to bed, Tyler?" I asked gently, reaching for his arm.

A sexy smirk spread across his face. "You want to go to bed with me?" His arms roughly found my waist, pulling me to him. I gasped as I looked at him wide eyed.

His mood went from attempting to be sultry to unsure. "Not sure why you'd want to go to bed with me, considering I won't get the job done. Well, at least not for you." He let go of me, pushing me away a little harder than I had expected. He turned to the kitchen, fumbling through the cupboards until he found another bottle.

"Ah... there you are," he murmured, untwisting the bottle and taking another swig.

"Ty, I think you've had enough," I said more sternly.

He turned to me sluggishly. "I think... you're too sober." He snickered as he slammed the bottle down then burst into a fit of giggles.

I rolled my eyes, moving to take the bottle from his hands.

"Nu uh uh, Becca... this is *mine*. If you want one I can pull another bottle down. I know you can't reach that high," he snickered again.

I furrowed my brows at him, yanking the bottle harder, but his grasp was too tight.

"This isn't how you need to deal with your feelings, Tyler," I grumbled.

He looked at me puzzled. "Feelings? What feelings? I don't have feelings." He gulped, completely yanking the bottle out of my hand and taking another swig.

"I won't let you hurt yourself because you don't know how to deal with RJ's death."

Tyler laughed whole heartedly. I was almost scared of his senile reaction. "RJ, a real actor." He shook his head while laughing, but his expression grew more somber. "Yeah... RJ. Maybe he wasn't such an asshole."

I studied him, hoping with all my heart he was finally going to open up to me, even if he were drunk.

"You want to know who the real asshole is?" he asked as he looked at the full fifth of alcohol in his hand. "Me. Because I'm a blind idiot."

Silenced passed through us. "You're not an idiot, Tyler."

He shook his head again, biting his bottom lip. "Yes, I am. I didn't realize who the real bad guy was."

"Who might that be?"

He looked at me, his eyes wetting. "My grandfather."

Now I was beyond confused. "Your grandfather?"

"Yep," he said, popping his lips. "My grandfather was a selfish son of a bitch."

"What?" Tyler always praised his grandfather. How he was a respectable businessman, always kept to his morals. He really looked up to his grandfather. Robert Senior took Tyler and his brothers under his wing when RJ wasn't ready to grow up and take responsibility.

"Robert Senior. So much for fucking morals."

"Tyler, stop it. Let's go to bed. You don't know what you're saying."

He slammed the bottle down on the counter, lowering his head so he could look me straight in the eyes. "I know exactly what I'm saying! My papa was a liar! He did bad business! And you know who covered it up? You know who almost had this Godforsaken business clean again?"

I stood dumbfounded, not understanding what he was saying.

"Come on Becs, you're smart. You've been standing up for him a lot lately, along with EVERYONE ELSE," he half exaggerated, throwing his free hand in the air.

I looked to the ground. I wasn't going to do this tonight, not while he was drunk.

"I'm going to sleep in one of the guest rooms," I said raising my hands in defeat.

"RJ!" he shouted, throwing the empty bottle across the room, the glass shattering into tiny pieces. "RJ spent the last five years digging this company out of the blood-sucking hole my papa built. Don't you get it? RJ wasn't the bad guy!" he practically screamed. The vein in his throat was popping out, and I was frightened and speechless.

Tyler's hand found his cheek as he looked at me, but he was looking past me into dead space. He dragged his hand down his face, his pinky pulling down his lower lip.

"My entire life was a lie, Becs," he whispered. Then he did something I never thought I'd see him do. He finally broke, falling to the ground, pulling his knees to his chest. He shook his head back and forth, his lower lip trembling as he was choking back tears. He was rocking his body, confusion and turmoil behind his features.

I knelt down beside him, contemplating if he would let me touch him. "Ty," I whispered in desperation. "Talk to me."

He shook his head faster, biting his lower lip to stop it from trembling.

"It couldn't be that bad," I whispered again, bravely bringing my hands to his knees. I was wracking my brain, trying to put together anything shady that had happened. "Nothing we can't get through."

"You should leave me now," he choked.

My heart dropped into my stomach. "Why would you say that?" I asked, fighting back tears. "After all we've been through, you want to give up now?"

"I'm no good, Becca. What good would a husband be when he's in jail?"

I stared at him wide eyed. RJ, or Tyler's grandfather, must have been involved with Chino's schemes. I thought back to what Connor had told me when we went to lunch, how Chino was heavy into narcotics, but they could never pin anything on Lee directly. Lee always had people to do his dirty work, and he must have been plotting for the Conklin's to be his next pawns.

"It's Chino, isn't it? Your grandfather used to sell drugs with him, didn't he?" I whispered, gripping his knees tight with my hands.

Tyler rubbed his eyes while taking a deep breath. "I can't prove it, but I'm pretty sure. I found paperwork today with my grandfather's signature on a residential subdivision as co-owner with Chino."

I stared at him blankly. What did that have to do with drugs?

Tyler let out a long sigh. "I don't want you involved in this."

"Too late. You put a ring on my finger, I'm involved," I said sternly.

He shook his head again. "This is business, and I won't let you get wrapped up in something like this."

"Like what? I don't understand how Chino's drug pushing would involve residential subdivisions?"

Tyler looked at me glassy eyed then slouched against the island cupboard, dropping his knees so his legs were flat on the floor, his arms dangled over his thighs. It was a purely drunken position. "Becca, I'm going to need to drink the rest of that bottle before I say something I'm going to regret," Tyler slurred.

I huffed as I stood tall over him with my hands on my hips. "You're done drinking for the night. Either you're going to tell me exactly what's going on or you're going to bed."

He raised an eyebrow at me, as if daring me to put my money where my mouth was. Then his eyes grazed from my face down my body, his jaw slacking as his tongue slowly traced his lower lip.

"Still sleeping in the guest room?" he asked as seductively as he could.

My heart beat faster as his eyes dilated, completely forgetting what we were discussing. I craved intimacy with him so badly and not just what happened in his office earlier. I wanted him to hold me and kiss me tenderly, not just hard grasps, rough thrusts, and biting.

I slowly shook my head no, putting my hand out for him to grab, hoping he would finally come to bed with me. Before I knew what was happening, he took my hand and harshly pulled me into his lap, forcing my legs to straddle him. He had my hands pinned behind my back as his eyes devoured me from head to chest. His mouth sloppily found my collarbone, making its way towards my neck. I tipped my head backward, feeling my body stretch from him pulling on my forearms. His tongue and mouth felt so amazing, along with the controlling grip on my wrists.

"It's so easy to get lost in you," he growled, his mouth finding my jaw.

"Why won't you talk to me," I said breathlessly. "I want to be here for you, Tyler."

He nuzzled my neck then took the strap to my camisole between his teeth, pulling it down over my shoulder. His breath was loud and heavy matching mine. Once the strap was past my shoulder, Tyler's eyes squinted, trying to focus on something.

I tilted my head, looking downward after he released one of my wrists, his hand shakily finding the mark on my shoulder from earlier.

"Did I do this?" he whispered in horror, staring at the teeth marks and faint bruise. It might get darker by tomorrow, but I doubted it would be bad. I wouldn't be able to wear anything with a strap or sleeveless the next few days, but I didn't mind.

"It didn't hurt," I said confidently.

Closing his eyes tightly, he let go of my other wrist, his head smacking back against the cupboard.

I reached for his face, wanting to comfort him. He turned his head away from me, trying to distance himself from any emotional connection that he could.

It tore me apart.

"You should go sleep in the guest room," he mumbled.

Tears fell down my face as he said the words.

"I want to lay with you," I choked.

He closed his eyes hard again. "I can't trust myself with you right now. I need time. I don't want to hurt you again."

"You're hurting me now," I said, catching a tear between my lips. I slowly stood, hoping he would grab me and pull me back to him, but he didn't. He kept his eyes closed, his brows creased. I watched him with the heaviest heart I had in a long time. Soon his brow smoothed over, and his breathing became deeper. He had passed out sitting upward on the kitchen floor. As much as I wanted to pull him into the bedroom with me, I didn't. He could sleep in this kitchen and feel like shit the next morning because he had just made me feel like complete shit as well.

Chapter Twelve

Tyler

My life was turning into a complete whirlwind, and I had no idea how to keep myself anchored in the tsunami that was happening.

When I woke this morning slouched against the kitchen cupboard, my clothing was disheveled and small shards of glass were all over the floor. I ran my hands over my face then checked my watch. It was 4:30am and still dark out. My head was foggy, but I remembered details of the previous hours. I can't believe I let everything slip, that I had an anxiety attack like a little bitch again in front of Becca. How was I ever going to convince her I was fine with all of this constant hyperventilating?

How could I tell her about my grandfather?

My chest tightened at the thought. I couldn't believe what I found when I started to go through RJ's office. I didn't want to, and I'm still not sure what drew me to that side of the office floor.

It was like a magnet, my heart beating faster every step I took towards RJ's office. The place where I was furiously stampeding because RJ had betrayed me exactly a week ago. Pretending to be a father, wanting a relationship. I shook my head, my anger sending tingles from my chest to my finger tips. My hand shook as I reached for the handle, expecting it to be locked like usual. Finally taking a breath, I pushed on the handle, swinging the door open.

The room smelled overly clean, no doubt from the special soap used to clean the carpets from RJ's... A shudder went through my body as I pictured the image in my head.

Push it away, Tyler. It'll only make you weaker.

My eyes examined the room, pictures on the wall and shelves, his tidy desk. Everything had a place, and I rolled my eyes when I saw th picture from my college graduation. I think that was one of the few times RJ had ever laid his arm around me. He was always one to put on a show for the cameras. There was a picture of Nathan and him as well, except it wasn't from Nathan's graduation. It was from the first project Nathan had contracted as the marketing coordinator with Conklin.

I remembered being happy for Nathan and embarrassingly envious. The way RJ looked at Nathan in that picture was moving. A father proud of his son and what he had accomplished. RJ never looked at me that way. In fact, he had never said he was proud of me, except for... No. I wasn't going to go there. I didn't need to feel guilty.

I ran my hand along the smooth mahogany, my fingers stopping at the random RJ brick dead center of the desk. I looked at it questioningly. Without thinking, I bent down, squatting in my expensive suit, my eyes skeptically looking for the notch. I reached for it, fingering the concrete until I found the knob.

The concrete slab popped open on the side. I gulped, afraid of what I might find. I thought maybe there would be some drugs, cash, the deed to the building, but never in my right mind did I think I'd find what my fingers pulled out.

The first item I found was a crinkled piece of paper, my jaw nearly dropping when I read the words.

RJ,

I'm sorry. I can't run away with you. I can't do that to your family. But know that I do love you. If things were different, we could be together.

Love Always,

Margo

Did he love her? My teen and young adult life flashed before my eyes, trying to notice any proof of them being more. Would that have changed my mind about Margo? Before Becca, I would have been more furious with Margo, using me as a pawn to get closer to my father. Did she really love him? Or was she playing RJ just like she played everyone else?

Truth be told, it didn't matter anymore. I had Becca. She was my love, who I would gladly escape with to a deserted island.

The next piece of paper literally brought tears to my eyes. It was a letter from my grandfather. God, how I missed that man. I wondered how he would deal with all of this. I'm sure losing a son would be excruciating, but RJ and my grandfather butted heads like no other.

Robbie-

The day will come when I won't be on this earth anymore, and I needed you to know I loved you so much more than I might have shown throughout the years.

The day you were born, my life felt complete. I had your beautiful mother, my parents, and the beginning of a company that would grow to be so much more than I could have ever imagined. I have never been more proud of how you have grown with the business. Your maturity and seriousness with your work is truly astounding. I know you will take care of this company and make it your life. For that I am grateful.

But don't forget about what really matters. We never had the normal father-son relationship, and I know that might hurt me more than it hurts you. I tried my hardest, but I created a working machine. As I said, I am beyond proud of all you have accomplished, but there is so much more to life than money and business.

Which brings me to the nitty gritty.

Your family.

Cherish them.

Mary loves you and respects you more than she acts. All she wants is your attention. Give it to her. It's impossible to find a good woman who will put up with our busy lifestyles. Like your mother, Mary understands. Don't lose her, and if you aren't willing to realize this, let her go. She isn't a trophy for you to display at company parties. She's the mother of your amazing boys. Be faithful to her, love her, and respect her. You'd be surprised the kind of affection and love you will receive in return if you give her what she deserves.

Work on your relationship with your boys. We both turned them into business monsters like ourselves. They all look up to you and want you in their lives. Please Robbie; give them more than two minutes of office time. Spend more than holidays and business functions with them. Like Mary, they deserve more. It's never too late to fix a broken relationship.

I love you son. Don't make the same mistake we did with our relationship with your boys. Your memories with them shouldn't be work related but focused on life and love.

Love always,

Dad

Rubbing my palms against both of my eyes, I tried to contain the tears and emotion I felt from the letter. I missed my grandfather, and I was angry RJ treated him so poorly. Reading my grandfather's words on that paper only brought me more confusion. When did RJ see this? Did it affect him? Was he trying to change?

The positive thought quickly left my mind.

No. He was trying to use me for the Chino deal.

Wiping my eyes one more time, I pulled out another piece of paper, but this one was more formatted and looked to be a legal document. Squinting my eyes, I read across the top—Put Option Agreement.

I hadn't dealt with these types of documents very often. To my knowledge, a Put Option agreement is when a purchaser is bound to complete a sale under the owner's wishes.

But this document didn't involve the Conklin Company and had two very familiar names.

Lee Chino's name was the Offeree, while to my horror, Robert Conklin Senior was the Offeror.

My eyes became wider and wider with each sentence I read.

The Offeror is the registered holder of ordinary shares in the company.

In consideration of the undertakings of the Offeror and of the Offeree under this Agreement the Offeror has the right at any time to require the Offeree to acquire the option shares (choice narcotic) for a purchase price of 12% over market cost per Ordinary Share.

The Put Option shall be excerisable by notice in writing service upon the Offeree.

Could this be possible? Did this really mean my grandfather was buying drugs from Chino? Not only was he buying them, they had a "legal agreement."

My grandfather, the man who valued morals and family, who cared about ethics in the business world, and refused to take the easy way out of any situation, because that wasn't how the world worked. The world didn't give out handouts, and he pushed for us to thrive to succeed on ethics and integrity.

My grandfather.
The well respected businessman.
The loving husband, father, and grandfather.
The morally-correct Christian.
My grandfather, the drug dealer.

I couldn't breathe. The only man I trusted and looked to for advice and counsel was a fake. He was a hypocrite, and I didn't want to believe it.

What hurt the most was the guilt in my gut as I read the large stamp over the contract that said VOID in red ink, followed by RJ's signature.

RJ had put a stop to the direct sales between Conklin blood and that sleezeball Chino. If my stomach could sink any lower, it would be in the pits of hell.

My chest felt like it was going to cave in as I tried to catch my breath, grasping the edge of RJ's desk making my knuckles white. I'm sure my face was just as pale as I threw up in the trash can underneath his desk.

The awful feeling was still there after I disposed of whatever was inside of my stomach. I couldn't see straight; I couldn't think straight. The only horrid thought running through my mind was that my entire life had been a lie, and I had no idea who the hell to believe. The worst part was, I couldn't confront them. They were both dead, and I had never had more of a conflicted love-hate feeling for anyone as I had for RJ and my grandfather.

I had approximately 45 minutes before meeting with the lawyers to go over RJ's will, and I had to get my shit together. I grabbed the three other envelopes from the RJ brick and left RJ's office without looking back.

I kept my head down as I power walked passed Cooper. Thankfully, he hadn't looked up from his screen to notice my frazzled state. I think I paced my office windows at least 15 times before Becca entered.

I never wanted her to see me so exposed and confused, so anxious and on the verge of losing my sanity. But there was no way I could hide it now. I was too wired and upset. The look on her face when she saw me gutted me even more. I couldn't bear the look of sympathy in her loving eyes. How could she love me? This giant asshole who disrespected the one man who was trying to keep our noses clean. I should have noticed. There had to have been signs while I worked so closely with my grandfather. How did I not see that he was a lying, good-for-nothing drug dealer?

Then she touched me, and I fell into my old miserable habit. She wanted to comfort me, and I used her like I had used every other poor girl that came in my direction when I was feeling lost and pissed off at the world.

I was a sick bastard and needed to completely disregard these feelings so I wouldn't touch my Becca like that again. I left marks on the one woman I loved and cherished. Even though I was mad as hell at my grandfather for being a lying son of a bitch, I would take the advice he gave RJ—cherish them. If by keeping my hands off Becca for a few weeks until I could get my head on straight was what I needed to do, then by God I wouldn't come within a hundred mile radius of her.

I darted to the bathroom, showering as quickly as I could. The throbbing in my head was getting worse by the beating of the water on the tile. I was going to need to give up drinking for a few weeks until I could control this awful pull in my chest. No more opportunities to be weak, and alcohol made me do exactly that. No one could know about this, at least not yet. Not Nathan, Mitch, or my mother. I had to wrap my head around all of it and try and figure out what the hell Chino was plotting.

I dressed quickly, brushing my teeth rapidly and as quietly as possible. I didn't want to wake Becca and face her. Thankfully, she was a hard sleeper and half the time didn't notice when I would get ready and leave.

Walking out of the closet, my heart tugged out of my chest as I saw her laying on my side of the bed, squeezing my pillow to her chest. Her hair was fanned out across the other pillow, and her mouth was slightly open. Her chest gently rose with the calmness of the room. I couldn't help but be drawn to come and look at her more closely.

She left her camisole on, and I cringed when I saw the faint teeth mark I left on her shoulder. My heart nearly stopped as my eyes wandered down her body, terrified I might find more bruises on her thighs from gripping them so hard when I used her.

Letting out a shallow breath of relief, I was happy there weren't any other visible bruises on her body from me. The urge to lay down and snuggle her was torture, but I couldn't be tempted. Knowing my Becs, she would wiggle her ass, and I would turn into a frenzied, leg humping disappointment.

Before giving in to my urge, I rushed out of the room, leaving Becca sleeping peacefully. She would understand my casual absence and blame it on work while I figured out these stupid mixed emotions.

The work wouldn't be such a lie. Nathan and I had to figure out how we were going to manage the company. RJ rightfully left the company equally to the three of us, providing we distributed the income properly between ourselves and our mother.

Mom might be crazy, but she would get her cut. She did put up with RJ and his unfaithfulness their entire marriage. It was the least the asshole could give her.

I sighed as I pulled out of the driveway, fighting the inner battle in my heart. Who to believe and who to trust.

***

"If you want to stay and manage this office the rest of the week, that's fine. I can handle bouncing from Cleveland to Chicago," Nathan said as he opened his portfolio of paperwork.

Reaching for my iPad, I shook my head. "Let me cover Chicago."

When I finally looked in Nathan's direction because of the silence, he was staring at me. "You can stay with Becca, Tyler. Really. I think you need to spend time with her."

I gulped, hiding any expression from my face. "She's busy with the Arena project. They're supposed to start the remodel in July and work through September."

"Don't the two of you have a wedding to plan?" he asked, leaning back in his chair.

My head started to pound again. "She doesn't need me to make decisions. I really don't care as long as Becca gets whatever she wants."

"I don't know about that," he said, scratching his chin. "But I would think Becca wouldn't mind having you around for your opinion. She's one to please."

"She knows all I care about is unzipping her white wedding dress at the end of the night," I said with a crooked grin.

Only if that were true. I fantasized about seeing her at the end of the aisle as the large church doors opened. She would be standing there, looking shy, but soft and vulnerable. Her blue eyes sparkling back at me, ignoring everyone else in each pew. I wanted to see Becca in that white wedding dress as much as I wanted to see her out of it.

"You're such a horny asshole," Nathan laughed, flipping through paperwork.

I laughed under my breath. That was true, but I had to keep it in my pants until I could control my strength and focus on lovemaking, not fucking.

"Gentlemen, glad to see we are both back in the office," Lee Chino said as he pushed open the door to Nathan's office. Nathan and I glanced at each other then back to Chino.

My pulse raced when Mitch followed behind him, dressed in his typical work jeans and boots. I clenched my teeth as they both stood casually in front of the desk Nathan and I were sitting at.

"Take a seat Mitch," Chino said while staring me down. Mitch obeyed, sitting next to Nathan, his eyes on the ground.

"I think it's time we discuss where this company is going," Chino said, putting his hands in his pockets. His eyes were serious, not matching his casual stance. "RJ agreed to become business partners. I think we need to continue in that direction."

Nathan stood tall from his chair. "RJ is no longer the owner of this company. We are, and our ideas for the future of this company are very different than RJ's."

A devilish grin spread across Chino's face. "Not too long ago you felt the same way, Nathan." His eyes moved from Nathan to me. "Tyler, have you had a change of heart? Or do you still not want this company to make billions?"

I stood along with Nathan, the testosterone thick in the air. I was a good five inches taller than Nathan and another two from Chino. My chest was puffed along with Nathan's while Mitch still sat in the seat between us. "I think you better be begging for us to keep any of your business, Lee. We are finally clean again. We're not about to go back to what you had with Robert Senior."

Mitch looked up towards me in confusion while Nathan didn't move a muscle. Right then I knew Nathan had known about our grandfather's dirty little secret with Lee Chino. I had a moment of stupidity from being blind as to what was going on right in front of me.

"Finally figured it out, did you Tyler?" Chino said with a sphinx-like smile. "Your grandfather and I had one hell of a business going."

I swallowed hard; paranoid I would start sweating bullets.

"He built this company for more than your drug money," Nathan said, interrupting our stare down. "I know you didn't like RJ voiding your deal, but that's where this company is going to stand. We'll keep contracting your subdivisions, but no other side deals. Our businesses WILL stay separate."

Chino began to laugh and not a small, under his breath laugh of frustration, but a full belly outburst. Nathan and I swapped a nervous glance. What the hell was so funny? He was damn near laughing into hysterics.

His lips finally met again, his mouth forming into a thin line. He took a large step towards me, his height having no influence on his confidence.

"You think RJ really cleaned this company up? You think he really stopped anything? He was going to sign that paperwork again. He just wanted to make sure those damn detectives wouldn't find anything."

My eyes found the floor. *Fuck.* If only I knew what to believe.

Nathan moved from around the table to the other side of Chino. "I don't believe he was going to sign. I think you are full of shit. "

Chino's eyes grew hard. "You have no idea who you are dealing with. There are more of your employees working for me than you realize. I get what I want, and I suggest you step over the line to my side." Chino's eyes darted to mine. "Both of you. You. Can't. Survive. Without me. This company will run into the ground without my subdivisions. And Tyler knows that. You both do. So I suggest you cooperate."

"You're bluffing," Nathan said, leaning back on the table, his hands firmly on each side. How he managed to stay calm and collected in times like this was beyond me. I was about twenty seconds from putting my fist through this asshole's skull.

"RJ was never going to sign that paperwork. You just sent that email to get us riled. Riled for our business meeting."

"Wouldn't riling you for your business meeting make him not sign the papers?" Chino grinned smugly. "After all, supposedly you were all on the same page."

Nathan smiled to the ground then stood tall from the table. "I think you were just trying to get RJ and Tyler to argue because you know when that happens, stupid decisions are made because they like to piss each other off. I hate to break it to you, but RJ wouldn't stoop that low just to get under Tyler's skin."

Was it that obvious?

Chino's lip quirked as he thought. "RJ is no longer in this equation. If I wanted to rile Tyler, I would go meet with Becca about my warehouses."

It felt like a mass of tiny bugs were crawling under my skin, trying to break through and tackle Chino to the ground. I hated Becca's name being in his mouth.

"The warehouses are to be dealt with Will, not Becca. She's busy with the Arena remodel. We haven't signed anything yet, so watch your tone," Nathan said, his demeanor changing from content to acid. "You don't run this business, I do."

"Such the big brother," Chino smiled. "I always knew you would take over for RJ." His eyes found mine, that same damn smirk on his face.

I huffed under my breath. We both were handling this company just fine. If only our idiot kid brother could help us pick up the slack. Instead, he sat there with a confused expression on his face the entire time.

"This isn't over," Chino said in a threatening tone. He stepped backwards. "I'll be speaking with you soon, Mitch," he said giving Mitch a nod. Both Nathan and my eyes darted to Mitch.

Chino's pompousness rang loud and clear as he walked out the door.

"Oh, and Tyler, Becca was lovely this morning when we spoke."

Nathan stepped in front of me before I could move. Chino laughed, his satanic sound mocking us throughout the halls.

Once we no longer could hear Chino's voice, Nathan paced to the door, slamming it shut. Mitch started to stand, but Nathan held an arm up to him.

"Oh no you don't. Your ass is sitting back down and telling me exactly what you have going on with Chino."

Mitch rolled his eyes. "It's nothing bad. He wouldn't jeopardize our business," Mitch sighed.

"Did you hear him? He's a fucking lunatic. He's unpredictable and dangerous. Whatever you are doing with him has to stop, NOW," I spat.

"Get off your high horse, Tyler. You don't tell me what to do," Mitch snapped. "Besides, the cops won't ever be able to find it."

Both Nathan's and I arched our brows. "So they are hidden? In the RJ bricks? Just like what you did at my house? How many places and where?" I shouted.

"That's not what I said," Mitch back peddled.

"Mitch, I want you to think long and hard. We have to get this shit off the properties," Nathan said, trying to stay calm. "RJ would have wanted that."

"RJ killed himself. He didn't give a crap about any of us," Mitch yelled. "At least Chino wants us to be a part of something."

"Chino is using you!" I shouted back, stomping in his direction while reaching for the collar of his shirt.

"Stop it! Both of you. Don't you both see he's trying to turn us against each other?" Nathan barked.

I let go of Mitch's collar, taking a few steps backward. Chino was trying to push all of our buttons. We couldn't let him get in between us. He was a master manipulator, and we couldn't lose at his game.

"Do we have to suspend you from the job sites?" Nathan asked calmly.

Mitch jumped from his seat, his chair nearly flying through the window behind him. "Don't go on some power trip Nathan. Dad left this company to all of us."

"If you can't be responsible then you can't handle the job," I said through gritted teeth.

"Whatever," Mitch said under his breath. "You two don't know what you're missing." And he stormed out the door before either of us could say anything.

Nathan let out a huge sigh as he sat in one of the conference chairs. "He's still upset about RJ," Nathan said, defending Mitch's actions. "He doesn't want to believe he killed himself."

"Do you believe it?" I asked quietly, walking over to look out the window at the summer day.

Nathan didn't say anything for a long moment, his silence answering my question.

"Who do you think killed him?" I asked.

Nathan's fingers tapped the table. "I don't know. But I do know, with RJ dying, that red void on Grandpa and Chino's Put Option Agreement no longer matters. Chino wanted to start over. And clearly, he's psychotic and going to do everything in his power to try and get us to sign his paperwork."

"I need to go find Becca," I said quickly as Chino's words kept repeating in my head.

"Tyler, I doubt he actually met with her," Nathan said.

I shook my head as I went to leave. "He won't ever meet with her."

Chapter Thirteen

Becca

I was frustrated and hurt from Tyler pushing me away last night. Shocked and dumbfounded by his admissions, I didn't know how to process all of the information. Was Tyler's grandfather really the drug dealer while RJ tried to stay clean? How messed up for Tyler to try and understand. He looked up to his grandfather and found out he was nothing but a fraud.

He didn't even say goodbye to me this morning. He always said goodbye or would kiss my head or cheek. Most of the time he thought I was sleeping, but I almost always felt his lips and hands on me. It was soothing and made me feel cherished knowing he took the time every morning to say a silent goodbye.

Work had been awful, and every five minutes I debated going to Tyler's office to confront him, but I didn't have it in me, not yet. My irritation with his behavior was near boiling, and soon we both could get burned.

Just as I was about to open a new file for the Arena, a small knock hit my door frame.

There he was, Mr. Conflicted and Beautiful standing awkwardly with both hands on either side of the frame. "Are you busy?"

I shook my head as I rolled to face him in my seat. Crossing my arms, I waited patiently for him to enter my office and start talking. Would he bring up last night? I secretly hoped he had a massive hangover with a killer headache.

He took a seat across from me, his expression antsy. "How has your morning been? Have any meetings?"

I shook my head no again. Were we really going to skirt around the elephant in the room?

He nodded, rubbing his palms against his knees, debating what to say next.

"Did you want to talk about last night," I asked, finally breaking the uncomfortable silence.

He blinked then looked uneasy. "I'm sorry."

I raised an eyebrow. "What exactly are you sorry for?"

His eyes searched my face. "Throwing the bottle of Jack Daniels?"

I huffed and turned back to my screen.

"Becca, come on," he pleaded. "I shouldn't have gotten that drunk, I'm sorry. It won't happen again. I didn't mean to scare you."

I swung in my chair back to face him. "You think you scared me? You think that's why I'm mad?" I said in a harsh whisper. He gaped at me. I huffed again and stood to go close my office door.

"Tell me what's going on," I demanded the second the door closed. "You said last night your grandfather wasn't who you thought he was, and RJ was cleaning up his mess. What did that mean? Does it involve Chino?"

Tyler leaned back in his chair, covering his face with his palms.

Feeling semi-guilty for acting like a complete bitch, I tried to calm down and speak to him rationally as I walked to lean on my desk in front of him. "Please talk to me. I can help you through this."

Tyler lowered his hands. "You want to know what will help me? If you promise not to meet with Lee Chino, EVER. No matter what he says, okay?"

His words were pleading and almost fearful. "Okay," I said, trying not to sound confused. "Is he dangerous?"

Tyler cocked his head to the side while closing his eyes. "I don't want you talking to him, please. Can we leave it at that?"

I glanced past him. Why did I have to have windows surrounding my office walls to the other cubicles?

"For now," I said under my breath. I took a seat next to him in the other chair across from my desk. "Can we please go get lunch together?" I asked, placing my hand over his.

We needed to spend normal time together. If we didn't soon, it would kill me.

He glanced downward then his eyes traveled up my body, stopping at my shoulders. A sad expression crossed his face. "I can't. I'm behind on a few things, and I won't be back in this office until next Monday."

My face fell. "Next Monday? That's an entire week, Tyler."

His eyes moved to my disappointed face. "Don't look at me like that." He pushed his chair back as he stood. "I have to leave by 6:00 a.m. tomorrow to catch my flight to Chicago at 7:30 a.m. I have a meeting at 9:30 a.m. that I still need to prep for," he said straightening and tightening his tie.

"Tyler, I don't want you to go," I begged.

His back was to me now, and I could tell he was rolling his eyes as his head fell backwards. "Becca, we've talked about this. I'm going to be gone for awhile until we sort out tasks."

I bravely walked to him, putting my hands on his shoulders, practically begging for him to turn around. "I miss you," I said, my voice cracking.

His shoulders slumped. "You can come to Chicago on Friday." I didn't like the clipped tone to his voice. He reached for the door and left without saying goodbye.

Instead of having wet eyes, I was red in the face from anger. I paced my office, floored and delirious from his harsh brush off. Didn't he want to see me as much as I wanted to see him? I understood he and Nathan had to figure out how to delegate responsibilities from RJ's death, but Grand Rapids needed him too.

Too frenzied to work, I decided to skip out and take my lunch break. I wasn't hungry, but focused on non work related tasks. I still needed some accessories for the wedding, but that would involve thinking positively of Tyler, and right now he was on my shit list.

By the time I got to my car and started to hear the crappy song on the radio, I knew just what I could do to fill my time.

***

Jimmy's Garage was on the southeast side of town. It wasn't surrounded by city life but was more country. There was an open space between the garage and the convenience store next to it. It probably took me a half hour to find it. I hadn't been to this shop since the summer before college, the summer I spent entirely with Gage.

Parking in an open spot, I climbed out of the car, stumbling from the gravel under my heels. I took a quick look around to see if anyone had noticed and was glad that no one was in sight. I straightened my coral colored shift dress and fluffed my hair. I had to wear it down. I was paranoid for whatever reason the broad shoulder sleeve might expose the bite mark from Tyler and thought my hair might make a good second cover.

Loud metal music was blaring from the garage entrance. I saw a pair of greased up jeans behind the hood of a car.

"Can I help you, sweetie?" a man in his early 40s asked as he approached me.

The pair of jeans stood tall from the car, his white grimy shirt showing off strong tattoo covered biceps and shoulders. My mouth gave a soft smile as he turned to face me.

"Bs!" Gage smiled, pulling a rag out of his back pocket to wipe his hands. "What are you doing here?"

The older gentleman walked to Gage, his eyes never leaving me. I felt uncomfortable by his stare as I covered my arms as if I were cold. "I was hoping your expertise could help an old friend out?"

Gage's dimples appeared along with his big white teeth. His skin was darker than normal, or maybe he was dirty. "Anything for you, Bs. What do you need?"

I looked at the other mechanic then back to Gage. "My car's out here. Something is wrong with the CD player. I'm not sure if that's something you usually deal with."

The older man chuckled then looked at Gage, slapping his shoulder. "Do your thing, slick. I'll be taking my lunch break."

Gage smiled then walked over to me, holding his hand out for me to lead the way to my car. I couldn't help but notice the tattoos on his forearm.

"So how have you been?" I asked, trying to make small talk.

"Busy. My boss doesn't give me much time off," he smiled as he pointed his thumb behind us in the older man's direction. "He wants me to become his partner. Really, I think he just wants to get in good with my mom."

I laughed, causing Gage's smile to widen even more.

"Surprised Stiff let you out of the city," Gage said.

I shook my head at him. I didn't want Gage to know how complicated mine and Tyler's relationship was becoming. "He's not that controlling," I said.

"Does he know you're here?" Gage asked, lifting a brow. We reached my car and he held his hand out for my keys. I bit my lip, and a slow sexy smile spread across his face. "Better make this quick then, huh?" he asked, his voice laced with innuendo.

I rolled my eyes at him, causing Gage to laugh again. "Meet me in ramp three." I shook my head and followed him as he pulled the car into the garage. Once he was parked, he rolled the window down. "Get in and show me what's wrong."

I opened the door and slid into the passenger side. "Do you want my honest opinion of what I think is wrong?"

He nodded his head. "That would help me fix it."

I told him about how I got a CD stuck and started to push buttons, and he laughed even harder.

"Let me get some tools and see what I can do. Has your check engine light been on long? This car seems too new for the light to be on."

I glanced over the steering wheel. I hadn't noticed. I shook my head no, and he rolled his eyes as he stepped out of the car, me following behind him.

"Stop acting like I'm some girly girl who doesn't notice anything," I said hitting his shoulder as he opened the hood.

"Those heels and that sexy dress aren't helping prove your point," he said quietly, his eyes shamelessly making a path down my body.

I hit his bicep. "Stop checking me out. You could at least try to be inconspicuous."

His eyes finally met mine then went back down to my hands that were resting on the car. He brought his pinky to touch my ring finger, the one that had the huge diamond making itself at home.

"No longer just a boyfriend?" he asked, his smirk fading into a faint smile.

I moved my hand from his touch. "Yeah. We're getting married in October."

"Look at you Bs. Finally getting your fairy tale," he said kindly then began to examine my car further.

"He's a good man, Gage."

"Oh, I don't doubt that. I just hope he's everything he seems to be," he said, fussing with different parts of the car. "If you're happy, then I'm happy."

Even though he wasn't looking at me, I knew he could sense my smile.

"You're such a girl," he teased. "I'm going to take a look under your car," he said, moving to press some buttons that started to raise the car. I didn't even realize he had driven it onto that kind of device.

He slid under the car then whistled. "You sure some big bodyguard isn't going to bust into this garage any minute and kick my ass?" he asked, his voice muffled from being under the car.

I made a questioning face as if he could see me.

Gage slid out from under the car and said, "Your car is wired so hot they'd know every time you'd changed the radio station."

***

I blew past Cooper, completely ignoring his greeting and yanked Tyler's office door opened. He was on the phone when his eyes flew towards my abrupt entrance as I slammed the door shut.

"I'll be there tomorrow morning. I'll transfer you to Cooper to sort out the details," Tyler said quickly as he reached to press the button to transfer the call. He held up one finger for me to wait, which only fueled my fire more.

"Cooper, can you confirm the details for tomorrow with Cortez? Thanks." He cautiously hung up the phone as he watched me intently.

"Do you have something to tell me?" I asked with a deep raspy voice. My arms were crossed across my chest as I stood in front of his desk.

His eyes searched the room as though looking for an answer. He actually looked completely dumbfounded.

"Something about my car," I asked slowly with narrowed eyes.

Tyler blinked again. "Becs, I don't know what you're talking about..."

"Oh? You don't?" I asked curiously.

Tyler bit his lip nervously.

I slowly walked around the desk as he rolled to face me in his chair. "So nothing rings a bell? No installations I should know about? Or something you *didn't* want me to know about?"

He swallowed again then became curious himself. "What's wrong, Becca?" he asked with a no non-sense tone.

"You wired my car! Why do you feel the urge to track where I'm going?" I said, trying to contain my anger. My teeth were clenched as I waited for him to reply.

But to my surprise, he looked thrown back. Did he not put the tracking system in the car?

"You didn't know?" I whispered.

Tyler stood from his seat so we were almost face to face. He was a good head taller than me, and my confidence normally faltered when he stood over me like this.

"How do you know there's a tracking device in your car?" he asked slowly.

Uh oh.

I looked to the ground then turned to walk back to the opposite side of the desk. "I just know."

"Becca..."

I sighed. "I went to get the CD player fixed."

"And the mechanic told you your car was wired?" he asked slowly.

I nodded my head. Maybe he wouldn't ask which mechanic I went to.

He put his hands on his hips and cocked his head to the side. "Why does it matter if your car is wired?"

I threw my hands in the air. "You are overly concerned about my safety!"

"Of course I care about your safety! With all the crazy shit that's been happening? How could I not be?" he shouted.

"So you did put the tracking device in my car!"

His eyes flew to the ceiling in annoyance. "Maybe I did. It's not that big of a deal, Becca," he grumbled.

"Why wouldn't you tell me? What is going on that's so dangerous? Is it because of the Valentine's Day fundraiser? I thought you said that was a prank?" I asked, trying to reign in my temper.

"It was," he answered quickly. "If it bothers you that much I'll have it uninstalled."

His mood changed from frustration to compliance way too suddenly.

"Okay," I said a little grouchier than I meant to. I crossed my arms again, feeling very small in the room. I didn't mean to come and pick a fight, and I didn't expect him to give up so easily. But he still wasn't telling me something.

He stepped around his desk so we were facing each other again. The urge to reach out and hold him was overwhelming. I hated being frustrated with him, and the only reason I was so edgy was because we hadn't seen each other nearly as much as we had grown accustom to. It didn't help how shut off he was from RJ's death either. I loved him so much. All I wanted was for him to trust and feel comfortable enough to rely on me to help him through his troubles. A tear escaped my eye before I could blink it away. I was emotionally drained.

He sighed deeply, the air taking its time to escape his nose. Then he raised his hand to brush the tear from my cheek, cupping my face with his hand. I guess I didn't move in time for him to not see. "Will that make you happy?" he murmured.

I nodded my head, still not looking in his eyes. He thought for a moment then lowered his hand to wrap his arms around me. I sank into him, craving his comfort and automatically wrapping my arms around his waist in return. This was what I needed, what I missed. Even though he was still hiding something from me, I wouldn't push it, not now. I was terrified he'd step away from this moment of solace that I wanted desperately.

He kissed my temple as he rubbed my back. "Where did you take the car? Maybe they can fit you in later this afternoon to get the tracking system removed."

I froze in his arms.

Tyler pulled back to look me in the eye. "Where did you take the car?" he asked more forcefully.

I swallowed hard. "I brought it to Gage's garage."

Tyler immediately dropped his hands. "Why?" he asked with disgust. "Why wouldn't you bring it to the dealership like I told you to? Did you just want to see him?"

I gripped his waist tighter, my body upset with me for causing Tyler to let it go. "I just, I'm not sure why I went there. I haven't seen him in a while—"

"You're not fucking him, that's why you haven't seen him in awhile," he bit.

My jaw dropped along with my arms. How dare he say that!

"No, I'm not fucking anyone lately," I said harshly.

His eyes grew narrow, and I instantly regretted what I had just said.

"Actually, I fucked you pretty hard yesterday if that mark on your shoulder isn't enough of a reminder. The world doesn't revolve around you, Becca! I have to uphold this goddamn business for my grand...," his voice faded. "I can't let this business fall through the cracks. You want that nice car? You want to get your hair and nails done? Have everything *waxed*? Have that house with lakefront acreage? Well, it doesn't come cheap."

I narrowed my eyes at him. "I don't need you to take care of me," I said through gritted teeth. "That's not why I fell in love with you! Although lately, it sure doesn't feel mutual!"

He stared at me, his jaw slacking this time. "Don't fucking say that, not to me, Becca. Everything I'm doing is because of you, for you!"

"What exactly are you doing? Because like I said, I don't need your money, Tyler. I won't ever need it!"

He rolled his eyes and walked away from me throwing his head back. "Oh, that's right, you have a daddy who can give you everything."

"Who are you?" I asked harshly. "You know I don't care about money."

He turned to face me again, but this time he looked defeated. I stood there, waiting for him to correct himself, to say he was sorry and tired and didn't know what he was talking about. But he didn't. He didn't move a muscle as though he were waiting for me to speak.

"I don't know how much longer I can take you acting like this," I whispered. He was still silent, but now he wouldn't look at me.

Even though my voice was strong and my shoulders were squared to him, my lip started to quiver. I wasn't one to argue and fight or point fingers. We always talked through our problems, but I was going to take the easy way out this time. I turned and walked out of his office, not saying a word.

***

Tears poured down my face like rain my entire drive home. Tyler's hurtful words were burned into my memory and kept replaying in my mind. Was this who he was going to be the rest of our lives? A cold hearted jerk who couldn't handle his emotions? A man who would do anything possible to not open up to me? And the secrets... I thought we were past that. How could he not realize one of the most important ways to keep me safe was by keeping me involved? Filling me in on anything suspicious. Shouldn't I know what to watch for?

Everything pointed to that slimy Lee Chino. I processed my thoughts, trying to calculate what I knew that was a threat.

Lee was into narcotics.

Lee had subdivisions and warehouses built by Conklin.

A very drunk Tyler insinuated something very illegal was happening with his grandfather and the company by talking about going to jail.

I shook my head, feeling dizzy from trying to put the pieces together.

When I got home, I methodically made dinner, not bothering to make something for Tyler. We hadn't eaten dinner together the past two weeks. I was losing faith in him coming home. He kept telling me he just needed time, but the nightmare of him being gone just as my father had been kept creeping in my mind. I didn't want that. I wanted him, all of him. No secrets, no traveling, just normal hours, dinners, and nightly love making. Was that too much to ask for?

I decided to call Jamie after I ate. She always made me feel better. Maybe she would be willing to make a trip out to see me since she was in town.

"Did you have another rough day? You sound beat up about something," she asked after our traditional greetings.

"I'm flustered and worried about Tyler. I never see him anymore, and he hasn't talked to me."

"I know you're sick of hearing this, but he lost his dad, Becca. Yeah, they didn't have the best relationship, but sometimes that can make losing someone harder. It's not easy hearing good things about a person at their funeral when you really couldn't stand being around them. He's probably feeling guilty for thinking his dad was such an asshole."

I knew he was guilty. Whatever he found out about the other night proved that. Remorse was written all over his face, even through his drunken state.

"I think you're right. I don't like how he's pushing me away."

"Time, Becca. If he doesn't shape up, then you bring in the gauntlet. Threaten to leave."

I gasped as my knees went weak, my hand catching my balance on the kitchen counter. My chest tightened and my breath caught in my throat. Leaving Tyler... I couldn't imagine.

"Let's hope it doesn't get to that," I said shakily.

Jamie laughed. "I doubt it will. I booked my flight from Miami to Chicago today for dress shopping!" she said excitedly. I was thankful for the subject change and enjoyed catching up on details about the wedding for the next hour.

"I'm SO glad I get to walk down the aisle with Nathan and not Mitch. That man is driving me bonkers! He keeps texting me!" Jamie exaggerated.

I laughed. "What is he texting you?"

"He's the king of sexual innuendos and cheesy pick up lines. UGH. He won't take the hint!"

I laughed even harder. Mitch was fun, at least I thought so, but I could see where his lack of smoothness could be irritating if you weren't interested. Mitch was very persistent though, and I couldn't help but wonder if he had any idea what was going on in the Conklin building.

After I hung up with Jamie, I hopped in the shower, feeling better about everything that was going through my mind. I was going to give Tyler until the wedding shower in Chicago to shape up, then as Jamie said, I would throw down the gauntlet, but not as harshly. He needed help, and if he wasn't going to open up to me, then he needed to go see someone who could peel back his layers. I frowned to myself, disappointed that I might not be that person.

Once I was cozy in bed, I reached for my phone. Tyler and I hadn't been sending each other many cheesy text messages lately. Maybe that would help us to get back into our normal routine? Still slightly mad at him for being so harsh earlier today, I opened up my messages.

I'm sorry I took the car to Gage. -Becca

I tapped my phone as I waited for a reply to come through. Feeling impatient, I sent another text.

I miss you, Ty. I want to cuddle tonight. -Becca

Still no answer.

Please hold me when you get home tonight. I need to feel like you love me. I need to know we are going make it through whatever is going on in your head. I love you. -Becca

I hugged my phone and screwed my eyes shut, hoping sleep would make him answer my texts or come home and show me his love.

A large thud jolted me from my sleep. Glancing over at the clock, I saw it was 11:30 p.m. Another loud noise came from the kitchen, and I rolled my eyes.

Tyler must have come home drunk again. I got that he wanted to drown in his sorrows, at least for the time being, but he never answered me if he drove home the other night, and that was something I wouldn't tolerate. If he were worried to go to jail for illegal working activities, he should be just as worried to go to jail for drinking and driving.

I swung my legs from the bed, reaching for my robe. Not sure why I felt the need to cover my silk nighty, but I wasn't exactly in the mood for a drunken Tyler to get grabby.

Tying the sash tightly, I took a deep breath, prepared to face another drunken fight and possible breakdown from Tyler.

My heart nearly stopped with what I saw when I reached the living room.

I covered my mouth so my breathing couldn't be heard, but it was too late. Searching, bloodshot eyes on yellow, taunt skin found me as I stood in the hallway.

The man was fidgety, his long greasy hair sticking to the sides of his face. His fingers were constantly moving along with his eyes. They sped up and down my body as his mouth ticked opened and closed.

I stood frozen, scared to move or speak. I was pissed off at myself for not remembering to turn the alarm back on once I locked the door for the night.

"Magic bricks. Where are the magic bricks?" he stuttered, his eyes moving rapidly around the room then settling back on me.

I opened my mouth, but nothing came out.

"Bricks... Bricks... Bricks...," he repeated over and over. He started to pace, his long sleeve shirt was covered in dirt along with his ripped and faded blue jeans.

My brain was scattered, trying to complete a rational thought. I couldn't freak out because this guy was already high strung and on edge. If I lost it, the chance of him doing something even more irrational than breaking into my house would be more possible.

Finally, I remembered about the safe buttons. The closest one was in the kitchen. I needed to figure out a way to pass him and make it to that button. It was my only option. Who knew where the hell Tyler was. He could be pissed still about Gage and staying at the condo downtown.

"I need the bricks," he said in confusion.

I gulped and took three slow steps towards the kitchen, my eyes never leaving him. "What bricks?" I asked calmly.

"He said there were bricks. Magic bricks. I need what's in those magic bricks."

I stared at him in confusion. In a brick? Bricks were solid concrete.

"I don't have any magic bricks," I said as best I could without my voice trembling. "Maybe I could call someone who could help you find them?"

I took three more steps but halted as he rapidly moved in my direction; my breath catching once he abruptly but clumsily stopped two feet from my face.

"He said they'd be here. In the house on the water through the trees. I need them," his voice was deep and scratchy. One eye went lazy and looked back towards my bedroom. He was close enough that I could see his lips were cracked and chapped, along with under his nostrils. His odor was unforgettable, and I held my breath trying not to gag.

I took another low breath, stepping two more steps towards the kitchen.

"What's your name?" I asked, my voice cracking. "Can I make you something to eat?"

His lazy eye circled again then came back to focus with the other. His eyes were deep in his head, and his cheekbones were scarily hollow. This guy looked like he could be on *Dateline*.

Not waiting for him to reply, I back peddled until I felt the tile of the kitchen floor, my body relaxing fractionally. Only 5 more steps around the island. How long did Tyler say it would take for the police to show up once the button was pushed?

"I don't want food; I want bricks!" he shouted then began pacing the room again. He was muttering under his breath, his head nodding in all directions.

Fear was taking hold of my body, terrified and searching for the right thing to say to help stall him from doing something scarring.

"I was going to make some tea. Can I make you some?" I moved to the kitchen drawers, letting out a small breath as I pushed the tiny button on the inside of the drawer. I glanced down, noticing the light turning from green to red, and the seconds started to tick by in my head.

"NO!" he shouted even louder, a howling screech followed. He gripped his hair tight and then found one of the floor lamps, grabbing it and chucking it across the room.

I covered my mouth, stepping back towards the refrigerator. Pleading with myself to not break down and be a victim. I hadn't watched too many crime shows, but I knew the weak ones never made it.

"Who told you about the magic bricks?" I bravely asked, desperate to calm him down and stall long enough for the police to get here.

His eyes still moved rapidly around. This guy must have been on some heavy medication, or he was having some really bad withdrawal symptoms.

"The builder. The big builder. He met me here once... but there weren't any lights," his voice shook with anxiousness.

I swallowed hard. Was he talking about Mitch?

"Did he have the magic bricks?" I asked slowly, my eyes bouncing from him to the clock on the microwave.

His head moved achingly slow until our eyes met. They were more focused now, and he took a step towards me. I held my breath again, wrapping my arms around my chest.

A slow nod came from him, and his head cocked to the side as he moved at an agonizingly slow pace from the living room towards me. It was like he was a snake, slithering his way towards his prey. The closer he came to me, the more steps I took back until I was backed against the sink. He finally stopped when he was two feet from me.

I was unable to breathe now, my face pinned to the side, my arms trembling as my knuckles were white from holding the silk robe so tightly. Why did I wear so little to bed again? I didn't even put any panties on, and the thought of him touching me brought an entirely new fear to my brain.

"Who. Are. You..?" he asked cautiously, studying the side of my face.

He was intrigued with me now, his mind taken off whatever the magic bricks were. "I live here," I whispered, trying not to cringe as I felt his hand touch my arm.

No no no no no!

"Let's find your bricks," I choked, desperate to not be pinned by this disgusting human being.

His lips curled, and I saw rotted teeth and black moldy gums. His breath was foul as he spoke. "What do I have to do for them?"

My eyes went wide as his other hand landed on the counter, caging me between his awful stench and the counter. That wasn't what I meant at all. My body shook, and I knew now was the time to be brave, to wrack through my brain about any type of self defense I had seen or learned in the past. The one target that my mother had always told me to hit was wide open, but I had to do it hard enough for him to fall to his knees so I could make a run for it... but where would I run? The two miles to the town in my bare feet and nighty?

He leaned his head down towards my neck, and I squirmed.

"You smell pretty," he said sadistically. "Don't be nervous, sweetheart."

A tear fell as he went to touch my hair as I continued to squirm, wondering why I walked myself back into the corner of the counter top in the first place.

My thoughts flashed to Tyler.

My heart was filled with sorrow as I thought about how I left Tyler this afternoon, not hugging him or kissing him, leaving mad and angry with him. I loved him, and if something happened to me tonight where we couldn't be together anymore, I'd be devastated.

Breathe, Becca. You can do this. Find your strength, just like a kickboxing class.

I needed to think quickly. I could lock myself in the closet. Yes, that's what I would do. I took a deep breath, trying not to vomit from the smell of body odor.

I slowly set my hands on his forearms, needing something to brace myself to make the impact. I had to do it gently, so he didn't think I was up to something. It killed me to touch his dirty shirt, but seeing his pleasing, rotting grin gave me all the courage I needed to get the hell away from him.

I looked towards him and gave him the best smile I could as I gripped his forearms tighter then rammed my knee into his groin as hard as I could.

A strangled moan escaped his mouth as he fell to the ground. "YOU LITTLE BITCH!" he groaned.

I jumped past him, but he caught my ankle with one hand while he held himself with the other. "I need my fix... I need my fix... NOW! If I can't insert it into my arm, I'm going to take it out on you!" he screamed.

I kicked my feet, desperate to break free from his greasy hands, finally nailing him in the head with the heel of my foot.

His groaning subsided as I scrambled to my feet, thanking God as I saw the flashing red and blue lights traveling the length of my driveway. I rushed to the front door, realizing it was open from the intruder as I shoved it completely open, running out in the front yard, the bite of the summer night feeling like freedom on my skin.

Chapter Fourteen

I sat staring at my computer screen, not sure what I was more upset about—the fact that Becca went to see that punk Gage, or how I was a complete asshole to her.

I shouldn't have said the things I said. I'm not even sure where my outburst came from. I was having so much trouble containing my frustrations that I said the first thing that popped into my head, not even meaning half of it. Yet when she gave me the chance to say something to fix it, I just stood there like an immature moron.

Even though I was pissed she went to see Gage, I was more fueled by what she told me he found in her car. It was nearly impossible for me to keep my cool and act like I was the one who put the tracking device in her car. I had no clue who did it, and the thought of someone watching Becca's every move made me uneasy. I wanted that tracking device out of her car as soon as possible, but didn't want to push the subject to the point where she would realize something was wrong.

At least I knew she'd be safe in our home. I made sure the most up-to-date security system was installed. As long as she remembered to turn it back on, no one would touch her. There were even safe buttons all over the house if, for whatever reason, the police needed to be called for an emergency. The buttons would alert each of our phones, in addition to her parents. She demanded that part more than me. After the incident at the Valentine's Day fundraiser, I wasn't about to take any risks, not when it came to my Becca's safety. With Chino being crazy as fuck lately, the top of the line security system helped ease my nerves, especially since I had been going out of town more.

I sighed as I aimlessly scrolled through the spreadsheet of numbers on my screen. Everything I had to accomplish was possible to finish in Grand Rapids, there was no real reason for me to go to Chicago. A shiver went down my spine as I thought of the bitemark on Becca's shoulder. I had to go to Chicago. Soon the numbness would settle in like always, and I could go back to being happy.

It was almost 11:30 p.m., and I was stalling going home. I didn't know what to say to Becca, and I was terrified she would be waiting up for me. She knew how to bring out that damn emotion, and I hated the thought of shedding any more tears in front of her. I'm sure the last thing she wanted was to marry a pussy. I thought about going to the condo for the night, but I wanted to see her. The safest time was when she was sleeping, and I felt peace watching her. I might steal a touch here and there but nothing more.

I reached for my phone, scowling to see it was dead. I kept forgetting to bring a charger into the office and would have to wait until I got to my car to plug it in and charge it. I wouldn't turn it on though, too afraid Becca might have sent me a hate text.

Although I doubted it. She wasn't like that. She was always the mature one, normally saying she was sorry first and wanting to talk things through.

I need to pull my head out of my ass.

Finally by 11:45 p.m. I gathered my things and headed home for another uneasy night's rest.

***

My heart leaped out of my chest when I saw the multiple flashing lights along my driveway. I looked down to my phone, cursing myself for not actually turning it on when I plugged it in to charge. What if Becca was trying to get a hold of me? What if she were hurt? I parked in the first spot I could around the cop cars, booking it up the lawn, dodging a few trees to get to my love.

What an idiot I've become! How could I be so irresponsible to let my phone die? With all the crazy shit that has been happening too. My Becs... What if something happened to my Becs? That panicked feeling was in my chest, and I couldn't reach the front door fast enough.

Swinging the front door open, I rapidly searched the turning heads surrounding my foyer and living room. There were at least twelve cops wandering around then I finally found my love, curled up in a blanket with tear stained cheeks, her mother and father protectively standing next to her with their arms looped through each others.

I swallowed the lump in my throat. I should have been here. I should be comforting her right now, not her parents.

She spotted me, her voice cracking as our eyes met. "Tyler!"

I ran to her, my arms wrapping around her like a magnet. I nuzzled my head into her hair, the smell of her shampoo calming me along with her presence. She was here; she was okay. My Bec's was in my arms and wasn't hurt, at least I didn't think she was hurt.

I held her at arm's length, surveying her for anything out of the ordinary or damaged. "Are you okay? What happened?" I asked in confusion.

She dropped her blanket to her feet and nestled herself back to my chest, squeezing my waist.

I held her again, waiting for her to answer then looked to her parents.

"Someone broke into the house, Tyler," Missy said quietly, holding onto Max's arm. "We got the alert on our phones and tried to call. Max and I headed out here when we couldn't reach either of you."

Max Stine's expression was unreadable as he stood next to his wife. I gripped Becca closer, hating myself even more for stalling at the office. The thought of someone in this house with my Becs, watching her, waiting for her, prowling. It made me sick to my stomach and even sicker with rage. Screw RJ. He was messing with my life, even when he was dead.

"My phone died, otherwise I would have been here sooner," I mumbled. "I didn't think to turn it on when I got it on the car charger. Did the alarm not work?" I was confused,

Max's and Missy's phones only got notifications if an emergency button was hit, not if the alarm was set off.

Becca buried her head into my chest even more. "I forgot to turn it back on when I got home," she whispered. "I'm sorry."

I furrowed my brows but refrained from scolding her. She had obviously dealt with enough tonight, and I was terrified to hear what happened. I was sure she'd never forget again.

"I didn't know you usually worked this late," Missy said looking at me intently.

"I don't. Things have just been a little hectic since RJ's death."

She nodded and leaned into Max, whose expression never changed from his blank stare. His look made me swallow the cotton that was forming in my mouth.

The sheriff walked over to join our awkward crowd.

"Mr. Conklin," he nodded towards me, holding out his hand for me to shake. Reluctantly, I took my hand from Becca's back and shook his hand.

"Thank you for getting here, Sheriff."

"The intruder has been taken to the county. He was pretty high strung, no doubt an addict of some type of amphetamine. We can talk more about pressing charges tomorrow. Becca gave him a swift knee and held her own," the sheriff said.

A thousand tiny prickles tickled my skin. The thought of Becca being attacked was horrible. I squeezed her tighter, holding her head to my chest. I felt her tremble, and my insides tightened.

"Well, I know Becca is in good hands now. We should be on our way home, Max," Missy said, tugging on his arm. She walked over to Becca, gently patting her head.

Max slowly followed, then looked me straight in the eyes as he put his hand on Becca's back. He was passing a subliminal message through his gaze, one that told me I better take care of his daughter, and I better not fuck up again. I had only seen these eyes one other time, and they sent a chill down my spine then as well.

She still had her arms tightly wrapped around my waist. Finally taking his probing eyes from me, he spoke softly to

Becca. "I'm proud of you, sweetie. Call if you need me. I'll always answer when my baby girl calls."

Becca turned her head to face him, giving him a gentle and grateful smile.

Once his eyes left Becca's, they were on me again until he and Missy walked out the door.

"We'll be out of your home in about twenty minutes Mr. Conklin. I'd like to get another statement from Becca tomorrow when she's not as shaken."

I gave him a nod, more focused on my love. Becca was shaking again, and I hated this feeling. Knowing I could have stopped something from crawling under her skin and causing her so much torment. "Want to go lay down?" I asked quietly with my lips to her temple.

She shook her head and nuzzled my chest more. "Only if you're going to lay with me."

"I will as soon as the police leave."

She shook her head rapidly. It felt like she was trying to burrow inside of me, getting as close as she could so nothing could get to her. I failed as a fiancé, as a lover. It's my job to protect her, and she was in serious danger tonight.

"What happened?" I gently asked, stroking her hair. We hadn't moved an inch since I walked through the door. The police officers had to maneuver around us as they left. I freed my arm for one moment so I could lock the door as they left.

"I heard a noise, and I thought it was you coming home. I thought the same thing was happening as last night," she squeaked.

My stomach churned, remembering how drunk and defeated I was last night. I slipped up with my emotions last night, saying details about the mess my family created that I didn't want Becca to have any idea about. But she was smart and caught on quickly to her surroundings.

"Normally I'm extra cautious if I hear a noise and I'm by myself, but I just thought it was you. I walked out into the living room, and he was standing by the fireplace." I felt tears penetrate through my button shirt, dampening my chest. "Tyler, I was so scared. I didn't know what to do. He kept asking for magic bricks."

I couldn't keep my body from stiffening.

Fucking Mitch.

Becca pulled her head back to look at me for the first time since I'd been holding her. "What are the magic bricks, Tyler?"

I looked down into her beautiful, probing blue eyes as I bit the inside of my cheeks. I didn't want her to know.

She took a deep breath, and disappointment filled her eyes. She turned to go to the bedroom, hugging her body. I followed closely behind her.

"What else happened?" I asked.

She halted abruptly just as we entered our bedroom. "I'm too tired to talk," she snapped.

I stepped back, shocked by her attitude. She had been clinging to me, skittish and hyper aware.

"Becca, did he try to hurt you?" I asked with a shaky voice, frightened what her answer might be. "Did he try to... touch you?"

She whipped around, her ponytail hitting the side of her face. "I told you I was tired, don't you understand?"

I flinched, unsure how else to react.

"Yeah, it's no fun watching someone who blatantly has something fucked up in their head but won't share, isn't it?" she shouted.

I narrowed my eyes at her. "This is different."

"How?"

"Because you're terrified. You were holding onto me as though someone were trying to whisk you away into the darkness. Becca, I need to know what happened so I can protect you," I pleaded.

"Don't you think filling me in on your secrets would help me protect myself?" she questioned. "Tyler, if there was a reason for me to be scared that someone could break in looking for 'magic bricks' then I might have thought twice about turning the alarm back on!"

I swallowed the lump in my throat.

She was right.

I shouldn't keep her in the dark, not anymore, and I made the decision to let her in on the Conklin and Chino predicament, at least some of it.

"Let's get into bed," I said calmly, picking at the buttons on my shirt.

"Of course, change the subject—"

"Becca, get into bed and we'll talk. You have a point," I mumbled.

Her mouth snapped shut as she dropped her silk robe, revealing a silky yellow nighty that had lace around the top and bottom.

Holy hell, maybe I should make her put on some sweats.

"Were you wearing that earlier?"

Her strong demeanor changed as she shriveled into the bed, covering her body the best she could with her arms and blankets. "I told you I thought it was you."

Something deep inside of me boiled. The thought of some sick fuck breaking into my house, ogling my fiancé. *He better not have...* "Did that fucker try to touch you?" I growled.

She curled further in the bed, covering her body up to her neck with blankets.

I ripped off the rest of my clothing, leaving my boxers on as I crawled into the bed with her. Tears were falling down her cheeks again, and that's when I knew he tried to touch her. I was shuddering at the thought. Rage and anger were filling every inch of my being. I was mad at everyone: myself, Mitch, RJ, fucking Chino.

"Tyler, he was awful," she whispered. I pulled her back to my chest, cradling her while stroking her hair, attempting to keep my hands from shaking with anger. "At first he kept his distance, mumbling about the bricks, but then he came on to me, like he had to pay me in sexual-favors for what he wanted," she sniffled and I pulled her tighter, wrapping my legs with hers. I wanted to cocoon her, protect her from any harm.

"Oh Becs," I said, kissing her eyelids.

"He was so dirty and smelled like sewage; his touch was like a thousand bee stings. His breath was foul and hot. I'm just glad I found the strength to knee him once he got close," she said shivering.

She nuzzled her head into my chest more, her hot tears rolling down my skin. "You're safe now. Don't be scared. I'll hold you all night, I promise," I murmured in her ear. She sighed and took deep breaths as she snuggled closer to my body, getting comfortable for sleep. I melted with her, wanting my anger for myself and everyone else to pass so I could get lost in my love, so I wouldn't worry about hurting her when we became intimate. All I wanted was to be able to focus on her without some messed up feelings or thoughts popping into my head every five seconds.

Just as I thought she was about asleep, her soft voice trailed across my skin. "You said I had a point," she whispered, tracing a pattern on my back.

I let out a breath of air. I had to tell her. "Chino is paying people on the inside of our company to hide his drugs and money in our unpurchased/empty/vacant buildings. He hides them all over his own properties, but RJ voided his contract with Conklin. From what I've learned, my grandfather used to sell drugs with him."

She was silent for a long moment, her finger pausing on my chest. "Hides them?"

I nodded then rolled us to our sides so I could look at her. "RJ invented bricks that double as a safe box. They're practically impossible to notice unless you know about them. RJ would always sell them to Chino, but he never let him use them on the subs while we were building. He didn't want Chino's dirty business to be pinned on us."

"Connor said something like that," she murmured.

I scowled at her. "Make a trip to see him along with Gage?"

She frowned. "No, and I already apologized for today via text. Not my fault you didn't notice it," she grumbled. "Not that I should have to apologize for seeing him."

"Okay, I forgive you. Now about Connor?" I prodded, ignoring her tail end of the sentence.

"Back when I went to lunch with him. He was warning me how he saw you meeting with Lee," she said, not looking me in the eye but focusing on her fingers tracing my skin. "He told me Chino has never been prosecuted because he gets everyone to do his dirty work."

I frowned. "Don't worry about this, Becca. Nathan and I are keeping an eye on him. He wants us to become partners on his subdivisions, but we are a firm and united no. I won't run a dirty business."

She kissed my chest then looked into my eyes. "Why was he asking about magic bricks here?"

The lump in my throat grew bigger as I blinked. I wanted to lie to her, tell her I didn't know, but that wasn't the case. I couldn't lie anymore. She needed to know what was happening. "Mitch installed a bunch of RJ bricks around our house. The fireplace, the porch. I found drugs in them."

Becca gasped. "He what? Why would he do that?"

"I have a feeling Mitch is the main guy Chino is paying to hide the drugs," I sighed in disappointment.

Becca sat up and looked down at me with a determined look. "Jamie said he's always talking about RJ bricks. Now it all makes sense. Have you talked to Mitch about it?"

"He hasn't admitted anything."

"Well, what do we do?" she asked, baffled.

"You don't need to do anything. This isn't for you to worry about. I've already put you at risk telling you all I know. I won't have you snooping around trying to help fix this. Nathan and I will hire a private investigator to find out who Chino is paying."

"And what if it is Mitch?" she asked sadly.

I blinked a few times. "I'm not sure what we'll do. But I know he's playing a part in Chino's game."

She laid her head back down on my chest, fitting her body completely on top of mine, her legs on either side of my thighs. "Tyler, could you get in trouble for this? Is this what you meant about being married to someone in jail?" she asked quietly.

I kissed the top of her head. "Yes. But hopefully we can figure out where the drugs are and get them out somehow. Nathan and I have this. Don't worry about it baby doll."

She looked up at me and smiled affectionately.

"What?" I asked, my lip quirking at her thrilled expression.

"You haven't called me baby doll in a while," she whispered. Her words sounded hurt, not matching her face. My heart pounded against hers, guilt for pushing her away thick in my chest.

"I know, I'm sorry," I murmured, stroking the silky night gown over her spine.

She bit her lip, giving me her all too familiar eyes.

"Becca," I said softly, pleadingly. "You've had a hard night, let me just hold you."

"Make love to me. Please Tyler... It's been way too long," she begged, finding my bottom lip and sucking on it gently. "I need this. I need you. Please." She kissed me harder, her hands traveling down my abdomen. My body was already responding to her, and she ground her hips down onto me.

The warmth of her felt amazing, and my foggy head was still running in a million directions. I wanted to comfort her as she nibbled down my neck and jaw, but I was terrified where my thoughts might go, especially with the intruder finding his way into our house, putting his sticky hands on my fiancé. I clenched my teeth tight as I pictured some sicko coming on to my Becs.

Her mouth found my lips again as my hands grabbed her thighs tighter, finding their way to her behind under the silk nighty. I squeezed her butt, and she moaned into my mouth, grinding down harder on top of me.

"Why aren't you wearing panties?" I asked harshly with a raspy voice.

She bit down on my ear then whispered, "Because I secretly hope every night my fiancé will come home and be turned on by me." She licked along my earlobe then brought her mouth back to mine. Goose bumps trailed down my neck and that was it—she had me. I was going to come at her full force.

Well, as full force as I could. "I don't want to hurt you," I murmured into her neck, kissing my way to the bite mark on her shoulder. My mind still wasn't stable, and I was terrified I wouldn't be able to control myself.

"You can't hurt me this way. Only your silence hurts me, Tyler."

"I told you everything I know," I groaned, hiking her nighty until it was completely off her body. She leaned back down on my chest once her clothing was discarded, kissing every inch of skin she could find. "I want to know what's going on in here," she said, kissing over my heart.

"I love you; that's what's going on in there," I groaned, lacing my hands roughly in her hair. "That's all that's ever gone on in there."

She nipped at my skin again, as though she didn't believe me. We stopped talking and both reached to pull off my briefs. I wanted to take this as slow as I could, knowing I needed to keep any upsetting thoughts out of my head. I tried to focus on her lips against my hot skin, the pads of her fingers exploring my arms and chest. Her gentle touch healed me to extremes, and I focused on her tenderness, her passion.

She hovered over me, and I grabbed her hips, wanting to completely fill her, drown in her until my heart felt normal again. When she finally did, it was frantic and frenzied. She moved too fast, pulling to a sitting position while resting her hands on my chest. The speed was overwhelming, fast like my racing mind. I moved my hands from her hips to grasp the sheets, my nails biting into my palms through the sheets instead of her precious skin.

Her eyes were screwed shut as she bit her bottom lip, her hips grinding up and down. My eyes were transfixed on her features, her breasts bouncing as she moved. The sight of her beautiful body moving against me helped me to focus on the now. I licked my lips, feeling the urge to taste her everywhere.

I leaned up on my elbows, my mouth finding her skin. She let out a loud moan, leaning forward more so I could fit more of her in my mouth. She was unraveling fast, and I was more than able to keep up with her speed. One hand cautiously found the curve of her spine, holding her down as she ground her hips into me, keeping the depth deep inside of her.

"Becca, when you move your hips like that," I groaned. She did it faster, her breath hitching along with mine. I was about to explode, secretly begging her to come so I could give in to the temporary pleasure of losing myself.

I could tell she was close by her movements finding a more steady rhythm. I moved my hands back to the sheets, knowing once we both let go my fists would ball into vices.

I pushed my hips along with her. She rammed her hips down hard, clenching her insides as whimpers left her lips.

"Yes...," I hissed, finally giving in and letting go, all tension leaving every strained muscle in my body. My elbows gave way and my back slammed against the mattress. Becca quickly followed but with her head on my chest, her breath slowing.

My hands were still at my sides, still gripping the sheet as I took deep, calming breaths.

Becca's hand found my chest, her fingers flexing gently as she spoke. "Ty, please, put your arms around me."

I tentatively smiled with my eyes closed. "Okay."

***

I wish I could say I slept peacefully all night, but that would be a complete lie. I jolted whenever I heard a sound. The air conditioner, leaves of the trees swaying in the breeze, the waves crashing against the beach. All sounds that used to calm me now made me paranoid that a drug addict my brother sold to was going to finagle his way into my home and try to hurt the woman I loved.

I wrapped my arms around her, holding on to her as my mind consumed any rationality I had. For whatever reason, I knew Chino wasn't lying when he said he had people on the inside of our company, my idiot brother being one of them. How could he betray us like that? Unless he was on RJ's side... but RJ wasn't on Chino's side, was he? I still didn't know what or who to believe.

Thinking about the mess of not knowing who my father and grandfather actually were was an anxiety attack creeping into my lungs, feathering throughout my body. Tingles of fear and uncertainty spread like wildfire, and I didn't know how to stop them. So I lay staring at the ceiling, my arms clinging to the only person who offered me any solace.

My eyes were heavy when Becca stirred awake. It was nearly 7:00 a.m., and she stretched on top of my body, wiggling her hips against my groin as she gave my chest butterfly kisses.

"Did you sleep okay?" she asked, nuzzling her cheek into my chest.

"Yeah," I said more gruffly than I meant to. She slowly lifted her head to meet my eyes, and worry spread over her face.

"Are you okay?" she asked with concern. "Your eyes are red and kind of puffy. Did you sleep at all last night?"

I blinked my eyes for a long second then looked out towards the porch. "Yeah, I slept fine. Well, except for your snoring," I teased.

She frowned, ignoring my sarcasm. "Why don't you go back to sleep while I make us breakfast," she said lovingly as she stroked my unshaven face. "This is so hot," she whispered, biting her lip in that seductive way.

My lip quirked. "Okay, I won't shave it off. Go ahead and make breakfast while I shower."

She frowned at me again. "Don't you want to shower together?"

I blinked. Of course I wanted to shower with her, that body wet and stretched for my eyes to watch. My dick twitched underneath her, causing a devious grin to spread across her face.

"That's what I thought," she flirted.

I shook my head. "No time, baby. I have to make it to a meeting by 9:00 a.m. for Nathan in Grand Rapids. I messaged him last night about needing to switch places for today."

Her face fell. "Oh. I have to go give another statement today at the police station. I wasn't planning on either of us working. I was hoping you could come with me after last night... Wait... did you say for today? As though you are going to leave for Chicago later in the week?"

My eyes darted away from hers. "I have meetings I can't miss."

I could feel her eyes on me, and I didn't want to look at her. I knew what they held— disappointment and fear. "Tyler, can't Nathan work in Chicago while you stay here? I think we need to spend some time together after everything that's happened," she said quietly.

Gently pulling her off of me so I could stand from the bed, I said, "Becca, I've told you over and over again. We have a lot to figure out with RJ being gone. I can't just fall off the grid with you right now, and neither can you. I know you care about your work."

Becca sat up, holding a pillow to her chest. "I know, but we can work anywhere. I just thought..." She swallowed hard as she looked to the ground. "With last night, I thought..." She stopped mid sentence.

Finally, I turned to look at her. "You thought what?"

Her voice was stronger when she looked up to me. "I thought last night was a turnaround. I thought maybe you could start healing."

I threw my hand towards her as I walked to the bathroom. "I don't need to heal. All last night proved was I need to spend more time at work to take care of the damage my father... or grandfather... put this company in. I won't have drug addicts breaking into my house, let alone our unpurchased/empty/vacant properties."

Becca rolled her eyes. "It's more than just work. You're different Tyler. You need to talk to someone," she pleaded while following me into the bathroom.

"Forgive me for being edgy after some creep broke into my house and tried to come onto my fiancé!"

I turned on the shower then walked to the sink to let the water warm while I brushed my teeth. I was furious and testy now, annoyed that Becca was trying to penetrate my unnecessary emotions.

Still holding the pillow to her chest, Becca nudged her way between the counter and myself. "Isn't that more reason for us to not be apart?"

"Whenever I'm in Chicago or Cleveland, you need to stay with your parents or sister. We should put this house on the market," I grumbled, pushing her to the side and wetting my toothbrush.

"No!" she whined. "I don't want to sell the house. Why don't you talk to Mitch about it?"

"We can build another one. One that doesn't attract junkies! Mitch is lucky I haven't killed him yet."

"I doubt we'll have any more trouble," she whispered.

I turned to her. "Yes, because YOU will remember to turn on the God damn alarm!" I scolded while pointing my toothbrush at her.

She flinched at my outburst. I was a bit harsh, but it was true. If she would have turned the alarm on, the guy would have been scared off or caught. He never would have laid a greasy finger on my Becs. I shoved the toothbrush in my mouth before I could say anything more, becoming angrier thinking about the previous night.

Just as I was about to spit toothpaste, Becca dropped her pillow and stared at me through the mirror her head cocked to the side.

My eyes traveled from her seductive stare down to her beautiful breasts, perfect stomach, gently curved hips, and well toned legs. Jesus, even her feet were sexy with bright pink nail polish. As my eyes traveled back up her body, they fixated on the bite mark on her shoulder. I closed my eyes. I was too upset for her to come on to me right now. Who knows what else I would be capable of, and we were lucky I didn't hurt her last night. It took all of my control to grasp the sheets and not bruise her body.

When I went back to brushing my teeth and looking down towards the sink, I heard her sigh then grab her robe and leave the bathroom.

I could feel the disappointment and rejection in the air. The awful feeling in my gut sat there throughout my shower, and I'm sure it would until I could see her smile again.

Chapter Fifteen

Becca

Last night my emotions were like whiplash. I was scared out of my mind from the crack head intruder, but Tyler's sporadic mood has been just as chilling. Last night he wouldn't let go of me, his arms were delicate and loving, yet strong and comforting at the same time. His voice was soothing, and he actually opened up to me.

We had made love for the first time in a few weeks, and even though I could tell he wasn't as connected and his mind was still in other places, he was trying to comfort me. I really thought we were turning around. Until he woke up and said he was leaving again, being agitated and cranky when I tried to get him to talk.

I pulled my robe tighter, fighting off the feeling of the rejected look from Tyler's eyes as I dropped my pillow this morning, baring myself to him, saying, *please, open up to me, touch me again, take me, I need you.* But his eyes only perused my body then continued to look at the faucet. My annoying insecurities popped up, saying he didn't like how I looked, but I knew it was more. After all he confessed last night, I knew he was carrying more than just guilt of RJ's passing.

Tears stung my eyes. One step forward and two steps back seemed to be our relationship lately. How many more times until we hit a wall?

I methodically moved around the kitchen, pushing back all of my self doubt and insecurities while making breakfast. I put together an omelet for myself then one for Tyler, praying he would eat it. I never knew what it was like to worry about someone who didn't eat. I understood now why he always kept a close eye on me. I always ate though. He was skipping meals and snacks all together because his mind was completely out of it.

I was gazing out the window at the lake when Tyler came into the kitchen, dressed handsome as always in his charcoal suit and matching tie. It hurt to see him purposely avoid looking at me.

"I made you an omelet," I murmured, continuing to look out the window.

"Thanks," he said in a low tone, standing in front of the coffee maker we rarely used. That was a sure tell he really didn't sleep last night. After he fussed with it for a few minutes, he leaned against the fridge with his eyes closed. I wanted to hug him. I needed to hug him, but I was so terrified of his rejection.

"What time are you meeting with the detective?" Tyler asked while keeping his eyes closed.

Startled he spoke to me, I replied, "I'm not sure. He said to stop in after 10:00 a.m. I'll probably go to the store when you leave then head over there."

He opened one eye then looked down at his watch, chewing on his lip as though he were thinking.

More silence passed between us.

Finally, I stood from the breakfast table and walked to the sink, disposing of my dish. "Don't let your omelet get cold," I said quietly.

I felt his gaze on my profile as I fiddled with the dishwasher then felt his hand finally touch my back. "Becca, I meant what I said about staying with your parents or sister."

I closed the dishwasher, leaning into his touch that I longed for. "Okay," I whispered, then reached for the lapels of his jacket, curling myself into his chest. "Please figure out your business soon."

***

Six weeks of bouncing from house to house and I was exhausted. I was ready to be back in my own home. I wasn't scared anymore, but Tyler wouldn't have it. He said if he weren't there, I wasn't allowed to stay.

My emotions were high, and I was losing faith in our relationship. We had only spent a handful of nights together, each of them brisk and painfully quiet. Every time my mother pulled out the wedding book I had to put on a face, trying to look excited when really I was a complete wreck.

Heather knew something was wrong, but I wouldn't talk to her. Same with Jamie. Even with Jamie being so far away in Florida she could tell I was upset over the phone and continued to tell me to give Tyler the ultimatum.

"Becca, you don't have to marry him yet. Just because you've said yes and have been making plans doesn't mean you have to go through with it." Jamie had said this numerous times. I knew I had this option, but I loved him so much, all I wanted was to help him through his storm. I wasn't about to give up on him. I knew in my heart he would feel the same way if the roles were reversed.

"Chicago's traffic is worse than Miami's!" Jamie grumbled as she weaved her way through the cars. Heather laughed in the backseat along with Josie.

"I know, right? Becca, hopefully Tyler won't want to move here permanently," Heather said.

"He practically does live here already," I whispered.

Jamie's eyes darted to mine, and I quickly changed the subject. "Mom and Mary are meeting us at Bella Vie. Then we'll get dinner. Tyler and the men are getting their tuxes fitted today too."

"I didn't know Tyler and the guys were coming! Maybe we could all go out tonight?" Jamie said excitedly.

"That would be so much fun!" Heather squealed. "And you could stay with Grandma, little missy!" Josie giggled in her car seat and threw her hands in the air with excitement.

I sat quietly in the front seat, biting my nail. With how Tyler had been acting, I doubted he would want to go out in the Chicago nightlife.

Jamie sensed my apprehension. "Maybe it will help them unwind with everything that's been going on at work."

I gave her a soft smile. I confessed to Jamie everything that Tyler had told me, but only because she already knew.

Nathan had filled her in, wanting her to keep an eye on Mitch since he had been traveling to Miami more frequently.

"I'm still amazed they all took a Friday off. You know how those men work!" Heather huffed.

It was shocking that Tyler, Nathan, Mitch, Ray, my brother Michael, and my father all weren't working. I felt like the world might stop. Guilt spread through me for having doubt that Tyler might not want this. Our entire families were putting their lives on hold for this shower and fittings, and our families never took time outs for anything.

Mary had been hanging onto this wedding tightly ever since RJ's death. It was the only thing that seemed to keep her together. She had called me every other day, asking what she could do and what my thoughts were on all the details, flowers, cake, centerpieces, favors, any small detail that involved a wedding.

Everyone seemed to take this wedding seriously, except for Tyler. Whenever I'd bring up the wedding, Tyler would just say, "Okay," or, "Whatever you want." He didn't care at all.

Jamie pulled into the parking ramp for Belle Vie, and we were greeted with warm smiles from the receptionist. Both my mother and Mary were already there. Mary was practically jumping with excitement, hugging me tightly.

"Becca, I've been looking forward to today!" She let go of me then turned me in the direction of who I assumed was the designer.

She had a big smile, but her eyes wandered over my body, making me shrivel as I shook her hand. My self image was better than it used to be but would always be damaged. Tyler being so distant didn't help either.

"Hi Becca, I'm Acra. It's so nice to finally meet you. Mary has been talking up how you are going to make a beautiful bride. Now that we've met, I completely agree!" She smiled while shaking my hand.

I smiled back, wondering if that was her traditional line for a new client.

"Well, let's get started! I pulled some dresses from what Mary said the two of you talked about, and if you don't mind, I'd like to pull some more once I get a full look at your figure." I nodded then put my head to the ground. Worry struck my nerves believing this might be more challenging than I pictured in my head.

Heather and Jamie both looped an arm through each of mine and gave me encouraging smiles as we followed Mary, my mother, and Acra to the fitting rooms.

The surroundings were so white and pure. Large mirrors and chaise loungers were placed throughout the space while soft music played in the background.

"Becca, stand on this pedestal. This is your day after all," Acra said kindly.

I slowly stepped on the pedestal, feeling awkward as I looked down at my family and future mother-in-law staring at me with doting smiles.

I tried not to fidget as Acra circled me, her mouth pierced and her expression of deep thought as she studied me. "Hmm... I think I have a few that will be perfect," she said then took off on a mission.

"Do you girls have your dresses yet?" Mary asked both Heather and Jamie.

"Yes, they came in a few weeks ago. I love the plum. It looks really good on Jamie," Heather said.

"Oh, please! You only saw a picture from your camera!" Jamie said.

Heather laughed. "At least it matches your complexion!" Heather whined. "But I'm not going to complain because I made Becca wear yellow."

My mother laughed. "Yes, that wasn't the best color for Becca at the time."

I shriveled on the pedestal. Tyler loved me in yellow. Maybe it was because I was pale and overweight for Heather's wedding and that was why I didn't look good.

"Becca," Jamie said sternly, causing me to lift my head in her direction. Her smile was strong, telling me to stop listening to my head. I gave her a gracious look. It's amazing how a best friend can read your mind and with one look tell you they understand and to stop listening to the monster inside your head.

"I'm sure you both will look beautiful," Mary said, grinning from ear to ear. "And you too, Miss Josie!" Josie smiled brightly. She loved her flower girl dress. Heather said she was constantly trying to wear it around the house.

Acra came back with two assistants holding dresses in bags then placed them in the changing room. "Ready to get started, Becca?" she asked.

I nodded and took her hand to walk into the dressing room.

I think I tried on at least a dozen dresses. My mother made a face at each and every one of them. It was fine because none of them felt perfect to me.

Some were long and very narrow through the hips. I didn't like the mermaid look they gave. Some were too puffy while others were too plain. Normally I liked sweet and simple. It matched my personality. But this was my wedding dress, and I didn't want any second guesses, even if it felt like the groom was second guessing me.

I was beginning to get discouraged, until Acra brought me one more dress.

My mother sighed, "I don't think that one is going to work for your figure, Becca."

"She should still try it on," Jamie said, helping Acra hold the train as we examined it from the hanger. It was strapless with very intricate beading across the bodice and down the hips. It intrigued me enough to step off the pedestal and take off the gaudy dress covered in tulle that I was wearing.

"I think this one will fit, too," Acra said encouragingly. None of the dresses we tried on fit, most of them were too small for my size six self. I guess that's what you get when coming to a designer who does weddings for movie stars.

"I think this one will take everyone's breath away, including yours," Acra whispered in delight as she zipped up the back. It actually fit and amazingly felt a little loose. "We'd have to take it in a little, and some from the bottom, but that's easy."

I closed my eyes, preparing to see at least one set of disappointed eyes in the tough crowd in front of me. Acra pulled back the curtain to the fitting room, and silence filled the room as she helped me step on the pedestal.

Afraid to open my eyes, I took a deep breath and was stunned to see their expressions.

"Oh, Becca..." Heather choked.

"It's beautiful. You look beautiful," Mary said, her voice thick with emotion.

Jamie nodded her head, tears of happiness threatening her eyes.

"Auntie B, you look so pretty!" Josie squealed.

I blew out air as I turned to my biggest critic who was standing by the three way mirror.

My eyes glistened as I saw myself.

The dress fit perfectly through my waist and hips, snug and flattering. I didn't feel huge or disgusting but pretty and graceful.

Acra must have noticed my stunned face, as she quickly grabbed a head piece. "Just to get an idea," she murmured so only I could hear.

I hadn't met my mother's eyes yet. I was terrified my happiness would be shattered with her disapproval and impeccable capability to squash my good feelings. Finally, she stepped in front of the mirror, head cocked as she studied me. A lone tear escaped her eye as a small smile played on her lips. "It's perfect."

I met her smile as I blinked hard.

Then all of my pent up emotions with Tyler and the Conklin mess rushed my head. A large lump formed in my throat as I did everything in my might to keep my chest from jolting and my tears from escaping down my cheeks.

I found the perfect dress and have gotten approving eyes from everyone I loved.

Except I doubted my groom's feelings for me. I doubted if he would ever be able to crawl out of the dark and dreary hole he found in his head with his father and grandfather. I bit my lip, trying to contain it from quivering. Sniffling once, I put my head down to try and hide from my onlookers, but it was nearly impossible when all eyes were on me.

"It can be overwhelming when you find the perfect dress," Acra said while smiling.

I nodded my head, hoping everyone else would buy that as the excuse for my emotions

Jamie stood and walked over to me. "Are you okay?" she asked quietly. I couldn't nod or say yes but looked back down towards the ground. Heather felt Jamie's concern and walked to my other side. "What's wrong?" she asked, not as quietly.

I shook my head. "I'm fine. Just happy to have found a dress everyone likes. I just hope..." I closed my eyes. A tear betrayed me and fell down my cheek.

Jamie tilted her head in understanding while Heather looked worried.

"Becca, why don't you let me help you out of the dress," my mother said quietly.

I was afraid to meet her stare. Her tone meant she knew something was wrong. I reluctantly stepped down, Jamie showing concern for letting me go in that room with my mother. Most likely she was fearful of my mother saying something to make me completely lose it.

"I think Becca needs a mother-daughter moment," she said kindly, ushering me to the changing room.

Stepping down from the pedestal, I walked to the dressing room, not meeting anyone's eye. Even Mary looked nervous now.

My mother followed, closing the curtain behind me. "Becca, you look beautiful in this dress. This is the one. If there were any time I wanted you to believe me, it's now sweetheart. I mean it when I say you will take everyone's breath away."

I choked back a sob. Her words were liberating from her usual judgmental self.

"Are you getting cold feet?" she asked sympathetically. "It's perfectly normal."

I shook my head. "He's different," I croaked. "He won't talk to me."

She took a step towards me, putting her hands on my biceps. "Sweetie, I think he's going through a very difficult time right now."

"I know, but I want to be there for him. But he keeps hiding in his work. You've seen how often we've been together the past six weeks. I've slept in your basement more then I've slept with him," I sniffled, feeling odd for admitting I was actually sleeping with him.

"Baby, he's a businessman like your father."

I shot my eyes to the ceiling, unsure if I should say what I was about to let spill from my mouth. "I know... but I don't want to marry someone like Dad. I don't want your life. I want my husband to be there for me and for me to be there for him. I don't want to live separate lives."

She bit her lip and stared for a second before she responded to my confession. "I know you kids wished your father was around more when you were growing up, and I tried to be there for you. I know I didn't always say the right things or treat each of you how you needed to be treated, but I tried Becca. Your father was there for me, more than you know. Physically, he was gone a lot, but we always communicated. Not for a second did I doubt the love we had and still have. Just because someone isn't there in the flesh doesn't mean they aren't in your heart. I know Tyler will always be there for you, and I wouldn't be surprised if he found a way to be around more if you talked to him."

I nodded my head, a rush of relief that she didn't take what I said the wrong way. "I wish he would open up to me, that's all. I think we could be okay if that happened."

"Sweetheart, men don't open up easily. From what I've seen, Tyler opens up to you more than anyone else. He's calm with you, at least that's what Mary says. But if you don't want this, you don't have to marry him."

I looked into her dead serious eyes. "You'd be okay if I didn't marry him?" I asked, surprised.

"Becca, you have to be happy. All I've ever wanted was for you to be happy. I don't care who you marry, as long as they treat my baby with respect and build her up, not put her down." She looked to the ground. "I know I didn't do a good job building you up, and I'm so sorry." Tears were in her eyes now, and guilt filled my chest.

"Mom, that's not true."

"Don't defend me because you feel bad. It's the truth. I've vowed to myself that I'm not going to be that mom anymore. But baby, know I've always loved you, more than anything." Her voice was choppy now, and I automatically reached for her, as though I was a little girl wanting to be comforted by her momma. She was always there for my siblings and me.

"I love you Mom," I said into her shoulder as I squeezed her thin frame.

I felt her shudder once then say, "I love you too." She backed away and looked me over again, with pure happiness in her wet eyes. "I know you love Tyler, and I know he loves you. I've seen how he looks at you. Your dad looks at me the same way."

We both let out small laughs then our eyes met again. "What do you think?" she asked softly, yet encouragingly. It didn't feel like she was encouraging me for something she wanted, but because she knew I wanted to marry Tyler. And I did. I knew we would jump over this hurdle, just like we had jumped all the other hurdles to get to this point. I was going to have to be the one to give the push start this time, and fight, as he had fought so hard for me before.

I nodded my head, smiling, wiping my eye with a tissue that was conveniently placed in the dressing room.

My mom smiled back at me then turned me to go back outside. "You are going to make the most beautiful bride. Don't tell your sister I said that though," she whispered in my ear. I could sense her smile. My grin was wide when I saw the three concerned faces that were very close to the curtain. No doubt they had overheard some of our conversation, but I didn't care. I looked to Acra and nodded my head rapidly, my smile almost hurting my cheeks from being so big.

"This is the one," I said confidently.

Chapter Sixteen

"Let's start measuring, gentlemen," Rocco, the tailor for Oxford suits, said while holding his piece of measuring tape. This wasn't anything new to me. Nathan would always drag me to places like this to get fitted for the finest suits. I couldn't care less, but for the wedding I was being a little more tolerable. I wanted to look my best for my Becs.

I had done well the past few weeks. I hadn't had any major panic attacks, and they only seemed to happen when I thought about RJ and my grandfather. I had almost pushed the feeling away, and I was sure by the time Becca and I were going to escape for a few days, it would be gone completely.

"Thanks for meeting us with some of your collection at the office, Rocco," Nathan said as he stretched his arms out. We had a few meetings this morning, and Ray, Max, Michael, and Mitch all met us afterwards to be fitted.

"How much purple do we have to wear?" Mitch asked.

"More than me," Ray said. "The joys of being an usher."

"I'm sure you'll get to wear a pretty flower though," Max said, patting Ray's shoulder. Ray looked backwards and gave him a stiff smile. "But this little guy is going to steal the show anyway," Max added as he knelt down to Emmett who was sitting in the stroller.

I was impressed Emmett hadn't made a peep.

"Are you sure she wants black tuxes?" Rocco asked as he finished measuring Nathan. "Gray would look spectacular with the plum lining."

I shrugged my shoulders. "She wanted black. At least that's what her email said."

Rocco came over to me with the tape measure in hand. "All right, but if she changes her mind, let me know. It'll be no trouble. Nothing but the best for the Conklins and the Stines."

I gave him a tight smile, knowing Becca hated how peoples' eyes grew big when they heard our names. She hated that we were associated so much with our parents. Sometimes I got just as annoyed. Lately the idea of running away together felt like the answer to all of my problems.

"Max, ever think of moving to Chicago?" Rocco asked.

Max shook his head. "Missy wouldn't like the city. Grand Rapids is about all she can take."

"I love Chicago, but Heather is like her mom. She wouldn't be caught dead in this city. Same for Becca," Ray said. "Although, I have been enjoying her babysitting the kids while you play in this city, Tyler," Ray teased.

I clenched my teeth. "I'm not playing."

Ray smirked. "I know, big guy. Just giving you a hard time. She has been in a funk though. Are you planning on moving here with her?"

"No, she's happy by the water," I murmured, giving Mitch a dirty look. He rolled his eyes at me.

I had given him a swift punch to the face after the intruder in our house. He didn't see it coming and thought it was a cheap shot, but boy did it feel good.

Mitch said he hadn't done any deals on our property and didn't know what I was talking about, but I was at my wits end with him and so ready to torture his ass until he told us where the bricks were hidden with the drugs. I secretly hoped it was all in Miami since he had been there more often. If they were in Miami, then they'd be far away from Becca. But I guess that wouldn't matter because they were still our bricks. Unless he was putting them on other clients' properties. My head spun. What the fuck would that mean legally?

Nathan was very monotone about the entire scheme. I think he didn't want to let off how truly worried he was with all that Chino was doing amongst our company.

"Becca always liked the beach," Max said. "That was her dream, to live on the water."

I smiled to myself, happy I was able to give her one of her dreams. I planned on giving her whatever she wanted.

"Now she's got her dream guy, even if the asshole went to Michigan," Michael piped in, slapping me hard on the back. I laughed to myself, knowing I would forever get his grief for going to his opposing school. Even though it might seem annoying, it made me feel accepted into their family. I was glad to have a place where arguing wouldn't take place over dinner on the holidays. Although that wouldn't happen anymore, now that RJ was gone.

My chest tightened, causing me to cough.

"You all right?" Nathan asked, studying my features. I nodded quickly to him, trying to regain my composure.

Taking away the attention from my coughing fit, Ray's phone chirped with a Dora the Explorer "backpack, backpack" chime.

His face lit up as he read his message. When his head popped up, we were all looking at him. "What?"

"Um, your ringtone?" Michael questioned with a raised eyebrow.

"Josie picked it out," Ray said offensively. "Anyway, the ladies want to go out tonight."

"That might ruin our plans," Mitch smirked. "We were going to have a pre-bachelor party."

"No," I clipped. "I'm not going bar hopping tonight."

"You will if Becca wants to," Ray said.

I bit the insides of my cheek. Bar hopping wasn't really my thing, and I didn't want to tempt myself into drinking around Becca, not yet. I still didn't trust myself to not go into a fit of rage or anxiety around her.

"Come on, just a few drinks, Tyler. It'll be fun. I've already made reservations at Enclave," Nathan coaxed. "Besides, who knows if we'll have time for another bachelor party."

"Don't have too much fun," Max interluded as Rocco started measuring him. "We have a tee time at 9:00 a.m. at Cog Hill."

Ray laughed. "I doubt we'll cause too much trouble, Max." Max gave him a stare, and Ray stopped laughing.

"Okay, fine. A few drinks. And this counts as my bachelor party," I said, pointing at Mitch.

"Aw, dude, they don't have strippers at Enclave," Mitch pouted.

I shot him a look. I didn't need to see any naked bodies besides Becca's.

***

The bar was loud and jam packed. It took us almost twenty minutes to find our VIP section. I was beyond irritated and drank my first Captain and Coke way too fast.

"Why don't we go find some chicks to dance with?" Mitch shouted.

"Go ahead," I waved to Mitch, happy to have his obnoxious self leave my air space. Michael nudged Mitch, and they found their way to the dance floor.

I sat down and sighed, closing my eyes while leaning back in the leather booth. At least they were comfortable. Nathan sat next to me, holding his scotch in one hand. "I talked to Anderson yesterday," Nathan said in my ear because of the thumping music.

I clenched my jaw. "What did he want."

"You know, beating around the bush about Chino's accounts. I told him I wasn't allowed to discuss our client's personal accounts, and he'd have to take up any matters he had with Chino himself."

I huffed. "He's a nosy bastard." Anderson was a little shit to me ever since he called RJ's death a suicide. That was bullcrap. I didn't believe it. I didn't like him constantly snooping around our office. I wished he'd get a fucking clue. If Nathan and I couldn't figure out where the illegal drugs were in our business, then he sure as hell wouldn't be able to either.

"I agree. But we need to keep him believing everything is peachy. So the next time he talks to you, put a smile on your face. You are getting married after all." I raised a brow at him. "You don't seem excited," he said, taking a sip from his drink as he looked down at the dancers. His eyes hardened for a second as though he saw something he didn't like. "I mean, shouldn't you be all doughy eyed?"

Ray came and sat down across from Nathan and me. He had a few beers already and was obviously feeling good. "He's not a chick. They are the ones that get all bushy tailed."

Nathan regained his focus from the dance floor then laughed. "Bushy tailed?"

Ray shrugged his shoulders and crinkled his nose. Then a sly smile crossed his face as he watched the stairs. "There's one sexy woman," he said in a deep voice. His eyes grew hungry, and I couldn't help but turn to see who he was looking at.

Oh, I was in trouble.

Heather and Becca were walking up the stairs, and I swear to God Becca was trying to kill me with her outfit. A super tight, hot pink dress hugged her body and was way too many inches from the top of her knee. Her hair was tousled from the Chicago wind, and her lips were bright along with her flushed cheeks. I was getting hard already, and I gulped with every step she took towards me.

Once they approached us, I realized just how short her dress was.

She snuck past Nathan, her eyes pinned to mine. A devilish smile crossed her lips as she slyly sat down on the bench next to me, scooting so her breasts were pushed against my arm. I couldn't stop the mischievous grin from spreading across my lips. She brought her hand to my tie, playfully tugging it with her fingers. She batted her eyelashes then leaned into my ear.

"What brings a stuffy businessman to the club on a Friday night?"

I grinned wider. So she wanted to play. "This is my bachelor party."

I felt her lips deathly close to my ear. "No strippers? Isn't that what bachelor parties are all about?"

I turned my head so I could look at her. I was met with sparkling blue eyes and long, dark, and sexy as hell eyelashes. "Haven't gotten to that part of the night yet."

She smirked again then moved her eyes down to my lap then back to my lips. "What would your fiancé say?"

I licked my lips, enjoying this playful side of her. We had hardly talked the past few weeks, and it felt good to see her smiling. "Mmm, I'm not sure she would approve, but I think it's customary for the bachelor to get a lap dance from a stripper on his supposed last night of freedom."

Her pupils dilated then her eyes turned hungry as she thought. What was my baby doll plotting in her head?

"The point of a bachelor party is no women," Nathan shouted. I turned my head from Becca, my eyes catching Heather damn near straddling Ray. She was wearing a dress almost as short as Becca's, the only thing keeping her ass from hanging out was Ray's hand holding the fabric down.

Heather turned to look at Nathan. "We're the strippers, don't you know?"

"Yeah, Mitch hired us," Becca flirted, running her hand up my thigh, getting very close to the bulge that was growing in my pants. I spun my head in her direction again, giving her a sultry stare.

"You didn't tell me you were a stripper?" I asked playfully.

She licked her lips and nodded. "Not sure if you can afford me though."

"Probably better, I think my fiancé would get upset."

"Oh Jesus," Nathan shouted, throwing the rest of his drink back. "I'm going to the bar."

Becca giggled. My smile widened. Her eyes caught mine again. "So, what strip club are we going to?"

I raised my brow at her. "We?"

She nodded her head while biting her lip.

"I don't think my fiancé would like that either."

"No? She sounds like a real stiff," she said playfully, reaching for my tie again.

I laughed under my breath. "She's actually amazing."

Becca's seductive look faded, and her eyes grew big. "Yeah?"

Swallowing the lump that was forming in my throat, I nodded my head yes to her. I'd been shutting her out ever since RJ left this world. That wasn't cool of me at all. That look she just gave me put everything into perspective. I was hurting her, causing her to question where my heart was.

"My fiancé is the most loving, caring, and precious person in my life. I would never do anything to jeopardize her," I murmured.

She bit her bottom lip again, but this time it was to try and stop it from trembling instead of looking devious.

"But, it might be hard to avoid someone as tempting as you the entire night. Especially if the waitress keeps refilling my glass," I said, shaking my nearly empty cup.

Her eyes filled with lust. "I guess I'm going to have to stick around and find out."

Her fingers traced the buttons on my shirt as the waitress brought more drinks. "Gin and tonic for my guest," I said without taking my eyes off Becca's.

"Top shelf," she added.

I smirked at her. "You're playing the part well."

She shrugged her shoulder's playfully. "Would your fiancé be upset if you danced with another woman?"

"I think she'd rather I sit and chat than grind against another woman."

Becca pouted her lips.

"Pouting those lips sure makes me want to kiss them," I murmured.

"I've been told my lips are like Pringles. Once you pop you won't want to stop."

"I think I'm willing to take that chance," I said, my words filling with a sudden need to kiss her senseless. To get lost in her like I had so many times before.

She yanked on my tie, making our lips practically touch. "I'm still charging you."

I grinned then grabbed her bottom lip with my teeth, nibbling and sucking, making her body go lax against mine. Her hand gripped my tie tighter, trying to pull me as close to her as possible while her other hand found my cheek, grazing the stubble as I tried to coax her to open her mouth and let my tongue go exploring.

Still kissing her, I set my glass down on the coffee table in front of me then reached for her thigh. My hand formed to her skin perfectly, hiking under her dress just enough so I could feel all skin.

She still wouldn't let me sneak my tongue inside but kept giving slow and steady kisses to my lips. We took turns sucking each other's bottom lip until the waitress came back with our drinks, clearing her throat loudly to get my attention.

Staring at Becca's beautifully plump lips from my tender nibbles, I told the waitress we were fine, hoping she'd leave again.

"Let me kiss you," I rasped, digging my fingers into her thighs.

Her smile was huge as she slowly shook her head no. "See, MY fiancé wouldn't approve of tongue."

"Oh, but letting another man suck on those delightful lips is okay?" I questioned.

She shrugged her shoulders again.

"We've popped, now I don't want to stop," I whispered near her ear. I heard her sweet giggle as she pulled my tie to bring her mouth back to mine.

"What the hell? What are you doing here? This is supposed to be a bachelor party!" Michael said, plopping down next to Tyler. "Can you not grope my sister in public," Michael scolded while smacking Tyler on the back.

I turned so I could face Michael, giving him a sly grin. "Sorry, can't help it. Besides, I'm being tame compared to your other brother-in-law." I laughed as I nodded across the seats.

Michael's eyes widened in horror as he saw Heather, who was now completely straddling Ray. If he was grossed out by mine and Becca's public display of affection, then he most definitely would be appalled with his baby sister's.

Michael stood up and smacked Ray in the head. "What the hell? Stop man handling my little sister!" Heather slowly slid to the side of Ray, laughing hysterically. Ray was laughing as well, but kept his hands on her.

"Michael, weren't you just grinding against some random chick? Now you're going to give me shit for cuddling my husband?"

Michael's eyes narrowed. "I would call it humping, not cuddling. Your ass was practically hanging out!"

"No, no, no. I made sure to keep my hands on both cheeks so her dress wouldn't ride up," Ray assured Michael with a sly grin then leaned in to kiss Heather again.

Becca and I laughed along with Heather and Ray. Michael finally gave in and let off a smile as he sat down next to me.

"Who knew my sisters were so sexually driven," Michael grumbled.

"Don't you know? That's what businessmen do to women. You picked the wrong field my friend," Nathan said as he walked back to our group with waitresses following behind him. "I got some shots! Pass them around, ladies." Nathan gestured to the waitresses.

"Um, there's more than shots, Nathan," Becca said as she took a glass from one of the waitresses.

"Ah, that's because everyone needs to have each hand full. Where the hell did Jay go? I saw her earlier," Nathan said with a puzzled look.

Becca looked more confused than worried. She stood from her seat next to me, her warmth leaving my side. I watched her walk towards the railing to look out at the dancers. *How did I miss those heels?* I had an instant fantasy of them being around my neck. Like a lap dog on a short leash, I followed her, my eyes never leaving her behind. Good thing the lighting was dim, otherwise my family might have seen more than they needed to. I covered myself with my wrist, just in case.

Walking behind her, I put my hands on the railing on either side of her, molding my body with hers. The curve of her back fit perfectly with my front, even with those heels she was a good six inches shorter than me. I kissed her shoulder gently and began to search the crowd for Jamie.

"Did she say she was going to dance?" I murmured in her ear.

Becca tilted her head so I could hear her. "She said she was going to get a drink. Unless she found a guy."

I skimmed the dancers the best I could with the flashing lights and loud music. Becca's citrus scent filled my nostrils, and my mind kept wandering back to her. I wanted to smell her everywhere, taste her everywhere. I wanted to get back to the hot and heavy that we once had. Before RJ was murdered.

For the first time when RJ's death came into mind I didn't feel like my heart was going to explode out of my chest. With Becca safely tucked to my chest and her head leaning back on my shoulder, I felt comfortable and relaxed. I was confident whatever was causing me stress with RJ and my grandfather was finally gone. Moving my hands from the railing to around her waist, I kissed her shoulder as tenderly as I could then nuzzled her neck.

"Is that...?" I heard her gasp then move her hand to cover her mouth. "Anderson's here," she whispered.

My head popped up from her neck, trying to find her line of sight. Quickly her head dipped down then turned to my cheek. "I think he's watching us, Tyler."

Finally finding him, his eyes were trained on Becca and me. He was sitting on the opposite side of the club with a few other men. His eyes were intense, and I felt him coaxing me to go talk to him. I stood tall from Becca, rubbing my hands on her sides.

"I'll be right back," I murmured in her ear.

"Tyler don't," she pleaded, spinning around to face me.

I put my arms around her again. "Baby doll, it'll be fine. I'm going to go talk to him."

Her eyes were unsure, but Detective Anderson followed us to Chicago for a reason, and I needed to find out why. I let Becca go then nodded to Nathan, silently telling him to follow me.

"What's up," Nathan asked once we were away from the group.

"That pain in the ass Detective Anderson is here."

Nathan sighed. "How are we going to approach this?"

I glanced at Nathan as I thought. "Start with small talk like he does." Nathan nodded and followed behind me.

"Detective Anderson, odd finding you in Chicago, at a night club," Nathan said as we approached Anderson's section.

Nathan had his arm out in greeting as I stood silently beside him.

"Hello, gentlemen. Would you like to join me?" he offered, giving his usual half smile.

"For a bit. As I'm sure you noticed, we're with our family and friends," I said in a low tone. It was hard for me to play nice with this asshole.

"Sit down," Anderson said evenly. Both Nathan and I took a seat and couldn't help but notice the few goons that were watching us like hawks. Why was I feeling like he wasn't a normal detective?

"Here for wedding preparations?" Anderson asked.

I nodded my head. "We are. What exactly are you doing here, in Chicago, miles away from your jurisdiction, watching us?" I asked curiously. I wanted him to know I meant business and that it was time for him to cut the bullshit small talk.

"Tyler, don't be so accusing. I'm not a bad guy. I'm just doing my job." A small smile played across his lips. "RJ used to come to this club and meet with undisclosed clients. I find it odd all three of his boys show up to the very same club."

"We're not doing dirty business, if that's what you're insinuating," Nathan said.

"Hmm, that's interesting. Because I want to know why the dirtiest businessman out there keeps coming around your office."

Nathan and I remained silent, meeting Anderson's stare.

"What the hell are you doing with Chino?" he asked meaning no non-sense. "That man will run you right to a prison cell."

"Chino is a client and nothing more. I assure you, our business with him is purely professional," Nathan said almost as a laugh. "Keeping our grandfather's name clean means a great deal to us."

Anderson took a long drink. "Your grandfather? Or do you mean RJ? From what I know, they were very different men."

I clenched my jaw, still baffled I was the only one who didn't know my grandfather was a drug dealer.

Nathan's voice was strong. "Both our father and grandfather cared about this company."

"Right, just in different ways? Ethical and unethical?"

"You didn't know either of them," I said in a low, threatening tone.

Anderson laughed then leaned forward so his elbows were on his knees. "I don't think you knew them very well either."

I swore I saw red. It took every ounce of self control to keep from tackling that mother fucker. Nathan took a protective step forward, probably because he thought I wouldn't be able to control my anger for much longer and would need to stop me from pummeling an officer.

"My brother and I have company we need to attend to. It was a pleasure, Detective," Nathan said as a dismissal.

Anderson's eyes wandered towards where we were sitting, and a suspicious smile crept across his lips. "Odd your company includes the very man both RJ and your grandfather periodically met at this very night club."

Nathan and I shared questioning glances.

Anderson nodded his head to our section. "Seems Mr. Chino has joined your party."

Both our heads flashed to our section.

Chino was amongst my family, sitting too fucking close to my fiancé. Fury filled my lungs as I darted past Anderson's goons and bolted to Becca.

I told that asshole to stay away from her, and there he sat, smirking playfully at Becca as though they were old friends. He even had his arm around the back of the booth, and I could have swore I saw him touch her shoulder. That was my shoulder. Only I could touch it.

Stalking past Michael flirting with the waitress and Heather and Ray molesting each other, I grabbed Chino's suitcoat collar and yanked him from MY seat next to MY fiancé.

"What the hell are you doing here?" I growled.

Chino raised his hands offering peace. "Tyler, I was just saying hello."

I noticed his thugs take a step towards him, but he put his hands up, ordering them to stay put.

"I thought I told you to stay away from Becca," I snarled in his face. I was close enough to smell the alcohol on his breath.

Chino's eyes had a cheeky gleam to them that only made me want to bury him to the ground. "I think it's up to her who she can and can't talk to."

"Tyler stop!" Becca begged, jumping from her seat.

I gripped his collar tighter, my knuckles turning white. "Don't fuck with me. One of these days I'm going to snap, and you're going to regret infiltrating this company."

"I already own this company," Chino whispered. "Try and stop me. See what happens." His head cocked to the side towards Becca.

The second his grubby eyes found Becca, swooping down her body like he were picturing her naked, I whipped his head by the collar directly into my other fist.

Nathan and Ray were by my side in a heartbeat, freeing my grasp on Chino's now bloody shirt. I got his lip good, possibly knocked a tooth loose.

Chino held his hands to his thugs again as he wiped his mouth with his sleeve. "Don't you know it's rude to hit your elders?" he said in a menacingly low tone.

"I've got a lot more coming your way if you don't stop with your bullshit," I growled, flexing against Ray's and Nathan's grasps.

Chino's snaky smile spread across his face, fat lip and all. Slowly walking towards me, I saw his pupils dilate. Even though he had his cocky smile, his eyes held the devil. Luckily I was floored and ready to pound his ass, otherwise I might be intimidated.

"You think I've got a lot more coming my way?" he whispered in a dangerously low tone. One more step, and he was so close I could smell the blood trickily from his lip. "You think tear gas is bad? You think drugs hidden in your house is bad? Even. A. Bullet. To. The. Head... is easy compared to what I'm capable of doing to your good for nothing punk ass." His voice went from a smug businessman to a crook off the street in the blink of an eye. His tone matched his stare—low, promising, and daunting.

The palms of my hands must have been bleeding from my nails digging into them. My ire was about to fly out the window, taking down Ray and Nathan so I could teach Chino a lesson. He just admitted to purposely hurting Becca, endangering my house with drug dealers, and killing my father.

Nathan felt my rage surfacing. "Anderson is watching you, along with everyone else in this bar," Nathan said calmly. "Let it go... for now."

As Chino took a step back, smug smile intact, Nathan spoke directly to him. "Conklin won't be backing your business nor start any new projects. Once your current projects are built, we are through. If you want to completely stop, I will order our attorney to summon the paperwork."

Chino eyes grew darker as Nathan stared him down. Nathan may not be all muscle, but he sure packed a punch with his words.

"Nathan... and I thought you had potential," Chino said tutting disappointedly. "I think you boys should sleep on that statement because I'm not going anywhere," he promised.

I jolted again, but Ray and Nathan held me back. "Anderson is watching," Nathan repeated, but more firmly.

I clenched my jaw as my eyes swept around my surroundings. Anderson was standing on his side of the club, eyes glued in our direction. The waitress had gotten a bouncer, who was standing only a few feet behind Chino and was grasping his knuckles. My soon-to-be family was off to the side looking unsure.

"He's not worth it," Ray said smoothly.

My eyes found Becca, and she looked horrified. Thank God the music was loud, and she most likely didn't hear anything Chino just cockily admitted to doing.

Chino took a few steps back, that damn smirk plastered to his face as he looked at me. He turned and showed concern towards Becca.

"See what I mean, Becca," Chino said as though he was a sympathetic father figure. "You call me, anytime." Once he was done giving Becca his bullshit lines, he turned and winked at me, his thugs following behind him.

Both Nathan and Ray grasped my shoulders, making it so I was unable to leap after him. I shrugged them off once Chino was out of sight then turned to Becca.

"What the hell was he talking about?" my tone was harsh.

Her eyes wouldn't meet mine as she stared at the ground.

Just as I thought I found peace, the rage was boiling inside of me again, laughing in my face for thinking I had any type of control over it. "Becca!" I said sharply, demanding her to answer me.

Her eyes were still on the ground as I took another step to her.

"Calm down," Michael said firmly, sliding in front of his sister.

My eyes grew big as I stared at him. "This doesn't concern you," I said in a low tone. Irritated that out of all the times Becca's brother could pick to be the protector, he picks now, when I was the only one who *could* protect her. Whatever mind game Chino was playing, I needed to know about, for her own safety.

Becca put a hand on Michael's shoulder. "It's okay, Michael. I think it's time Tyler and I take a cab home."

Michael turned to Becca, looking for reassurance that everything would be okay. She gave him an assuring nod then reached for my hand. "Let's go, Ty," she said soothingly.

I gulped, my eyes hitting the ground, feeling foolish for losing my head in front of everyone I wanted so badly to fit in with.

Nathan patted my shoulder then nodded to Becca as we left.

"I'm going to call a cab, unless you think we can walk home," Becca said softly, making a circling motion on my palm with her thumb as we exited Enclave.

Closing my eyes, I felt that familiar suffocating feeling in my chest. The one I had been fighting so badly to stop from creeping in and screwing up my life.

"It's about a fifteen minute walk," I answered.

Becca nodded and tugged on my hand. "Lead the way."

I let go of her hand and put them in my pockets as my mind reeled. Chino, Anderson, drugs, RJ, Papa... It was all such a head rush that I clearly didn't have a grasp on at all.

Becca crossed her arms and silently walked beside me, her heels clicking against the cement.

"Tyler, can you slow down, please?" I turned back to see her feet shuffling to keep up with me. "These heels will be the death of me," she laughed uncomfortably.

I narrowed my eyes at her. She was trying to make small talk and dodge what happened in the club. I wouldn't reprimand her until we were secluded in the condo, and I needed to not let those heels distract me from what I was so angry about. She caught on to my lack of small talk and didn't say anything the rest of the walk.

When we finally passed through the door frame of my condo, I turned on her, my arms firmly planted on my hips, eyes boring into her. She shriveled at my glare, but I didn't care. I needed to know.

"What is going on between you and Chino," I said slowly, trying to reign in my anger.

She tossed her heels to the side and walked into the living room, completely ignoring me.

"Becca, I swear to GOD you better start talking," I said, my voice rising.

"Tyler, it's nothing," she sighed as she turned to face me. My scowl was in full force as I waited for her to continue. There was no way I was going to let her off the hook with this.

"How am I supposed to keep you safe from the monster if you are making deals with him?" I asked, now inches from her face. "You can't keep secrets from me, Becca."

Now her eyes narrowed as she crossed her arms, meeting my stare full on. My skin prickled while waiting for her to talk. Finally, beyond frustrated, I turned and groaned, throwing my phone onto the couch and kicking it angrily before I sat down, holding my head in my hands.

"That's what he was talking to me about," she said loudly. "The fact that you have an awful temper and how he's worried about me."

My head shot up from my hands. "You're joking," I said, now more mad than ever. I stood from the couch, pacing the length of the windows looking over the city. I stopped mid step, realizing what else Chino had told her. "He was the asshole who told you about my record, wasn't he?" I growled in her direction. My mind started reliving the awful night I beat a dumbass college kid so badly that he had to eat through a straw.

Her eyes found the floor again, arms still firmly grasping her chest. "Yes," she said quietly, losing her strength. "He was telling me I could trust him and come to him if you ever... hurt me..."

My breath caught in my throat, realizing how uncomfortable my unstable state was making Becca. Was she worried I would hurt her? I could never hurt her. But then that awful bitemark came to mind, the unknown bruises I most likely left on her hips from my uncontrollable hands. Anxiety in my chest squeezed my lungs, slowly suffocating me from my own mistakes. "Becca, I'd never," I whispered, leaning back against the window with my hand to my chest. My other hand rubbed my face. How fucked up had I become?

Her head cocked in understanding as she slowly walked towards me, her arms open to reach out and touch me. "I know, Ty." Becca put a gentle hand over each of mine.

"Don't you see he's trying to get a rise out of you. I think he's trying to break us."

"Why would he care if we are together or not?" I asked, dumbfounded. "I don't know what angle he's coming from with you, Becca. I don't know why he's trying to involve you in this."

"He's trying to get into your head Tyler, make you weak, so you give in to what he wants. Don't let him win," she pleaded. She grabbed my face with both hands now, causing me to drop my own hand. "Please don't let this break us."

Closing my eyes, I took a deep breath. "I don't know what else to do. Maybe I should just go through with the deal. Give him his partnership," I conceded. "Maybe that would stop me from feeling like I'm going to have a heart attack every five minutes."

She shook her head rapidly. "No, that makes you no better than him. We'll figure this out. Maybe... Anderson could help you and Nathan? Neither of you know where he's hiding people in your company. Can't you plead ignorance?"

"I don't think there's an out for this, Becca. All I know is, if I sign that paperwork for him to become a partner, his drug scheme will take over our company. Everything I stand against would become a part of what I've helped to build." I had never felt so defeated in my life, and that prick Chino was pinning me down by the balls.

"Promise me something," she said quickly.

I nodded my head.

"Promise you won't ever sign those papers," she begged.

I swallowed hard. I just had my biggest moment of weakness ever when it came to the company. Hearing Becca's voice make that plea helped me to snap out of joining the dark side.

"I promise."

"We'll get through this, Tyler," she said soothingly again, her thumbs making those circles that helped temporarily calm every bone in my body.

Chapter Seventeen

Becca

My mind was preoccupied throughout the entire wedding shower. Sure, I smiled and nodded, said hello and thank you when it was appropriate, but I kept reliving last night. After I made Tyler promise me he wouldn't give in to Chino's outlandish demands, we made our way to the bedroom. I stripped off my clothing but was surprised when Tyler threw a t-shirt at me. Once I was dressed for bed, he scooped me in his arms and lay with me, clinging to me for dear life the entire night. My poor, handsome man. He was like a little boy, snuggling me as though I was a teddy bear. Throughout the night I could feel his pulse start to race, his heart pump faster. Whenever this would happen, I'd trace circles on his back and shoulders, kiss his forehead gently, trying to give him a sense of comfort. His breathing would typically go back to normal, but my heart slowly broke each time he had a minor panic attack.

What astounded me the most was his demeanor in the morning, acting as though nothing had happened. He showered, got ready to go golfing, then hid in his office the rest of the weekend. He only came out for dinner Saturday night with the wedding party.

It took all of me to stay strong when he said he was staying in Chicago for the majority of the next week when I thought he would be in Grand Rapids. He just gave me his same spiel, *I need more time to get things in order from RJ's death.*

Tyler was more messed up than I thought he was. He was like an egg that had been dropped too many times, cracking and barely holding itself together. I was scared he was going to shatter the next time he was dropped. I needed to figure out how to help him. I knew he didn't want me involved, but the truth was I had resources, and I was sitting in the waiting room of one of them.

"Miss Stine, Mr. Prince will see you now," the receptionist said at the law firm Connor was working for.

I stood and smoothed over my skirt, waiting for the receptionist to point me in the right direction. Connor beat her to it, giving me a great big bear hug. "It's so nice to see you, Becs."

I gave him a big smile once he finally let go of me and lead the way to his office.

"What brings you to my side of the tracks? Need a pre-nup?" He laughed. "I saw your engagement photos. They were nice." His eyes were sparkling, but I could see a trace of hurt behind them.

"No, we've already taken care of those things," I said quietly while taking a seat in front of his desk. "I just had a few... hypothetical questions."

Connor cocked his head and leaned on his desk in front of me. "Okay... shoot."

I took a deep breath, wanting to make sure I said what I needed to say in the right way. I didn't want to give away exactly what was happening and needed to be as vague as possible.

"What happens if something bad is happening in a company you own, but it wasn't your fault?"

Connor raised a brow at me. "Well, it depends on the factors and the jury."

"So say someone was paid by another person outside of the company to do illegal things, who would be held responsible?"

Connor's features evened then a knowing look crossed his face. It wasn't a happy one, but a sad expression. He knew Chino was trying to get at the Conklin business.

"Becca, if there's something going on, you need to get out, now," he said firmly. "You can't fall in this city or be associated with anyone who will bring down your reputation or your father's."

He was talking about Tyler. He already knew. I was stupid for thinking I could beat around the bush with Connor. He was too smart and already had an inkling of what could possibly be going on in my future husband's business.

"But what if they were thrown in the middle of it," I asked in horror. "What if they didn't know it was happening?"

Connor's shoulders fell. "Becca, it all just depends on the case. If it's what I'm thinking you're talking about, the chances aren't good."

A tear escaped my eye. "What if the person who doesn't know were to go to officials and explain, maybe help catch what's happening?"

Connor's jaw ticked as he thought. "It could either end good or very badly on their behalf." He grabbed my hands and pulled me from my seat, looking at me intently. "Becca, if you're scared..."

I shook my head rapidly, pulling my hands from his grasp. "I'm not scared. I just know someone is hurting when they shouldn't have to be." I turned on my heel, shaking my head and wondering why I even bothered coming to Connor for advice.

Connor raced past me and put his hand on his door so I couldn't leave. "If Tyler is really worried, tell him to come to me. Everything will be confidential, and we can figure something out. I can't guarantee him going to the authorities unless I know every single detail."

I nodded. "Thank you, Connor. But I'm not sure Tyler will be ready to take that step. I guess I blew my cover," I softly laughed, dabbing under my eye with my finger.

He leaned on his door and smiled. "You've always been easy to read, Becs."

I rolled my eyes. "I'm working on that."

Connor's grin widened then he became serious again. "I mean it Becca. Don't get wrapped up in this. I can help you only to a certain point."

"I know," I said gratefully.

"I'd still do anything for you, Becs. But I really don't want to represent you in a criminal case," he half smiled.

I returned a similar smile, although both of us knew that could be true someday if things went according to Chino's plan.

***

After denying an invitation for lunch with Connor, I headed back to the Conklin building. There was no need for lunch with Connor. I had said what I needed to say and didn't need to become any more involved with him on a personal level.

I sat at my desk, staring at the finished prints for the Arena. They would be breaking ground on the remodel on Wednesday and would be finished by mid November. The Griffins would start playing in their new Arena by December. My father was impressed it would only take three months.

Just as I was beginning a new project, a knock came to my door.

"Hey Becca, do you have a minute?" I was stunned to see Detective Anderson in my office door frame. After witnessing the odd encounter at Enclave in Chicago this weekend, I had no idea what he could possibly want.

"Yeah, sure," I said quickly, standing from my chair, gesturing him to sit down as I closed my office door.

"I wanted to apologize if I antagonized Tyler this weekend," he said smoothly as he sat down. "I didn't mean any harm."

I shook my head. "Don't worry about it. He's been easy to rile ever since RJ's passing."

Anderson scratched his chin. "Yes. It was a shame. RJ was so young. Tyler made it sound like he didn't think it was a suicide."

I blinked at him, feeling slightly hurt that Tyler had talked to the detective about RJ's death and not me.

"I wonder sometimes if it was foul play. To be honest, a lot of fingers point in Tyler's direction, but his alibi is too clear. Surveillance cameras catch him entering the building after RJ's time of death. I don't think Tyler is capable of killing anyone anyway..." Anderson said, trailing his last sentence as he looked at me.

"Of course not!" I gasped. "Tyler would never hurt anyone, especially his family."

Anderson raised an eyebrow at me.

"Look, I know RJ and Tyler's relationship seemed unconventional, but deep down they cared about each other. They just had a weird way of showing it."

Anderson nodded in agreement, and a huge sigh of relief escaped my mouth. No way would Tyler kill anyone, and the thought of Anderson pinning his father's death on his son's hands sent a shiver down my spine.

Anderson leaned forward, his eyes intently looking at me from across my desk. "Becca, this is going to be off the record."

I gulped, unsure if I could trust him.

"I know Robert Senior did dirty business and that RJ covered it up somehow. If Tyler is feeling pressure from anyone, he can come to me. Deals can be made."

We stared at each other for a moment then Anderson stood. "I should get back to the office. It was nice seeing you again."

"Same to you," I said quietly, getting up from my seat to let him out.

"I mean it Becca. This city isn't what you'd think it'd be, and I'm willing to get help from anyone to make it a better place."

"Corruption seems to be taking over everywhere," I agreed.

The detective nodded then left.

Slowly closing the door, I tried to recollect what he and Connor had said. There just might be an out for my Ty.

Chapter Eighteen

Tyler

My Chicago office was bigger than both my Grand Rapids and Cleveland offices combined. The space was too quiet, and the sounds of my keyboard reminded me how separated from people I had been the past few months.

Glancing at the clock, it was almost 7:30 p.m.. Becca would be home from the gym, cooking dinner. She decided to start staying at the condo in Union Square instead of her parents' or sister's. I didn't blame her for wanting her own space. No one would be able to break into the top floor of Union Square, so I felt she would be safe without me there.

My door slowly creaked open, and I was shocked with who passed through the door frame.

"Why are you here, Tyler?" my mother's voice rang through the stillness of my office.

I scowled as I looked up from my computer screen. Since when did she come to my office? And why did my receptionist let her back without telling me?

"I'm obviously working, mother."

She rolled her eyes and marched to the front of my desk. "Why aren't you in Grand Rapids with Becca?" she asked harshly.

I squinted at her. "Again, I'm working."

"You need to stop this, Tyler," she said sternly.

What was she talking about? "Stop what? Building this empire?"

"Stop turning into RJ."

I stood from my seat, glaring at her. "I'm nothing like RJ," I sputtered. Then that awful thought crossed my mind that maybe he wasn't so bad after all.

"You're sure acting like it. Have you actually talked to Becca lately?" she accused, her hands firmly on her hips.

"Of course I talk to her," I snorted. "She's my fiancé. I talk to her every day." Maybe we weren't as connected as we should be, but I was trying. So what if our main communications had been through texts... or text...

"She's been a mess. She broke down when we were wedding dress shopping."

My heart sank. *Broke down?*

"Don't start treating her like RJ treated me all those years. I thought you knew better from watching him while you grew up," she chastised.

"I'd never cheat on Becca," I growled, appalled she would even insinuate such a horrid idea.

"You are right now!" she shouted, throwing her hands around my office. "It might not be some sleazy woman, Tyler, but you're obsessed with work! Stop putting this before Becca! It'll destroy you!"

My jaw clenched as I stared down at my desk. I wasn't obsessed with work. I was using it as a distraction.

"I know you love her. I've seen how you look at her," my mother said more softly. "But sweetie, you need to put Becca first."

I closed my eyes. "Like you put us first all those years?"

She looked like I stabbed her with a knife, turning it deep inside her.

"Okay, I get it. I was a horrible mother." she exaggerated. "I left you with your grandmother and nannies. But I was trying to please my husband. Just like Becca is going to try and please you. Don't take advantage of her, Tyler."

"Becca won't put up with this lifestyle for long," I said quietly. "She won't jump when I tell her too, not anymore."

"Good," she said, nodding her head. Silence passed through our stares and a tear fell down her cheek. "I'm sorry I wasn't there when you were younger."

Now I was uncomfortable with her apology. It was easier to be mad at her, resent every missed moment of my youth.

How could we start over? I stayed quiet, not sure how to address her comment.

She turned to leave then saw a photo of Wrigley Field on the wall. She traced a finger on the frame, a small smile played on her lips, countering her wet eyes. "I remember when you were ten years old and went to Wrigley Field for the National Anthem with your little league team. You were so excited. I don't think you slept at all the night before. You were bouncing off the walls, talking about how you wanted to get all of the players' autographs." Her smile widened at the memory and tugged at my heart. I thought she was too drunk to remember anything from my childhood.

"Just like your first high school game, when you got pulled up to varsity. You were so nervous yet focused when I watched you on the bench. Your leg was bouncing. You wouldn't talk with any of the other team members."

She turned to look at me, happiness shining through her tears. "I always talked about you and your baseball at brunches. The other wives got annoyed and bored I think, but I didn't care. I was so proud of you for being focused on something other than that stupid business."

I swallowed hard. She did come to all of my games, even a good portion of my college games, and I just ignored her. Not caring or being grateful for her support. She typically had a drink in her hand, and I always thought it was just a reason for her to escape her confinements with RJ.

"I'll never forget how disappointed you were when RJ missed your first college game." The life left her eyes. "He never told you, but he tried his hardest to get there. He called me at least six times during the game, wanting to know what was happening."

My chest felt like it was going to collapse. "He did?"

She nodded her head. "Tyler, he wanted to come to your games. He used to play you know. He got suspended from his high school team because of bad behavior, but he could have been good. You got your talent from him."

My eyes stung as I screwed them shut. "Then why didn't he ever play with me? Why didn't he ever show interest? I never once knew he even wanted to come to my games."

She shook her head sympathetically. "RJ never wanted anyone to know how he felt. He always had to be the calm and witty one. He never let his guard down. A lot like someone else I know," she murmured with an arched brow.

I scowled at her. "Why was he so different from Papa?" I asked in confusion.

My mother sighed loudly then walked over to one of the plush black leather couches. "Your grandfather and RJ were a lot alike, but your grandfather wanted everyone to like him. He was two faced in other ways."

I blinked at her intently, a small part of me terrified what more I was going to find out about the man I had so much respect for.

My mother crossed her legs and took another deep breath. "I've heard the ugly side of your grandfather. He could be downright nasty to RJ. What he said to him on your very first college game....," her voice faded, anger creeping into her words.

"He was mad he missed it," I assumed, taking a seat back at my desk.

My mother laughed while shaking her head. "I'm not sure if I should tell you this, but your grandfather was the reason why he didn't show."

I shook my head, knowing they had probably gotten into a fight and RJ couldn't stand being in the same vicinity as his father.

As though my mother read my mind, she said, "Tyler, it wasn't because he was mad at Robert but because Robert made RJ stay and do his work so Robert could come and watch your game."

I looked at her in bewilderment. *"What?"*

She shook her head. "I loved your grandparents Tyler, more than anything. They have done so much for me, but they could be nasty when it came to you boys. They didn't want to miss a thing, even if it came down to between them and us."

I rubbed my eyes with both palms, feeling more confused than ever.

"They always came first, whether RJ and I had an opinion or not." She sniffled for a moment then continued talking. "I wanted to leave so many times, take you boys out of your beds and disappear. I wanted to be your mother so badly, Tyler. Sometimes that house felt like a prison. Things got better when we were in our own house, but they still had a hold on us. When RJ would be demanding I attend certain functions and parties, your grandparents would be insisting to spend time with you and your brothers. At the time I didn't have a voice to say no."

Tears spilled down her face, but she quickly dabbed them away. "Please, don't let this change how you thought of your grandparents. They loved you and provided for you when I couldn't." She sniffled loudly again, and my heart twisted into a noose, hanging itself for thinking so poorly of my own mother.

"You knew about Papa, didn't you?" I choked.

"What? That he was a dirty crook?" She half laughed again, standing from the couch. "Yes, unfortunately I got the heads up from your father. RJ and Robert's relationship was a lot like the relationship you had with your father, Tyler."

I hit my fist on my desk, furious for how stupidly blind I was. "How come I never saw it? How come I never figured it out?" I stood from my chair, covering my mouth and holding my chest.

My mother rapidly shook her head, making her way to stand by me. "No, Tyler. Don't beat yourself up about this. You were so young; you still are. You've always held too many responsibilities. You need to remember the good in your grandparents and in RJ."

Mary took a step closer to me, her emotions radiating into mine.

"I know it's hard to find good memories of RJ, but..." She quietly laughed. I let out a small chuckle, but turned into an embarrassing sob. Covering my head with my hands, my chest heaved as I fought back tears of regret and guilt.

"Tyler, sweetie," my mother comforted. Then I felt her hand on my back, my body shuddering, making my cries harder to control. She rarely touched me, and I never wanted her to until now. Her hand was soothing like Becca's as it made circles on my back.

Mary gently pulled my body into hers, holding me the best she could while I cried like a little girl. I had so many emotions, so many feelings that I didn't know how to control or what to do with.

I felt her chest stutter, knowing tears were falling from her face as she got to hold me for the first time since either of us could remember.

"Everything will work out Tyler," she hushed. Her body was so tiny but offered so much condolence and compassion. "Let me help you through this. Nathan and Mitch too. We all need each other even more so now. Don't push us away. We all love you. Especially Becca."

I moved my hands from my face to wrap around her thin frame, my body crouched so I could put my head on her shoulder. Her smell of fancy flowery perfume reminded me of when I was little, maybe the first memory I had of her.

Sometimes she would let me sit on her bathroom counter while she got ready. I remember looking at all the different bottles of perfume and makeup, wanting to touch all of them to see what they did. She would sing as she applied the contents of the funniest looking bottles to her face and body, smiling periodically at me. She was pregnant with Mitch in this specific memory. She would rub her belly then encourage me to feel it too. Her smile was like diamonds, and I let out another ugly tear for forgetting how she looked at me as her little boy.

Then I remembered my grandmother coming in, scooping me up and taking me to the kitchen to feed me sweets or play games with me. The look on my mother's face when she did that never affected me until now. It was one of sorrow and hurt, like she was stripped of her own right as a mother.

"I love you Mom," I muffled between huffs of catching my breath and shedding tears. It was all I could say, the only way I could apologize for being such a dipshit of a son. The only thing I could do to make her realize she was important and that I was sorry I didn't put my faith in her, that I didn't fight to spend more time with her.

"Sweetie, I love you so much," she choked, squeezing me the best she could. "Don't feel guilty for anything. We can make this better from now on, okay? No more shutting out the people you love."

I nodded my head quickly, giving her another squeeze.

Once my tears subsided, I pulled away from her, feeling sheepish and less of a man for breaking down. She touched my cheek and gave me a warm smile, letting me know all was forgiven between the two of us.

I swallowed hard, my heart beating faster, needing to find Becca.

My mother sensed my anxiety then reached into her purse, pulling out a piece of paper. "I have a ticket to Grand Rapids. The flight leaves in an hour. Take it," my mother said with a knowing smile. She took out a prescription bottle as well, handing it to me. "Take these too. They'll help with your anxiety. I know a good doctor who can get you your own prescription. They'll be a life saver," she said sincerely.

Gratefully, I took the ticket and the pills from her hands, kissed her cheek then bolted out of my office without any of my things. They didn't matter right now. I needed to get to Becca as soon as possible.

Chapter Nineteen

Becca

Here I sat in my office at 10:15 p.m. at night staring at multiple sets of blueprints. I was the only one on my floor and most likely the only one in the building. Monday nights weren't really popular when it came to working late.

I rubbed my eyes with my palms, frustrated I couldn't find any correlation within each print. I wanted to find where the drugs were being hidden. Maybe if we could figure out a system Chino had then we could figure out how to either get rid of the drugs or tell Anderson.

I stood and stared, my palms now flat on my drafting table. I was beginning to feel so defeated, lost in my thoughts of how to fix things. Then out of nowhere, my heart started to calm, a sense of softness and caring rushed through my body, causing me to close my eyes.

Warm breath touched the back of my neck, along with a hand sliding between my waist and the hand that was flat on my desk. I looked down to find a familiar hand slipping a yellow rose with a ribbon attached on the prints I had been studying for what felt like hours.

"Hey," Tyler's soft and raspy voice said against my ear. I leaned back into him, craving his touch more than anything.

"I thought you were in Chicago?" I asked, the back of my head finding his chest.

"Well-" he paused, reaching for my hand and turning me to face him. His expression was different from what it had been in months. It was calm, loving, maybe even playful. "... I miss you," he finished, swiftly wrapping his hands around my waist, pulling my body so it was flush against his.

"I miss you too," I said quietly, my heart filling with emotion.

Bringing a hand to my cheek, he didn't say anything, but just gazed into my eyes like he hadn't seen me in years. "I'm sorry," he murmured, "Sorry for not being here, with you. My mind has just been..." His voice drifted as his expressions tightened on his face.

I brought my hands to his face, wanting to cradle my lost boy from any pain he had been enduring on his own. "I know, I understand. I'm here for you Ty, always," I consoled.

His smile was warm and affectionate, melting my heart like always.

I missed that smile.

He leaned in to kiss me tenderly, his arms firmly holding me to him. It was sweet and reuniting, something I had craved for months now. I knew from that kiss that we were on the upswing, that we would get through this.

Pulling his lips from mine, he smiled then turned me back around to face my drafting table and the plans I had been getting lost in the last few hours. My eyes found the single rose, making my heart flutter as it always had whenever I saw those roses. Reminiscing about how he first made amends, his compliments, his apologies... when he told me he loved me.

"I haven't brought you a rose in a while," he murmured in my ear. He kissed my shoulder while lifting the rose so I could read the tag.

Let's go away together- Ty

"Really?" I asked, a huge grin on my face as I cranked my head back to see him. His smile was infectious and wholesome.

"Yes," he whispered into my neck, followed with a nuzzle, making me giggle. Oh, how I missed his affection! "I told you I wanted a pre-honeymoon. Besides, I have a place I want to show you, but we have to wait a few weeks. I have some important potential clients I need to hook and reel." His mischievous Conklin grin spread across his face, and I couldn't help but turn to kiss him. Full out hands in hair, tugging him as close to me as physically possible with clothing between us.

His grin was huge as we kissed, his hands still wrapped around me, enjoying my need for him.

"Get. A. Room," Nathan exaggerated in disgust while walking into my office.

Tyler pulled away, throwing his head back and laughing. I blushed, hiding my head in Tyler's chest. To my surprise, Jamie walked in behind him.

My face lit up with even more happiness. "What are you doing here?" I'd seen her most of the weekend but assumed she was flying back to Miami.

She rolled her eyes dramatically. "I told you I was going to be in Grand Rapids this week. We have to finalize things with that crazy artist for ArtPrize."

I blinked, aware I didn't remember a lick of anything she just said. I wasn't surprised. I was completely out of it after our over-stimulating time at Enclave.

"What are you doing here so late?" Tyler asked, bringing my body back to his. He didn't want to let me go, and it felt comforting.

"We had a meeting," Nathan said. "We were discussing Chino."

Tyler's arms tightened around me. "Yes, we need to address that situation."

"I don't know how to get that asshole out of here. He doesn't seem to take no for an answer. I think we need to force our lawyer on him," Nathan sighed, taking a seat in one of the office chairs.

"I say we find his drugs and dump them in a large body of water," Jamie huffed while taking a seat next to him.

Nathan shook his head. "That sounds like a sure way to get ourselves killed. That man is a lunatic. I think he's using again and a lot more than any time before. I'm shocked he didn't pull a gun on us last Saturday." He glared at Tyler.

"What?" Tyler said defensively. "I'm sick of his shit. You probably wouldn't have told him we were cutting ties unless I would've almost lost my head."

Nathan laughed, then leaned forward in his chair. "Hah! Almost? Tyler you punched him in the face!"

Tyler's cocky grin radiated throughout the room. "Yeah... I got him good didn't I?"

Nathan rolled his eyes. "Purely unprofessional."

"That asshole needs more than a swift punch to the face," Tyler growled.

"I agree, but we need to fight dirty with him. Chino plays mind games. Jamie might be on to something. We find his drugs and use them against him."

I wanted to open my mouth about Anderson's morning visit. But I needed to talk to Tyler about that before anyone else. His head might seem better now, but he would only really listen clearly if it were just the two of us.

"How do we plan on doing that?" Jamie asked, baffled.

"Why don't you talk to Mitch? Maybe find out some of Chino's insights," I said. There wasn't a doubt in either Tyler or Nathan that Mitch was involved in some way.

Nathan shook his head. "Mitch won't say anything. I've tried every aspect possible."

"Yeah, the only way through his thick skull is through a woman," Tyler grumbled.

I stood up straight then glanced at Tyler. He looked at me for a moment as if reading my mind then his eyes found Jamie.

Nathan watched our interaction then a small smile played on his lips. He turned to face Jamie as well, who was playing with her nails. "Yeah, too bad we don't know any single, desirable women who could handle taking advantage of him."

All eyes were on Jamie. As though she could feel the unsaid conversations between the three of us, she looked up, eyeing each one of us slowly.

"Oh no... don't y'all give me that look," she pleaded, her Florida accent thickening. "I am NOT going out with that loser."

"Come on Jay," Nathan said, putting his arm on the back of her chair. "I'll give you a bonus."

"I don't want a fucking bonus! I'm not going out with him!"

"Jamie, we could all be in a whole heap of trouble if we don't figure this out," I said softly, glancing up at Tyler. His jaw was doing his nervous tick, and I reached my hand up to calm him.

Jamie's eyes swept back around all of us again then she groaned. "Fine! I swear to God, if he makes a move on me, I'm kicking him in the nuts."

Chapter Twenty

Tyler

Top Ten Moves To Make Her Come. This was the headline in the magazine I was reading in Becca's old apartment. No one knew, but I already subscribed to this magazine on my iPad. They gave good advice most of the time; at least I believed it was good because it worked. I'd planned on using some of it next weekend when Becca and I took our trip.

I managed to get a three day weekend for both of us. Clearing our schedules wasn't always easy, but I knew we needed to get away.

Our relationship had been better, but I still had business to attend to in Chicago the past week. I couldn't swap with Nathan because he would be mainly in Miami. Tonight was the first time Becca and I had seen each other in over a week.

Becca was helping Jamie get ready for her date with Mitch. Jamie was being a poor sport, complaining there was no way Mitch would tell her anything and how he would never leave her alone after tonight. I guess he'd been hitting on her constantly since she had been stationed in Miami, making landing a date with him easy.

Both girls came walking down the hall, Jamie's heels clicking loudly on the hardwood. My brother would eat her up in her short tight dress, but she didn't compare to my Becs and her little shorts and comfy t-shirt. Becca's hair was pulled back in a messy bun, and her face was fresh without makeup, just how I liked it.

I threw the magazine down, not wanting them to know my secret as they approached me. "You look like Mitch won't be able to keep his hands off you," I teased.

Jamie narrowed her eyes at me. "I meant what I said. If he touches me, he won't ever be able to have children."

Becca laughed. "Maybe we should put a cardigan on you and dress pants."

"No, because a girl only gets what she wants if she looks the part. How else am I supposed to tempt him into telling me what I want to know if I don't seduce him a little?"

"Jamie, I think you are underestimating your ability to control my little brother. There isn't that much going on up there," I smiled, pointing a finger to my head.

She let out a growl and stomped to the kitchen the best she could with her dangerous shoes. I never understood why woman put themselves through wearing those things.

The buzzer rang, letting us know Mitch was here.

"Okay, put on your game face. What do you have to do?" I asked, standing from the couch.

"Try and get Mitch to spill about the RJ bricks. Find out if he's working with anyone on the side and where and how many properties," she answered as if I were an idiot.

I nodded my head, wrapping an arm around Becca's waist.

We heard a knock at the door, and Becca left my side to open the door for Mitch.

To no surprise, he showed in jeans and a button shirt with boots. No flowers. I shook my head. How did he ever expect to charm a woman this way? I guess it didn't matter to him; he wasn't looking for the one, only the one night. I felt slightly guilty for throwing Jamie into this situation.

"Hey Becca," he greeted, giving her too friendly of a hug. I cleared my throat as I gave him the death glare.

Mitch looked passed Becca's shoulder and gave me a smirk. Ass.

"Surprised to see you here, Tyler. This isn't a double date, is it?" he asked, showing concern.

Jamie walked from around the island loudly. "Nope. Just you and me," she said, popping her lips.

Mitch's eyes grew wide as he took her in, and I knew he was thinking the same as any other warm blooded male. My guilt for Jamie just doubled. She might have a hard time fighting him off her leg by the end of the night.

"You look amazing," Mitch said.

"Thank you." Jamie smiled then turned to roll her eyes at me. I stifled a laugh and shrugged my shoulders. "What do you have planned?" she asked, batting her eyelashes in Mitch's direction.

Mitch licked his lips, proving Jamie might be able to pull off our plan. "Let me tell you on the way out," he flirted, actually holding the door open for her. He gave a wink with his sleazy grin, and I only shook my head in disgust.

Becs came back to my side, wrapping her arms around my waist. "Have fun! Be good to my best friend!" she called after Mitch.

He gave another wink to Becca as he closed the door.

"We owe her big time for this," Becca said, nestling her head into my shoulder.

"Yeah, we'll think of something," I said, rubbing her back with my arm. "I just hope it'll be worth it."

I sensed her thinking then pulled her away so I could look at her. "What's wrong?"

She shook her head then headed back towards the kitchen. "Nothing. I bought ingredients to make fish tacos. Does that sound good?"

I nodded my head, following her into the kitchen.

***

After cleaning the mess from dinner, we settled ourselves on the couch, waiting like anxious parents for Jamie to come home.

"Dinner was great," I murmured, touching my lips to her hair. I inhaled the smell of her shampoo, feeling calm and collected. It was a big change from my normal anxiety.

"I'm glad you liked it. I enjoy feeding you," she smiled, running her hands along my full stomach.

I wrapped my arm around her shoulder, enjoying the small and rare moment of peace between us. Is this what our Saturday nights were going to be like? Cuddled on the couch, gentle caresses and conversation? If so, I could really get used to it.

"Our schedules are set for next weekend. I hope you don't mind me talking to Will for you."

"No, it's fine. Where are we going?"

"Somewhere that means a lot to me," I said, swallowing for a moment before I continued. "My family has a cottage in the Upper Peninsula on Lake Superior. I thought it would be nice to disappear for a few days."

Becca turned to me and smiled. "I'd love that. What days?"

"Friday through Sunday. We'd be back in time for work on Monday." She slowly brought her hand to my chest, tracing circles with her finger. Her eyes wouldn't meet mine. Something else was on her mind. "Spill the beans, baby," I said in a teasing tone.

She glanced back to my eyes from my chest then continued her pattern. "Will you be here on Thursday night? I'm supposed to do the food tasting for the caterer for the final menu. It'd be nice to have your opinion." Her voice was small, acting as though it wasn't a big deal even though it probably would mean the world to her if I could come.

"I can probably make it. Did you not think I'd want to come?" I asked with concern.

Her smile didn't meet her eyes when she looked at me. "No, I just didn't know if you'd make time. You haven't shown interest whenever I mention anything about the wedding."

I furrowed my brows, not really knowing what to say. "It's your special day."

"No, it's our special day."

"You're right. It is our special day. But what matters to me most is that you're happy with everything. I'll love whatever you choose," I reassured her, rubbing my nose with hers. My absence the past few months made her lose faith in me and that sick, guilty feeling went straight to my gut.

She let out a soft smile but still wouldn't meet my eyes.

"Tell me about everything you've chosen so far," I said, sitting up straighter on the couch to give her my full, undivided attention.

She sat up alongside me, a hesitant look on her face. "Really?"

I nodded my head in all seriousness.

"Do you want to see the wedding book?" she asked, even more puzzled.

Oh boy, there was a book. "Yeah. Show me."

She bit her lip then stood, walking towards her old room. "Let me get it."

When Becca came back, her face was brighter. The book she was carrying was massive, making my eye twitch.

"We don't have to do this," she said, a bit of life fading from her eyes. I shook my head, pulling her to sit down next to me.

"I want to. Show me."

She smiled brightly again, getting cozy next to me while crossing her legs. Once she opened the book, my eyes went wide. There were magazine pictures, color swatches, printed pictures of everything wedding related. Pamphlets and business cards, spreadsheets with finances. Becca was more in to this than I thought.

She smiled widely when talking about each subject from the cake to the DJ.

"We should set a time to meet with the DJ, soon. He's been hounding me about songs. And so has the wedding planner about our vows" she sighed. I frowned. My lack of involvement was stressing her out. More guilt passed through me. "Don't take it the wrong way, but I wanted to keep them traditional."

"That's fine," I agreed quickly. I loved Becca more than anything, but I liked telling only her. Spilling my guts in front of 600 people didn't sound fun to me. Becca and I were personal and quiet. No one needed to see my emotions for my wife.

My wife.

My heart sped faster at the thought. Becca was going to be my wife in a month's time.

She continued going through the book but quickly passed through the wedding dress portion.

"Hey, I want to see that," I teased, reaching for the book.

"No! You have to wait!" she scolded, pulling the book from my reach.

"Oh, come on, Becs. A picture won't do it justice. I probably won't even remember the photo," I teased, reaching across her lap.

She shoved my chest with her free hand, holding the book as far away from me as she could. "No!" Becca giggled. Instead of trying to grab the book, now I was tickling her sides, making her shriek, flailing her arms and legs. I pinned her to the couch, laughing along with her.

I studied her beautiful features as she laughed underneath me, realizing how lucky I was to have her. Once her giggles subsided, she met my gaze, her smile still wide as I moved a stray strand of hair from her face.

"What?" she asked, matching my grin.

"I can't wait to see you in your wedding dress," I murmured, still brushing the hair from her forehead.

She raised a brow in question.

"I think... seeing you in that dress, walking towards me... is the biggest fantasy I've ever had. I think about it a lot."

Her smile faded and wonder was heavy in her eyes.

"And of course I can't wait to see what's underneath it," I joked, causing her to roll her eyes and laugh again.

We stayed like that, gazing at each other. I must have looked drunk with love because I couldn't stop smiling at her. She reached her hands so they were cradling my face.

"Will you keep this," she whispered, running her hands along my thicker stubble.

"You really like it, don't you?" I asked. She had seen my beard a lot lately. It only took a few days to grow and typically every Sunday it was a full on beard.

She nodded her head, her look becoming deeper. She bit her lip, and I couldn't help but follow her lead. Becca's lips found mine and tenderly locked together, slowly moving in a grateful way. Kissing her like this felt amazing and well needed. We hadn't taken our time together, cherished each other in so long. This was my fault, and I couldn't wait to have a normal schedule together. That was my next project. Figuring out how I could stay in Grand Rapids and be with my Becs more.

Becca's tongue swept into my mouth, sweetly entangling with mine. I was getting excited but was enjoying the innocent vibe we were taking. We loved kissing and touching, really awakening our depth of feelings for one another.

Just as things were going to heat up, Becca slowly pulled her face from mine, her breathing heavier than before. "We should wait until Jamie gets home," she whispered, biting her lip while looking back into my eyes. "Then we can go to my room."

Tilting my head, I reluctantly agreed, resituating so we were both sitting upright. I pulled her close to my side, my arms firmly wrapped around her as she continued going through her wedding book.

Our wedding book.

***

My eyelids were heavy as I kinked my neck, the sunbeams seeping in through the half drawn blinds. I was slouched on the couch, Becca sprawled across my chest. After rubbing my eyes with my palm, I checked my watch. It was 7:30 a.m.

Did we really fall asleep out here? I hadn't slept that hard in a while. Maybe it was the prescription I just started taking this week. How did we not hear Jamie come back? And why didn't she wake us?

I lay my head back further into the couch cushion, attempting to stretch my neck the best I could without waking Becca. She felt so peaceful, and I enjoyed her cozy on my chest.

Just as I was about to drift again, the door creaked open, and a disheveled Jamie tiptoed across the hardwood floor in escape to her room.

"What happened?" I heard Becca's morning voice accuse.

Jamie stopped dead in her tracks, not turning to face either of us. "Nothing. I didn't get any information out of him. Sorry."

Becca quickly sat up, fussing with her hair. "Jay, are you just getting home?" she questioned.

"Um… yeah," Jamie muffled. Both Becca and I waited for her to continue talking, but she said nothing and proceeded to her room.

"Jamie!" Becca called, standing from the couch and following her down the hall.

I raised a brow. Holy shit, did she spend the night with Mitch? I shook my head, trying to contain my smirk. Poor Jamie, making the walk of shame.

Running my hands through my hair, I made my way to the kitchen, rummaging through the fridge to find something to cook for breakfast. Never fails, eggs are always in the fridge. I kept searching to find other ingredients to add, warming the pan then chopping veggies.

By the time I was almost done cooking the veggies, Becca padded her way to the kitchen, her arms crossed and heavy in thought. She took a seat at the island, staring at her hands, a small smile creeping across her face.

"Well?" I finally asked.

Becca looked my way then shook her head. "She didn't get any information out of him."

I cocked a brow at her, waiting for her to say more. "Is that all?"

"Yep."

Chuckling, I turned back to the skillet, stirring and flipping the egg mixture. My Becs was one loyal girl.

Chapter Twenty-One

Becca

Our weekend was finally here. Tyler and I were going to spend the next 72 hours together. Alone. No interruptions, no RJ bricks, no crazy detectives or drug dealers bothering us. This weekend Tyler and I were going to shut off our phones and reconnect before the wedding.

The wedding was shockingly in order. Everything was scheduled and planned, merely waiting for the day to come. We had three weeks until the big day. Three weeks until Tyler and I were married. Giddiness ran through my veins as I thought about having him be completely mine.

Tyler's mood was better. He was calling me more, asking about wedding details, telling me he loved me and couldn't wait to be married. His anxiety attacks were fewer, only happening in the night. I'd hold him to my chest, rubbing his back and shoulders, smoothing his hair with my hands, kissing his forehead and cheeks until he'd calm down.

The psychiatrist was helping. Of all the people, his mother recommended someone based in Chicago. Some nights, I would give him a Xanax to help him calm if I couldn't do it myself. Tyler seemed to be healing, and I was relieved.

I tried not to be disappointed in his lack of ability to confide in me. Tyler wouldn't talk about the psychiatrist but acted as though he never went. He was embarrassed, but I was so thankful he had been making the appointments. I knew it would take time for him to open up to me, and we had the rest of our lives.

"Ready?" Tyler asked as he tossed one last bag into the back of the Lexus LX.

Nodding my head enthusiastically, I stood on my tip toes to give him a kiss on the cheek, putting my hands in the back pockets of his jeans. His Conklin grin made an appearance as I squeezed his butt. Seeing Tyler dressed casually in jeans and a t-shirt made my insides tingle. Reluctantly pulling my hands from him, I hopped inside.

"This is a good way to celebrate your birthday," I giggled.

Tyler rolled his eyes as he closed my car door. "It's about a six hour drive," Tyler said as he slid into his side of the car, completely ignoring my birthday comment.

I ran my hand along his thigh. "Is that why you made me get up so early?"

"Yes. I want to make it to Mackinaw City for lunch. I haven't eaten there since I was a little boy," his smile faded and his face became somber. Was he having a flashback?

"I can't wait for you to show me. I haven't been to the bridge since I was young either, Tyler." I traced his knee with my fingers. Tyler took my hand in his and kissed my knuckles, still holding the same bleak expression.

We went between small talk and silence, and that was okay. A few weeks ago Tyler would have been stone faced and put off the entire ride. My Ty needed to take this slow, and I would be beside him through the journey.

The weather at Mackinaw was shockingly warm for being mid September. Sunny and 75 degrees made me wish I would've worn shorts or a skirt instead of jeans. Tyler put his aviators on as we walked to find something to eat. I enjoyed him grabbing my hand and leading the way, another aspect that helped me to feel we were moving forward from the death of his father.

The town wasn't very busy. Most tourists were getting back into their fall routines. Stepping into Dixie's Saloon, I took in the rustic, log cabin environment. We were one of three customers and the waitress was anxious to seat us.

"Want to split some cheese curds?" Tyler asked.

My focus derailed from the menu to raise a brow at him. He laughed when he saw my expression.

"I hate cheese curds," he smiled. "I just like to get a rile out of you."

I shook my head and continued to look over the menu.

"I'm going to get the fish and chips. Something greasy sounds good." He folded his menu and contently looked at me. "What are you going to get?"

"Probably a salad. I have a wedding dress to fit in to," I said still examining my choices.

"Fine… but you still need more meat on your bones. I was inspecting you from behind as we walked inside," he flirted.

Oh, I missed this fun, playful side of my Ty.

"I should say the same to you," I said playfully back, although I was serious. He was thinner. I understood how hard it was to eat when your mind was elsewhere, so I didn't like to bug him about not eating.

"Hence the fish and chips," he smirked. "Watch out, I'm going to let myself go when we get married. I hope you'll still love me with a beer gut."

I practically snorted into my menu. "Well, I am only marrying you for your charmingly good looks," I sighed.

His lip quirked. "Wow… and I thought it was because of my money?" he teased again, reaching across the table for my hand.

I shook my head at him, reminding myself he was only joking. He knew I didn't care about money.

Setting down the menu and holding his hand with both of mine, I looked him in the eyes. "When I say our vows, I'll mean them. I'm looking forward to sitting with you on a porch, gray-haired and barely moving. I love your mind and personality, and if it happens, your beer gut will be loved just as much."

A grateful smile crossed his lips. "Same to you Becs. It's okay if you don't count every calorie and skip the gym from time to time. I love you for you, no matter what. I'll be turned on by your body, even when I can't get it up."

We both laughed. While staring at our hands intertwined, I knew he was telling me the truth. Tyler loved me with stretch marks and love handles, and I didn't have to be physically perfect for him.

***

Napping in the car with a full belly was way too easy. Maybe that's why the last few hours flew by. It was a good thing because the only scenery was woods. I probably would have been constantly checking the gas gauge, worried because I didn't think there were any gas stations close by.

I stretched my arms as we pulled into a very wooded driveway.

"Sleep well?" Tyler asked as he patted my thigh. I nodded my head and groaned, blinking a few times as I tried to wake from my nap.

"The cabin is a few miles down. I hope you like it."

Finally, the trees partially cleared and a small, wooden cabin appeared.

"It's probably not what you were expecting, but I have a lot of memories here," Tyler said quietly as he unbuckled his seat belt.

Stepping out of the car, I took in the humble cabin. "I think it's wonderful. I'm looking forward to hearing your memories."

His grin faded slightly, as he thought intently about something. Shaking his head as though riding his memories, he went to the back of the Lexus and grabbed our bags. I followed him, reaching for the few groceries we packed.

Tyler unlocked the door, nervously ushering me inside.

The cabin was smaller than it looked on the outside. The walls were actual logs, with a fireplace in the center of the one main room with a few beat up couches. A shelf with unorganized games and books was shoved in the corner. The kitchen was a part of the big room, only a few cupboards and refrigerator and stove, no microwave or dishwasher.

The only table in the room was petite and round, four chairs clustered around it.

My smile grew wide. I loved this cabin. It was everything you'd imagine Tyler wasn't by his expensive suits and cars. Turning to meet his beautiful, worrisome face, I whispered, "This is perfect."

This cabin was the Tyler I grew to love, the basketball shorts and t-shirts Tyler. The guy who wouldn't shave or do his hair the entire weekend while we lounged because he really didn't care. Tyler was more laid back than most people assumed.

His nerves washed away as he met my smile. "Let me show you the loft."

I nodded, dropping the groceries and following Tyler up the open stairs. The lack of railing made me uneasy. He dropped our bags on the floor in the wedged space to the side of the full size bed. A flowery patterned comforter with matching pillow cases covered the bed. There wasn't a headboard or matching furniture and only one dresser with a mirror attached. A picture of who I'd assumed were Tyler's grandparents with him and his two brothers was taped to the mirror.

"Hope you don't mind cuddling at night," he murmured, referring to the small bed.

I wrapped my arms around his waist. "I guess I could put up with it." We both laughed but then my smile faded. "Wait, there is a bathroom, right?"

Tyler slowly shook his head, no, and my eyes went wide. His lip twitched, giving away he couldn't lie to me.

Smacking his chest, I said, "That's not funny!"

He laughed whole heartedly again then led me back downstairs. "I'm sorry but yes, there's a bathroom. Wow, you should have seen your face, Becs."

The bathroom was as tiny as a bathroom could be, a simple standup shower, toilet, and pedestal sink. "We're going to have to cuddle in the shower, too," Tyler murmured in my ear, his hands finding my waist. "The other bedroom is over here, but it only has a couple of bunk beds."

"Where you slept when you were younger?"

He nodded his head as I walked into the room. The bunk beds took up most the space. Envisioning Tyler and his brothers rambunctiously picking which bed they'd sleep in, excited to be away from the busy city life, made my insides warm.

"Let me show you the lake," Tyler smiled, pulling me out of the room. The slider to the back deck stuck and took Tyler a few moments to crank it open.

I nearly lost my breath with the view.

It was... so, beautiful.

The water was crystal clear. I hadn't realized the cabin was on an inlet of the lake. We could see Pictured Rocks about a half mile out. The beach had only a few feet of sand

and was covered in stones from Lake Superior. Tyler reached down to pick one up, throwing it across the water making it skip.

"This is wonderful, Ty. Look at the rocks!" I said enthusiastically.

Tyler turned to me and smiled as he bent down to pick up another rock. "We can take the kayaks to get a better look if you want."

My smile widened along with his. "Yes! That'd be so cool!"

Tyler laughed and skipped his stone then pulled me to his side. "I never would have pegged you for an outdoorsy girl."

My smile straightened. "I can guarantee you I'm not," I said seriously then my smile shyly returned. "But this place is important to you, and I want an insight on a young Tyler. A Tyler who isn't all business and numbers."

His face relaxed, but his features still seemed tight. I reached my hand to caress his jaw, enjoying the neatly trimmed beard that took place on his face. "I love all sides of you Ty, but this side doesn't come out too often," I whispered.

Tyler's arms wrapped around my waist, pulling me tight to his chest while his chin found my hair. "Lately I don't even know who I am," he murmured into my hair.

My heart nearly shattered at his broken expression. "You'll find yourself again," I whispered into his chest. "And I know I'll be even more in love with you when it happens."

His grip tightened on me as he buried his face into my neck, his actions speaking louder than his words.

***

Oranges, pinks, and purples filled the skyline as Tyler built a fire. The scenery of the woods and crystal clear lake was breathtaking with the sunset molding them together. Except my view kept getting distracted by my hand swatting bugs out of my face.

"Once the fire's lit, the bugs won't be as bad," Tyler laughed.

I swatted another bug away, crinkling my nose in discomfort. We had an awesome day in nature, but I was a true city girl. Thankfully, we were only staying a few nights.

The afternoon had been perfect. We cruised in the kayaks around the inlet, taking in the beauty of Pictured Rocks. I was amazed by how clear the water was as I saw fish swimming at least 40 feet below me. The other scenery was pretty distracting as well. Tyler using his strong arms to row his kayak, his jaw ticking as he was deep in thought. He looked beyond yummy, even in his backwards Cubs hat.

To be honest, he was looking pretty scrumptious right now. He was cutting wood, using those same strong arms. I couldn't help but lick my lips, watching him, enjoying the veins in his forearms flex against his muscles.

I pouted when he was done and watched as he fiddled with how the chopped wood should be placed in the fire pit. Once Tyler was pleased with his handy work, he took a seat next to me on an old, pine swing. His arm made its way behind me on the back of the swing.

"Nice fire," I complimented.

He glanced in my direction, his Conklin grin sneaking towards the side of his mouth. "I guess you would know since you couldn't take your eyes off it."

A blush crept to my cheeks. I had been caught ogling him.

"You get to make the fire tomorrow night. Naked," he teased. I laughed and snuggled into his chest.

The flames of the fire danced as the warm colors of the sky began to fade into darkness. The air was calm and peaceful, so different from the city life we were used to.

Tyler's hand methodically rubbed my shoulder to my bicep as he watched the fire. I peeked up at him, watching the shadows of the fire dance along his face. Something was troubling him again.

"Penny for your thoughts?" I asked.

Tyler was quiet for a moment then shook his head. "I was just thinking about when I came here as a kid."

The fire crackled as I patiently waited for him to say more.

"I think I was about three the first time I remember coming here. Nathan was so excited throughout the car ride. I was too, mainly because Nathan was. Life has always been so fast paced, and when we came here everyone went slower. My papa would sit and fish while we played on the beach. My nan would collect rocks with us." He paused, thinking intently. "So many memories have been coming back to me," he whispered.

"Good memories?" I cautiously asked.

He didn't say anything at first then nervously laughed. "Both. I um... I remember missing my mom."

I studied him intently, trying to grasp what he was feeling.

"Did she ever come here with you?"

He shook his head no. "When I was showing you around, I remembered waking up at night wanting her. My gran would come in and try to soothe me, but I only wanted my mom." I could barely hear his voice because it was so soft. "I just remember nan telling me how my mom didn't want to come with me, and that she wouldn't play on the beach with me if she were here anyway."

He looked so troubled and hurt.

Tyler's chest started to rise and fall faster. "We should bring your mom with us next time. I bet she'd like that," I murmured, tracing a circle with my fingertips on his chest.

His eyes closed as he took a deep breath. "Maybe."

More silence passed between us as Tyler's breathing slowed back to normal. Just when I thought Tyler was going to be done talking about his childhood memories, he began to speak again.

"I wonder if my mom wanted to come, but RJ wouldn't let her," he said quietly, his hand stopping on my shoulder. A slight laugh escaped his lips, "Or my grandparents wouldn't let her."

I furrowed my eyebrows at him. "What do you mean?"

He shrugged his shoulders then continued rubbing my shoulder and bicep. "What do you want to do tomorrow?" he asked while sighing.

I frowned at his change of subject but didn't push him to keep talking.

"Doesn't matter. As long as neither of us is working."

I sensed Tyler's grin. We left our phones in the car for a reason. I'm sure we'd eventually go check them for emergencies, but I didn't want Tyler to hole up in the cabin, stuck on the phone with a client or the office.

"I doubt we'll have good service anyway. Might have to find a bar so we can watch the Cubs game," he teased, pulling me closer to him.

I groaned loudly.

"The Tigers play tomorrow too. Would that convince you to go find a television somewhere?"

"I guess," I sighed dramatically.

Tyler laughed, pulling me on his lap with both arms so I was straddling him. I squealed by his sudden movement, grabbing his biceps to steady my balance. We both were laughing from his playfulness, but the air quickly turned thick, immobilizing our laughter into passion.

Heat rushed through me as our eyes met, dilating into one another. Tyler slowly bit his bottom lip then released it as his eyes locked onto my mouth.

We hadn't been intimate in a while. His head wasn't there, and I hadn't had the urge to push him until now. I knew he was worried about hurting me, worried his emotions would get the best of him. He always wanted to be gentle with me, cherish me. The thought of grabbing onto me and pounding his frustrations and confusions into me terrified him. At first I wanted him to use me for a means to escape his own demons, but now I understood. He did that for ten years with Margo, and our relationship was so much more than that. Mixing the two together was sickening, and I was all for giving Tyler space until he could control his emotions. And he was getting better, maybe enough for us to rekindle on a physical level.

My sex was aligned perfectly with his, and I'm sure one, tender, kiss would cause the space between us to disappear. I was throbbing to move, the ache low in my belly wanting me to make that simple gesture with my hips.

Tyler's chest started to rise faster as his grip around my back tightened. I brought my forehead to his, silently praying he was ready, and hoping my body wouldn't push him to do something he'd regret.

Moving my lips so they were barely a centimeter apart from his, I waited for him to make that final move. Our breath was intermingling, building a frenzy of lust that I couldn't control any longer.

I moved my mouth to his, sucking hard on his bottom lip. His groan of pleasure vibrated through me, causing my hips to move downward on his lap. Tyler's hands held a firm grip on my waist, finding their way up the back of my shirt, fiddling with the strap of my bra.

Our heads automatically shifted the opposite directions, our mouths opening wider for our tongues to dip and dance with each other. My hands found his face, one creeping up to tug his hair while the other cradled his jaw.

Just as my hand was contemplating finding the inside of his shorts, Tyler slowly pulled away, his eyes closed, but his hands still firmly placed on my back. The struggle was obvious on his face by how his eyes were screwed shut and the heavy breaths coming from his nose as his nostrils flared.

I gulped, fighting the urge to feel disappointed that our kissing was about to come to an end instead of building into passion.

Tyler's head suddenly jerked back to mine, finding my mouth hungrily again. His desire was stronger now, his hands pressing harder into my back. I whimpered from his unexpected drive, but he misunderstood my cry.

"I'm sorry," he gasped, catching his breath, his hands moving like lightning from under my shirt to the wood of the swing.

My hands gripped his face; my head drastically shaking back and forth. "No, no, I liked it, please, don't stop."

His eyes searched mine as his jaw ticked. Tyler's hands slowly found my thighs, making their way back to my waist as he continued but with slow, tender kisses.

The feeling of his lips caressing mine so lovingly, his hands moving in a simple rhythm up and down my spine, made my heart pound faster in my chest.

My hands gripped his hair tighter, my hips pressing into his reaction further, making it blatantly obvious what I wanted.

Tyler grabbed my thighs, standing from the swing in one fluid swoop, carrying me back towards the cabin, our mouths never separating.

My back bumped into the screen as Tyler struggled to open the slider, holding me close with one arm. I moved my mouth down to his neck, nipping at his collarbone.

His breath was harsher now, letting out a frustrated grunt as he finally got the door open. Tyler nuzzled into my neck, his mouth sucking furiously on my skin as we made our way up the stairs to the loft. The lights were off, and our bodies would randomly hit objects on the way.

Finally reaching the bed, Tyler set me down gently, his body pressing into mine. Our lips locked again, hands feverishly pulling at his shirt. I swore I could have ripped it right off him.

Grabbing the back of his shirt, Tyler pulled it over his head as my hands greedily swept over his chest and stomach. The ripples of muscles were so hard and taut, I wanted to trace my tongue along each line. Before I got the chance, Tyler tore my sweatshirt over my head, my tank top along with it. His hot breath traveled down my neck to my collarbone, his tongue anxiously dipping into the cup of my bra. He was so close, and I groaned, arching my back, wanting him to meet my skin with his soft tongue.

Fighting him long enough to yank my bra over my head, I laid back down, pulling his face back to my sensitive skin. The sucking and the nibbling felt like heaven, and I never wanted it to stop.

Then he bit a touch harder, his arms wrapping underneath my back, squeezing me tightly. It felt amazing, and I knew it did because of my state of mind. His teeth tugged on my skin again, and I knew it would leave a mark. Not wanting to upset him, I forcefully rolled so I was on top of him, taking control.

I kissed down his chest while I held his forearms on either side of his head. Strangled moans escaped his mouth the further down my tongue traveled. I kissed him through his shorts, running my nose along his length.

He quickly sat up while taking a sharp breath, grabbing my wrists from his forearms. "Don't tease me, Becca. Not tonight. It's been way too long," he groaned, yanking me upward and claiming my mouth with his.

His grip on my wrists was like vices, and I struggled to free my hands. I wanted to hold him, not let him hold me down. As bad as I wanted aggressive, teeth clenching, and controlling sex with Tyler, I knew it would only end badly in the morning.

Finally pulling my hands free, I cradled his face, slowing down his demanding and urgent kisses. His heaving chest slowed some, but his hands were still roughly holding me, pressing me as close to him as possible. His erection was digging into me. I needed him deep inside, my calm and soothing hands turning frantic, pulling off my shorts then tugging wildly at his.

Tyler grunted and released me, helping me rip his shorts and boxers off completely. Before I could mount him like I had planned, he flipped me to my back, wedging himself in between my legs. The shadows in his face were laced with lust and need as his desire filled eyes locked with mine.

I whimpered from his stare, my heart pumping blood loudly throughout my body. Every nerve was on edge, and I felt the second he'd enter me, I was going to explode and never stop.

Grabbing my palms tightly and pinning me to the bed, Tyler's breath was hot on my lips. "Becca, I love you so much."

I groaned at his declaration and lifted my mouth to meet harshly with his, my tongue swirling and pulling him into me. Finally, his hips thrust forward, entering me forcefully and sharply. My moan vibrated through our kiss. Tyler pulled away, his ragged breath rumbling into my neck as he pushed deeper into me.

I gripped his hands, digging my nails into his skin, wanting him to drive harder. "Tyler," I moaned, meeting his hips roughly with my own. "I'm so close."

He cursed under his breath, raising his hips higher and pumping faster. The angle his hips were taking and the arch of my back gave his mouth direct contact with my heavy breasts. The second his mouth clamped on to one, I came, spiraling hard and fast. My body twitched and trembled as he kept his steady pace, carrying my orgasm further and further. My moans were high pitched and pleading now, fearing I'd never see the end of this miraculous oblivion Tyler brought me into.

With five or six hard and unsteady thrusts, Tyler was grunting into my chest, his mouth still clamped down on my breast. Our moans peeked together, making me thankful we were miles away from anyone else. Tyler's jaw twitched as he slowly took his mouth from my skin, his breath fast and inconsistent. I could feel his heart hammering against my abdomen, and I'm sure mine was thumping loudly in his ear.

"That was incredible," I sighed in deep breaths.

Tyler nodded his head into my chest. After our breathing calmed, I felt his soft, gentle kisses along my chest. "I bit you too hard, didn't I?" Tyler gulped, rolling to my side while caressing my breasts as if to give them comfort. "Fuck," he mumbled under his breath, holding his head low in shame.

I rolled to face him, barely being able to see his face because it was so dark. "What part of incredible didn't you understand? Ty, I don't mind if you're a little rough when we make love. The way you hold me so tight and put so much passion into us... it's so hot. I feel unbelievably loved."

If I had to guess, his eyes were as big as saucers. "I never want to hurt you, Becca. I love you so much."

Tyler Conklin stole my heart, and I fell recklessly in love with him. He cared about me so much more than his own self, and that made me realize just how undeserving I was of his love.

But he wanted me.

Cared for me.

Tyler loved me, and I was going to do everything I could to keep him safe. I was going to do everything in my power to be deserving of this humble and broken man that I adored and cherished more than my own life.

Because I needed him.

I craved him.

We belonged together, forever. Even if the most dangerous man in Grand Rapids was doing everything in his power to destroy my Ty.

To destroy us.

I wouldn't let it happen. The villain wouldn't break what I've fought so hard to find.

Chapter Twenty-Two

Tyler

"Tyler, he's trying," Nathan exasperated.

"No, he's not! I'm so sick of everyone saying that! He's not trying!" I shouted. "This bull shit business deal has gone far enough," I said through clenched teeth. I shoved past Nathan and stormed out of his office.

"Cooper!" I heard Nathan yell from behind me.

I pounded on RJ's office door.

"Tyler, you're being irrational right now. Calm down before you talk to him," Nathan tried to convince me.

I hit the door harder with both fists. "RJ, open the fucking door!" I yelled.

"Buddy, it's not worth it. Don't lose your head," Cooper said on my other side.

"RJ!" I shouted again. I was going to break the fucking door down. I grabbed the door handles, figuring they would jiggle from being locked, but shockingly they clicked free.

"RJ I swear to God—" I lost my voice and my train of thought as the doors flew open.

The puddle of blood streaming out from under RJ's desk caused my breath to hitch, but the bullet in his forehead stole my breath completely.

"Oh my God," Nathan gasped, sprinting towards RJ's desk. "RJ! Wake up!" Nathan yelled, shaking RJ's lifeless, hunched over body. "Dad!"

My feet wouldn't move as I watched Nathan drastically try to stir RJ awake. Cooper jolted past me to the other side of

RJ, tugging him to the ground. "We have to start CPR," he said firmly to Nathan as he positioned RJ on his back.

My eyes were fixated on the puddle of blood making its way towards my expensive shoes. The thumping of Cooper's palms on RJ's chest rang like the pulse in my ears.

Holy fuck, blood... so much blood.

Nathan flung his coat off, kneeling next to RJ. "Come on, you asshole... wake up!" His head swung in my direction. "Tyler, call 911, NOW!"

I couldn't move my hands to my pockets. I couldn't move my feet from the oncoming blood. I couldn't even move my jaw from its detached position.

"TYLER!" Nathan shouted.

I shook my head, my unsteady hands fumbling as I tried to retrieve my phone from my pocket.

As I dialed 911, Cooper and Nathan switched places. "Come on," Nathan's voice cracked.

My nerves took over as the phone rang. Nathan's voice didn't crack; it never cracked. He was always so sure of everything.

"911 what's your emergency?"

My lips trembled as my eyes watched Nathan shift so his pants were completely in RJ's blood.

"911, what's your emergency?" the teleprompter said more forcefully.

I shook my head to bring me back to what was happening. "Yes, someone's been shot. Downtown at the Conklin building. The top floor. Please, come quickly." I dropped the phone on the floor, directly in RJ's blood.

I took a quick step to the side, not realizing what I had just done.

"Come on, RJ!" Nathan's hands were drastically pumping, his chest beginning to shudder with each thrust. "Dad, come on! Please!"

Cooper pushed Nathan out of the way, continuing the process.

"Tyler, come take a turn."

I heard my name, but I couldn't move. My eyes were fixed on RJ and the giant bullet wound that blew off part of his head.

"Tyler!"

"Tyler!"

My body bolted upright, my chest feeling like a python was wrapped around it. I couldn't breathe. I was suffocating, my heart pounding so fast it felt like a hammer continually banging a nail through a board.

"Tyler! Baby, it was just a dream," Becca's soft voice said. It only barely registered as I gasped for air. "Just breathe," she soothed again, her hands tentatively wrapping around my back and chest.

My hands were gripping the sheets on either side of me so tightly that my knuckles must have been whiter than snow. *Damn it, where is all the oxygen in my lungs?*

"Have you taken your pills?" she asked calmly.

My head shook rapidly back and forth. I hadn't taken any in almost two days. Becca and I had been making such happy memories that I didn't need them. Maybe I should have kept a small amount in my system.

"Where are they?" she asked, running her fingers along my spine.

I blinked rapidly, trying to think where the prescription bottle was. "I... I... I think..." I gulped, moving my hand to my chest. Fuck, I couldn't calm down. The brick in my chest was making breathing and thinking impossible.

"Are they in the car? Your bag? Did you unpack them in the medicine cabinet in the bathroom?"

I nodded my head rapidly at her last statement.

"The medicine cabinet?" she confirmed.

I nodded my head again, bringing both hands to the back of my neck, pulling my head in between my legs.

She quickly stood, turning on the light by the stairs as she made her way to the bathroom.

Just as I was going to look up, she was already by my side of the bed, unscrewing the cap to the Xanax.

"Here, take two. Put them under your tongue," she commanded, her thumb finding my lip to help open my mouth. She dropped the pills into my mouth then pulled my head to her chest. She ran her fingers up and down my arms, kissing my forehead and whispering that I was going to be okay.

After a few minutes, the medicine kicked in, and I could finally breath again. I was in a cold sweat, goose bumps forming on my arms. Becca pulled me so we were laying down, my head still on her chest.

As much as this moment comforted me, it bothered the hell out of me at the same time. I felt like such a pussy, my fiancé holding me like I was some little toddler having a night terror.

Mine was a nightmare... completely different.

"Do you want another one?" Becca asked gently, running her hands through my hair.

I shook my head no, pulling away from her.

"No... I'm sorry I woke you," I mumbled, grabbing the pillow and hugging it to my chest.

Becca pulled on my bicep, forcing me to turn to face her. "Don't hide from me, Tyler."

I sighed, debating if I should tell her about my dream.

"Tell me why you had an anxiety attack. Maybe talking about it would help. I know I'm not your phsyciatrist, but..."

I groaned, rolling to my back, rubbing my face with my hand.

"I'm sorry, I know you don't like talking about going—"

"I hate that I have to see one of those doctors, okay? I hate that I have fucking panic attacks and have to be coddled like some little kid. It's embarrassing, Becca," I grumbled while interrupting her.

She sat up straight, pulling my hands from my face. I didn't like that she could see my expression because of the light. I liked being able to hide in the dark.

"You should never be embarrassed by needing to talk to someone. The doctor has helped you."

"No, the medicine has helped me. Do you know how awful it is sitting in a room with your mother spilling her guts to you for an hour? Feeling like a complete asshole for ignoring and resenting her your entire life because you didn't know the truth? You didn't know she really wanted to be there for you but didn't know how and was constantly shoved to the side?" I rambled.

Becca's eyes went wide as I realized what I just told her. I closed my eyes, slowly sitting up next to her. "I hate that my mom comes with me," I whispered. "I hate this awful feeling that seeps into my chest. I hate all these memories of her flooding back into my mind." I paused, shaking my head in disgust. "My grandparents wouldn't let her be a mother," I confessed, my heart breaking at the same time.

"Becca, I have all these memories that I somehow pushed away. I remember her rushing to get me when I had bad dreams, but my gran would race past her, reaching for me. I remember sitting next to her watching cartoons, but my gran pulled me away to go do something with her. She'd kiss me goodnight, read to me, but my gran would hover over us."

"My mom admitted giving up after a while, letting my grandparents take over. She let them control her; she let RJ control her for so long."

I dipped my head back between my legs. Becca raised her hand to touch my back again, but didn't say anything.

"I feel so terrible for hating her all these years when it wasn't her fault. But she doesn't care that I've been an asshole. She doesn't care that I haven't given her the time of day the past 20 some years. She still *loves me*."

I let out a huge breath, feeling a portion of the weight that had been on my shoulders lifting. It felt good to finally let out some guilt for my mother.

"It's not too late, Tyler. You can tell her how much you love her. You can still have a relationship," Becca said calmly.

"I know," I whispered.

We were quiet for a few moments then Becca tentatively asked, "Was your dream about your mom?"

My eyes screwed shut. Did I really want to talk about that horrific morning?

I felt pain and hurt radiating off her when she spoke. I knew it was hard for her when I wouldn't open up, but my throat felt like it had needles surrounding it, waiting for me to speak so they could penetrate.

Running a hand through my hair, I decided the risk of spilling my guts was worth it.

"It was about RJ. How he... died."

Her hand tensed on my back, and I was pretty sure she stopped breathing until I started to talk again.

"There was so much blood," I whispered. "I just stood there... I couldn't move. Nathan and Cooper kept yelling at me to help... but my feet wouldn't budge."

I scrunched my eyes; the picture so vivid in my mind.

"We all knew he was dead, but Nathan kept trying. Then after paramedics came and declared him dead, Nathan cradled RJ's bloody head. He was crying. I've never seen him cry before." I closed my eyes, fighting tears. "I couldn't touch him, but I couldn't take my eyes off him either. Part of his skull was showing."

I heard Becca gasp, catching a glimpse of her hand covering her mouth.

"Tyler," she said sympathetically.

I shook my head, not finished telling her my story. "You want to know the worst part? I was mad at him. Furious. I kept seeing red, and for the slightest moment... I was happy he was dead," my voice cracked. Uncontrollable guilt filled my lungs as I choked back a sob.

Becca dropped her hands from her mouth, instantly reaching for me, cradling me the best she could.

"He called the night before, after we'd made love. You were asleep, and I crept up to my office. He left a message, telling me he wanted a relationship, that he wanted to start fresh. He told me he loved me... that he was...proud," my voice cracked and I hated feeling so remorseful. "My hand was on the phone, Becca. I could have picked it up and talked to him, but I didn't."

"The next morning, Chino emailed me with lies, and I believed him. Chino wanted RJ and me to fight so RJ would sign the deal in spite of me, but it didn't matter. That fucker killed him, Becca. He practically admitted it."

Becca gasped again, holding me tighter. "What do you mean he admitted it?"

"When we ran into him at the club. He hinted towards killing RJ. I don't know anyone else who hated RJ enough to put a bullet in his head. And I know damn well RJ didn't pull the trigger. He also hinted about the tear gas and the drugs hidden in our house."

I pulled my head from Becca's chest, wanting to see her reaction towards Chino infiltrating everything. Shockingly, she didn't look as terrified as I thought she would. Her mind was ticking, and I got the feeling she was keeping something from me.

"What is it?" I asked, trying not to sound too stern.

Her eyes found her hands, pulling the pillow to her chest. "Promise you won't get mad?"

My jaw ticked. What was she keeping from me?

Without my answering, the words began to spill from her lips. "I went to Connor. I didn't tell him anything specific or names."

"Becca," I scolded.

"No, just listen," she pleaded, her big blue eyes finally meeting mine. I sighed, laying back down on the bed with my hands behind my head.

"After talking to Connor... I think you should talk to Anderson."

Was she crazy? "Becca, that sounds like a terrible idea."

"Tyler, you have no control over what Chino is doing. Anderson obviously wants to take Chino down, and you can help him. Maybe if you told him everything, showed him everything you've had to put up with, things he's said and emailed."

I shook my head. "I don't see that ending good for me or the Conklin empire. I may have different feelings about my name lately... but this company is all Nathan has and wants. I couldn't jeopardize the status of the company. Nathan would spiral out of control if he weren't distracted by work."

"Maybe Nathan would agree to go to Anderson with you. After all, neither of you have taken part in what's going on. You have proof with the legal papers you've found that RJ stopped it. I'm sure Anderson will take those papers as a sure sign for RJ's death being a murder." Becca moved the pillow to lay on top of me.

Any uneasy feelings in me evaporated from the skin on skin contact. My hands instantly wrapped around her. She ran her fingertips along my eyebrows to calm them. I guess I was scowling without knowing.

"I think you can trust Anderson," she whispered.

I was apprehensive still. Maybe a phone call to Nathan should be in order. For the most part, Becca was right. We had no idea where he was hiding drugs and never authorized him to do so on our properties.

"Let's go back to sleep," Becca said softly, leaning in to give me a peck. "I don't want to worry about Chino this weekend. I want the next 52 hours to be about you and me."

Her hand stroked my jaw, and my eyes fluttered closed. She was right. My Becs deserved to be the center of my universe this weekend, and every other second of my life.

Chapter Twenty-Three

Becca

Tyler's confessions last night were sobering and terrifying at the same time. He'd never had an anxiety attack that bad, at least not since the one time I found him struggling to breath in his office. I was thankful he brought the Xanax, and I was going to slip it in his food if he didn't start taking it regularly.

I wasn't going to bring up Chino again this weekend. I told him what I needed to and was going to leave the decision up to him. I knew he'd make the right one. I believed in my Ty. He'd know the right thing to do so we could have our happily ever after.

When I woke this morning, it was after 9:00 a.m., and I was relieved Tyler was sound asleep next to me. I longed to run my hands through his brown hair but resisted. He needed to sleep. The dark circles under his eyes when he came home from Chicago or Cleveland proved he rarely slept when we were apart.

So I silently watched him sleep, taking in his relaxed features. He was so handsome, and he was going to be mine forever.

Tyler's eyes fluttered open, catching me studying him. He stretched and ran his hand over his face, letting out a groan at the same time. I smiled at his morning routine that I hardly saw. He normally always woke before me.

"Happy birthday. Sleep good?" I asked.

He took a deep breath then pulled me to his chest. "Thank you, and yes I did," he said bashfully. I grinned as I pecked his cheek. "What would you like to do today?"

I nuzzled his chest. "It's your birthday. You pick."

"Well...," he murmured as he rolled me to my back, pulling the sheet from my chest. He scowled as he looked down then his face smoothed as he met my eyes. "I think I need to kiss these better." His hand roamed to my chest, gently caressing.

I glanced down, noticing the few bite marks then looked back to his face. He didn't look as upset as the last time he left a mark on me, and I was thankful.

Rolling to my side, I gave him the most sultry look I could while my hand roamed down his abdomen. "Sounds like a perfect start to the day."

***

We didn't move from the cabin until well after lunch. After a morning session on the cozy bed, followed by breakfast and a long steamy shower, we needed another nap. And of course, another happy wake-up.

Tyler was finally coming around. He seemed happy here after airing some of the baggage he'd been carrying with him the past few months about his grandparents. The guilt was evident on his face when confessing everything about his mom and RJ. I was so happy he could confide in me with his gut-wrenching feelings. Tyler and Mary's relationship was going to be on the mend, and I was so happy for him.

Hearing about RJ was devastating. The fear and sorrow in Tyler's eyes was heartbreaking, and all I wanted was to take away his pain. I couldn't imagine seeing anyone in my family die, especially from a blow to the head.

"Want to go for a hike?" Tyler asked as we finished cleaning the mess from our late lunch.

I turned and nodded while putting the last dish away.

His mischievous Conklin grin shown on his face as though he was up to something.

"Now I'm nervous. What are you plotting?" I asked.

Kissing my cheek, his grin grew wider. "Get your shoes on and come find out," he flirted while smacking my butt harder than usual. He laughed as I yelped, walking backwards to the screen door that lead to the backyard.

After giving him a glare, I hung the drying towel and went to find my tennis shoes. The weather was a bit cooler, so I opted for jeans and t-shirt.

Tyler had on his typical gym shorts and a t-shirt. His hair was rugged and flipping in the back from our nap. He was skipping stones into the lake when I came out to meet him for our hike.

"Where are we hiking to?"

Tyler tapped my nose. "I told you, it's a surprise." I rolled my eyes and followed behind him, noticing two towels draped across his shoulders.

We walked along the water, crossing through the mixture of trees and small beaches. The bugs weren't being friendly either. I kept swatting them away while Tyler would look back and smirk at me. He teased by calling me a city girl. I laughed when midsentence he swallowed a bug, swating the air in front of his face just as I was doing earlier.

"Okay, this is it!" he said excitedly. Pushing back a branch from my face, I searched our surroundings. The shoreline was right on the lake, and two ropes were attached to one of the bigger trees.

Tyler ran to the ropes, untying them from the branch after dropping the towels on the ground. "We used to come here as kids. The owner of the property is never here. At least we've never seen him."

"So you just crash his rope swings?" I asked.

He nodded his head with his boyish grin. Once the rope was untied, he tugged on it a few times, his smile wider. "Want to give it a try?"

I gaped at him. "That water is freezing."

Tyler rolled his eyes. Tugging off his shirt, he teased,"Don't be such a girl."

"It's not even 70 degrees outside! And I'm sure the water isn't even in the 50s this time of year!"

He dropped his shorts, stepping out of them and his shoes and came towards me. "Come on Becs, you know I'll warm you up," he flirted.

"You've been warming me up all morning and afternoon!" I laughed. "How about I just watch you?"

He shook his head no then pulled at my shirt. My eyes darted around, tugging back on my shirt. Tyler scowled. "No one's around. Come on... it'll be fun. It is my birthday."

I gave him a dirty look but couldn't resist his charm anymore. I hopped out of my clothing down to my underwear, feeling goose bumps creep along my skin.

"Those are cute," Tyler smirked, running his hand along my lace panties. I slapped his hand then pushed him to the tree branch with the rope.

"Now's not the time to flirt. You go first."

"I love when you're feisty," he smiled, reaching for the rope.

"I'm going to get real feisty depending on how cold that water is," I grumbled.

Tyler wiggled his eyebrows as if it were a dare then climbed higher in the tree. "Okay, so you make sure the rope is tight then swing and let go," he said enthusiastically.

I shook my head, thinking he was crazy to jump into the 40 degree water.

He swayed a few times, getting geared up to fly through the air. The look on his face was serious at first, but once he finally pushed off the tree, he was radiating happiness. I watched him soar then let go of the rope, dropping into the water, his arms flailing as he splashed down.

The water rippled as he rose to the surface, spitting water out as his head found the cool air. "HAH! That was great! Come in, baby!" he shouted, his smile pure and innocent.

I took a deep breath, wandering over to the tree where the other rope was. "Is it cold?"

"No, it feels great," he shouted back as he treaded water.

I pulled on the rope, making sure it was as taut as possible, trying to find courage to swing into the water with Tyler.

"Just do it!" Tyler coaxed.

I shot him a glare, took another deep breath, and swung into the crystal clear water.

You know why the water is crystal clear? Because it's fucking cold. My lungs felt like they were going to crush as my back stiffened with the icy greeting the water brought upon me. My body shot up out of the water, spitting water from my mouth.

"You're so full of shit! It's fucking freezing!" I chattered, splashing water at Tyler.

Tyler howled whole heartedly, reaching for me and holding me close to his chattering skin.

"You're right. I'm sorry I lied," he murmured against my lips.

A shiver went down my spine, but I wasn't sure if it was from the arctic water or Tyler's raspy voice.

Before I could make a smart remark back, he was kissing me, full on open-mouthed make-out. At least my head was heating up, along with other parts of my body.

I was breathless when Tyler pulled away, fighting my hands trying to pull his head back to my lips.

"Let's get out of this freezing water," he whispered. "Your lips are turning purple."

Reluctantly, I nodded my head, shocked I had forgotten just how cold I was.

We both quickly found the shore, wrapping the towels around our bodies. Tyler made his way towards me, rubbing my back and shoulders, trying to warm me up with his heat.

Tyler found a seat on the ground and pulled me into his lap, cocooning me with his strong arms and legs. The sun broke through the trees, and even though the air temperature was only in the 60s, the heat of the sun felt like heaven.

"You did way better than Mitch just now," Tyler laughed, rubbing my arms. "Nathan had to practically push him out of the tree."

I laughed, picturing Mitch whining just as I had about jumping in the cold water.

"He eventually did all right though," Tyler said, for the first time ever sounding soft for Mitch.

We were both silent for a moment, looking out over the water.

"Do you really think he's helping Chino?" I asked, breaking my own 'no talking about Chino the rest of the weekend' rule.

Tyler sighed then said, "I'm not sure. He was always so fond of RJ. I doubt he would go against his wishes if RJ didn't want him to. But... he's not so fond of me..."

I turned my head to look back at him. "You can change that too, Tyler."

He stared into my eyes for a moment, weighing my words. "I know," he whispered. My heartfelt smile earned me the prize of one in return, Tyler rubbed his nose against mine. "You know what today is?" he asked against my ear.

"Um... your birthday?" I laughed.

He laughed with me then reached for his shorts. "Actually... it's something else, too."

His arms found their way around me then handed me a small box.

My heart stopped. Did I forget something?

"Open it," he murmured in my ear. My now warmed hands found the small box, pulling out a twenty dollar bill. I looked at it in confusion, trying to figure out why a twenty dollar bill would be significant.

Underneath it was a small velvet bag.

Tyler gently took the bag from me, pulling out a ruby red stone shaped heart. "A year ago from this very day, I was a bitter, angry man, waiting in line at a coffee shop with my ignorant brother. A beautiful blonde caught my eye. She was in the line next to me then pushed her way up to the front."

My eyes widened as I recognized what he was talking about.

"She was so kind, paying for a few items for another customer with a twenty dollar bill."

Tears threatened my eyes as Tyler continued.

"That day, she started to melt my icy heart, and I wanted to pay her back for her good deed," he whispered, placing the ruby heart in my hand along with the twenty.

Salty tears fell down my face as I turned to kiss him.

"Now that you've thawed it, take care of it for me, please," he whispered against my lips.

"Always," I murmured back, squeezing the stone.

***

We made foil packets of food to throw on the fire for dinner, eating and enjoying the sun setting for the second night in a row. The temperature dropped even more, causing both of us to throw on hoodies.

"Want a drink?" Tyler asked as he took the empty foil from my lap to throw it away. I nodded my head as I curled my legs into my chest. This cabin was so perfect, and I kept picturing Tyler and I bringing our family here in the future. Tyler bringing our kids to his favorite rope swings, tricking them into flying through the air into the cold water. Even though the water felt like ice cubes, they would love it.

"What are you thinking about?" Tyler probed as he handed me a glass of wine.

I blushed, not sure if I wanted to tell him about my fantasy. I still didn't know where Tyler stood with kids. He told me he wanted to make babies with me, but that's completely different than fathering them. He sat down next to me, wrapping an arm around the back of the swing, a beer in his other hand.

"Just how much I like it here," I said truthfully.

"Is that all?" he asked with a raised brow.

I smiled and leaned into him, nestling my head into his shoulder.

"I was thinking about our future, you know... maybe we could have family trips here," I said shyly.

"Yeah. Maybe," Tyler replied as he took a swig of his beer.

The fire crackled with our silence. I didn't need to bring up kids, not now. We'd cross that bridge more seriously when we got there.

"Oh my gosh!" I shouted, jumping from the swing.

Tyler jolted along with me, worry apparent on his face. "What's wrong?"

"I can't believe I haven't given you your birthday present yet!" I shrieked as I ran to the cabin.

"Gosh Becs, give me a heart attack," Tyler chided, making himself comfortable in the swing again.

Excitement filled my body as I rummaged through my bag. I couldn't wait to give Tyler his present. I always had to be creative. What do you buy a man who has more money than he knows what to do with it? After our very short lived bachelor/bachelorette party, I knew just the gift.

I snickered as I found the shoe size box, grabbing another smaller box to go with it.

Tyler's eyes were bright as I handed him both gifts.

"Baby, you didn't have to get me anything," he said sincerely, even though I knew he was thrilled.

"It's not much," I giggled.

"What one do I open first?"

I shrugged my shoulders. "Doesn't matter."

He looked at me curiously, a smile creeping across his lips. To my surprise, he opened the big box.

His deft fingers worked their way on the paper then tugged the top off, his eyes growing bigger as he pulled out the black negligee, complete with a matching thong and see through bra.

"Well, you can't go wrong with this," he said, his eyes heating as he held the garments in front of him. "Let's go to bed," he said quickly.

I laughed, taking the lingerie from him and handing him the smaller box.

Tyler groaned, unwrapping the box while pouting his lips at me. I could barely contain my excitement. This was going to throw him for a loop.

Finally looking down at what was inside the package, he furrowed his eyebrows. "Why would you give me a wad of cash?"

"They're all ones," I said seductively, standing from the swing.

He studied the cash in his hands then it clicked what I was hinting at.

"Better not tell your fiancé," I winked.

A devilish grin spread across his face as I slowly walked backwards to the cabin. Tyler anxiously followed, his fast pace walk turned into a run, grabbing me and lifting me the rest of the way.

Chapter Twenty-Four

Tyler

Never did I ever think Becca Stine would give me a strip tease, and tease being the key word. The shy, timid girl who wouldn't let me see her naked turned into a full on vixen of a woman, and I was sure I'd be supporting a constant hard on the rest of my life whenever she'd be near me.

She shoved me on the beat up couch, making me wait way too long for her entrance. I'll never forget her wild hair, big red lips, and smoky eyes. She really went all out. She even made me keep my hands to myself, only letting me slightly touch her whenever I'd slip a dollar in the scraps of fabric, per her request of course.

Once all the ones were on the floor, along with her clothing, she straddled me, and I couldn't help but stare into her eyes, wondering if it were all real. She was too perfect, too special. I could never take her for granted or risk hurting her in any way.

That's when I knew I had to go to Anderson. Becca was right. He would help us, and I had a good feeling we might not get into too much trouble if we cooperated.

Becca would have ripped off my clothing right there, riding me hard until my mind was blown. But I didn't want that. I needed to be close to her, go slow like I used to. I cherished my Becs too much, and I needed to remind her just how special she was to me.

So I made love to her just as I did the first time I knew I loved her, in front of the fire on the floor amongst pillows and soft blankets. I constantly reminded her to keep her eyes open, kissing away her tears of emotion. Except this time, I told her what was in my heart instead of holding it inside. How much I loved her and every single inch of her mind, body, and soul.

***

"Want to come back for our honeymoon?" I asked as we both strapped on our seatbelts.

She almost snorted her protein shake all over the dashboard. "Don't get me wrong, I love it here, but I'd prefer a hotel."

I laughed as I pulled out of the cabin that held so many good childhood memories. Memories I decided I needed to hold tight, along with the good memories of my mom, RJ, and my brothers. I didn't need to dwell on the bad anymore. All it did was make me angry, and I had nothing I needed to be angry about anymore.

"I have a wonderful spot for our honeymoon. Don't you worry," I assured Becca.

She huffed. "I think you should tell me. I don't like being kept in the dark when it comes to vacation plans."

"Oh, you love my surprises," I smirked.

She shook her head, a full on smile breaking through her lips. "I guess so."

"I almost forgot. Tomorrow I told Heather and Ray I'd go see ArtPrize with them and the kids. Louis' pieces are pretty amazing," Becca said. "Can you come with us?"

I turned to look at her, nodding my head. "Why don't we take another day off?"

She looked taken aback, surprised by my suggestion. "Really? That would actually be great. I need to find a hairpiece for the wedding. I think I'm going to check out some of the smaller shops in Grand Rapids. Everything mom picks out is way too gaudy. The wedding is already big enough."

"Whatever you get will be beautiful," I assured her. "I set up a meeting while you were in the shower." I gulped, my stare becoming semi serious. "I'm meeting with Anderson."

Becca's eyes looked hopeful as she read my mind.

"I think you're right. Anderson could help us."

"Did you talk to Nathan, too?"

I shook my head no. "I'll call him once you fall asleep and convince him it's the right thing to do."

She narrowed her eyes at me then shook her head in disgust. She smiled though, knowing I was right and that she'd pass out as soon as we were passing the bridge.

"We'll see who falls asleep," she said confidently.

***

About two minutes after we were off the bridge, Becca was leaned against the window, mouth open and softly snoring. I laughed quietly to myself as I reached for my phone. Nothing was going to wake her up now.

"Have a good getaway?" Nathan said after the second ring.

"Shockingly, perfect," I said truthfully.

"Oh," Nathan said, surprised. " I wasn't sure how the cabin would treat you."

I gulped, knowing Nathan was worried about the memories that would come back to me once I was in our old stomping ground. He knew what I had been going through. Sometimes I wondered if we were twins because of our brotherly connection.

"It was good," I said reassuringly. "But I thought a lot, and I want to go to Anderson."

"Tyler," Nathan sighed. "Stop instigating him, he's not—"

"No. I want to ask for his help. I want to stop Chino."

Nathan was silent for a long moment.

"Do you really think that will work? What happens when we catch him? The press will catch the Feds finding millions of dollars worth of cocaine on our properties." Nathan wasn't happy. This was exactly why he would be afraid. Nathan didn't want to get a bad reputation, and neither did I, but sometimes you have to do what's right.

"I don't think we have any other option," I finally said.

"What about Mitch?" Nathan said with a scared undertone to his voice.

The only person I was worried about was Mitch. I loved him. He was my little brother, and along with memories of my mother, I had memories of him when we were younger. I forgot how much I wanted to protect him, and I forgot how often he'd sneak into my bedroom when we were kids, but in reality, we both snuck into Nathan's. I'd never admit that to anyone else though.

"We send him to Miami, permanently. Then he can't get into trouble. If Anderson wants to go south, then we bring him into the offices. I won't let him go down with Chino, even if he's his right hand man."

Nathan was silent again, but then sighed, "All right. I'll set up the meeting."

"I already did."

***

Becca and I rode together into the city for the first time in what felt like ages. I enjoyed seeing her smiling next to me, giving me her random shy glances as I'd stroke her knee. We were both dressed down, jeans and fleece jackets. The weather turned cooler again, closer to the lower 60s.

While I'd be meeting with Anderson, Becca was going to do her shopping, and then we were going to meet up with Heather and Ray and the kids. I didn't really care about ArtPrize, but Becca did, so I wanted to support her.

We parked in the basement ramp of the Conklin building, an eerie feeling spreading throughout each of us. My biggest fear could take place in moments, me being handcuffed and taken in, leaving Becca with a convicted fiancé. The Conklin reputation would be destroyed forever because of drug trafficking accusations.

She reached for me, wrapping her arms snugly around my waist. "It'll be okay. Tell me everything will be okay," she whispered.

I nuzzled her hair. "Everything will be fine. I'll meet you in an hour."

We still didn't let go of each other. "I love you, Ty," she murmured into my chest.

I reached for her face, my eyes boring deep into hers. "We'll be fine. This was your idea, and you're always right," I said with a smile.

She half laughed then took a long blink. I kissed her before I saw her tears of fear. I needed to be strong now. I couldn't let Anderson think the wrong thing. I needed a clear head, to be focused. I had to do this for my Becs.

"I love you," I said, finally let her go, turning to ride the elevator up to my fate.

Chapter Twenty-Five

Becca

I wasn't sure why my nerves picked until stepping out of the car at the Conklin building to make an appearance. The thought of Tyler confessing every detail he knew about Chino ending badly had only been in the back of my mind. But when I saw him heading towards the elevator, I couldn't stop myself from shaking. It wasn't the fact that Tyler could be falsely accused or have a bad name that I was worried about. I was terrified how it would affect his mind. He was finally coming around and getting comfortable in his own skin again, who knows what a whole legal mess could do to him.

And I really didn't want to talk to him through a glass window. Ever.

Letting go of his waist was damn near impossible, but it was the only way we could move forward and get Chino out of our lives. Tyler wasn't going to let him harm his family any more.

After watching the elevator doors close, I turned on my heels and headed to find some shops downtown. I needed to not think about what my Ty was doing but pretend this was going to be a normal day.

I took my time finding shops, enjoying the large sculptures and artwork on the sidewalks and intersections of the city. ArtPrize helped keep my mind from not being so fuzzy.

A store caught my eye after I walked passed it. Curiously, I walked backwards while looking into the window. It seemed to be a small boutique, probably a new designer getting their feet wet for the first time. Maybe they had bridal accessories?

A bell rang as I stepped through the door, and a gentleman around my age greeted me from the counter.

"Hi! Can I help you find anything?" he asked sincerely as he nudged his glasses higher on his nose. His hair was tousled and his clothing was average, jeans and a t-shirt, nothing over the top or fancy.

"Hi, do you have any bridal accessories?" I asked, searching the store with my eyes, thinking I might need to find a different shop.

"Um, I'm not sure. Let me ask my girlfriend, hold on. Hey Ash!" he said, turning into a backroom.

As I thumbed through a rack of clothing, a voice I thought I'd never hear again whispered through the store, sending a chill through my body.

"Hi ma'am, what kind of accessories were you looking for?" Her voice faded as her face went pale. She gulped hard, running a hand through her tousled pony tail.

Living and breathing, there she was, my nemesis.

Ashlynn.

She looked totally different. Her hair wasn't as blonde as usual, and there wasn't a lick of makeup on her face. Her clothing was simple and respectable, not flashy and eye catching like normal.

The gentleman watched as Ashlynn and I took each other in, confusion spreading over his face.

"Everything okay?" he asked tentatively.

Ashlynn looked horrified when she realized the three of us were in the same room. It was like she didn't want him to know who I was.

What a bitch.

"I was just leaving," I said confidently, turning to walk out the store.

"No, Becca, wait!" Ashlynn pleaded.

My mind fought against my muscles, every single one of them wanting to walk through that door, throwing my middle finger in her direction. But my heart pounded, telling me to be the bigger person. But I was always the bigger person when it came to Ashlynn. I was done with her shit and had been more than happy ever since she was permanently out of my life.

"Becca, I," she hesitated, her words sounding so broken, so hurt, so... real.

"Would you mind going and stocking the new merchandise in the back?" she asked the gentleman who was watching us skeptically.

I slowly turned, noticing concern wash over his face as he watched Ashlynn. She gave him a gentle smile, and he returned one, kissing her forehead and heading to the backroom.

He must have had money for her to be with him. Shallow Ashlynn would never be with someone so normal.

I didn't say anything as I watched her fumble with her hair. She wouldn't meet my eyes for the longest time, and just as I was about to turn around and finally leave, she spoke.

"Becca, I'm sorry. I know I was horrible to you our entire lives. I can't change that."

Wow... that wasn't what I was expecting. Ashlynn had never apologized or took responsibility for her actions. I simply watched her, wondering if she would ever get the courage to look me in the eye.

"What are you looking for?" she asked quietly, finally meeting my gaze.

The look on her face was sobering and humbling. The urge for me to coddle her like I always had crept up, but I quickly pushed it away.

"Well... I was looking for a hairpiece."

Her lips slowly quirked up, and a hint of smile took over. "Let me show you what I have."

Reluctantly, I followed behind her through the tiny store. My heart pounded with every step I took. Was she going to secretly jump me and pull out all of my hair? Make my appearance terrible for the most important day of my life?

"This is what we have. I assume it's for your wedding? I saw the spread on MLIVE. You and Tyler looked amazing. You both looked happy."

"We are," I said quickly, not wanting her to think anything was ever wrong between us.

Her smile faded as she nodded. She hung her head then slowly started to walk away.

Fuck. Why was I feeling so guilty for being bitchy? This girl typically radiated bitch. But her fakeness wasn't there, and her tone was normal. She seemed remorseful and hurting.

"I, um... How have you been?" I stuttered, pretending to look extra carefully at all the hairpieces.

Her head popped up as she turned back to face me, a small ounce of hope in her eyes.

"Well, after Connor and I broke up, I did some changing. I didn't realize how much of a bitch I was until Connor let me have it. Well, until you said the things you said." Ashlynn's normal confident self shriveled like a dead plant.

I blinked for a long second. Was I too hard on her?

"Becca, you needed to say what you said. I needed to hear it. I can't be so superficial and chase things I can't have. I'm not going to get anywhere being fake and treating people the way I did. My whole life I've gotten everything that money could buy, yet I still wanted more. Trying to take someone's love from them, and twice... was the most selfish thing I could have ever done. I'm sorry it took me so long to figure it out. I'm sorry I ruined our friendship."

I was speechless by her confession. Her ability to realize what she was doing shocked the hell out of me. This was so unlike Ashlynn. I kept waiting for the cameras to come out and say, JUST KIDDING! YOU'VE BEEN PUNKED!

"But I can understand why you'd never forgive me."

Shit.

"Ashlynn... " I paused, taking a deep breath. What was I supposed to say? I always forgave everyone and anyone so quickly. But I just wasn't ready to mend things with Ashlynn. I didn't want her to try and come into my life again. I didn't trust her and never would.

She shook her head, a small smile playing on her lips. "Why don't you try this one on?"

I stared at her for a moment then nodded my head. I was thankful she realized how uncomfortable I was with her apology.

"Are you wearing your hair up or down?"

"I, um... I haven't really decided."

She gave me a warm smile, picking through different pieces and holding them up to my hair different ways. She was always good at helping me figure out what to wear.

"Is everything else ready for the wedding?" she asked.

"Yeah, for the most part. It's been fun, stressful, but... Well, you know how my mom is." I laughed. She let out a giggle as well.

"Yes, Missy can be a bit much. I'm glad you've enjoyed wedding planning." Her smile faded, and hurt crossed her face. "Maybe one day I'll plan my wedding."

"Hey babe, are these supposed to be on sale?" the gentleman asked who greeted me earlier.

Ashlynn turned her head and looked at him adoringly as he held up a pair of shirts with a confused expression. I smiled, enjoying his less-than-perfect appearance.

"Yes. Thanks, Alex." He grinned wide at her as though he was her puppy, like she had just patted him on the head for doing a good deed.

She blushed as he turned back into the back room then met my eyes again. "He's still learning," she said softly.

"Your boyfriend?" I blurted.

She nodded her head. "He's different from anyone else I've known. He's pure, and I've learned so much from him. Maybe one day." She was insinuating marriage, I'm sure.

"You'll get your fairytale," I said sincerely.

Her eyes watered as she nodded her head at me. "Do you like any of these?"

"Yeah, I think I'll take both. I'm not sure which one I like more," I said truthfully. They were gorgeous. Intricate beading that I'm sure she did by hand. She was always creative when it came to designing. I'd imagined when we were younger that she'd be the one to make my wedding dress.

I followed her to the register, an awkward silence passing between us.

"You're going to make a beautiful bride. I can't wait to see pictures," she whispered, pain laced with her words.

"They won't be on MLIVE," I half laughed. Tyler promised, and I would personally go to the news station and have a major freak out until the photos were taken down.

"Oh, well... maybe we could have lunch after and you could show me sometime," she asked timidly.

My eyes widened, that same fear of her creeping back into my life.

I paid her for the headpieces then offered her a smile. "Maybe."

She nodded her head with a small bit of hope twinkling in her eyes.

Turning to leave, I felt a peace in my heart. I didn't hate her, not anymore, but I wouldn't be showing her my wedding pictures either. Forgiveness was something I was willing to give, but I wouldn't let her back into my life. Maybe that was low of me, but some things just can't be repaired completely.

The sun was warm on my face as I left the store. I took my time walking back to the Conklin building, reaching into my pocket to rub the ruby heart Tyler gave me. My breath hitched with worry. Just as I was reaching for my phone, it chirped.

We're by one of Conklin's pieces at the Public Museum. They look awesome! Meet us here?- Heather

Sure! Let me get Tyler and I'll text you when we're on our way- Becca

Oh, Tyler! My heart raced as I went to dial his number, but a FaceTime message from Cooper's phone came through. Odd. Cooper rarely called me. I only had his phone number if there was an emergency.

Oh my God, Tyler! Anderson must've thought he was suspicious and took him into custody! My heart dropped, breaking into a thousand pieces as I slowly hit accept. A million thoughts rushed through my head as I waited for the phone to connect. What were people going to say? How was I going to tell Mary her sons were in jail? What was bail all about and would I be able to get Tyler and Nathan out? Maybe I should go see Connor?

Finally the phone connected... and Cooper wasn't on the screen. A snaky, smiling older man was on the other end.

"Hello, Miss Stine," Lee Chino greeted. His voice was friendly, but his eyes held something completely different. The Devil.

"Hi Lee... I wasn't expecting to see your face. Why do you have Cooper's phone?" I asked, trying not to seem completely shaken. I began to walk faster, my eyes searching the streets for anything suspicious happening. Maybe Tyler would still be with Anderson, and things were going smoothly enough that we could catch Chino saying something Anderson could use against him.

"I borrowed it. I figured you wouldn't answer an unknown number, but that doesn't matter right now. What matters right now is that you listen to everything I say."

The phone he was holding rotated, making its surroundings shake. Finally, it focused on what appeared to be a mock of one of the ArtPrize pieces Louis made for Conklin.

"Now. I need you to cooperate for me, Becca. If you don't... I'll show you what's going to happen." Chino zoomed into the piece as worry struck me. What was he up to?

Just as I was about to say something, the mock up of the Public Museum exploded into a million pieces, spitting debris all over wherever Chino was.

I gasped in horror, stopping dead in my tracks. Then something even more terrifying came on the screen as Chino turned, showing a video of Heather and her family standing outside of the museum. Josie was patting the small version of the building, and I was about to vomit.

"I see your family likes the artwork. Every single stupid little model that crazy ass artist made has an explosive inside of it. And see this," Chino moved the video to a list of buttons, 18 to be exact. 18 models. My mind went back to when we first met with the artist.

"Can't you see it?" he said in frustration. "It will be a masterpiece. I will need at least 18 spaces throughout the city."

"These buttons, all 18 of them, are connected to each art piece. If I'm not mistaken, that's your sister and her family? Right?"

I couldn't answer him; my mouth was trembling along with my hands and heart.

"Answer me, or I'll push this button right here—"

"STOP! Yes, that's them. Please, don't hurt them! This isn't about them! What you want doesn't involve my sister and her kids! Please!" I begged, tears running down my cheeks. I had never been more frightened in my life. I wanted to sprint to

Josie, grab her from that small mock up building, and run thousands of miles away.

"Now that you're being so compliant, I want you to listen and do exactly what I say. Come to the Arena remodel. I have some paperwork that needs to be filled out," Chino's slimy voice said over the phone. "If you're not here in ten minutes, I'll push this little red button. If you call the cops, I'll push two more, if you call your precious fiancé, I'll push five. Get what I'm saying, Becca?"

I nodded my head as though he could see me, trying to catch the wind that was knocked out of me from pure fear.

"Good. Hurry up. The clock is ticking."

Chapter Twenty-Six

Tyler

Every single document that Nathan and I found from Robert Senior and RJ involving any business with Lee Chino was spread across my desk.

Anderson was holding the Put Option Agreement that RJ had voided once my grandfather died. He didn't say a word while Nathan and I fed him our story: how we had no idea what was going on until RJ died, all the threats Chino had sent and told us. Every little bit of information I'd stored in my mind was now in Anderson's hand, and my palms were sweaty as I waited for him to speak.

Nathan was as cool as a cucumber, sitting in the chair next to me. He was pissed I didn't wear a suit, but quickly forgave me once Anderson came in wearing jeans.

After what felt like hours of silence, Anderson finally spoke. "So you don't know who his snakes inside your company are?"

Nathan and I both collectively answered no.

Anderson sighed, setting the document down on the table, collecting all the others and throwing them in a pile together.

"Well?" I asked, doing everything in my power to keep my nerves from taking over.

"Well... let's catch the fucker."

I let out a huge breath of air. *We were going to be okay.* We had Anderson on our side, and that brought us one step closer to getting Chino out of our hair.

"So, what do we need to do, and how is this going to affect the company? I don't want any bad publicity," Nathan said quickly.

Anderson chewed on his lip as he looked up towards Nathan. "I can't guarantee the press won't find out about it once we catch him, but I'll try my best to keep everything under cover."

Nathan nodded, clearly not happy with his confession.

Anderson stood, and Nathan and I quickly followed. "We'll get this sorted out. For now, keep contact with Lee as much as you normally do. I'll go over all this and get our own privates in your company. If you want to walk free from this, we'll do it my way. Understand?"

"Yes, sir," Nathan and I said in unison.

He nodded his head then eyed the liquor on the table off to the side of my office. "Do you mind?"

"No, please, help yourself," I said. My heart was finally starting to calm. We were going to be okay.

Nathan's smile was wide as he joined Anderson, pouring himself a glass. "Want one, Tyler?" he asked. I shook my head no, still ravishing in the bit of hope I had in my heart.

Then that hope was whisked out of my chest.

"Tyler!"

I turned to face the frantic voice, hoping to God it wasn't who I thought it was.

Margo stood in the doorway, her clothing disarranged and rumpled. What the hell was she doing here?

I looked at her features. Her cheek was bruised, her eyes wet, one swollen. Her red hair was scattered on top of her head, not bouncing and around her face like it usually was. She looked like she had been knocked around.

"Tyler, it's Becca," she said, her breath heavy and uneven.

My eyes widened. Becca? Was she talking about my Becs?

"Chino. He's going after her," she said through heavy breaths again.

My jaw dropped along with my heart. I made a dash for the door, but Margo stopped me.

"You have to listen, Tyler!" she said more frenzied than before.

Anderson's and Nathan's heads turned then Margo realized we weren't alone.

Her eyes found the floor, realizing she just walked into a whole lot more trouble than just with me.

"Oh, no... you better start talking now. I don't give a shit if they hear. What's he doing with Becca?" I could barely get the words out of my mouth fast enough as my eyes bore into hers.

She gulped, her shoulders slumping. "He wanted me to come here to coax you to go to him. He's kidnapped her. I don't think he'll hurt her, but God Tyler, I don't know..." her voice faded as she covered her swollen eye. "He's gone crazy," she sniffed.

"Did he do that to you?" Nathan asked, taking a step towards us. Margo slid to my side, as though shielding herself from Nathan.

"Sweetheart, if he did, we can stop him. I'm the detective. Tell us what you know so we can get him out of your life. He won't hurt you again if you help us find him." Anderson said softly. It was the softest I had ever heard the nosy prick speak.

"You need to go to the Arena. That's where he's going to take her. But Tyler, be careful. He's going to try and get you to sign the agreement with the residential properties. I'm afraid if you don't sign, he's going to take it out on Becca."

My eyes hardened as I pushed passed Margo. I had to get to her and fast. I pulled my phone out of my pocket, hoping to God he hadn't found Becca yet.

Her phone rang and rang as I ran to the elevator.

"Tyler, wait!" Anderson and Nathan shouted after me. "We have to come up with a plan!"

Once I heard Becca's voicemail, I cursed then turned to face Anderson and Nathan. "You're a detective. Get your swat team out. My fiancé just got kidnapped! If that's not enough, throw Max Stine's name in there, that will get everyone moving!" I shouted, making my way to the staircase.

I heard Nathan and Anderson curse then follow after me.

"Come on, let's take my car," Anderson said with a heavy breath as we made our way down the crap ton of floors.

"Fine," I mumbled. "Just fucking hurry." My legs bounced as I sat in the front seat. I constantly called Becca, my heart shattering every time I heard her sweet, loving voice from her voicemail.

"FUCK," I shouted in frustration as she didn't answer for the fourth time.

"We'll get her, Tyler," Nathan said calmly, putting his hand on my shoulder. "She'll be okay."

"I really don't think he'll hurt her if you sign, Tyler," Margo said from the backseat next to Nathan.

"Margo, how did you get involved in all of this anyway?" Nathan questioned.

Margo pretended to pick a piece of lint from her jeans. "Lee and I have been on and off for a while. But once my father got sick, he offered me help."

"Money," Nathan said knowingly.

Margo's shoulder sagged. "I couldn't ask your family for money, and Chino willingly gave it to me. But..."

"But what?" I snapped.

"He wanted me to flirt with you. Chino told me I should go to you, Tyler. He wanted me to break you and Becca up. I'm so sorry," Margo sniffed.

"After all I did for you and your father!" I shouted.

Margo started crying, and I didn't care if she were upset. I called Becca again, hoping I'd get through to her.

I held my head in my hands, listening to Becca's voicemail over and over again. I had to hear it in person. I couldn't lose my baby doll. I just found her. She was the only reason worth living. If I didn't have Becca, then Chino might as well take this company because I'd rather be six feet under than walking around without my Becs on this Godforsaken planet.

Chapter Twenty-Seven

Becca

My legs couldn't move fast enough as I darted through the crowded sidewalks of the busy city. People from all over the country were here for ArtPrize, and I suddenly hated being a part of the festivities. I never should have encouraged having an artist represent Conklin. Then my family wouldn't be in danger.

I found the Arena, covered in construction tape. Big machinery surrounded it, along with concrete slabs and dirt. It wouldn't be done for another month, and my gut thumped as I tried to find a way into the building.

My phone rang again, Cooper's number showing on the screen.

"Glad to you see you made it. You have two minutes to get to the back entrance. Someone will meet you there to let you inside."

"Two minutes? That's impossible!" I shouted into the phone. It clicked, and I only heard a dial tone.

Sprinting as fast as I could, I found the back of the Arena, having no idea if I made it in time. I looked around, confused that no one was there to greet me. Did I not run fast enough? Was I too late? Oh my God, Heather! Ray! Josie and Emmett! I'd never forgive myself if they were hurt!

Then I saw movement, and the urge to crush someone fueled my fist as I swung at Mitch.

"You fuck! How could you be a part of this?" I shouted. "He's threatening to hurt my family!"

"Becca, stop! He's not going to hurt anyone!" Mitch said, grabbing my wrists. I was furious, still trying to beat the shit out of him even though he was twice my size. "Becca, he just wants to talk to Tyler and Nathan. He knew the only way he'd be able to talk to them was if you're here."

I shook my head in disbelief. "How could you?" I screamed. "He's crazy! I was on your side, Mitch! I didn't think you were working with Chino!" Hurt spread across his face as he shook his head. He was about to say something, but all I remembered were his eyes widening before I blacked out.

***

A pounding pain aggravated my head. Where was I, and what the hell happened? I tried to move my arms, but they were too heavy. I finally found the strength to squint but only because a bright light flicked on above me. I couldn't adjust my eyes, and I still couldn't move my hands. Then I realized I couldn't move them because they were tied down to the chair where I was sitting. My legs were tied too.

I went to yell for help, but I couldn't because duct tape was wrapped around my mouth.

"This is fucking ridiculous. Why the fuck did you hit her so hard?" Mitch's unloyal voice asked.

"She was going ape shit on you, dude! I figured it'd be easier to just lug her inside. Not to mention easier to tie her up," some other voice said.

I squinted my eyes, trying to focus, but my fucking head hurt. We were in the middle of the Arena, tarps and dust everywhere. Then I saw Mitch, his eyes holding fury as he talked to some other guy.

"You didn't need to tie her up! She would've calmed down! Chino is going to kick your ass when he see's this!"

The other guy looked at Mitch cockily. "You really are dense. He doesn't give a shit about her. He only cares about your brothers signing that contract."

"Tyler won't sign if he sees Becca tied to a chair with tape over her mouth," Mitch roared as he began walking towards me. Once he was done shouting at the thug, his eyes found mine and guilt filled them. "Becca! I'm sorry. I didn't know they were going to do this!" he said in a rush, beginning to untie me.

I choked out a sob, terrified of what was going to happen next. Tears ran down my cheeks as Mitch tried to free me.

"Don't fucking touch her," the mastermind of this sickening plan said. Mitch's head shot up but froze when we heard the sound of a gun cocking. He slowly rose, putting his hands in the air. He turned, blocking me from viewing Chino point a gun in my direction.

"What the hell is going on? This isn't going to get Tyler and Nathan to sign anything," he said, attempting to sound calm.

Chino's cocky grin spread across his face. "We'll see who gets their way." A sinister laugh escaped his mouth as Mitch shook his head.

"She's not a prisoner. I'm untying her," Mitch said, turning to face me.

My eyes went wide, and a muffled shriek escaped my mouth through the duct tape as I heard the gunshot.

Mitch fell to his knees, yelping while grabbing his leg. Chino just shot him, and I was tied to this chair and couldn't help him.

My cries were uncontrollable, choking on my own tears because I couldn't stop.

Chino slowly walked towards me, putting the gun behind his back, tutting with each step. One of his goons pulled a whimpering Mitch to the side.

"Don't worry, he'll be fine. I've got good aim. If I wanted him dead, he wouldn't be crying like a little bitch right now."

I shook my head, frightened to hell with every step he took closer to me. Chino bent down so his slimy face was right to mine. He took the gun from behind him and ran it down my cheek. "You sure are pretty," he sighed.

My body seized, my muscles clamping as tight as they could to shut him out.

"What do you want Chino?" My heart sped faster. Nathan was here.

That meant Tyler was close by. Hope rushed through my blood stream, a tiny part of me thinking everything might be okay. That Tyler was here to save me, even if Chino was in control.

"Nathan!" Chino smiled brightly as he turned to face him. "I'm so glad you could join us! Now where is Tyler? I'm sure he's not far behind."

"He'll be here. What do you want? I'm sure we can compromise on this... misunderstanding. In the mean time, I'd like to know why my little brother seems to be in searing pain," Nathan said calmly with his hands in his pockets.

"Mitch wasn't following directions. I suggest you take that into consideration while we discuss the future of RJ bricks and the Conklin empire. Everything we need to make this all go away lies on that desk."

Nathan let out an amused laugh. "Chino, I thought I told you, our business with your enterprise is done." Nathan began to walk over to Mitch, putting a hand on his shoulder. Mitch was grasping his leg, scrunching his face in pain.

My heart sped up but quickly calmed when I felt a familiar hand on my wrist, deft fingers untying me. "You're going to be okay, baby doll," Tyler whispered near my ear. More tears sprung from my eyes. All I wanted was for him to hold me and to believe what he had just said.

Just as my hands and legs were freed and I was ripping the duct tape from my mouth, Chino turned to find Tyler pulling me from the chair.

His devious smile egged Tyler on, goading him to say something snarky as his trigger happy-hand shook.

"I'll sign your agreement," Tyler said stiffly. "Let Becca go with Mitch to the hospital, and we can do this like men, in an office, with suits and ties."

Chino laughed, full on belly laughter, holding his stomach as he bent over. Holy shit, he really was losing it.

"You know... I tried really, really hard to break you two apart." Tyler and I glanced at each other, not sure what I had to do with him getting his way. "See, if you marry him, that means I don't get what I want."

"We wouldn't sign your deal even if Tyler wasn't marrying Becca," Nathan said sternly, wrapping his tie around Mitch's leg.

Chino shook his head, his sinister grin still in place. "A broken hearted Tyler would. And I'm willing to go just that far."

If my heart could race any faster, it would have popped right out of my chest and ran clear cut to Tokyo across the ocean.

Chino nodded to his thugs, and each of them made a grab at each Conklin brother, including Tyler.

"NO!" I shouted, but I was grabbed as well, forcefully being pushed and held down in the chair I had been tied to.

"Chino, what are you doing?" Tyler's voice broke, his eyes consumed with fear.

Chino raised his gun as he looked at Tyler, pointing it at his head.

Tyler's hands instantly flew from the thug that was holding him back to the air. "I told you, I'll sign. So will Nathan and Mitch. Just let Becca go," he begged.

Chino thought for a moment then cocked his head to the side as though he were contemplating what Tyler was saying.

"Nah... I don't think that's good enough," he whispered, then turned to me, the arm holding the gun making a snail's pace in my direction. "I think you might need to be heartbroken after all."

The gun cocked, and my life flashed before my eyes.

Being young, going on family vacations. Smiling with my brother and sister, enjoying being around my loving father when he was home. I remembered the good of my mother, all the fun times we'd spent together without her cryptic remarks. My complex relationship with Ashlynn. Gage, losing my virginity. Meeting Jamie, falling in love with Connor, my heart breaking from his and Ashlynn's betrayal. Then more tears flooded my eyes as I saw Tyler for the first time, his scowl plastered to his deep in thought face in our first meeting. His gentle voice in the elevator asking how my first day went. The roses with the sweet notes, our first kiss, our first touches, and ups and downs.

If I were to die right now, in this very moment, I would know one thing: I experienced the most passionate love that could be found, and I was lucky enough to have gotten it for so long. The fantasies of our future would have to be enough to hold on to in heaven until we met again. I closed my eyes, preparing for the inevitable.

Only God can stop a moving bullet.

Or the strong voice of your father.

"Leeland... is there a reason why you're pointing a gun at my baby girl?"

My eyes popped open as my head jerked to see my father, standing in his pristine suit with two men on each of his sides. Three of the men I had seen before. Two were twins, one bald, but both had red facial hair. They were always with my father. I remembered people always joking about them being his bodyguards. One I didn't know, but the other... *Detective Anderson?*

The hands that were firmly holding me down disappeared from my shoulders, his footsteps crunching on the gravel ground as he backed away from me.

Tyler's and Nathan's mouths were gaped open, shocked to see him as well.

Chino's mouth went into a thin line; his head dipping low as he slowly dropped the gun to his side. "Your family isn't cooperating with my plan," he said in a low tone.

My father cocked his head to the other side then glanced at one of the men to his left. The man I didn't know looked at him then to Mitch, making his way with a duffle bag while putting rubber gloves on his hands.

Max began to walk towards Chino. He looked so strong and confident, standing taller and broader than times before. His eyes were hard as they pinned to meet Chino's stare. He didn't look like one to be reckoned with and surely didn't look like the man who brought me into this world.

"I thought I told you to stay away from the Conklins," Max said as he approached Chino.

Chino stood tall, meeting my father head to head. "I had them first Stine. You already took Martel's business from me; I won't let you take Conklin's too!"

Martel? Holy shit! Ray! Heather's husband!

My father shook his head, a small smile playing on his lips. "Oh Leeland, if I remember correctly, RJ Conklin put a squash on that a few years ago. If a business says no, you back away. You know the deal. You keep your shit away from my daughters and son."

"It's your shit too, Stine," Chino snarled.

I held in a gasp. *His shit too?*

Max's eyebrows narrowed as he studied Chino. Then his head tilted to the side again, his eyes finding Tyler being held down. "Let go of my future son-in-law."

"Yes, sir," Chino's thugs said compliantly, immediately taking a step back. They looked terrified, as though they didn't realize who they were holding down.

Who exactly was in charge here?

I ran into Tyler, my body still trembling as he wrapped his protective arms around me. He looked just as confused as I was. His lips found my forehead as he squeezed me, moving me so my body was out of the direction of men with loaded guns.

Max turned back to Chino, closing his eyes briefly before he spoke. "It is my shit and my rules. You know what happens if you break them."

Chino laughed, but his eyes held a different expression. Max licked his lips in contemplation then searched Chino's face. He tilted his head, communicating with Anderson. Anderson obediently took a step forward, handing my father a gun.

I let out a loud shriek as my father lifted the gun to Chino's head. Tyler covered my mouth and eyes with his hands, pulling me as close to his chest as he could.

A gunshot rang through the Arena then a loud scream belonging to Chino roared through the air.

"You fuck! I never thought you'd do it!" Chino shouted at my father.

I peeked through Tyler's hand, seeing Chino curled on the ground, holding his foot.

"It'll be your head next time. Don't forget, I'm in charge," my father growled. He bent down so he was level with Chino. "Stay the fuck away from my kids. I won't give you anymore warnings." Pulling the gun to Chino's forehead, he continued in a dangerously low tone. "Next time, I'll use the right piece to drive a bullet clear through your head and into any goon who's helping you."

Max stood up, turning to look back at the man who was working on Mitch's bullet wound. "Tend to this prick when you're done with him. He still has work to do for me." He turned to Anderson, giving him another nod. Anderson proceeded to walk towards Tyler and me. Tyler's grip tightened on me, moving me behind him even more than I already was. "Let her go, Tyler. I promise he won't hurt my little girl. I can keep her safe... which you keep failing to do."

For the second time in my life, I was torn from Tyler's arms, and everything faded to black.

Chapter Twenty-Eight

Tyler

"What are you doing?" I shouted at Anderson as he jabbed a syringe in Becca's neck, making her melt in my arms. Her eyes rolled shut, her head lolling to the side.

"Give her to Anderson," Max commanded. "Like I said. She won't get hurt."

I reluctantly complied, swallowing the lump that formed in my throat as I lifted her, handing her to Anderson. Anderson gave me a sympathetic nod as he walked out of the Arena.

I should have known that asshole was a dirty cop.

"Nathan, take your brother to the hospital. I need to have a word with Tyler," Max said, handing the piece he used on Chino to the bald headed twin.

Nathan looked around then to me, his eyes terrified.

"I'm not going to kill him, Nathan," Max said irritably. "Now get your brother to the hospital before he bleeds all over my Arena."

Nathan obeyed, giving me a nod as he helped Mitch walk after Anderson.

Watching Nathan leave caused my heart to constrict wildly in my chest. I was so confused with what just happened. I knew Max Stine was someone you didn't mess with, but I never believed any rumors about him having a dark side. How Becca talked about him, and the few interactions we'd shared, he proved him to be a harmless, hard working man.

Maybe when I asked him for his blessing on marrying Becca his tell showed, but I always thought the gun cabinet he constantly referred to was just a joke.

I was obviously wrong.

Chino whimpered while Stine's henchman worked on the bullet in his foot, and a sick feeling found its way right to my gut, knowing I would most likely be on the ground next to him in the matter of moments.

Max was quiet like usual, but this type of quiet was agonizing. He was plotting in his head. There were two types of businessmen: the fast paced, smooth talkers like Nathan, and the silent, well thought out stone faced ones like Stine.

His hands found his pockets then his eyes met mine. "I wasn't sure about you at first, Tyler." He took a step towards me then looked around the Arena. "There's something to say about a quiet man. Everyone assumes they're harmless, but I beg to differ. Silence just means you're thinking thoughts most people shouldn't hear."

I gulped, terrified where he was going with this.

"But then I saw you with Rebecca. She had a little more life in her eyes than normal when she looked at you. I had my doubts, thought maybe you'd treat her poorly like your father treated your mother. But... you're just as much like your father as you are different."

"I love Becca, more than anything. I'd never hurt her—"

"I know," he cut me off. His eyes were hard as they bore into mine. "There's more than one way you can hurt someone though. For instance," he walked over to Chino, tapping his shoulder with his foot as he lay on the ground in pain. "With wealth, there's always going to be some idiot trying to gain your power. They'll do anything to get it. Including threatening the ones you love."

"I want you to know, I had nothing to do with your father's death. That was a mistake," Max scowled down at Chino then turned back to me. "If I had any indication that was going to happen, I'd have put a stop to it."

So it was true. Chino killed my father, put the bullet in his head. What a sick and twisted man. Then play it off like it was a suicide. Pushing all my anger and hurt away, I remained on topic, simply nodding at Stine so he knew I believed him.

"I wasn't going to sign Chino's deal," I said quickly. "Only because he was going to hurt Becca. That was the only reason I said yes just now. I'd find my way out of his deal once she was safe. I couldn't risk him shooting her."

He nodded his head. "I had Anderson checking up on you, making sure you were staying away from Chino's outlandish propositions. And you passed. I even smiled when he told me how you hit him."

Amusement crossed his face, and for a split second, I let my lip quirk at the memory. It felt good to punch that asshole square in the jaw.

Any trace of amusement left Stine's face, and I quickly followed.

"I let the tear gas incident slip, figuring that really was out of your control. The junkie breaking into your house... that hit a nerve, but Chino kidnapping her, taking her here and tying her up... it's unacceptable."

My eyes widened.

Max made his way to me; now we were toe to toe. It didn't matter that I was taller than him, I was still scared shitless.

"I'm going to take care of this fuck. He won't be doing business in Grand Rapids anymore. If he tries to make any type of contact with you, you tell me, got it?" Max said, his calm demeanor still in place.

I nodded my head. "Of course," I whispered.

He patted my shoulder with one hand, a satisfied smile on his face. "Good. I sure hope we won't have any more trouble."

Sighing with relief, I thought I might be off the hook after all.

I was wrong.

With his silent communications, the red headed twin walked towards us, handing Max another gun. My eyes widened.

Fuck.

"I want you to know I mean it when I say if you ever hurt my little girl, or let anything happen to her, you'll regret ever existing," he murmured, his breath hot on my face.

Grabbing the gun, he held it up to my trembling arm and cocked the trigger.

Bang!

I immediately fell backwards on the ground, my heart racing as I reached for my arm. Holy shit, he just shot me! I must have been in shock because it didn't hurt nearly as bad as I thought it would. My head whipped to my arm, waiting to see blood trickling from the new hole in my jacket. But there was hardly any. Would it take time for it to surface?

I looked up at Stine as he stood over me, handing the gun back to the red head. He began removing the handprints from the piece just as he did when Stine shot Chino.

"Now you and your brother-in-law, Ray, will have matching scars to remind you whose little girls you're meant to protect. The only reason it grazed your arm instead of going through your foot like Ray's is because you have to walk Becca down the aisle in two weeks."

Holy hell. Ray. I remembered Stine saying a shot to the foot was the price for knocking up one of his daughters. I thought he was joking. Apparently not.

"That'll be sore. He'll take care of you once he's done with that asshole." Stine said, nodding his head in Chino's direction.

My arm started to hurt the second he pointed it out, and a few trickles of blood were making their way on my hand that was covering it.

Max silently walked away, turning just as he was about to leave the Arena. "I trust we can keep this between us. Becca is going to be groggy, and hopefully won't remember much. I know you'll do your best to keep it that way."

"Yes, sir," I obeyed, more frightened than ever of my future father-in-law.

"Oh, and Tyler? Don't mess with the tracking system in her car either."

Wow. So it was Stine who had that thing installed, not Chino.

Stine turned his back, walking casually out of the Arena like nothing had just happened.

***

Anderson was waiting for me in an SUV outside the Arena. He tilted his head to the back for me to join him.

Holding my now bandaged arm from Stine's on call medic in an expensive suit, I opened the door to find Becca sprawled across the seat.

"Jesus, what did you put in her?" I asked in horror, lifting her head so it was in my lap. It felt good to run my hands through her hair. It took all of me to not lift her completely on my lap, kissing every bit of exposed skin I could. She was safe, and that was all that mattered right now.

"I'm sorry, I had to give her a sedative. Trust me, it was best for everyone involved. If Becca knew about her dad...," Anderson trailed off as he made his way onto the highway.

"What? Knew he was fucking crazy? I always thought Chino was the bad guy controlling everyone. Never did it cross my mind that Max Stine was really his puppet master," I said still in shock.

Anderson glanced in the rearview mirror. "I bet he grazed you, didn't he?"

"Yeah," I answered softly, still stroking Becca's hair. "Said he only did it that way because I had to walk Becca down the aisle. How the hell am I supposed to keep this from her?"

"Unfortunately, that sedative won't completely erase her memory. In time, she's going to remember everything. It might feel like a dream for a while, but Becca's smart. She'll start to put the pieces together," Anderson sighed.

"How did you get mixed up in all this?" I bravely asked.

"I've known Stine for a long time. Back when I was in the academy. They breed criminals as well as cadets. But as far as criminals go, Max Stine is the most like a Robin Hood."

I stayed silent, knowing my opinion was completely different from Anderson's. Maybe Anderson didn't have anyone and found companionship with the bad guy. That seemed to be the usual case. I could have easily gone down that path if I didn't have my Becs.

The news of who her father really is would crush her. I was going to have to be there to pick up the pieces just like she did when I found out the ones I loved really weren't who they said they were.

***

Anderson wanted to help me with Becca, but I didn't want him stepping foot in my house. I laid Becca down in our bed, stripping her of her clothing and dressing her in one of my t-shirts the best I could. The lump on the side of her head was pretty big, but the swelling would go down as long as I put ice on it.

After I stripped down to my briefs, I rummaged the freezer to find a cold pack, wrapping it in a cloth so the sting of the cold wouldn't startle her awake, although I was positive she'd be asleep for quite a few hours, if not a day or two. Anderson said a medic would stop by in the morning to check on her when he dropped us off earlier.

I gently moved her head so the cold was being applied to the lump. Hopefully the swelling would go down by the wedding. She'd still be beautiful, but I'm sure her mother wouldn't let her forget it was there.

Running my fingers down her face, my emotions hit me like a ton of bricks. I kept picturing Chino holding that gun to her head, my heart shattering with what felt like the inevitable. I used all my strength on those goons to try and get to her, but I couldn't move from their grasp. It was the worst feeling ever, seeing the one person you love more than life itself in the path of destruction and being helpless. If she would have been shot, I think I would have begged Chino to shoot me in the head too.

I bit my lip, the sting of tears escaping my eyes. I knew I should have left her alone so she could rest properly, but I had to hold her, bask in the fact that she was here with me, a few bumps and bruises, but she was safe.

I kissed her eyelids, her nose, cheeks, forehead, breathing her in as though I needed her scent to survive. My hands found her smooth, warm skin, making a path to find out if there were any other cuts and bruises that needed to be tended to.

I hated how her body just lolled when I pulled her against me. That awful sickness formed in my stomach, making my hands rub her skin at a faster pace, relishing the fact that she was warm and alive, not cold and comotose like RJ's body was.

I squeezed her, letting my tears escape like a faucet. I couldn't control it and just cried. I cried until I passed out with her warm and safe in my arms.

***

The loud chime of the doorbell startled me awake. It was dark out now, and I was still clinging to Becca's body. She hadn't budged. I felt her chest, just to make sure she was still breathing.

The chime rang again, and I reluctantly stood from the bed, covering Becca with a blanket and kissing her one more time before I went to see who the hell was at my door.

Pulling on my jeans, I checked the time on my phone.

"11:00 p.m.?" I said out loud. I didn't need anymore drama today, let alone the rest of my life.

I squinted as I tried to see through the window before turning on the lights.

"What are you doing here?" I asked Nathan as I flipped on the lights and opened the door.

"Jesus, you're okay!" he said with a tremble in his voice. His pale white face was shocking as he practically leapt at me, wrapping his arms around me tightly. "Fuck, I thought I'd find you in a pile of blood at your front door."

I tentatively wrapped my arms around him, my body sinking into him. It felt good to have my big brother here.

"What the hell happened?" Nathan asked, letting me go and finding a seat on the couch in the living room.

I closed the door, taking a deep breath before I told him everything.

He sat quietly, but was mainly stunned, only speaking when I got to the part about Stine grazing my arm with a bullet.

"Holy shit! He actually shot you?" Nathan gasped as he stood to examine the bandage on my shoulder. "Another reason why I'm staying the fuck away from women. I don't need some chick's dad putting a bullet in me."

I thought of bullets then thought of Mitch. "How's Mitch?"

- 315 -

"He's in the car. They cleaned and cauterized the wound. Stine must have people everywhere. They didn't even ask how the bullet was taken out of his leg. Took forever to get out of there."

"In the car?" I asked, puzzled.

"I told him to stay there while I made sure you were okay. I didn't know if you'd want to see him or not, you know... put another bullet in him for being such an idiot. He feels awful for believing Chino wasn't a lunatic. He tried to help Becca, that's how he got shot."

Nathan sighed as he went to search through my cupboards. Most likely he was looking for liquor.

My jaw ticked, and surprisingly, I wasn't upset, but wanted to make sure my little brother was okay. I'd already lost one family member before mending our relationship. I needed to make things right with Mitch before it was too late. "Becca's passed out in our bed. Can you keep an ear out for her? I doubt she'll wake up, but just in case."

Nathan nodded. "Don't strangle him, please."

I rolled my eyes as I walked out the front porch to the driveway.

Opening the car door, I slid into the driver's side. Mitch didn't look at me but stayed silent. We sat there for a few minutes, not saying anything.

"How's the leg?" I finally asked.

"Hurts... but not as much as my conscious," he gulped.

"Thank you, for taking that bullet for Becs."

"How'd you know?" he asked softly.

"Just a guess. She's okay. I'm not sure what I'm going to tell her when she wakes up," I said, taking a deep breath. "Today was the scariest day of my life."

"I'm so sorry I didn't believe you and Nathan about Chino," he choked, putting his head in his hands. "I'm such a fuck up."

"I know, I believe you," I said, putting my hand on his shoulder. He didn't need me to tell him he was wrong. I'd been doing that his whole life.

"When Chino came to me, it was all supposed to be on the side. I'd only hide the drugs or money on his subdivisions, not ours. Your house was a royal fuck up. I didn't even realize that many RJ bricks were installed. My guys can't disguise them, and Chino switched the packaging. That's why there were so many at your house. Chino told me today was going to be a meeting. He never said anything about kidnapping Becca or threatening her family."

"Threatening her family?" I asked.

Mitch nodded. "I guess he made Becca believe there were bombs in the pieces the artist built for ArtPrize. He said he'd set them off, hurt everyone downtown with the explosion, including her sister's family."

I frowned in disgust. My Becs, always caring about everyone else first. Of course she would do or go wherever Chino asked her to in order to keep others safe, especially her niece and nephew. A sudden urge to protect those little ones came over me as well, wishing I'd beat the shit out of Chino when I'd had the chance.

"When I saw Becca tied to that chair, that's when it all clicked. Chino is dark and will do anything to get what he wants. I'm so sorry I didn't see it sooner," he choked.

"I was scared when I saw you on the ground with a gunshot in your leg," I confessed.

His head popped up, "Really?"

I nodded my head, looking out into the darkness. "We already lost Dad. I don't want to lose a brother."

He bit his lip, nodding his head, tears threatening his eyes. I had to look away. I was sick of crying like a girl. "Why don't you come inside? You and Nathan can sleep in the guest rooms."

Mitch nodded, reaching for his door handle.

I walked slowly along side Mitch as he used his crutches up the path to the front door.

"I was worried blood would be shed. We good now?" Nathan asked with a raised eyebrow as we both entered.

Mitch and I exchanged glances, giving Nathan a nod. Nathan let out a full on smile, nodding happily towards both of us. "Who wants a drink?"

I shook my head. Some things might never change.

Chapter Twenty-Nine

Becca

Either I was having a very realistic dream about Wack-A-Mole or Josie and Emmett were actually playing and using me as the mole while I slept. My head was killing me. I was afraid to open my eyes and groaned out loud.

I heard rustling then felt a dip in the bed. "Here, take some Tylenol," Tyler murmured.

I threw my hands out aimlessly, looking for the drugs and water.

I popped three pills then rolled over, burrowing in the covers. "Ugh... I don't even remember falling asleep last night," I grumbled into the pillow.

Tyler's hand found my back over the blankets, gently massaging.

"What time is it?" I asked, my voice muffled in the pillow.

Tyler paused before he answered me. "It's about ten after noon," he said quietly.

I shot up from the bed, the sudden movement making my head hurt worse. My hand found the back of my head, and I gasped when I felt the huge lump.

"Oh my God! What happened?" I exclaimed, bringing my now wide-open eyes to Tyler. His expression was timid, and I was confused.

"You, um, hit your head really hard."

My eyes narrowed at him as I continued to feel the bump. Why wasn't he telling me the truth? I closed my eyes, my heart pounding along with my head... then memories came flashing back...

But they couldn't have been true? They must have been a dream.

"Gosh... I had this awful nightmare," I groaned into my hand. "It felt so real."

I slowly rubbed the back of my head then found Tyler's expression again. His cheeks were clenched, and I could tell he had more to say.

I shook my head again. "Was it a dream?" I slowly asked in confusion.

Tyler took a deep breath then rubbed my leg. "Why don't you go back to sleep. I can lay with you if you want."

I started to lie down then stopped. "Wait, why are you home? Shouldn't you be working? It's Tuesday, right?"

Tyler's face fell again, pity filling his eyes. "It's Wednesday."

"Wow... must not have been a dream," I whispered. My eyes were searching, the urge to freak out nearing.

"Hey, hey... you're okay. You need to rest, baby doll."

I shook my head, tears streaming down my cheeks. "No... I need to get up and process this." When I stood it felt like the floor was removed from my feet, the blood draining from my head down to my toes. Tyler rushed to my side, helping me sit back down.

"Look, I'm not sure what you remember. But you took a really hard hit to the head. You should just try to relax."

Taking another deep breath, I stood again, but this time slower. "I need a shower."

My body felt clammy, and a shower would help.

Tyler followed me into the bathroom. After turning on the shower I took off my clothes, now anxious to feel the warm water and soap after sleeping for so long.

"Are you joining me?" I asked Tyler, curious why he was following me.

At first he looked tempted, but then shook his head no, rubbing his bicep. "I've already showered. I'll go make breakfast."

I was a bit stunned by him turning down a shower, but the throbbing in my head said a quick shower might be better. When Tyler and I showered together, it was anything but quick.

The sound of the water hitting the tile was surprisingly soothing to my aching head, along with my hands gently massaging the shampoo into my hair.

I didn't want to believe my faint memories that began to clear in my mind. But they all started to add up and make sense.

The obscene amounts of money.

The hushed phone calls in his office.

My mother pacing the kitchen some nights, waiting for him to come home.

The late nights.

All those nights…

My tears blended with the water, sinking to the bottom of the drain along with my heart.

"You okay, Becs?" Tyler asked as he tapped on the shower door.

"I'm fine," I lied, putting on my best attempt to sound normal.

Tyler stood in front of the foggy door until I turned the water off, greeting me with a towel. His expression was unreadable, and he knew I'd figured out I hadn't been having nightmares. They were all a reality. We didn't say anything as I curled the towel around my body. I refrained from snuggling into Tyler like I normally would.

"I'm guessing you can't talk about what happened," I whispered into the towel. His head cocked as pity filled his face. I watched the lump slide down his throat as he studied me. "It's okay. You don't have to," I said a little louder, walking past him into the closet.

Tyler audible sighed as he followed me. "Becca, I—"

"It's fine," I said flatly. I quickly rummaged through my drawers, trying to find clothing as I mumbled, "I just feel like such an idiot. All this time…" I shook my head. How was I fooled for so long?

Understanding and sympathy spilled out of Tyler's voice. "I know, baby. I know."

My hands found my head as silent tears dripped down my cheeks.

Tyler hugged me from behind as he hushed into my ear. "It'll be okay. I love you. I'm here; I'm always here to listen and comfort you. You could cry until our house became an indoor swimming pool, and I'd still be here." He spun me around as gently as he could, my towel falling and baring my body to him as he pulled me in close. "I'm always going to protect you, even if it's from the man who brought you into this world."

I cried harder, my naked body trembling with his embrace. "I'm more worried about him hurting you," I croaked.

I felt Tyler's heart speed up from my head being pressed against his chest. "Yeah, I think I'll be okay," he murmured into my hair. "Max and I had a talk. We're good."

My arms found his waist, securely locking around him.

My tears finally dried as I unraveled myself from Tyler's hold. His eyebrows furrowed when I turned to find clothing.

"I have to see him," I said, amazed by the strength in my voice as I sniffled.

"Becs..."

"No." I spun quickly to face him. "I have to. I don't care what he told you. He needs to hear my two cents on his lifestyle he's kept hidden for so long." Tyler looked torn. "I'm going, and you're staying here."

***

Tyler wanted to drive me to my father's Grand Rapids office, but I refused. I needed to do this myself. I had so many emotions running through my head you'd think I was an experienced marathon runner.

I decided to bring the gift I purchased for him for our wedding, figuring it would make for a good opener to conversation. I hadn't put a lot of thought into the gift until the ride into town, but it seemed perfect due to recent events. I figured I could give it to him early since the monogram was finished. Besides, I needed some excuse to barge into his office.

I was furious the entire car ride from Grand Haven to Grand Rapids. I was plotting out everything I needed to say to him. The fight I was preparing to have with my father played at least three times in my head as I drove through the parking ramp under my father's building.

Flying by my father's assistant, I opened his door, surprised to see him standing and staring out the window.

When he turned to see me, his soft brown eyes taking me in, all my anger rushed out of my body. The timid, quiet Becca made her obnoxious appearance, and I knew she was going to need more of a push to come out of her shell.

"Becca, sweetie, I didn't know you were stopping by. You should have called. We could've gotten lunch," he said in his kind, soft voice.

I swallowed hard, taking my eyes from his and finding the floor. "Sorry. I didn't mean to stop by unannounced. I just wanted to give you your wedding gift from me."

"You're always welcome in my office, Becca. Why are you giving me a present for your wedding? Isn't it the other way around?" he said softly. I could sense his loving smile.

I stood still for a moment then forced my legs to walk towards him. I pulled out the small package from my bag and handed it to him. He looked taken aback as he studied the package. "Go ahead, open it. I want you to have it now," I whispered.

A small smile played on his lips as he eyed me then began to unwrap the present.

How did he act so calm and like himself after all I remembered happening? He'd shot a man! How was my caring father, who'd never hurt a fly, not a huge mess right now?

His eyes twinkled as he pulled the watch from the box.

"This is great, sweetheart. Thank you," he said sincerely while examining the platinum Cartier watch.

Cartier, yes. I'm sure you can guess who helped me pick it out. We still had one in a box somewhere that was meant for RJ. I think Tyler was going to give it to Nathan instead.

"I figured you could always use another source to keep time," I said, my eyes finally finding his.

For the first time ever, Max Stine couldn't meet my stare. For whatever reason, his discomfort fueled my desire to speak up and tell him all that had been ticking in my head. A bomb of emotions was about to explode, and I wasn't sure if either of us were going to survive by the time I was done.

"Time's a funny thing," I said a bit louder. "It's funny how so much time can go by, and you don't even realize what's been happening around you."

My father looked out the window, licking his lips as he took in what I was saying.

"Why?" I whispered. "Why?" I asked again, gritting my teeth.

"I don't know what you're asking, Becca," Max said, making his way to his desk.

I shook my head rapidly back and forth, irritated he was going to try and keep me in the dark.

"I know Anderson drugged me."

My father's eyes shot up, meeting mine, a touch of anger in them.

"Tyler didn't tell me. Please don't threaten him," I said sternly.

Max took me in, his expression unreadable now.

"How long?" I asked, my tone meaning no nonsense.

Leaning back in his chair, he sighed heavily as his hands found the arms of his chair. "I don't know what you're talking about."

I crossed my arms. Fine. If he were going to sit there and play dumb, then he could sit there and hear everything that was heavy on my heart.

"Have you always lived two lives? The good, church going, ethical businessman that I knew you as? The father who worked so hard to make something for himself? The father whose kids looked up to him because they thought he was a good man, who preached morals and the importance of integrity?"

I shook my head at him in disgust as he watched me with a still presence. "That man... he wasn't in that Arena two days ago. He wasn't there when my future brother-in-law was lying on the ground with a bullet in his leg. He wasn't there when a gun was pointed directly at my head. That man wasn't the one who shot someone, bringing him to his knees just to remind him *who was in charge*." My voice rose with each word, anger and hurt bluntly laced with each tone.

"All those late nights you were gone, all the golf and tennis matches, choir concerts, teacher conferences and open houses, the daddy-daughter dances you missed... was it because you were being this other man? The man who basically admitted he was a drug dealer and partners with someone who tried to rip me apart from the only man who's ever truly loved me?"

His eyes darted up to meet mine at that last sentence, and I almost felt bad for the words leaving my lips. But the way his eyes found his desk again only encouraged me to keep going.

"All the money you donate? The millions of dollars... is it all dirty? Did you earn any of it legally?"

He sighed heavily. "If money is doing good for someone or a community, it isn't dirty. It helps provide for people in need."

I stared at him, emotion thick in my heart. "Dad, you make enough money with your business investments. Why risk everything to make more?"

He leaned forward in his chair, resting his arms on his desk. "I want to provide for people who don't have anything, including my family. Someone has to take risks to help others. When I was in foster care, I knew I'd need something to make money when I got booted from the system. I had kids who looked up to me for whatever reason. They did all transactions while I planned everything."

"You mean Chino?" It was a question, but I knew that was the answer.

"Yes. Leeland and I met in a foster facility when we were young. Somehow we kept getting placed together. We ended up being in the same school district. I stayed with the same foster family my last two years of high school, but Lee kept getting moved around."

"You liked them. I remember Mom telling me she liked them too." My parents met in high school. My mother always talked about how my father's foster family was well off.

He nodded, a slight smile framing his face. "My foster father was a business tycoon. He's who I learned how to run companies and make proper investments from. Most people don't know this, but they actually adopted me right before I turned 18." My father's face went blank. He stood from his chair, finding the window and began gazing out as he continued. "They paid for my schooling. My adopted father was my role model. He taught me everything he knew about business."

"I'm sorry you lost them in the car accident," I whispered.

He gave me a thankful smile. "Sit down, sweetie."

I followed my father's gentle command, sitting obediently in one of the leather seats while he talked.

"The police came and got me. Brought me into the station. My father's number one business partner was there, telling me I owned everything that had belonged to my adopted parents, including a very large check. They didn't have anyone else, only me."

I nodded my head. I knew this. This was why our attendance for holidays was so important to my mother. She loved having us all together because we were all each other had.

Max half sat on his desk in front of me, his hands finding the edge of the desk on his sides. "My first purchase was a diamond ring for your mom." He grinned softly as though recalling the moment. "Once I graduated college, I took over my adopted father's business. But my side jobs with Leeland and the others continued to grow. Before I knew it, we were pulling in all kinds of money, and every single person took orders from me. By the time I was 26, I started to realize this other job was getting out of hand and was extremely illegal. That's when I met Anderson. He was 18, started joining the crew. He didn't have a record yet like the rest, so I sent him to the academy."

"Only Anderson?" I questioned.

His eyes left the floor to find my face. "There were a few others. I began sending other kids in certain directions, figuring in time I'd need knowledge in other areas. I paid their tuition. It felt good."

That explained the doctors, lawyers, detectives. Who knew how many other random people were on his payroll.

"What about Lee? He pointed a gun at my head. Threatened to kill Heather and her kids. Your grandkids!"

"Leeland won't be doing business anywhere near Grand Rapids," Max promised.

"But you're still going to do business with him?" I asked baffled.

Max sighed heavily, drinking me in while biting his cheeks.

"You're unbelievable. How can you be a drug dealer?" I asked in horror, tears filling my eyes.

"I don't do the drugs Becca. I rarely come in contact with them."

"So that makes it okay?" My whisper turned into more tears.

He sighed, cocking his head in my direction. "No, it doesn't. Becca, I've only ever wanted to give you, your siblings, and your mom the world."

"We didn't need to have everything money could buy," I whispered, tears shamelessly escaping my eyes. "All we needed was you. All those nights you were gone... you make so much money from your investments. Why not leave the bad business behind? Stop risking getting caught and thrown in jail!"

His head dipped down in shame, one hand reaching for his forehead. "Sometimes, it's easier to stay involved than to leave, baby."

"Does mom know?" I asked boldly, standing from my chair so he would look at me. He was still silent. Not speaking, only thinking like he always did. Finally he nodded his head.

"And she's okay with it?"

"Your mother understands that some things can't be changed," he said softly.

"No," I said, shaking my head drastically. "You can. I don't even know who you are," I added, fighting back the urge to cry ugly, hateful tears.

When he didn't say anything, I knew it was time for me to turn around and leave.

I meant to walk slowly, but I stomped to his office door.

"Becca," he said firmly, causing me to stop dead in my tracks.

I didn't turn around, but only listened.

"Do I still get to walk you down the aisle?" he asked, emotion thick in his voice.

My eyes closed tight, all the good memories of my father flooding my brain. There were only a few, but they were strong, and I held on to them with everything I had.

We'd go golfing on Sunday afternoons together. Our rides in the cart normally quiet. I'd never forget his proud and kind brown eyes watching me, no matter what type of shot I took.

Every Christmas we'd be in charge of fixing the nativity. He'd tell me the story of Christmas, reminding me that the smallest of things can change the whole world's perspective.

The day I graduated from college. He hugged me and held me tight, telling me how proud he was that I made it through one of the hardest times in my life. Now I knew he was talking about Connor and Ashlynn's betrayal and not getting through school.

My father's life was consumed by always being let down, and for the longest time I thought he'd gotten the best of all those miserable people.

He was so intelligent, so giving, and caring. The amount of empathy the man had was astounding. I just didn't understand how he could be two completely different people.

Was he a dark knight? A modern day Robin Hood? Selling drugs to the bad guys so he could feed the poor?

Would I let his other life ruin the good memories we'd created?

"Of course I want you to walk me down the aisle," I murmured. I paused for a long second then walked out the door.

Chapter Thirty

Tyler

The neck of my suit felt too tight as I fidgeted with the plum tie. The wedding planner was trying to pin my boutonniere on my breast pocket. She'd already poked me twice. If I weren't so nervous I wouldn't have scowled at her the second time the pin dug into my skin.

"Sorry! These pins can be so difficult sometimes!" She laughed, finally putting the flower in place.

I gave her a wry smile as she scurried towards Mitch. His eyes widened as she came at him with her pins.

Mitch and I had been good the past few weeks. He was trying to grow up; at least it felt like he was. He'd come into my office a few times, asking questions about the business. Maybe he'd want to help out more with the business side than on the construction sites. Nathan was unsure Mitch could handle it, but maybe we needed to give him a chance. After all, we were all Mitch had to look up to now that RJ was gone.

RJ.

My back pocket burned as I thought of his name. There was an envelope in the RJ brick that I found on his desk with my name on it. I found one for Mitch and Nathan too. I gave it to each of them last night after the rehearsal dinner. I had no idea if either of them had opened their letter.

I still wasn't ready, but for whatever reason, I felt I needed to have it with me today. My father wouldn't be walking with my mother down the aisle before Becca. I would be escorting her. He wouldn't help my mother light the unity candle. No toast would be made on his behalf. We weren't going to have a parent dance because RJ wouldn't be there.

Swallowing the lump in my throat, I reached for my back pocket and brought the letter to the breast pocket of my suit. I'd never know if RJ would've come around and been a father to me, but I'd like to think that if he were here today, he'd be pouring me a drink, putting his hand on my back, and telling me he was proud of me.

And of course he'd make some inappropriate comment about our wedding night. A smile snuck up on me, and Nathan caught me in my daydream.

"You ready?" he asked, setting his hand on my back, just as I imagined RJ would have done.

I nodded my head. "Never been more ready."

We exchanged glances then smirks.

"Ugh... you all have that same cocky grin," Jamie groaned, barging into our room at the church.

"You know, you're not supposed to be here," Nathan said, failing to sound annoyed. "What if I wasn't dressed?"

She completely ignored him and walked in my direction. "I'm making a delivery. Here." Jamie handed me a single red rose with a note attached.

I looked down at the rose puzzled.

Jamie rolled her eyes. "It's obviously not from me. Becca wanted me to bring it to you."

My lip quirked. She stole my move. "How's she doing?"

Jamie smiled. "Shockingly well."

I gulped and nodded.

"And you?" she asked with a knowing smile.

I tilted my head to the side as I played with the envelope. "Today is the happiest day of my life... and I've never been more nervous," I laughed.

"He'll be fine," Nathan said confidently.

"I need to get back. I want to make sure I'm there when they zip up her dress."

My eyes lit up. I couldn't wait to see Becca in her white dress.

"Hey Jay. Lookin' fly," Mitch said, wiggling his eyebrows.

Jamie audibly groaned in disgust as she walked out of the room.

"Leave her alone, Mitch," Nathan scolded.

Mitch smirked as he checked himself out in the mirror. "She secretly loves me."

I laughed. I'll never know what happened that night Jamie went out with Mitch, but the satisfied grin on Mitch's face whenever she walked into the room was obvious.

The wedding planner came back in the room, grabbing Ray and Michael to start seating guests as they arrived. Knowing people were here made this all feel real. I was pacing now. My anxiety was high but a completely different high than normal. I popped a Xanax, closing my eyes and taking a deep breath.

My mother and Missy came in randomly to check on me, both of them giving me hugs and words of encouragement. The only person I hadn't seen yet was Max Stine.

Becca didn't talk to me about the day she confronted him. I assumed she didn't say anything too revealing to piss Max off, otherwise I'd be six feet in the ground next to my father. Maybe one day she'd tell me what they said, but I was ready to put everything behind us.

I hoped he'd show. Even though Becca was deceived and traumatized by finding out who her father really was, I knew in her heart she'd want him here. My Becs was forgiving, and in time she'd forgive her father. For all I knew she'd already forgiven him.

Once I was finally in the room by myself, I opened Becca's note.

Tyler -

I think for the first time in my life, I'm not terrified. Marrying you is the only sure decision I've ever made. I love you, and I can't wait to spend the rest of our lives together.

Love Always,

The future Mrs. Becca Conklin

P.S. I hope the rose brings you as much joy as every single rose you've ever given me.

Her note made me smile and washed away my nervous twitch.

"Tyler, it's time for you to seat your mother and Missy," the wedding planner said. I took one last glance in the mirror, running my hand over my neatly trimmed beard. Becca begged me to keep it, and who was I to say no? I might have trimmed it shorter than she liked, but I like to think she really enjoyed how it felt on her fingers, neck, thighs...

"Tyler! Come on, let's stay on schedule!" I jumped from my thoughts that were going down south, giving me an extra pep in my step thinking about our wedding night and honeymoon.

I couldn't wait to surprise Becca with where I planned on consummating our marriage.

My mother was anxiously awaiting my arrival in the foyer, along with the rest of the wedding party. Everyone except Becca and Max.

"I know I keep saying it, but you look so handsome, Tyler," my mother gushed, putting her hands on the lapels of my jacket.

I smiled down at her, thankful she was bright and perky like usual. I was worried she might have trouble with RJ not being here to share this day with her.

"RJ would have been proud," she whispered, nodding her head at me for reassurance.

"I know," I said confidently.

Taking her arm, I tried to walk down the aisle without seeing the 600 and some people who were attending the wedding. I didn't know many on a personal level besides Cooper and his family. The rest were work associates or friends of my parents and grandparents. The same went for Becca. I never liked standing in front of people; that's why Nathan always talked at meetings.

Kissing my mother's cheek, I went back to get Missy.

"Oh, Tyler! I'm so thrilled for you and Becca! She couldn't have picked a better man!" she said with enthusiasm.

I tried not to laugh at her giddiness. I had to know about Max before I started to walk her to her seat. "Max is here, right? I haven't seen him all day."

"Of course he is! Max wouldn't miss today. He loves Becca more than anything in this world," Missy said as we began moving down the aisle.

I knew Max loved his daughter. I had a knick from a bullet on my arm to prove it.

"Don't worry about Max, Tyler. I promise he's a good man," she murmured as she smiled at everyone in the church.

I knew she was talking about our run in at the Arena. Max and Missy shared everything.

I nodded my head as I ushered her to her seat.

Once she was in her seat, I began to walk back towards the lobby.

Josie ran towards me, leaping into my arms once I passed the threshold of the sanctuary.

"Uncle Tyler! Auntie B looks so pretty!" She giggled.

"Just as pretty as you I bet," I smiled, kissing her cheek. She giggled again then squirmed to get down, finding Heather holding Emmett. Becca was hoping he'd be ready to walk down the aisle, but he was still too little. So instead, he'd be sitting with Roger, the Stine's butler who was more like an uncle, and next to Becca's parents.

The pastor patted me on the back, his gesture for me to follow him. This was it; I was going to see my bride. This was the moment I had fantasized about for so long. I anxiously waited, trying not to fidget as I watched the bridal party walk down. Both Jamie and Heather looked beautiful. My brothers didn't look too bad themselves.

Josie received a room full of awes as she threw plum rose petals on the white aisle runner. She was super cute. So cute I forgot about the time she threw up on me.

My heart started to race once Josie made her way to Missy in the front row. I tried to stand still and not twitch while I waited to see her. My palms were starting to sweat along with my forehead. I dabbed my forehead with my palm, not wanting to look sweaty for my beautiful bride.

A song started to play, and I cocked my head when I listened, trying to figure out which one it was. My heart thudded even faster as I realized it was our song. The song I was going to surprise her with as our first dance. The song I sang in her ear at the Valentine's Day party, telling her every single beat of my heart was hers to keep, that she was the one who always pulls us through. That had never been truer these past few months. She's the reason why I'm still breathing and why I finally feel safe.

Then, like a goddess, she moved into my vision.

The sight of her was even more intoxicating than I'd imagined. My chest rose as my breath was taken away by her beauty.

Her dress was stunning, showing off those curves that I loved. It was as if she were floating like an angel towards me, her baby blue eyes shining brighter and brighter the closer she came. Her light brown hair was curled elegantly, falling down her shoulders and just above the small amount of cleavage of her breasts. Her flawless smile captured my heart, and it took everything in me to not meet her halfway, scoop her in my arms and call her mine forever.

My eyes were wet, but I didn't care. Tears of joy were allowed for my Becs. I barely looked at Max as he handed his daughter over to me. He gave me a loving smile, one that I actually believed. Maybe I was just seeing love everywhere. Becca's image burned in my mind.

I reached for her hands. They were trembling from anticipation and excitement. Her eyes were glistening like mine as she whispered, "Hi."

I mouthed hi back as well, but only because I was choking back my emotion.

Men don't get to experience their dreams in a lifetime.

Becca was my dream.

My Becs.

Forever and Always.

Epilogue

Becca

"We're home, baby doll," Tyler said gently as he pulled the Lexus in the garage.

I stretched my arms, feeling groggy from our long few days of traveling. It was nearly 1:00 a.m., and our families were coming over at 11:00 a.m. bringing brunch and all the gifts from the wedding.

Even my father was taking another Saturday off to join in on the fun. I still had my reservations about him, but was trying to put his double life behind me. He was still my father, provided for me and offered guidance my whole life, even if he were a complete hypocrite.

Our father-daughter dance was fortunately not as awkward as I thought it was going to be. I was too high from marrying the man of my dreams to have any doubts or negative feelings.

Max was teary eyed and emotional which helped to make him seem to have a heart. I was glad the side of the man I knew my whole life showed up for my wedding, not the terrifying monster who was at the Arena.

My body felt heavy as I stepped out of the car, but I was quickly lifted off my feet, curling myself into Tyler's chest. He rubbed his nose with mine, giving me sweet Eskimo kisses, causing me to giggle.

"Why aren't we going in through the garage?" I asked sleepily as Tyler carried me through the lighted path to the front door.

"I have to carry you across the threshold. Marriage tradition," he said as a matter of fact.

I wanted to roll my eyes but refrained. He was eating every bit of this marriage up, and it was adorable and very unlike Tyler.

I loved every second of his traditional attitude.

The lights inside slowly started to dim on as Tyler impressively finished putting in the code with one hand. "Welcome home, Mrs. Conklin," Tyler's deep voice said as he nudged the door open with his elbow.

My cheeks heated as he called me Mrs. Conklin. I was really his, branded with his name.

I began to squirm, expecting him to put me down, but his grip tightened. "I can walk now. I'm sure after all that island food I'm at least fifteen pounds heavier," I grumbled.

Tyler ignored my request, walking straight towards our bedroom. "I'll set you down once I pass the most important threshold. Our bedroom," he said, his voice turning sultry. "Besides, you saying I can't handle another fifteen pounds is offensive."

I smacked his chest playfully, enjoying seeing his ever-famous Conklin grin slowly spread across his face.

Finally making our way to the bedroom, Tyler laid me down gently, his body covering mine.

Bringing my hands to his cheeks, I pulled him in for a sweet and tender kiss.

When we pulled apart, Tyler looked into my eyes filled with love and desire. "You're not too tired to relive our wedding night, are you?" Tyler's mischievous grin made me melt, and my sleepiness from earlier evaporated.

"I guess I could muster enough strength for that. As long as we can relive some honeymoon sex later this week," I flirted.

Tyler's eyes smoldered into mine as his grin grew wider.

"You can count on that for the rest of our lives, baby doll."

***

After our family brunch, we opened all the extravagant gifts from the mile long list of guests. Overly priced crystal vases and glasses that we would hardly ever use were piled in our living room. The gifts I enjoyed the most were, per my request, the envelopes holding cards with donations to the Conklin's fund for building shelters and low-income housing. I was extremely grateful for everything but guilty in return.

Over our honeymoon, Tyler and I discussed revamping the shelters and low-income housing project. I couldn't wait to start giving back. We both agreed any wedding checks that were made out to us would automatically go into that fund. We didn't need any more money. We were fortunate enough as it was.

After every present and envelope were opened, everyone scurried in different directions. My father and brothers went down to the cigar cellar, while our mothers, Heather and the kids went into the kitchen. Nathan, Mitch, and Tyler escaped to the deck. Probably discussing work. Tyler and I had been gone for three weeks. Of course he still had a few conference calls, but I made sure to be a very big distraction. A welcomed one at that.

"So anything wild and crazy happen on the honeymoon that you can tell me now that we're not surrounded by your family?" Jamie asked, raising a brow.

I laughed and blushed at the same time. "It was very memorable."

"Oh, come on, you can give me more than that!" she pestered.

I laughed then whispered, "I'm not going to kiss and tell, but Tyler Conklin may have a thirst for kink."

Jamie gasped, taking a look around to make sure no one was watching. "I knew it! I told you the quiet ones are always the kinkiest!"

I hushed her. "Stop! He'd kill me if he knew I said that to you! My lips are sealed now."

She shook her head rapidly. "Oh, no you don't. You can't drop that bomb and not finish. Just wait, I'll get you drunk and you'll spill."

I laughed again, standing from the couch to go find Tyler. Jamie followed, bickering more about keeping her in the dark. I ignored her and then tried to dismiss the pull low in my belly from memories of our very delectable honeymoon.

Then I found my love, sitting on a lounge chair, his body relaxed and happy, practically begging me to find his lap.

I gracefully walked past Mitch and Nathan on separate sides of the outdoor couch, setting myself in Tyler's lap. He was startled at first, but quickly wrapped his arms around me, kissing me softly.

"Gosh, I can't WAIT for the honeymoon phase to be over," Nathan said in mock disgust. Jamie hit Nathan's shoulder while both Tyler and I laughed. We knew it'd be a long time before we'd be able to keep our hands off each other.

Jamie sat down in the chair between Nathan and Mitch, swatting Mitch on the arm for putting his feet on the outdoor coffee table. That caused Nathan to mimic Mitch, earning him a glare from Jamie. I loved their interactions, and I was so glad to have them all in my life.

Tyler gently nuzzled my neck, his scruffy beard causing me to giggle.

Of all the people in my life, I was the most grateful for him.

My husband, Tyler Conklin.

"So what now, Mrs. Conklin?" Tyler asked, his hands making affectionate circles on my back and thigh.

As I stared into his eyes, admiring how they were changing color from green to blue, I was reminded of the first time in the elevator when I saw them. He hypnotized me from the beginning with those beautiful eyes. He stole my heart soon after.

Our life was finally starting. All scary drama was over with, and I was thrilled to begin our quiet life together.

He chuckled as I smiled like a love struck idiot at him, waiting for my answer. "Well?"

I blinked my eyes, my heart beating steadily for him in my chest.

"Babies," I murmured, my voice never faltering.

He searched my face. "Babies." He tested the word.

I nodded my head, my smile never fading.

"Babies," he said more confidently, a slow smile tugged at his lips. "I think we could manage that."

I kissed him, knowing one day he'd fulfill another dream and all of my dreams to come.

Today, tomorrow, and forever.

Acknowledgements

This is always the hard part. So many people have been supportive throughout my journey with Tyler and Becca. To be honest, this part could easily be just as the long as the entire Conklin Trilogy!

First I'd like to thank my cousin, Jen. Without you pushing me to do this and encouraging me that my rambles were more than just crazy thoughts inside my head, I would never had hit publish. Thank you for having faith in me. Your supportive texts and emails mean the world to me, and I'm so thankful to have you in my life.

Sam Hondorp-we did it! I can't believe we actually made it through THREE books! I know we've both learned so much from this experience, and I'm grateful for your willingness to answer my crazy texts on silly things I could probably just google! Cheers!

My amazing Beta readers. I value every single bit of your feedback, whether it be positive or critical. You helped to mold this book into a beautiful sculpture. It takes real guts to tell someone whether you like their work or what they could do to make it better, and I'm so thankful to have you all do so.

Emily Hamilton- I'm so thankful Christine gave me your name! Thanks for proofing my book and making it squeaky clean! You rock girl and I can't wait to work with you in the future!

Andrea and Melinda- Thanks for being another set of eyes. I love that you've taken the time to read through Becca and Tyler's story!

Sommer- Oh Mr. Handsome... you've made my book come to life again! Keep working your magic girl! Can't wait for more future covers to be done with you and Perfect Pear Creative.

Tonya- Oh My God. You are so amazing. I'm scattered, hairbrained, unorganized, and act like I live on a cloud most of the time, and you love me STILL!! You do so much to help me gain control over everything, and I'm so thankful! You're honestly my best friend, I wish more than anything that we lived closer. I know you're only a phone call away, but holy hell a hug would be nice! Or a trip to the bar, we could get into some fun trouble I'm sure! I'm so happy Eye Candy Bookstore gave my book to you for a review, otherwise I we wouldn't have met. You rock chica, and you do deserve all the good in the world! Love you to the moon and back babe!

Karen- To my author Mamma! My face lights up whenever that facetime call comes through or a message pops up on my phone or computer! I know we'll always be friends until the end, and I can't wait to come visit you and your family. Also, my husband loves you, so there's no way you can ever get rid of me!

Amanda- You are my author bestie. Your snapchats and phone calls make my days better. I know I can go to you for anything, bookworld or real world and vice versa. It's nice being able to talk with like minded people, and our dirty minds together create for an interesting convo. You say you ramble, and well...you do, but I love it! I can ramble back to you and not feel like an idiot doing so. I can't express how much of an impact you making me go to NOLA with you had on my life and my personal growth. It was great finding someone who likes to randomly break out into song, take shots like a champ, and be myself with!

Angela- I still always text you, and you always respond! I hope one day I can offer you a fraction of the advice you've given me. You've helped me grow as a writer (and marketer!). I will forever be indebted to you for that.

Trudy-Can you believe this is my third book?? Seems like just yesterday we created our facebook pages! You've been there since the beginning, and I'm so glad to call you friend!

You offer advice like no other, and I'm so thankful for all your advice.

Jen- You're always so chipper and right to the point! I love your boldness and positivity! You answer your phone at all hours it seems, and I love that we can chat for just that long about random shit! You're the first one to share and see how I'm doing, and I'm thankful Karen bugged the crap out of me to do a takeover for Just One More Page! Love ya girl!

To all my fellow authors who give me support daily. We are in this together as one, and I'm so thankful every time I see a share or supportive like/comment. Authors unite!

To my NOLA crew- Amanda, Trudy, Jen, Brandee, Renae, (and of course Brad and Kevin!) That was an experience of a lifetime. I was pushed completely out of my comfort zone. Who hops on a plane to New Orleans to stay with a bunch of people they've never met in person before? I changed for the better after that trip. Thank you all for being a part of it!

Christine with The Hype- I'm thrilled to be working with you for the release month of Corruption! I see big things in our futures, and I can't wait to see how it all plays out. Thanks for your constant support and advice!

Bloggers- Thank you to all of the bloggers out there. If it weren't for you, my books wouldn't be out there. Especially to those few who took a chance on a brand new author with a flower on the cover of her book.

Tyler's Blueprint Babes- I'm lost for words when it comes to all of you. Your pimping is inspiring, and I'm still in awe by all of your constant support and faith in me. Know you all are appreciated and loved, and can message me any time and as much as you all want! I love talking to my babes!

Last but certainly not least- I'd like to thank my loving husband for all your constant support. I can't wait to grow old with you. I love you more than cupcakes. And thank you to my babies. Lincoln and Hannah, you are my world. I strive to succeed because of the two of you. You're the reason for every breath I take, and I love to continue watching you both grow.

www.ingramcontent.com/pod-product-compliance
Lightning Source LLC
Chambersburg PA
CBHW070734180626
46818CB00007B/2844